P9-BVM-617

THE
EXECUTIVE
ORDER

DAVID FISHER

ST. MARTIN'S PRESS
NEW YORK

This is a work of fiction. All of the characters, organizations, and events portrayed in this novel are either products of the author's imagination or are used fictitiously.

First published in the United States by St. Martin's Press,
an imprint of St. Martin's Publishing Group

THE EXECUTIVE ORDER. Copyright © 2021 by David Fisher.
All rights reserved. Printed in the United States of America. For information,
address St. Martin's Publishing Group, 120 Broadway, New York, NY 10271.

www.stmartins.com

The Library of Congress Cataloging-in-Publication Data is available upon request.

ISBN 978-1-250-18345-3 (hardcover)
ISBN 978-1-250-18346-0 (ebook)

Our books may be purchased in bulk for promotional, educational, or business use. Please contact your local bookseller or the Macmillan Corporate and Premium Sales Department at 800-221-7945, extension 5442, or by email at MacmillanSpecialMarkets@macmillan.com.

First Edition: 2021

10 9 8 7 6 5 4 3 2 1

3836960

*It is with great pleasure that I dedicate this to
the real Brian McLane, my friend, my teacher, and the most
courageous person I have ever known. Few people have fought so hard and
made an impact on so many lives for so long. Brother, brother.*

THE EXECUTIVE ORDER

Prologue

It was twenty minutes after eight on the island of Oahu. The morning mist Hawaiians call Kupanaha was starting to lift over the waters of Pearl Harbor. According to legend, this was just the ghosts of the deepest waters cautioning all who traveled the seas to be wary.

The sky was the clear blue of an angel's eyes. The first Navy-operated ferry from the beach had just arrived at the USS *Arizona* memorial, which gracefully spanned the remains of the battleship sunk by the Japanese on a cold December morning. The ferry carried 128 properly solemn visitors from numerous countries, including Japan, who had come to pay their respects to the 1,102 men entombed in the wreckage. Many of them were standing at the railing looking at the renowned "black tears," the eerie drops of engine oil that had been bubbling up from the ship for more than eight decades. Some people referred to them as the last breath of the dead.

Without warning, the memorial shivered. The earth seemed to growl. The ocean bubbled. The six park rangers stationed at the memorial exchanged curious glances. The senior officer was reaching for the emergency phone when the first explosion erupted. It was followed an instant later by two more massive explosions.

The jagged remains of the great warship *Arizona* rose off the ocean floor. Shards of rusted metal ripped through the water and into the air, slicing into bodies in a rain of death. The massive concrete memorial lifted from its moorings as if being pushed upwards by Neptune's hand. It flipped onto its side, and shattered.

Those visitors and rangers who survived the initial blast were tossed into the water. Several of them were crushed instantly by the debris.

Then the sea caught fire.

Thousands of gallons of released oil gushed to the surface. It ignited with the whoosh of a fire racing through dry forest, turning the harbor into a boiling cauldron. The screams, then the pleas of the victims ended quickly, and mercifully. Of the 128 visitors and six guides at the memorial that morning, eight survived. Even that number was considered a miracle.

Minutes later the bones of the men who had died on that Sunday morning in 1941, ash-gray bones that had rested undisturbed for most of a century, began drifting up on the beach.

FRIDAY, JULY 11. MORGAN CITY, LOUISIANA

The early afternoon sun was sparking diamonds of light in the ripples of Louisiana's Atchafalaya River. It was twenty minutes after one on a steamy July afternoon. A cloud bank the color of hardened cement was forming on the horizon. The shrimpers were mostly out of port working, but a threatening weather forecast had limited the number of pleasure boats on the river. In the nearby swamps, visitors drawn to the area by the popular cable program *Swamp People* were happily slapping mosquitoes as flat-bottomed boats glided through the dense marshes. Just a bit downriver, the chinquapin run had just begun on Flat Lake and fishermen were pulling out panfish fast as they could toss a line, while paddlers and kayakers were working their way across the four-mile-wide lake. On the banks of the river, small groups of picnickers and sun worshipers were resting on blankets and brightly colored towels.

The boaters, the fishermen, the picnickers, and the sunbathers had no way of knowing that almost thirty miles upstream, without warning, nine of the eleven 44-foot-wide concrete and steel gates comprising the massive Old River Control Structure had begun rising, freeing the pent-up power of the mighty Mississippi. Billions of gallons of water surged through the opening gates, following the natural course of the river, creating a massive wave of churning energy.

The Army Corps of Engineers had built the ORCS in the 1950s to control the Mississippi River, to prevent it from joining the Atchafalaya channel and carving a new shorter, steeper path directly to the Gulf of Mexico. It had mostly successfully fought nature, keeping the Great Muddy on its historic path between New Orleans and Baton Rouge. Designed partially by Hans Albert Einstein, son of the great mathematician, it had corralled the Mississippi River system, ensuring it would remain the world's most significant navigable river highway.

The shift supervisor in the control room made a heroic but futile effort to override the system, trying desperately to manually close the gates. There was no response. Finally, cursing with the frustration of a doomed pilot in the last seconds of flight, he activated the emergency warning system.

"Oh my god," he whispered, watching the raging waters overwhelming the Atchafalaya.

The people along the banks of the river or at play on Flat Lake and other nearby lakes may have noticed the leaves of the cypress trees rustling. Some of them certainly would have felt a new urgency in the gentle current. In Morgan City, a broken traffic signal had caused an irritating traffic backup, and several motorists began honking.

Those people on the river heard it first. A growing rumble, as if a fleet of jumbo jets was thundering across the sky. Then they would have felt the river rising. The massive wave hit Morgan City first; within minutes the curious trickle of water in the streets had become a flood, catching people in their cars or in shops, overturning trucks and buses and smashing them into storefronts, an unstoppable rage carrying tons of debris and bodies into Flat Lake.

Billions of gallons of water barreled forward, playing in this new freedom, racing toward the Gulf, changing the river's course forever. Carrying with it everything in its path. Boats were capsized as easily as toys in a bathtub; fishermen, sunbathers, and picnickers were swept up and carried downriver. Within a half hour Morgan City ceased to exist, as did several smaller towns in the floodplain. Highways, railroad tracks, bridges, and gas and oil pipelines crossing the Atchafalaya were destroyed, disrupting the nation's flow of natural gas. The lack of water flowing into the Mississippi forced refineries, petrochemical plants, and two nuclear power plants to shut down immediately, leaving millions of people with only emergency power sources. As sediment flowed into that river, barges carrying vital grain and materials to the Gulf sunk into the mud.

By the time the floodwaters reached the Gulf of Mexico, much of its strength had dissipated. A news helicopter in the air to film a police-preparedness drill followed a sixteen-wheeler for miles as it bounced off buildings as easily as a pinball hitting bumpers, until it finally crashed into a pleasure boat and settled on its wheels in the middle of a parking lot.

Washed-out roads made it impossible for rescue, recovery, and repair crews to get near the damage for several days. Initial estimates put the number of dead and injured at more than 23,000. It would be several months before the roads and energy systems were mostly restored, at an estimated cost of $45 billion.

FRIDAY, JULY 11. NEW YORK CITY

It was twenty minutes after two in the permanent twilight of the Lincoln Tunnel. Its three tubes had been cut into the bedrock beneath the Hudson River beginning in 1934 to connect New York to New Jersey and the "west of the nation," as Fiorello La Guardia had proudly announced. Not unusually, the two lanes of traffic in the northern tube leaving Manhattan were backed up to a standstill; apparently a rental van had stalled just before exiting into Weehawken. Three men were leaning casually against the emergency catwalk guardrail, ignoring the cacophony of angry horns, presumably waiting for assistance. Then, oddly, a white Bronco stopped alongside the stalled van, blocking the second lane. Three more men quickly got out of that car. The Jersey end of the Lincoln Tunnel was now effectively sealed.

The six men appeared to be in no rush. They were practiced and prepared. One of them opened the rear doors of the van and handed each man an automatic weapon. Each of them fired a burst into the tiled ceiling to test his weapon. Shards of broken tiles rained down. The drivers who were trapped directly behind them realized what was happening, got out of their cars and started running back into the tunnel. They were screaming, warning people to run, run, run. The terrorists let them go, pleased they were spreading the desired panic.

After checking their weapons one more time they started walking back into the tunnel, firing several rounds into every car. One of the terrorists climbed onto the catwalk and fired down through the car roofs as he casually walked along. Some people escaped; many more did not. It made little difference to the killers; their objective was to create terror on a level no one would ever forget.

Those people trapped in the tunnel scrambled for their lives. They threw off their jackets, they ran out of their shoes, but they ran. They squeezed between cars, the most fit among them running on top of the cars, chased by the incessant chattering of automatic rifles, the echoes inside the tunnel magnifying reality. They ran as fast as they were able, which in many cases was not fast enough. They clogged the narrow spaces between cars, then began pushing others out of their way; if someone fell, he or she had little chance of getting up. Taxi and limousine drivers abandoned their passengers, but a Pakistani Lyft driver carried a grandmother from Linden a full half mile to safety on his back. The crush was so great drivers were unable to push open their doors against the human tide. Many of them escaped through their sunroof.

The fleeing mob made it impossible for the soldiers and police officers who had been positioned on the Manhattan side for just such an attack to get into the tunnel. There was nothing they could do but help people get to safety. But from the Weehawken end responders began moving cautiously into the hell, moving slowly, wary of booby traps. The firing coming from deep inside the tunnel seemed relentless, the echoes reverberating through the entire tube.

Then the explosions started.

As the terrorists moved past deserted cars, they casually tossed time-delayed grenades through broken windows or now-open sunroofs. They moved slowly and deliberately, stepping over bodies, being in no hurry to meet their own certain death at the mouth of the tunnel. The cars well behind them began exploding. Large segments of concrete fell from the roof, blocking access for those responders.

The attack continued for almost an hour. It ended when the terrorists finally reached the perimeter formed just inside the mouth of the tunnel by the U.S. Army-NYPD joint antiterrorism squad. After a brief firefight, the attackers blew themselves up. The explosion blew a massive hole in the tiled ceiling and bedrock, arousing fears of a complete collapse.

The tunnel held.

At the press conference at the site hours later, Police Commissioner Rogers said his people believed all of the attackers were dead but admitted that conflicting descriptions from survivors made it impossible to even determine with certainly how many of them there had been. Mayor Rose was forced to admit that it was possible, although not probable, he insisted, that one or more of them had escaped by joining the fleeing survivors.

Four hundred and fifty-six bodies were eventually recovered; many of the victims had been trampled to death. Optimistic Port Authority officials predicted, with luck and good weather, the tube could be reopened within four months, while damage to the tristate economy was guesstimated at "more than $28 billion."

1

This is my all-time favorite *Far Side*: Two turkeys are sitting at a small round table. There are cups of coffee in front of both of them. One of them, wearing black-rimmed glasses, is reading a newspaper dated Tuesday, November 23. In the distance a coveralled farmer carrying a hatchet is walking toward them. The caption reads, "I always feel sorry for those chickens."

Don't say you weren't warned. Please, don't ever say that.

Looking back, the damage that had been done to American democracy by the Trump administration was almost incalculable. It was as if someone had lifted the Constitution out of its bulletproof, moisture-controlled sealed case in the Rotunda of the National Archives and edited it with a Sharpie. First Amendment? Ah, not so much. Fifth Amendment? Nobody needs all that stuff. Fourteenth Amendment? Don't worry about it. With the grace of a defensive tackle at a ballet recital, Donald Trump and his sycophants had undermined the foundations of our republic; they had introduced new forms of vulgarity to the political system, inflicted terrible damage on the authority of the judiciary and the credibility of the media, coarsened the national dialogue, and emboldened hatred in all of its disguises. The Trump administration was the political version of the comedian's fabled Aristocrats—the most vile, repugnant act in history.

Whatever chance at reelection Trump might have had disappeared with his fumbling response to the pandemic. I remember playing Covfefe Scrabble his last few months in office: any combination of letters that looked like it might be a real word was legal. Jenny and I had just started dating and I usually zayed her! Trying to find the right person to follow Trump was like watching a blind man in a dark room stumbling to fit a plug into a socket. There was no right answer.

In those last days of that administration I actually believed the worst was over. According to the pollsters, "any breathing person" was about 10 points more popular than Donald Trump. "Any dead person" was only 6 points more desirable. Ah, the innocence of a middle-aged journalist.

The big question was how much of the chaos was permanent. One terrible night in the sandbox years earlier we'd been dropped into a firefight to reinforce a patrol that had been ambushed. When we hit the ground, I looked around at the wounded and the dying and wondered, *Where the hell do I start?* That was what the whole world was wondering six years ago: *Where does America go from Trump?* My boss at the *Pro,* Howie Bernstein, summed up the problem in his most colorful journalese, pointing out, "You can't push crap back up an asshole."

In retrospect, it didn't really matter who came next. We could just as easily have elected the grizzled old guy with the missing teeth who took the tickets at a traveling carnival as the Democrat. In a desperate effort to return to normalcy, the Biden administration shined up old ideas and pretended they had discovered gold. But those officials who filled the so-called Black Hole of Leadership either didn't fully understand the extent of the damage or lacked the capability to respond to its economic aftermath. Our national foundations had been destroyed and even MacGyver with a 102-piece Craftsman tool kit couldn't fix it. An anonymous poster on Facebook compared the Dems to housekeepers walking into a hotel room after the Stones had spent a week there. It was as hopeless as trying to glue a patch on the *Titanic.* Any chance they might have had to keep the ship of state afloat ended with the drought and resulting famine that plagued half the world.

The result in 2024 was the election of President Ian Wrightman. Ian Michael Wrightman was a career politician who until that time had been considered such a lightweight he had to be tethered to his Senate desk to prevent his floating away. While he lacked substance, he did have the distinct political advantage of not being one of them, whichever *them* you supported.

But that was not what I was thinking about when I woke up that morning, July eleventh. Jenny had stayed over that night and as usual was up before me. I had laid in bed watching with silent admiration as she slipped into her professional life. She glanced at me and, seeing I was awake, smiled. We made plans to meet for dinner unless, as always. She kissed me lightly, wrinkled her nose, picked up her briefcase, and was gone. The warmth of her next to me dissipated slowly.

"Cher," I said when she was gone, "come here, please." Mighty Chair rolled to the side of the bed, red and white side lights blinking happily as if saying good morning.

I almost beat the sunrise to the gym. The first embers of the morning were sneaking into the night. About half the members of the Light Brigade were already there, clacking away on the weight machines, grunting with pleasure. Although the mandatory face-mask rule had been lifted years earlier, several people still wore the popular designer coverings. "So you're keeping banker's hours now?" Hack Wilson greeted me. Hack was my friend and workout partner. He was built like a mountain range but moved with the ease of a Steinbeck sentence. As we got to work, the banter was the stuff of daily life: relationships, new restaurants, Netflix series, kids leaving for sleepaway camp (his), work, vacations, and eventually, politics.

The wisps of optimism that had greeted President Wrightman's inauguration were long gone—blown away by the random breezes of time. As we'd feared, the structural damage done by the pandemic and other natural and unnatural disasters had continued to reverberate throughout the entire world. Wrightman had made temporary repairs where that was possible and had slowed the decline in other areas, but his attempts to rebuild vital international relationships, restructure the economy to relieve the pressure on the middle class, salvage affordable healthcare, and begin healing the chasm ripping apart the nation had pretty much failed. The country was stagnant, as if 350 million people were stopped at a traffic signal, waiting patiently for it to change. In one of my columns I had written that Wrightman reminded me of the caretaker at a graveyard, who dutifully clipped the grass once a week to preserve the illusion of life.

So our once-hopeful workout conversations had transitioned into complaints and jokes about his ineptitude.

By the time I'd finished, the summer morning had sucked the air out of the city. It was typical Washington weather: 91 degrees, 100 percent humidity, no chance of rain. On the way to my office, I stopped at Nonna's. As usual, there was a long line at the takeout window. "The usual?" George asked. "The usual," I told him. "Cher, good morning," he said.

"Good morning, George," Cher responded evenly. George and I laughed; Cher was silent.

Everything flowed together, everything fit. The people, the places, the normalcy of a hot July morning in Washington made it a day that otherwise would have been enjoyed, then stored somewhere in my memory and forgotten.

Admittedly that's a pretty big *otherwise.*

As usual when I got to work during the morning rush, I took the freight elevator to the seventh floor. While the thermal security camera signaled I was a healthy 98.6, I still didn't think it was fair to squeeze Mighty Chair into a crowded elevator, no matter how much some of those people enjoyed teasing Cher. I walked into the *Pro*'s office a few minutes after nine o'clock. Sometime during the night two coffee cups had been added to the tower growing on the edge of my desk. It was now a rigid twelve cups high—substantial but not close to the record.

July eleventh began as what we in the journalism game call a slow news day. The media was still suffering through what was referred to as the post-Resurrection malaise—what stories might attract readers two weeks *after* Jesus had risen. During Trump's regime and the worldwide pandemic, digging up a story among the hustlers, scoundrels, liars, incompetents, and dolts who had profited from the chaos had been easier than finding shells on a beach. We had so many stories to choose from that anything involving an official lower than a Cabinet undersecretary got thrown back into the press pool.

The Democrats had given us the excitement of bureaucratic competence and natural disasters. In contrast, the Wrightman administration took great pride in its boring normalcy. Rather than those provocative red *Make America Great Again* caps or *I Survived 2020* T-shirts, Wrightman supporters wore lime-green caps reading *Reboot Government to Original Factory Setting*. This White House stressed quiet professionalism: no leaks, no turmoil, no fuss, no big-bucks bestsellers. As much as possible, everything was done behind closed doors. This quiet was welcomed by everyone except reporters, who once again were forced, as my great editor in chief Howard Bernstein urged, to do journalism.

Our newsroom at the *Pro* was a large open space plan with small glass-enclosed conference rooms and offices running almost the full length of both side walls. While we had the option of working remotely, most of us chose to come in at least several days a week. Co-cuddling, we called it. My desk was at the farthest end of the office; on a ship it would have been the lookout perch. Each desk had a low-backed rolling chair, except mine of course, with a visitor's chair on the side. While the desks were all the same standard office gunmetal gray, every side-chair was different. That was our big perk: express your inner self in your choice of a side chair. They ranged from Costco folding chairs covered by bright cushions to style editor Katy Fitzgerald's circa 1960s strapped-plastic lounger. I'd brought in one of the inexpensive dining room chairs my sister and I had saved from our parents' home when it was sold: a brown wooden ball-and-claw with a scrolled back and a long-faded green cloth seat. The gnaw marks chewed into the arm made me confident it had been mine.

On the wall directly in front of me, four large-screen Samsungs were set permanently to the four major networks. Smaller monitors were mounted above the offices along the side walls. They were set to various cable stations, including BBC America. There were twelve screens in all—four in front, four along each wall—enough monitors to enable us to simultaneously watch an entire season of the newest *Star Trek* series. Each monitor was numbered, and headphones enabled us to select the channel we wanted to hear.

The fact that twelve TV sets were required to enable us to produce digital stories did not escape my somewhat overdeveloped sense of irony.

I was developing several stories. I had the reporter's itch, a feeling that deep below the placid waters of the administration the waters were roiling. The Wrightman administration had failed completely to fulfill any election promises and seemed bogged down. The nation remained so politically divided that any kind of progress was almost impossible.

Unlike Trump, who had governed with the stealth of Inspector Clouseau, or the befuddled Democrats, who had raced around trying to quench an erupting volcano with fire extinguishers, the Wrightman people were tunneling into the bureaucracy. Its appointees were quietly consolidating power, taking esoteric but legal steps to harness and control the remnants of the legislative process. Their actions were too subtle to raise any alarms and too complicated for anyone other than policy wonks to understand, but in some ways they portended far more danger. Obviously these people knew what they were doing. The question nobody seemed to be able to answer was what did they want to do?

I spent that morning investigating dry ditches. I had a nice off-the-record lunch with the Director of Befuddlement at the Department of Bureaucracy, as the Pythons might have identified him. He actually was the second assistant to an assistant ($85,000 annually) at Interior, a seemingly decent guy who actually had a roving eye. (I don't mean he liked to scope out women; I mean he had a floating blue iris that wobbled like a duck in a bathtub.) The secretary had just spent several hundred million taxpayer dollars refurbishing the Stewart Lee Udall building, including the installation of Neo Deco murals, so I told him I intended to write a wry feature about the new interior of the Interior.

In fact, the secretary had quietly proposed amending several regulations and codes that would give the department considerably more oversight of state spending on public projects like roads, buildings, even airports. While on the surface it didn't seem like much more than bookkeeping, in actuality these changes granted to the federal government approval power over significant portions of state budgets. Several governors had complained about it, but there was little fuss. After the sins of the past administrations, this story raised about as much interest as a pothole on the highway of life. I thought there might be a good story there, but the most I got out of this lunch was an off-the-record hamburger.

When I walked into the office a little after two o'clock, it was the unexpected silence that puzzled me. Newsrooms by definition are loud, raucous, alive with energy and enthusiasm. People are always in motion; you can feel the determination. Not this time. Just about everybody in the office was standing, staring at the large monitors in front. A couple of people were shaking their heads. Someone was crying.

I caught Joanne Curtis's attention. Auntie Jo was our high priestess of punctuation; she had never met a semicolon she didn't like. "What's going on?"

She took her headphones off and looked at me as if I had just arrived from another planet. "Mighty Chair didn't tell you?"

I shook my head. I'd turned off Cher's alert system for the interview and neglected to turn it back on.

She indicated all the screens with a wave of her hand. "Somebody attacked Pearl Harbor."

Rod Serling was the first thought that popped into my mind. I was floating through time. But an instant later I snapped back to reality. Each of our twelve screens were showing essentially the same disjointed images: visual bits and pieces of whatever they could grab as local crews scrambled to get cameras to the site. Reporters stepped in front of the camera, several of them donning headphones as they got there, like soldiers gearing up for battle. Chyrons at the bottom of the screen summed up what was known: EXPLOSIONS ROCK ARIZONA MEMORIAL IN PEARL HARBOR. Some stations were already reporting mass casualties. The recently issued government seal appeared on each screen: a red, white, and blue badge mounted by a bald eagle, with a bold *N* in the middle confirming this was actual news, not opinion.

The professional images were mixed with pickup shots from people who had rushed there and uploaded video to YouBroadcast.

I slid in behind my desk. The attack was coming to life in disparate pieces. Cameras were sweeping the area, searching for that one symbolic image that would visually sum up the story. The Pacific Ocean was on fire; thick plumes of ugly dark smoke spiraled triumphantly into the air. On CNN a reporter in plaid Bermuda shorts was doing his stand-up in front of a large block of jagged concrete embedded in the white sand.

Bits of unrecognizable debris were floating on the tide. Fox focused on a body floating facedown; it was up only a few seconds before the director cut to another image, perhaps deciding it was too gruesome even for their audience. There were several pans of spectators with the usual horrified expressions on their faces: an older woman covering her mouth with her palm; two teenagers crying and hugging each other; cops pushing people back, back. Swirling responder lights colored the scene. Suddenly, there it was, the shot of gold.

As soon as I saw it, I knew that this was the image that was going to be looped endlessly for the next few days. It was going to be splashed on the front page of newspapers and the opening image on news sites: a single tannish bone on the shoreline, shifting just slightly as it was nudged by each rippling wave. I knew what it was, the remains of one of the men of the *Arizona*. Free, finally free, coming home.

The horror delivered by that simple image was astonishing; I puffed out my cheeks and released a long, thin breath to maintain control. "Whoa," I muttered.

As the numerous visuals began to coalesce into a story, the office came alive as if someone had double-tapped the play button. Howie clapped his hands sharply three times, shouted, "C'mon, people, let's do some journalism." He started rattling off assignments—gather, organize, report. This was Career Day for reporters; this was the type of story that made reputations and led to promotions and bigger jobs. This was Murrow in the blitz, Dan Rather on a rooftop after a Dallas flood. Maybe the attack took place some five thousand miles away, but we were in Washington, D.C., and the response would come from right around the corner. That was our bailiwick. Track down sources and find out how the government was responding. What was the military doing? How did our intelligence community fail? Three claps, and it was as if the starting bell had rung, the gates had sprung open, and the horses had burst onto the track; in an instant the newsroom had been transformed from startled spectators to journalists reporting a story.

"Cher," I said, "call Jenny." I'd start by finding out what was happening on the Hill. But two rings into the call I was stopped by the traditional newsroom expression of surprise. "Hol–lee shit!" someone shouted. "Heads up, everybody. Look at this."

I swiveled Cher around. One of the side monitors was showing an entirely different scene. Several other monitors quickly switched to it. Thick smoke was pouring out of the entrance to a tunnel. An aerial shot from a helicopter or drone showed people scrambling out of smoke, through a gridlock of stalled vehicles. Soldiers, or maybe cops, were going against the flow, trying to get into the tunnel. It was like a scene from a monster flick. Only apparently this was real. The chyron reported: TERRORIST ATTACK INSIDE NEW YORK'S LINCOLN TUNNEL.

The other networks picked up this second attack. Screens were split between rescue operations in Pearl Harbor and the ongoing fighting in New York. Fire. Smoke. People running. Cameras were moving quickly, sweeping across the sky, then over the ground—visual panic. Accurately capturing the confusion.

I put on my headphones and began clicking between channels. Mostly I heard sirens, some shouting, gunfire in the background. Little of it matched any images; all of it reinforced the chaos.

A series of explosive flashes lit up the tunnel mouth, like lightning illuminating storm clouds; but victims continued emerging from the smoke. NYPD officers and firefighters were pushing, dragging, even carrying people to safety. Two officers crouched behind a ballistic shield and disappeared into the cloud, walking into the attack. It was a level of bravery I'd seen over and over, first in Iraq, then in the Big Sandbox. I was still awed by it. I could feel my heart being ripped open.

I closed my eyes. I was back in the mix. Rushing into the firefight carrying seventy pounds and seven years of combat experience. The world around me was exploding. Back in my personal comfort zone. It felt right.

When I opened my eyes Howie was standing in front of my desk, his back to me; his sleeves rolled halfway up, hands resting on his hips, looking straight ahead at the wall of monitors, shaking his head. Even Howie was having difficulty organizing this reality. It appeared that for the first time in our history America had been attacked simultaneously from the East Coast to the farthest West Coast. Howie was wrestling with how to cover it, what angles we could take that would set us apart. How do we "do journalism" here?

"All right," he snapped, turning around to face the room. "Bart," he said, pointing at our youngest reporter. "You do the history. Every domestic attack since . . ."

"Howie!" another voice shouted with hesitant astonishment. We turned again and looked. The newsroom went silent. Two of the screens were now showing a still photo of a summer lake. Sailboats, children floating on inner tubes; it looked like a travel poster. "There's another one."

"Jesus. What?"

"They just blew up some dam in Louisiana."

The story spread to the other networks. None of them had visuals, so they went back to their anchor desk. I began switching through the channels, catching snippets. The same words were repeated: *Explosions. Gunfire. Casualties. Multiple deaths. Reporters racing to the scene. Information as soon as we get it.* Some of the stations were broadcasting Google Maps footage from a place called Morgan City. It looked like a pleasant place. Seventy miles west of New Orleans. Sixty miles south of Baton Rouge.

Seconds later every cell phone in the newsroom began ringing, chiming, singing, and vibrating. The soundtrack of social media. Every single device. I glanced at my iPhone. Big red caps announced: PRESIDENTIAL ALERT! This was the first real-time use of FEMA's new Wireless Emergency Alert System:

> This is a message from the president of the United States, Ian Wrightman. Our country has been attacked on several fronts. We are meeting this threat with all appropriate measures. The greatest military and civilian police forces in the world remain ready to protect all Americans. We ask that everyone shelter in place until we can be certain these attacks have ended. We will keep you informed. We assure you that this attack on the foundations of our democracy will

be met with our entire arsenal of weapons, righteousness, and the American spirit, and that those responsible for it will feel our wrath. God bless you and God bless America, President I. M. Wrightman.

I stared at that message, letting it sink in. Three simultaneous attacks, west to east and one in the deepest South. The meaning was obvious, delivered clearly: No American is safe, from west to east, on land or at sea, from the sophisticated cities to the deepest swamps. Every American is now vulnerable. Your government cannot protect you. We can strike anywhere.

The problem was identifying the *we*. Who launched these attacks? Where'd they come from? How many more would there be?

The Promethean had been founded in 2015 to provide context to current events. We did background digging to help readers better understand our world. We focused on the why rather than the what. We took great pride in fitting somewhere between breaking news reports and birdcage lining. My interior-of-the-Interior story, for example, was actually part of a series I was writing about the billions of taxpayer dollars wasted annually. We weren't set up to report breaking news beyond doing wraparounds, brief summaries of known facts. We didn't have a budget to physically cover events, so we gathered details from numerous other sources—twelve TV networks, for example—added our own indepth reporting, and then tried to make sense of it.

Howie took it all in, considered the possibilities, then decided with a dismissive wave, "Fuck it! You guys know what to do. Do it." Get on the phones. Dig up your contacts. Use every source you've ever developed. Do journalism.

Over the next hour we all began filling in the details. I clicked among the different stations and internet sites, making notes while reaching out to my sources to try to find something, anything, I could turn into a story. It looked like the actual attacks had ended, although in New York cars were still burning in the tunnel, and in Louisiana the flood damage continued spreading. The scope of damage was beyond easy comprehension. New York had lost a vital connection to New Jersey and beyond. In Louisiana, the Mississippi River had cut a new course to the Gulf, destroying everything that had stood in its path.

But from the muddle, some basic facts were emerging. The first attack had begun at approximately twenty after eight in Oahu, just after the Navy-operated ferry carrying an estimated 130 passengers had arrived at the USS *Arizona* memorial . . .

I could visualize the place. I had rotated through Pearl several times during Special Ops training. I'd paid my respects at that memorial. I'd been to New York too, paid my respects there too. I'd driven through the Lincoln Tunnel, the gateway to everywhere that is not New York, at least a dozen times. At that scene, a female reporter was pushed back against a brick wall, glasses perched on the tip of her nose. As she spoke, she leafed through loose pages. I thought she was doing a good job in a really difficult situation. Screeching sirens forced her to hold the mic against her mouth to be heard. She was dressed casually, in pants and a glittering gold Harmony Street T-shirt, as if she had rushed to the site. Descriptions of the terrorists varied, she said, but several survivors described them as "Middle Eastern looking."

Maybe, I thought, *probably, but expectations always color memory.*

The reflection of flashing emergency lights bouncing off the wall and the shadows of people rushing in different directions made it look like a scene from a David Lynch movie. She read from her notes, talking to an anchor named Bill. The terrorists had taken automatic weapons from the back of the van. They began firing indiscriminately into the trapped vehicles.

I had shifted into journomatic. Whatever sense of panic or fear or distress or even sympathy I should have been feeling wasn't there. I had no time to waste on emotions. That wasn't my job. Gather, organize and filter, spew it out. The adrenaline had lifted me into a different consciousness: Once again I was operating on training and experience. In an odd way it was like being in combat again; I was right in the middle of it with no time to realize I was right in the middle of it.

The reports continued from a plain outside Morgan City. The city itself had been inundated. A debris field had flowed into Flat Lake. A minute earlier I had never heard either name; after this no one would ever forget it. Jet-skiers, swimmers, picnickers, boaters and fishermen, the whole gamut of people working or enjoying a day on the water—gone. Just gone. A male reporter was standing in front of two police cruisers blocking access to a highway, explaining that the entire area was in lockdown. No one other than first responders was permitted on what was left of the roads. *What was left.* It was too soon for any damage assessments. "Everything is just gone," he said, shaking his head in disbelief. He tossed his free hand in the air. "The whole city, it's gone."

Initial reports indicated the dam had been blown up by a sudden explosion, but that was just a bad guess. Authorities now believed it was a cyberattack. Techno-terrorists had hacked the computer system controlling the Old River Control Structure. Without warning, the huge steel gates suddenly had begun opening. Inside the control room the staff had made a heroic but futile effort to manually shut them; one of them was quoted as saying, "We never had a shot."

The reporter was holding his palm against an earpiece, committing the broadcast sin of looking down to focus on what he was hearing rather than looking into the camera. He was repeating information in bursts, not worrying at all about turning it into sentences. Watching him, I could feel his despair.

Frankie B. Goode carefully set another cup of coffee in front of me. Frankie was my deskmate, sitting directly across from me. Frankie was a burly, round-faced guy; I always thought he had a vague resemblance to the man in the moon, if the man in the moon had a mustache. On some days I spent as many as twelve hours watching him twisting the drooping ends of his handlebar stasch while he reached for the right words. He carefully avoided tipping over the growing tower of used cups on the corner of my desk as he sat down. I already held the office record at twenty-eight, but this stack looked promising. Some people were betting I would make thirty. "Anything?" he asked.

I shook my head. "You?"

"Nada," he said softly.

On a large monitor, the Louisiana reporter kept going, but whatever he was hearing in his ear was shaking him up. He was fighting to maintain his composure. He swiped at the corner of his eye. The engineers in the control room had engaged the emergency alert system, he reported; maybe it had saved some lives. No way of knowing. Those people who heard it had only a few minutes to respond. People usually eat up most of that time looking around curiously, trying to figure out what that warning means.

I switched from monitor to monitor:

. . . large pieces of the memorial were blown several hundred yards, crashing into the reception center . . .

. . . limousine and taxi drivers abandoned their passengers, but a Pakistani Lyft driver had heroically carried an elderly female passenger more than half a mile to safety . . .

For some reason, camera operators at all three sites decided to focus on abandoned clothing. Shoes especially.

. . . floodwaters reached the Gulf, carrying tons of debris . . .

. . . children were among the missing at Pearl Harbor . . .

. . . terrorists inside the tunnel had engaged those troops Wrightman had initially sent to New York to enforce federal immigration policies. It was believed all of the terrorists were killed in the series of explosions that had rocked the tunnel, although it was not known if those blasts had been caused by Homeland Security forces or if they had blown themselves up to avoid capture.

Did they get them all? I wondered. No way of knowing for sure. The problem we'd faced in the desert was how to identify the bad actors who slipped away with fleeing survivors. It was frustrating as hell, and we never solved it. At her press conference early that evening NYPD commissioner Rosemary Rogers admitted, "While we believe all of the attackers are dead, as I'm sure everybody understands it is a very confusing situation. To allow our people to do their jobs, we are imposing a curfew on the city tonight. Beginning at nine P.M., we will stop, question, and detain if appropriate anyone on New York's streets without proper cause. This is for your own safety, people." Rogers reminded New Yorkers to check Twitter hourly for further information.

Gradually the breaking news morphed into features. At first we heard the uplifting miracle survival stories: A baby had been found floating in its stroller in the Pacific. A pregnant woman had been carried out of the tunnel and had given birth in an ambulance. A teenager claimed to have ridden his Jet Ski through the floodwaters. Estimates of casualties were all over the place—*casualties* being the acceptable term. Nobody wanted to put a number on the death toll.

I watched Howie moving around the office, reading over a shoulder, making a brief comment, laying a reassuring hand on someone's back. Keeping control. That was no surprise. Howie Bernstein had spent four decades preparing for this day, rising from covering local schoolboard meetings to the national desk of *The Washington Post*. After taking his buyout, he had helped found the *Pro*. There was no hesitation in him; he put on his green plastic printer's visor given to him by his former colleagues at the *Post* and dived into the story.

Howie had created the *Pro* to tell stories in human terms, focusing on those events that emotionally touched our readers. Dogs in floodwaters, he called them. We were working on a limited budget, a Velcro budget he called it, the staff consisting mostly of experienced journalists laid off by the big boys—the major newspapers, networks, and cable channels and young people willing to trade salary for opportunity. When necessary, as it would be for this story, he hired freelancers living near the site (no transportation costs!) to inject a local element.

Several of our people spent the rest of the day and into the night cutting and pasting, finding the common denominators and combining reports from all three attacks into one cohesive story. The lede was obvious: "The United States was simultaneously attacked by terrorists in three regions, as the yet-unidentified attackers proved their ability to strike anywhere in the country. Although casualty reports are still sketchy, this is believed to be the worst attack on the homeland in American history."

In the safety of the early evening, politicians had begun showing up on television to express their outrage. They became more courageous and defiant as time passed. Senator Lindsey Graham reminded us that once again we had all suffered the terrible loss of innocence. New York State governor Andrew Cuomo was filmed at a recruitment center trying to volunteer. Senator Ron Johnson (R-Wi) sent heartfelt prayers to the victims through a spokesperson, who explained Johnson would have a statement to make in the near future.

I finally got hold of Jenny. "You okay?"

"I guess," she said, but I could hear the quiver in her voice. As usual, she tried to lighten the load. "Although they canceled an important hearing on milk subsidies."

I leaned way back into Mighty Chair's soft cushions, closed my eyes, and took a long relaxing breath. Until then I probably hadn't realized how deep into the day I had dived. Her voice had brought me back to the surface. I coughed my throat clear and went back to work. "Your guy hearing anything?"

Her "guy" being Congresswoman Martha McDonnell, the powerful chairperson of the House Intelligence Committee.

"On or off?" For attribution or deep sourcing?

"Pick one."

"Off."

"There's a feeling that it's homegrown. It just feels like there're too many moving parts for it to be away teams. Somewhere along the line out-of-towners would've tripped a wire."

"Well, that's not good." I let the thought run out. Launching three simultaneous attacks required sophisticated planning and meticulous co-ordination. People had to be in place. They had to have weapons. They needed to be in frequent communication with home plate or their team-mates. We'd spent several trillion dollars after 9/11 to prevent a single attack; it looked like we didn't get our money's worth. "Any guesses?"

"That's what Martha has been asking. Nobody wants to make any bad guesses. This is a career killer, and everybody wants to be on the safe side."

"You hearing anything from the Wrightman people?"

She forced a laugh. "All dressed up and no place to go."

We didn't bother pretending to make plans.

I could imagine the panic taking hold inside the White House. There was nothing the administration could do until they were confident the attacks had ended, other than issuing vague statements reassuring the public that everything was being done to protect them, then offering the usual sincere prayers for the victims and their families. The White House did release an official photograph of the president and first lady, Charisma Wrightman, in the Situation Room. In the photo he is lovingly reaching over and wiping a tear from her cheek. It instantly went viral, within minutes achieving the same level of historic symbolism as the image of George W. Bush standing atop smoking rubble with a bullhorn in his hand.

The what, when, and where were finished, the why was pretty obvious, so it was time for the how and the who. As horrific as it was, even I had to admit pulling off an attack of this magnitude was an impressive feat. It had required a level of planning, logistics, and security our intel hadn't believed the known terrorist organizations were capable of pulling off, especially considering all of the safeguards the Wrightman administration had put into place in its first few months.

My military background and the sacrifice I had made for this country, which admittedly I was not above exploiting when useful, had enabled me to make some pretty good background source contacts in the dark world. I threw out lines to the initials—the CIA, the NSA, the FBI, and other lesser known smarties. The damage done to the American intelligence community by the Trump/Pence administration had been substantial, cutting their budgets, their staffs, and their capabilities. The Biden people had plugged the dam but hadn't rebuilt it. Today was the payoff for that. Those people who would talk to me had zilch. One of them, a liaison to the White House, told me off the record that when Secretary of Defense Eldon "Rip" McCord saw that macabre video of the bones floating in the Pearl Harbor surf, he had exploded in anger, screaming, "Fuck 'em! Fuck all of those bastards!"

In response, President Wrightman had asked the obvious question: "Fuck who exactly?" That same deep source told me that when it was clear the attacks had ended, the president had leaned back in his chair, spread his arms in dismay, and asked his assembled cabinet, "Now what the fuck are we supposed to do?"

No one had responded.

Within hours I had posted several stories. My first piece confirmed what everybody already knew, that no one knew anything. I had actually become pretty good about writing convincingly about nothing. I included several quotes from my "well-placed anonymous sources" inside the government telling me knowledgeably that they had no new information and nothing to say "at this time." I had learned early in my career that putting quotation marks around a few essentially meaningless words gives readers the impression that those words must have some deeper meaning.

My second piece focused on the new role that social media was playing in American society. Had this taken place only a few years earlier, the vast majority of people would have told their phone to speed-dial family and friends. No longer. Seconds after the initial bulletin, people had begun reaching out to me through social media platforms, in particular Facebook, Twitter, and Instagram. I just assumed that was typical, that everybody had the same experience. To be candid, who was going to know if I was wrong? I turned to my experts in academia, who were always available and always good for a quote, knowing they could use the tear sheet to demonstrate their importance in their field. My go-to sociologist, Dr. Richard Soll, noted that the fundamental change caused by these platforms was that "Rather than contacting loved ones to make sure they were safe, as was traditional, people immediately posted their own feelings in response to these events. That demonstrated society was becoming considerably more 'me-oriented.'" (Notice my use of quotation marks!) For me, the real importance of this piece was that it kept Howie off my back for an hour.

My third story also focused on social media. The price was right for our shop; to report it all I had to do was open my phone and laptop. It was a roundup of the rumors, gossip, theories and speculation being spread on social media. The wild days of the internet when anyone could post anything had ended three years ago with the Supreme Court decision in *Trump v. Facebook et al.* Citing special prosecutor Robert Mueller's attempt to prove Russian elements had used social media to illegally influence the 2016 presidential election, the Court had ruled finally that the government did have a compelling constitutional right to determine the source of potentially seditious comments on the public media. Several people had been indicted, and while no one had been convicted, the chilling effect on free speech was obvious. With the protection of anonymity gone, people tended to be a bit more cautious with their comments. It also put additional pressure on the media; our lawyer had cautioned us about repeating unfounded allegations.

The reaction made a great story. The legendary comedian Jimmy Durante had a popular catchphrase, "Everybody wants ta get inta da act!" Social media provided that platform. A large number of people offered their prayers, others announced Kickstarter campaigns to provide assistance to affected families, and a sizable number advocated using nuclear weapons to destroy any country that had assisted the perpetrators. Some posters blamed the Wrightman administration for failing to protect the homeland; others suggested the Wrightman administration actually might be behind the attacks as an excuse to further erode constitutional rights. A surprising number of people blamed the Kardashian family for creating the culture that made these attacks possible. And, of course, several posters boasted about how much money they were making working at home.

I was finishing my story on social media reaction when Howie plopped himself down in my dining room chair. "We havin' fun yet?"

"Life's just a bowl of cherries."

"They just announced a press gathering at the White Castle," he said. He had begun referring to the White House as the White Castle several years earlier, after Trump had served cold hamburgers to the visiting national college football champions from Clemson, and it still delighted him. "Why don't you just roll on over there and see whose life you can make miserable." He Groucho-ed his eyebrows and stuck his imaginary cigar in his mouth. "Toodle-oo," he said, pushing himself out of the chair.

"Cher," I commanded out loud, "play *Victory at Sea*." And as I set out in pursuit of the truth, with maybe a quick stop to grab something to eat, that soaring score came through the seat-speakers Y had installed.

Maybe five thousand years ago I would have been carving my story, this story, into a stone. I would have depicted myself as a stick figure in a seated position on wheels; I'll bet that would have confused the archaeologists. Somehow, though, I would have gotten it down on rock or paper or now in cyberspace. I'm certain of that. It's all up there, taking up too many bytes of my memory.

As I sit here tonight, so many months later and miles away, telling you how it happened, committing it to history, I hope it serves some purpose. Maybe it's already too late. Who knows? In the end, I guess, that's up to you.

But as I remember that terrible day, I know now I made one significant mistake: I thought that the worst was behind us.

2

As I walked over to the White House I glanced at the half moon; it was startingly bright—the yin of a glass half-full. At that moment, I was pretty certain, the people in New York and Louisiana and Hawaii were experiencing the dark side of that moon.

I'd been to the White House numerous times for press conferences. I still loved the place, but as I waited in the security line I remembered my first meeting there with the new administration. That had been a memorable visit, as meaningful as the starter snapping the green flag at Indianapolis. Less than a week after Wrightman's inauguration I had been invited to meet privately with Vice President Arthur T. Hunter. I suspect I was selected thanks to Mighty Chair. I've never forgotten the advice I'd been given by the late paraplegic columnist Charles Krauthammer when I rolled out of Walter Reed into journalism. "That chair makes people uncomfortable," he said. This was even before Mighty Chair was a dream, when I was still using a standard ride. "They may dismiss you, they may be overly solicitous, or they may try to use you, but they can't ignore you. Don't ever hesitate to use that to your advantage."

It was valuable advice. I'd gotten quite adept at reading people's response to the chair, then turning it into a benefit. I'd learned to be whatever they needed me to be. In addition, I'd found that many people underestimated the physically handicapped. Some people actually spoke

louder and used simplistic language when speaking to me, as if not having
the use of my legs had affected my brain.

I didn't care. It didn't matter at all to me if I got an interview because
someone felt sorry for me. My disability wasn't exactly a use-it-or-
lose-it situation. But I did use it.

Vice President Hunter, "Artie the Hun," had been properly solicitous
as I walked into his office that afternoon. (Point of explanation: Handicapped people use the language just like everyone else. We walk into
rooms, we run to the store, and we're always ready to roll!) As I walked
into Hunter's White House office, he cleared a spot between two large
chairs for me and I eased Mighty Chair into it, maybe exaggerating the
difficulty in maneuvering into that space a little.

"Captain Stone," he greeted me, tenting his hands in front of him
and bowing gently. The elimination of the firm look-right-in-the-eye
handshake had robbed him of his opportunity to demonstrate he was a
man's man.

Artie Hunter was a bull in a $2,000 suit. He had that kind of intimi-
dating size the military has always loved. The first thing I noticed about
him was that he had suspicious hair. It was too full, too dark, too immo-
bile. It was perfectly squared away, like everything else about him. He
was the kind of man who made Mike Pence look scruffy. I wondered if
he had his general's stars tattooed on his body. Artie Hunter, it was clear,
was a man comfortable in front of a mirror.

"Hooah, sir," I responded passively. And added a good-old-boys wink.
While Hunter and I had never crossed careers in the military, I knew
his reputation. He was known for riding a desk hard. The joke in Special Ops was that he had been awarded his Purple Heart for dropping a
cassette of *Saving Private Ryan* on his big toe.

Like the man himself, his office was shipshape. He could have been
in there for years rather than just a few days. His career was neatly
framed and displayed on two walls, each photograph precisely the same
few inches from those next to it or above and below. It took two entire
walls to make the full impression, from West Point to a few doors down
from the Oval Office, from Ronald Reagan to George Clooney. And
just in case anyone doubted his toughness, eight large copper-jacketed

projectiles were lined up in ascending order on the buffed mahogany cabinet behind his desk.

Hunter was generally considered Wrightman's spine. The president was as firm as a feather in a nor'easter, bending with the winds. But the Hun fancied himself a tough Patton, who would force those winds to reconsider.

He settled into his desk chair, reminding me of Captain Kirk on the bridge of the *Enterprise.* Sunlight filtered through open blinds behind him, forcing me to squint. A power move. "This is impressive," he'd begun, tapping his computer screen. "Captain Roland Stone." Obviously he was looking at my military jacket. He nodded approvingly. "Yeah, yeah. Nice." Glancing across the desk he added, "Your country's proud of you, son."

"Rollie," I said, with an abundance of humility.

He smiled. "I know. Rollie Stone. The Rolling Stone." He clasped his hands behind his head and leaned back into that nest. Body language for "We're all guys here. Let's just relax." "I appreciate your coming by."

I shrugged. "I was in the neighborhood."

He tipped forward and clasped his mitts on his desk. "Let me be honest with you, Rollie."

(Here's my first tip to all you aspiring young journalists: Any politician who tells you he is about to be honest is *not* going to be honest.)

"That'll be a nice change around here," I responded.

A young aide entered carrying a silver tray. He laid a coaster bearing the Seal of the Vice President of the United States on the edge of the desk, then put a glass of ice water on it. He did the same thing for Hunter. I noted that he'd placed my glass just beyond my easy reach. Maybe he was just inconsiderate, but I thought more likely it was a subtle message. I'm sensitive that way.

The vice president picked up his glass and clearly enjoyed a long sip, then laid out the ground rules: "You understand this is off the record, but we have no objection to you discussing it with your colleagues. Here's the thing, Cap . . . Rollie. You've already given more than most men to this country. We're asking you for a little bit more."

He raised his eyebrows and looked at me, as if they formed a question mark. I guess I was supposed to ask what more I could give for my country. If he was looking for working legs, he'd come to the wrong person. "As I'm sure you know, this country has never been so divided ..."

Well, there was that pesky Civil War thingy.

"...and with the challenges facing us now, that god-awful mess the Trumpers created. The Democrats ..." He clenched his lips and shook his head in disdain. "I don't have to tell you what a shitstorm we've inherited. The pandemic. The drought. Famine. That whole Trump thing about the election being fixed. The Iranians, North Koreans, Putin." He shook his head. "The whole China debacle. The Palestinians. The French are laughing at us." He paused to muse over that. Apparently the French were not supposed to laugh at us. "We've even had to reestablish relations with Canada. Canada, for God's sake, how the fuck do you fuck up relations with Canada?

"The whole fucking world is ready to blow up and we can't even get the two parties to agree that we should clean our water and fix the roads." He took a long and thoughtful breath. "Frankly, Rollie, we no longer can afford that division. The future of this country is at stake. 'A house divided against itself' and all that stuff. It's right. We've got to figure out some way of putting this country back together. Whatever it takes. That's why I asked you to come in."

He paused again to await my reaction. I wasn't quite certain what I was supposed to say. I couldn't even convince a plumber to come on a Saturday, yet somehow I was supposed to bring the entire country together? I flipped up my hands in confusion.

"Here's the deal. Among journalists here in Washington you're an influencer. Editors and reporters know who you are. They respect you. The president asked me to tell you that he would welcome your support." He took another sip of water to allow that compliment to sink in. Then he smiled his most insincere smile—the one in which his lips are so tightly closed they might have been sewed together, and only one side of his mouth curls up—and added, "But honestly, Rollie, we don't need it."

I assumed this was where I was expected to respond with some level of dismay. Well, we both knew I wasn't going to stand up and walk out in a huff. Instead, I smiled back, although both sides of my mouth curled. I'd found mirroring an expression often was far more effective than words. And in my humble opinion my insincere smile was far superior to his. Then I lightly pushed the toggle switch on Mighty Chair's armrest. With barely a whisper the extendible arm emerged from the armrest. I guided it to the water glass on his desk. Holding my hand above the AI command screen, I closed my fingers as if squeezing a toothpaste tube. In response, the steel fingers at the end of the arm mimicked that motion, closing around the glass. Using the toggle switch, I deftly brought the glass to me and set it gently on my tray without spilling a drop. I picked it up, tipped it toward the vice president, and enjoyed an equally long sip.

I loved doing stuff like that. Admittedly, Jenny thought it was immature. But she would be humming a very different tune after I told her I was an officially certified influencer!

Hunter and I sat there smiling insincerely at each other until the silence became too loud for him. "This administration has great respect for the First Amendment. Great respect. I give you my word . . ."—he patted his heart—"no one in this administration will ever interfere with your right to write whatever you believe. Ever." One, two, three. Here it comes. "However . . .

"By law the government of the United States has the absolute right . . ." He shook his head, then corrected himself. "Check that, it's more than that." Shaking his index finger to make sure I understood the importance of each word, he continued, "We have a constitutional and moral obligation to protect this country from anyone who would tear it apart. That goes all the way back to the Sedition Acts. That's one reason Congress was given the power to regulate the public airways . . ."

I went into frozen-face mode, trying not to show any emotion. It was hard. But this was a direct threat.

He rambled on, ". . . times of crisis . . . spread propaganda . . . further inflame the division . . . unfair criticism . . . the Sedition Act . . . the Espionage Act . . ." It was a history lesson. Well taught, to be honest (wink, wink). He navigated through the long history of the federal government's invoking emergency powers to achieve its objectives while limiting criticism. While eventually the salient parts of almost all of them were ruled unconstitutional by the Supreme Court, he told me that the administration was willing to take its chances, "especially given the *current* makeup of the court."

He hit the word *current* hard, reminding me the Dems had threatened to add members to the Supreme Court to tip the balance to the left, but had backed off after the huge negative response. The implication was obvious. Wrightman's spine was not going to be bent by the complaints of a hundred million people.

As he continued this lecture, he stood and walked around his desk until he was behind me. Another power move. "Cher," I instructed, "turn around, please." Mighty Chair turned; its GPS system locked on him and followed as he moved. I turned up the motor volume, so each step he took was followed by a brief and, I hoped, disconcerting whir.

He wet his lips and looked down at me. "Look, Rollie, we know the press isn't on our side. That's okay, that's your job. But we also have a job to do and we intend to do it . . ." His tone was battlefield firm. "Do you know why Wrightman was elected?"

(Here's a second tip for future journalists. When the person you are interviewing asks you a rhetorical question, the best way to answer is to wrap the question in your own words and hand it back. Regift it.) I responded. "Why was Wrightman elected?"

"He promised the American people three things. One . . ." He held up his index finger like a magician displaying his deck of cards. "We are going to make people proud to be American again. Two." He added his middle finger and pointed the *V* right at me.

I held up my index finger and middle finger to confirm that I was counting with him.

He blipped, like a tape skipping a frame. Generals aren't used to having two fingers waved at them. "Two. We are going to reunite this country. And three." He added his ring finger and concluded loudly and firmly, "We are going to keep America safe! Whatever it takes to do that." He repeated that last line slowly, emphasizing each word as if in warning: "What. Ever. It. Takes." He took a step back, satisfied.

I guess I was supposed to get caught up in his fervor, but I was no longer capable of a standing ovation. Whatever his objective, I didn't like being threatened. "Is there something specific I'm supposed to know," I wondered, "or is this just a, you know . . ." It was my turn to emphasize the words: "*General.* Warning."

In my last life we'd told every possible variation of that old joke: Did you hear about the general who made the mistake of being specific? But to my surprise it almost slipped by Hunter. I can report from experience that most general officers are about as funny as a six A.M. barracks inspection.

The meeting continued this way for several more minutes. While Hunter never made any direct threats, his belligerent and dismissive tone made the point. He reminded me that on the battlefield we'd had to deal carefully with reporters to prevent them from disclosing strategic information. "We used to say the media was an important tool," he explained. "It can help you hammer things down or screw things up." Then he flashed me a smile, displaying a mouthful of sparkling white teeth.

If the intent of this meeting was to intimidate me, it failed. Woe was he. As I was leaving his office, he made the mistake of stepping quickly in front of me to open the door. I'd neglected to turn off Chair's GPS system, which continued to target him, and somehow I ran right over his highly shined left shoe, digging a dirt-brown tread mark into the soft European leather.

Hunter was stunned silent, having no idea how to respond. His jaw opened and closed as he searched unsuccessfully for the right words.

Cher spoke up in her decidedly feminine voice. "Rollie, I'm sorry we hit that bump."

The vice president was confused. He began looking quizzically around the office for the source of that voice.

"Oh, sir, I'm sorry," I said as earnestly as I could manage. I lowered my voice and said, "That's just Cher. You know women." And winked.

As I left, I heard him ordering an assistant to find a shoeshine kit.

When I got back to the office, Howie had asked what I'd learned.

"I'm an influencer," I said proudly.

"Wow," Howie said, "that's great. Who are the influencees?"

"He didn't tell me."

Howie tapped his index finger against his lips to show me he was considering the value of that information, then decided, "I'd put it on my résumé."

After that meeting I'd never heard directly from the Hun again, other than bouncy ecards "With best personal wishes" every Christmas. The security line was moving even more slowly than usual that night. The guards always pulled me aside to do a complete scan of the chair. I had this thing I always did; when they ran the metal detector up and down Cher giggled and said girlishly, "Don't you touch me there unless you're serious." No one was kidding that night, though. I passed through three levels of security before being escorted to the James S. Brady Press Briefing Room in the West Wing of the White House. The press room is considerably smaller than it appears on TV. Mighty Chair just barely squeezed through the door. But a large wheelchair did have its advantages; while everybody else had to take an assigned seat, I always had mine with me. Officially I was assigned a spot in the rear, supposedly so I didn't block the emergency exit, but no one dared complain when I eased closer to the front.

As I sat waiting there on arguably the worst day in American history, I thought about Hunter's three raised fingers—and that line from my favorite Meat Loaf song popped into my mind: "Two out of three ain't bad."

That third one, though, keeping America safe—that one was a bitch.

I glanced at my watch. As usual, press secretary Kaufman was late. "Preparing to make up," Frankie B. Goode had called it. As I'd walked in I had been handed the list of approved subjects I could ask about and several suggested questions. The briefing room was already way overcrowded, but people made way for me. Hunter had been right about one thing, most members of the Washington media knew who I was; I had never heard a single person claim they had gotten me confused with some other guy in a large, black-leather-covered wheelchair. With cool signal lights! A few people screamed greetings to me above the din. It wasn't really going to be any kind of conference in the traditional sense of the word; that once-normal televised Q and A had ended forever with Trump. Press secretary Eunice Kaufman responded only to preapproved questions. Now it was what was more accurately described as a "media opportunity." The only reason any of us were there was to be able to report to viewers or readers that we were there. "White House press room" made a great visual for stand-up reports and print bylines.

I'd attended my first White House press conference in 2015. Obama. Josh Earnest. I'd sat there hoping I would be called on to ask a question and terrified I would make a fool of myself if I was. Press conferences mattered then; we were doing a vitally important job, holding the administration to task for its actions. Making politicians accountable. While sometimes we failed, at least we were making an effort to represent the interests of the American people. We asked the questions that needed to be asked, admittedly not always with good manners, but there was at least a modicum of respect between the administration and the media. I'm smiling as I write this just thinking about those days. Imagine being nostalgic for organized chaos.

That first time I was there, I'd turned Mighty Chair into a corner, hunched my shoulders so no one would see me, and called my sister. I later learned that this was the standard "Guess where I'm calling you from?" call that just about every first visitor makes. Press conferences were fun, as much a social gathering as a serious meeting. Meet, greet, and apply the heat, as we called it. But we believed we were acting as the vox populi, the voice of the people.

It didn't seem possible so much could have changed in such a brief period of time. The easy answer is to blame it on President Trump, who so casually destroyed American traditions and conventions without understanding their importance. But honestly, relations between the White House and the media had begun fraying long before him.

The competition between the cable networks—and between reporters for TV face time—had resulted in a little too much media showboating. Asking probing questions became less important than those gotcha moments. Maybe too many of us card-carrying correspondents had embraced the (Sam) Donaldson Rule: Confrontation makes good TV. The Obama people had been able to handle it; they didn't like it, but they understood it and learned to deal with it.

Not the Trumpers. None of them. Spicer. Huckabee. Sanders. Conway.

What's her name, the Invisible Woman. The mandatory blonde. None of them. Paranoia had enveloped their West Wing. Every question we asked was treated not only as a challenge, but also as a rebuke. It is inaccurate to claim the media was treated as an enemy; Trumpers appeared to respect America's enemies far more than the press.

Trump and his people had screwed things up so badly that the Dems had about as much chance of putting the economy back together as the king's men had with Humpty. The Bidens suffered under the mistaken belief that restoration of traditional government was possible.

The Dems got caught cleaning up the mess, but never figured out how to properly restore the relationship between politics and the media. They assumed we were naturally on their side because they weren't Trump, and they assumed that until we began calling them on their mistakes. Then we became the enemy again. I remember once being chastised by Senator Klobuchar, who told me, "You're not helping us do our job."

Well, yeah, I'd responded, actually that was our job.

The damage done to that traditional relationship had served the needs of Wrightman. During his campaign he had made a big deal of refusing to be interviewed one-on-one, explaining he wanted to speak directly to the American people without any filter.

The appearance of press secretary Eunice Kaufman, finally, took me out of my reverie. I liked Eunice, most of us did. At first the selection of a Jewish grandmother had been criticized as an attempt to further reduce the importance of the office, but Kaufman changed that quickly through the force of her personality. With her platinum-blond bouffant hairstyle, her blue-rimmed glasses and matching nail color, and her omnipresent pearl necklace, set off by a rollicking personality, she became a popular face of the administration. Although she had no previous journalistic experience, she explained that she was quite capable of handling a press room full of "busybodies" because she had raised two daughters, "One's a doctor and the other one's one of those fall-down lawyers, who must do okay because she has a pool," and "a smart boy who maybe could have married better, but you didn't hear that from me."

She entered without her usual pratfall; usually she made a show of adjusting her glasses, which caused her to fumble the loose papers she was carrying while muttering under her breath. She often began with a friendly insult: we were "ink-stained wretches" or "typewriter terrorists." But not this night. She wasn't even wearing her trademark rhinestone-framed glasses. "Hello, people."

A couple of people in the back, probably White House staffers, shouted back, "Hello, Eunie!"

The job of the press secretary had changed considerably. Kaufman's job, rather than answering questions, was basically to tell the media what the administration wanted the public to know and to do so in an entertaining way. She was sort of a human press release. And she was so entertaining that the public either overlooked, ignored, or just didn't care that few questions were asked or answered. As long as she did her act, nobody other than a few reporters really cared. When a reporter did ask an unapproved question, she peered over the top of her signature glasses, threw her hands in the air, and issued what had quickly become a national catchphrase: "Why are you hocking me with these questions?" Perhaps her most oft-quoted line was, "Listen to me, Mr. Big Shot Reporter, I don't need you to give me agita. I've got my own kids for that." And the most cutting line of all: "Does your mother know you're out here badgering an old woman?"

It was a reality show and she was the star. The reporters in that room were willing props, the audience was out there in Televisionland, on the far side of the remotely operated cameras. Not this night, though, not at all. Not while corpses were still floating off Pearl Harbor and through Louisiana streets, and body parts were being scraped off the walls of the Lincoln Tunnel.

Kaufman provided no useful information and did so with great confidence. No organization had claimed credit for the attacks. The intelligence community had promising leads it was pursuing but had no statement to make at this time. Our troops around the world were on high alert. Homeland Security could not yet provide any estimates of killed, wounded, or missing. The president, the first lady, and most of the cabinet had spent the day in the Situation Room, monitoring events. The president had spoken with European leaders, who had offered their prayers and condolences. They promised their cooperation in any investigation and stood ready to provide whatever aid was necessary. To avoid any sense of panic, the president had asked the stock market and banks to remain closed until further notification. A temporary eleven P.M. local time national curfew was being imposed in cities with a population of more than 100,000 for safety. The aviation industry would be reopening in the morning, although many flights would be delayed. It had not been decided when the president would visit any of the sites.

She continued for about ten minutes, mostly reading from the handout we had been given. When she finished, she perched her glasses on the end of her nose and looked over the top of them at us. "Okay, who's got a question?"

Every arm in the room snapped up. "Jane," she said, pointing at the very pregnant Jane E. Stein from Fox News. "Okay, what?"

Stein wobbled out of her seat, glancing at her notes. She inhaled deeply, shook her head in disbelief, and then asked simply, "What happened? How could this happen?"

There wasn't a sound in the room. In another life Eunice might have been the famed madam Polly Adler, the flamboyant character Diamond Lil, the restaurateur Elaine Kaufman or some mysterious Russian temptress. Those of us in the room had the good fortune of knowing her as a wise political operative who had promoted the chutzpah of a Jewish grandmother and the instincts of Catwoman into a successful career. She was a showwoman with situational ethics, which made Washington the perfect place for her to be: There was no place else in the country with more people for sale. She also understood she had one job: Protect the president.

Eunice cleared her throat; being somber wasn't part of her shtick. She had the impossible task of threading a needle with an anchor chain. She couldn't admit we were completely surprised, which would be admitting the most significant intelligence failure in our history; but she couldn't claim we had any advance knowledge, either, and failed to act on it. "If we knew the answer, it wouldn't have happened," she said, flipping up her palms in wonder. "Here's what I can tell you: We will get to the bottom of this. We will answer all of your questions." She swept her hand around the room. "This isn't the time for it, though. But what I am going to tell you is that there is a lot going on that I can't tell you about."

Ollie Casperson, the veteran MSNBC correspondent, went off-list to ask what steps the administration was considering to prevent another significant economic hit. The country had barely recovered from the full effects of the pandemic. The damage had been filtering through the entire economic sector for years. All the economic indicators had been flat for months. Unemployment was still over 7 percent, and the department stores had never fully reopened, causing malls to go out of business. Banks had been devastated by people defaulting on loans, which limited available capital and led to a depressed real estate market. Commodity prices were way up. Only the stock market had continued to do well, but these attacks were going to change that. Panic and fear drive the market down.

"Mind your own business, Ollie," Kaufman responded pleasantly. Mind your own business was Wrightman's basic economic philosophy; it is up to each person to tend to their own economic situation. He'd run on the premise that the government couldn't possibly create a one-size-benefits-all program, and no one cares about your own situation more than you do. The most the government could do is create a climate in which business can flourish. "The president is well aware of the danger," she continued, "and he has been conferring with his cabinet and financial industry leaders to determine when the markets can safely reopen. But he does want to reassure all Americans that our economy remains healthy."

Having successfully said nothing, she pointed at me. "Rollie?" In unison the pack of reporters turned toward me. I wanted to ask which cabinet member was going to be resigning to spend more time with their family, meaning who was going to take the fall to insulate Wrightman. That subject, however, was not approved. I could have asked my snarky question and risked losing important national exposure for the *Pro*; or I could have tossed her a softball.

I already was a certified "hero." My hard-hitting question was "Has the first lady decided which designer to wear when she goes with the president to visit a disaster site?" Okay, maybe not exactly that, but it was just as innocuous: What actions would the military take in the next few days?

When I strolled into the office later to write my follow-up piece, everybody pretty much ignored me. I expected that. After all, the nation was still in shock, we had suffered three successful, massive, simultaneous attacks and rescue and recovery operations were ongoing. The coverage on every one of the dozen monitors was different, although the floating bones of Pearl Harbor showed up regularly.

But sitting in the center of my desk was the infamous Golden Plunger. This spray-painted gold toilet plunger was awarded by the staff on precious few occasions to assist the recipient in retrieving his balls from up his ass. I did catch a few people snickering, then turning away. Actually, receiving it was the best thing that had happened on this dreadful day.

A few seconds after I got settled, Howie plopped down in my dining room chair. "Congratulations," he said, nodding toward my prestigious trophy. He leaned forward, resting his right forearm on my desk, and said quietly, "Thanks. I know it wasn't fun." Then he pointed at the plunger with his thumb and added, "In case you're wondering, no stipend comes with it."

I placed the plunger on the floor, carefully avoiding the growing tower of cups. But deep down, deep inside my gut, that place where knowledge meets intuition, I knew somehow this was going to alter my life. "Cher," I said, trying to dismiss that feeling, "buckle up."

"Rollie," she replied with sufficient huff, "I'm a disembodied voice. I don't have a seat belt."

3

I love the clacking of a typewriter. The sound stirs a vestigial emotion buried in my ancestral DNA, so long ago I had downloaded a program that synced the tick and *bringg* of an IBM Selectric to my computer keyboard. But those reassuring sounds were lost in the din of our newsroom. Making journalism is supposed to be loud and sweaty. My story began, "'This was probably the worst day in the history of the United States,' White House press secretary Eunice Kaufman admitted today. As individual acts of incredible heroism continued into the evening, and responders began the painful task of recovering the bodies of many more victims, the questions remain: Who is responsible for these attacks and why wasn't this nation better prepared?"

"C'mon, Rollie, we need it!" Howie screamed at me. "Let's go. Let's go."

I pecked away, the words coming as easily as if I were pounding them into a cave wall. I leaned way back and stared at my monitor. Words dug into my soul: *killed, crushed, children, families, bloody, explosions.* I released a long controlling breath, reminding myself I was a reporter; report it, don't feel it. There had been a lot of bad days in the past eight years, more than I could count even if I took off my shoes, but there had been nothing as stomach-churning, black-pit awful as this day had been. I reread my words, my head shaking back and forth like I couldn't help wondering, how the fuck did we get here?

Like so many others, I had assumed that no administration could be worse than Trump/Pence. In those days we had been thankful for the Trumpers' ineptitude: The pit bull trainer put in charge of the pandemic response. The twenty-four-year-old college graduate running banking policy. The son-in-law who made a full-sour pickle seem warm and fuzzy apparently in charge of everything else. We used to joke about how much real damage to the country, to the world, they would have done if they had been competent. Then the pandemic came along and the laughter stopped. Then the drought and the subsequent famine.

I remember that incredible sense of relief that we had survived Trump. Well, those of us who had survived. I still have the T-shirt. Looking back on it, I am reminded of Steve McQueen's story in *The Magnificent Seven*, about the guy who fell off the roof of a ten-story building; as he passed each floor, people heard him say, "So far, so good."

Any chance Biden and Democrats had to lead the recovery had disappeared with the drought and the subsequent famine, not to mention Superstorm Malika, which had further devastated the Gulf Coast. The Democrats' efforts always reminded me of that classic 2022 photo showing disbelief, frustration, and helplessness on Dodgers outfielder Cody Bellinger's face as he watches Aaron Judge's World Series–winning home run sailing into the Yankee Stadium bleachers.

As much as possible throughout my career, I've been an equal opportunity smart-ass. I poked at both sides equally, or in the last election all three sides. About Wrightman I had written: "Senator Wrightman's record in the Senate has been unblemished by achievement or conviction. He established his legendary 'independent streak' by refusing to support controversial legislation proposed by either party. When criticized for this lack of achievement, he responded by railing against both parties for 'their transparent efforts to silence the only truly independent voice in the Senate.'"

While John McCain had once described him as having "the depth of a puddle after a light drizzle," he proved to be the perfect political package for the moment: a walking antidote to chaos and controversy. He was, as his campaign slogan promised, *The Wrightman for the Right Time*.

He certainly looked right for the part. His trim body seemed made for Italian suits, which never wrinkled as he walked; his full head of silver hair was so perfectly flaked with hints of black that Benjamin Moore might have manufactured it, and his teeth were whiter than a Trump rally.

He was a terrific politician. He smiled easily and often and had mastered the complex skill of never being caught by photographers between friendly expressions. There were no Dukakis's head popping out of a tank or John Kerry sailboarding pictures of Ian Wrightman. He brought to mind that great Nixon political credo: Never wear a hat or stay for dinner. Early in his political career he had found the comfortable ground between self-deprecating and acceptable opinion and couldn't be moved off it with a backhoe. He spoke in a deep and mellifluous voice that resounded with profundity; Wolf Blitzer once noted Wrightman could make a mattress label sound profound.

But mostly, Senator I. M. Wrightman understood completely that the most important skill for an American politician was to be first to be second. He never actually staked a position on an issue. Instead, he had the rare ability to catch the most desirable breeze and make it his own.

That campaign slogan was right; he probably was the right man for the time. After the daily chaos of Trump/Pence, followed by the aggressive flailing of the Democrats, more than anything else Americans craved normalcy. They wanted a decent person who had a pet and watched the same TV shows they did.

Senator Wrightman announced his independent candidacy after both parties had made their choice, claiming he was reluctantly running only because neither nominee was capable of reuniting the divided nation. As his running mate, he picked the respected former chairman of the Joint Chiefs, Marine general Arthur T. Hunter. Wrightman's choice of the Hun was meant to send an unambiguous message to our allies and enemies, a list that had been jumbled during Trump, that the United States was willing and able to defend our shores, wherever in the world we decided they happened to be.

While Wrightman's opponents made grandiose promises about restoring basic American values, uniting the country, and regaining our prestige in the world, he did no such thing. His campaign slogan was concise: "Restore Order." It was presented as a social, economic, and diplomatic doctrine, and rather than being pinned down to any specific policies, he urged voters to define it in their own best possible way. *Restore order.* That allowed people to interpret it to mean whatever most appealed to them. The one thing few experts realized is that it meant exactly what it promised.

The essential feel-good highlight of his campaign had been the gleeful announcement that his and Charisma's twenty-two-year-old daughter, America, had become engaged to a Marine combat vet who had lost an arm fighting in Afghanistan, a man she'd met while volunteering at Walter Reed. His Republican opponent, former vice president Mike Pence, who had begun wearing pre-wrinkled jeans to prove he was just an ordinary guy's guy, had skillfully countered that by tearfully putting down his previously unknown fifteen-year-old border collie, Abraham Lincoln. He was accompanied to the vet's office by his family and a media horde, but America Wrightman had still snared *People*'s cover while the photograph of a tearful Pence carrying Abe's lifeless body was relegated to an inside quarter-page.

Running as an Independent who was "not beholden to any special interests," Wrightman benefited from the disarray in both parties. With the lovely, oft-blushing, and unthreatening Charisma at his side he ran a feel-good campaign mostly free of specifics other than *I'm not the other guys.* With his campaign song, "There's a Great Big Beautiful Tomorrow," playing in the background, he had been appropriately sympathetic to the plight of the unemployed renewable energy workers, he had stood next to dour farmers whose silos were filled with rotting corn, potatoes, and soybeans, and he had been supportive of congressional efforts to pump money into the system while proclaiming himself fiscally conservative.

He was folksy when necessary, admitting sheepishly to voters during the first debate that it was Charisma who had urged him to get into politics after he had sold the family publishing empire, "mostly because she wanted to get me out of the house, where I was spending way too much time disagreeing with Judge Judy's verdicts."

As he had done in the Senate, during the campaign he mostly laid back and let his opponents destroy each other, busying himself shaking hands, kissing babies, and reminding voters that "America's future is still ahead of us." People believed Wrightman was a nonentity who slipped into office because of the disdain voters had for both political parties. But the actual key to his success turned out to be twenty-four-year-old wunderkind Raymond Munchmeyer, a lanky, quirky cybermarketing genius who teamed with veteran pollster Nolan Noyes to create the social media effort that shaped each of Wrightman's images. Reign Man, as Munchmeyer was known inside the campaign, lived by the motto "You are what you share."

Noyes's polling data determined what people wanted to hear and Munchmeyer's manipulation of social media fed it to them, making it possible for Wrightman to simultaneously be all things to all voters. To young people, for example, he was the sometimes forgetful but lovingly supportive dad, even when befuddled by technology; to Southerners, he was a down-home guy who loved banjo music, William Faulkner, Friday-night football, NASCAR, and the American flag; to Northerners, he was the egghead who sang along with Springsteen, recommended Walter Mosley, and loved his daughter's rescue labradoodle, NBA basketball, and the equal protection guarantees of the Constitution as symbolized by the American flag.

It was a marketing technique that worked equally well for selling diapers and electing a president. According to various media, his inauguration marked "a new dawn," "a new beginning," "a new era," "a rebirth of the American spirit," and "a new day" on which "it is time to turn the page" on the "darkest moments in our history" and "bring forth a renewed spirit of cooperation" or "a rebirth of American democracy."

Admittedly I had been as guilty as anyone else in creating that positive atmosphere. A couple of those phrases had come from my computer, which makes it difficult to deny I wrote them. It is amazing how easily we all bought into that. All of us. I understand the general public falling for this—after all, campaigns spend millions of dollars to accomplish that—but me? On Inauguration Day I had written that the voters had "saved democracy." I admit that; those were my own words. But as the immortal Eric Stratton pointed out in *Animal House,* "You fucked up. You trusted us."

The entire *Pro* crew watched the inauguration on the TVs above the bar at Lucille's Ballroom, our local hangout across the street from the office. "Cut-rate coverage," as we referred to it. We rarely sent a staffer to cover any event viewers could watch on TV. Wrightman's inaugural address had been somber and realistic. "As we approach our two hundred and fiftieth anniversary," he told the huge crowd, "our democracy faces grave challenges from many quarters, among them from rogue nations and terrorists both across the oceans and close to home, as well as our fellow Americans who have lost faith in our shared American values of life, liberty, and the pursuit of happiness. Damage has been done to this country that will take considerable time to heal. The foundations of our financial security have been hobbled by irresponsible fiscal policies. Hatred based on race, religion, creed, nationality, political status, and gender has been exposed to light and has grown. Our physical infrastructure and the value system that had made us great among nations has deteriorated and is danger of collapse.

"And yet it is a great day . . ."

My own feelings were a mix of relief and trepidation. I loved this country with all its faults; I had never bought into the American myth, but I always appreciated the potential greatness of this country. My grandfather, Aubrey Stone, had emigrated here from Eastern Europe. Sometimes at night, after he'd had just enough to loosen his memory, we'd sit on the porch swing and I'd listen as he described the terrors of his adolescence. "It may not be so perfect here," he'd say with the last trace of an accent he tried so hard to overcome. "Americans like that Disney stuff because they got good at pretending, but you listen to me, here is much better. There we carried around our fear with us like we were walking in a shadow. We were wondering always what was waiting around the next corner. The people here, they wouldn't never let what happened there happen here. They'd see it for what it is and stop it quick." Then he would launch into one of his stories about a neighbor disappearing or hiding a radio under the floorboards at the first sound of boots on cobblestones or his walk over the mountains to get out.

I voted for Wrightman. I know, I'm not supposed to reveal that. Journalism 101. But as I write these words, I think it's important to admit that. Considering . . . well, considering. I believed that this nation, America, needed a president who lacked sufficient passion to alienate anyone. A healer, someone dependable; a decent, reasonably intelligent guy stuck firmly in the middle. I actually found his lack of grandiose plans far more honest and appealing than the hollow promises made by his opponents.

On his first day in office Wrightman began fulfilling the only promise he had made, restoring order. "A free society relies on a trustworthy, vibrant media," the official announcement began. To rectify the damage done to the media's credibility by President Trump's continued accusations of "fake news," broadcast and print media henceforth would be required to post either a news, fact, or an opinion logo, a shield with an N, F, or an O on its stories. Significant penalties, including loss of license for multiple offenses, would be levied against any outlet mislabeling its content. This was necessary, the announcement continued, to protect the First Amendment. It was not intended to be any restriction on free speech, which would of course be unconstitutional; instead, it was simply a matter of extending the movie and music industry rating systems to news outlets to assist viewers and readers in separating actual news from opinion or "fake news."

The reaction surprised me. I expected most journalists to be outraged. And in fact some news outlets did object, pointing out that government officials would be empowered to designate stories as real news or opinion. In response, to help viewers and readers understand the objectives of this system, those officials gave these complaints the very first O rating.

While people like Howie were furious, to my surprise many outlets accepted it, even praising the administration for its efforts to combat the concept of fake news. They were okay with it, so long as the government did not impose any restrictions on what to report. When Chuck Schumer warned in a tweet, "He who controls the media controls the American people," he actually received more responses correcting his misuse of gender—"It should read 'He or she who . . .'"—than criticizing the policy.

4

liked to walk to work. The combination of my handicapped placard
and D.C. journalist plates would have allowed me to park Van on the
White House lawn if I wanted to, but unless the weather was awful,
I put it in a garage that formed the third point of a triangle with the
gym and the office. That morning ramble, with Cher playing soft music
through Chair's speakers, gave me time to sort out my thoughts, plan
the day, and make sure I kept in touch with the street.

In the desert, it had been essential to maintain contact with the so-
called Arab streets. We gathered considerable intelligence from watching
and listening and noticing even the small changes. Who had disappeared
from a stall? Why was the price of figs going down? Where did a fruit
peddler find the money to fix his truck? It was a learned habit that I'd
carried with me through the years.

I tried to take a slightly different route every day to sample as many
streets as possible. I'd gotten to know the area well. I knew the shops
and their keepers; I had befriended the homeless and knew what spots
they'd staked out—once even mediating a turf dispute over rights to a
warm Metro grating. When I was on schedule, I got to know people
on a similar schedule, and over time I had developed a sense of the
Washington street. It got to a point where I could identify what street I
was on by the scents from the stands and shops. Even sometimes by the
cracks and divots in the sidewalks that rattled Mighty Chair.

In the days following the attacks, the streets turned cold. It was like an old friend avoiding me. People averted their eyes, mumbled a few words, and shook their head in response to a familiar greeting or simply turned their back to me to avoid contact. There was nothing to say. The audacity of the attacks, their success, the relentlessly mounting toll of dead and wounded, the endless photographs of known victims and those who were still missing, the reports of funerals, the stories of miraculous survivors and those who missed their fate by a seemingly innocuous decision—all of this shattered the last fragile hope that Wrightman could somehow bring America together. The dark, quiet anxiety that had been hanging over the country finally settled down as completely as if someone had simply put the lid on a Crock-Pot.

The depression was psychological. It spread as easily as dandelion seeds floating on a breeze. It seeped into every aspect of American society until it finally impacted the economy.

The worldwide economic collapse didn't start here. It resulted from the confluence of several factors that had been percolating for years and exploded with the pandemic, which finally caused our markets first to freeze, then to begin the long decline. The damage throughout Europe began with Brexit, followed by the anarchy in Venezuela that eventually bled into other South American nations, the unchecked Russian aggression, the relentless Chinese economic expansion, the political unrest throughout the third world, and the growing belligerence of Iran against the OPEC nations and North Korea against South Korea and this country. All of this was made significantly worse by the mass migration of desperate populations caused by war and climate change. The coronavirus finally collapsed the already weakened global economy. The vaccine might have stabilized the situation had the drought not led to famine, which devastated the remnants of the third-world economies. The result was global insecurity, which morphed into global instability.

But what actually caused the collapse was fear—the fear that finally reached the street. As long as we all held hands, sang "Kumbaya" by the campfire, and ignored reality, somehow we kept chugging along. I'll tell you the event that I believe made a significant difference. In late August 2022, just as the economy was stabilizing, Amazon received an order for a Kenmore microwave from Mr. and Mrs. Rob and Jeni Farwell of Mesa, Arizona. It was one of about 13 million microwaves that were sold in America that year. Rob Farwell had placed the order online. It was forwarded by Amazon's internal computer system to the computers operating their warehouse. A robot in the Phoenix fulfillment center was directed to pick the item off the shelf and place it on a truck. The self-driving truck delivered it to a warehouse in Mesa. From there, the self-operating mini-system delivered it to the Farwells' address, depositing it in the Nest delivery security system. An alert was sent to both Rob's and Jeni's cell phones, informing them that their new microwave was waiting on their front porch. The Nest locked it in its secure box until one of the Farwells got home and opened the box with their password. It was a dazzling display of technology. Not a single human being touched that carton from the moment the order was placed to its delivery a day later. Amazon was justifiably proud of this display of excellence and boasted about it on a Super Bowl commercial.

But the estimated 110 million people who saw that commercial had a very different reaction: Not a single human being touched that carton from the moment the order was placed to its delivery a day later. They were horrified. They saw their jobs disappearing. Rather than marveling at this feat, they wondered how anyone was going to be able to pay for the microwave. Any hopes that the jobs that had been destroyed by Covid-19 would be coming back disappeared that day.

Here, here's an example: During my military career every time I boarded one of our Globemasters, I'd wonder how the fuck anything that big could get off the ground. It made no sense. How could thin air support a hundred tons of steel? But somehow it did. I decided what made it possible was the collective belief of all the people onboard; as long as we believed it could fly, it could fly. I worried that if any one of us dared admit the truth, that airplane would not get off the ground. What kept us all sitting there quietly was that cool guy in a crisp uniform wearing aviator shades—*aviator shades,* they even named them after him—and smiling confidently as he stepped into the cockpit. Our captain. All the Sullys in the world, even before there was a Sully, we trusted that he knew what he was doing. He said it could get off the ground, it could get off the ground. We had a leader who would take care of us so we could sit back with confidence and watch a boring in-flight movie about marching penguins.

As far as I was concerned, for several years that same sort of belief system was the only thing holding together the American economy. It really should have collapsed decades earlier. It made no real sense: it was too big; it had too many structural problems; it was inefficient and unfair. It was capricious and disorderly and depended as much on luck as on ingenuity and innovation. The distribution of wealth created the very rich and all the rest of us. The only reason the economy worked was because people believed it would continue working. That some-how, whatever the problem, the smart guys would figure it out. Even the pandemic hadn't destroyed that pioneer optimism. Whatever prob-lems existed, somehow our Sully would come along and solve them— just as had happened throughout our history.

That Amazon commercial terrified everyone.

To the surprise of most experts, the American economy wheezed and sputtered through the disasters but did not totally collapse. It proved to be too big, with too many moving parts. But it slowed, and the more it slowed, the more concerned people became, which caused it to slow even more. As I wrote in one of my most widely reposted columns:

> We've lost our Hojo. We are about as far as we can be from the promise of post–World War II America, when our factories were bursting with economic potential and our politicians were determined to export our unique democracy to the world, when you could find the security of an orange-roofed Howard Johnson's on every spanking new highway crisscrossing the nation, knowing that a coffee-pot-carrying waitress named Esther would be pleased as punch to serve you apple pie a la mode topped with any one of its 28 flavors of ice cream. We've lost that American can-do spirit in which we once so confidently believed, and it has been replaced by . . . an array of overly-confident cats on Facebook.

It was the perfect climate from which a candidate like Ian Wrightman could emerge. He understood, or someone in his campaign understood, what Americans so desperately wanted: someone to believe in. A Sully to convey the message: *Trust me, everything is going to be all right.* The only thing Wrightman was missing were the aviator glasses. So while the Republicans were warning Americans about encroaching socialism and the Democrats were promising economic equality and affordable healthcare, Wrightman positioned himself as the plumber who could fix the leaking pipe. He shrugged his shoulders and agreed that all those promises the other guys were making were great, we all want everything they were offering, but meanwhile that leak is destroying your house. It really was a brilliant metaphor; millions of Americans easily related to fear of plumbing.

The usual *Meet the Press/This Week/GPS* panelists characterized his campaign slogan, "Restore Order," as a code phrase for either fascism or neoliberalism. But what they failed to understand—okay, I missed it too—is that order was exactly what people wanted. Wrightman paid attention to what was happening around the world. The Russian people loved Putin. The Brazilians elected Jair Bolsonaro, a former army captain—note that, a captain!—who proclaimed, "A good criminal is a dead criminal," and set out to prove it. In the Philippines, President Rodrigo Duterte became wildly popular by detaining small-time criminals for loitering and smoking and even drinking outdoors while sanctioning executions for more serious crimes like dealing drugs.

Wrightman came into office with a smile and a fist. The smile provided cover for the fist. Day after day his administration announced seemingly minor changes and restrictions that taken as a whole gave the impression that he was going to do exactly as he promised: restore order. After the endless chaos of the Trump White House and the intense ineffectiveness of the Democrats, the belief that an intelligent adult was flying the plane allowed people to sit back and enjoy the penguin movie. It worked—as long as nobody looked behind the curtain.

With great fanfare, Homeland Security introduced the new Cyber Card program, creating an app that allowed everyone to download their national driver's license—which also could be used to bypass long security lines at airports and to prove voting eligibility—on their smart-phone; but registering for it required providing proof of citizenship and other personal documentation. In reality, it was the country's first national identity card, and it allowed any law enforcement officer to instantly learn numerous private details about you simply by scanning the bar code. The whole concept made me feel uncomfortable—in fact a lot of the questions that had to be answered were invasive—but as much as I didn't want to register, the card offered a lot of convenience that was impossible to ignore.

I started to get really uneasy when the Defense Department, citing the founding fathers' belief, as directly expressed in the Second Amendment, that a national militia "was necessary to the security" of the nation, urged gun owners to voluntarily form militias to assist local law enforcement. This was taking the actions of the Trump administration in sending armed DHS troopers into our cities a great step further; it proposed granting limited law enforcement powers to private organizations. To facilitate this, grants were given to cover start-up costs and buy locally designed uniforms; blanket liability insurance policies were made available. Within days, militias began forming all over the country—"Elks with guns," joked Fox News anchor Trevor Roberts. To ensure these militias remained in-dependent of the military and were not directed by the government, the NRA was placed in charge of the program.

To better fight global terrorism, the Treasury Department joined the new International Bank Database, which allowed the government access to all domestic bank records, as well as any overseas transactions greater than $5,000.

The hits kept coming. Almost every day the new administration an-nounced a new initiative. Jenny began referring to it as "the daily di-saster." Health and Human Services began providing five-minute-long "Morning Announcements" to every American school. This was a na-tional version of the opening announcements most schools broadcast over their PA systems, reminding them about everything from club and athletic schedules to upcoming vacations. "Morning Announcements" was strictly voluntary. At eight A.M. each morning students could join their peers from around the country online to hear a celebrity provide information the government believed it was important they know. In addition to showing the Clip of the Day, generally something heartwarming or guaranteed to make students laugh, it reminded them about upcoming events, urged them to stay away from drugs, provided a three-sentence history lesson, and only occasionally slipped in some political content.

Few of these actions attracted significant complaints. They were rolled out over a period of time, often without an official announcement "for security reasons." And if there were protests or legal challenges, they were dealt with quickly—and always legally. When the ACLU attempted to enjoin the government from activating its National Surveillance Camera Center, which connected all public surveillance cameras (and interior cameras from any entity that volunteered to join, which eventually included major retailers, most stadiums and arenas, even homeowners), the FISA courts ruled secretly that this system was an invaluable and entirely legal resource for law enforcement.

While there was some minor grumbling, the most controversial action taken by the Wrightman administration was granting presidential immunity from prosecution to Donald Trump, ending years of legal wrangling. Legally the power of the president extended only to federal cases, but several states had indicted Trump, his oldest son, Trump Junior, and his daughter and son-in-law, Ivanka and Jared Kushner, for crimes that included tax evasion, money laundering, bank fraud, misappropriation of funds, and perjury. In total, the disgraced former president was facing more than seventy-five criminal charges that together would have put him behind bars for several hundred years. Channeling Gerald Ford, who had pardoned Richard Nixon upon ascending to the presidency, Wrightman said that while prosecuting Trump might make many people feel good, it would do nothing but distract us from the serious problems the nation was facing. Attorney General Richard Langsam issued the first presidential immunity. It was of dubious legal value, but Wrightman made an impassioned speech to explain his decision. While the cable stations that would have carried the trials were unhappy about it, complaining about lost commercial revenue, most people agreed it was the right decision. Trump paid significant fines and was allowed to retreat to Palm Beach, where he remained a recluse at Mar-a-Lago.

Every one of these new programs was supported and reinforced on all the popular social media platforms. Reign Man Munchmeyer supposedly employed as many as five hundred young men and women, working out of a converted airplane hangar at CIA headquarters at Langley, to apply and improve upon the lessons we had learned from Russian hackers in the 2016 elections. The existence of a social propaganda unit obviously was a major story, so I tried to track it down. I cultivated a couple of promising sources, but I was never able to get anyone to go on record, which meant my story would get the dreaded *O* rather than a desirable *F* or *N*. I was told, for example, that the kids in Hanger P had successfully defused a scheduled National Day of Rage by promoting fictitious marches that were to take place on different days in numerous places. But I couldn't nail it down. I didn't stop trying. As far as I know, it's still sitting in that pile of "working stories" on my desk. Wherever that desk is today.

You know what surprised me most about all of this? Besides those usual nattering nabobs of negativism (that's you, Howie, if you're reading this), few people seemed to care very much. Unfortunately, that included me. I didn't object. I complained, I gradually got better at adding cups to my tower, but I didn't do a damn thing. I was just another fly on the cheese of life. Other than the rating system, little that Wrightman did seemed to intrude on my everyday life. I went to work every day, I wrote my stories and worked on my next book, I fell in love, and lo and behold, I actually felt a little better about the country.

Writing that line right now—"I actually felt a little better about the country"—gave me pause. But at the time, the situation seemed to have stabilized. And that was enough. Maybe my professional self didn't like it, but that old military me accepted the command structure working around me. And like so many other people, secretly I even liked it.

I certainly talked about it enough. Understanding, interpreting, then explaining politics basically defined my job. My mother told me I talked about politics too much, reminding me that I always was a complainer (although she still loved me!) and suggesting I take more of an interest in sports and theater. Or cooking! Why don't you write about cooking? she asked, pointing out the popularity of the Food Network.

Most mornings I discussed it with my boys and girl of the Light Brigade. This was the close-knit group of people with whom I worked out
before going to work. There were fourteen regulars in the bunch who
worked in a variety of industries and professions, ranging from sugar industry lobbyist Charlie Fitzgerald to my workout partner, Hack Wilson, a
computer guru who hinted he had some vague connection to some unnamed government agency (cough, NSA, cough). As a result, at least one
of us could offer insight about whatever was going on in the news. Jenny
and I talked politics all the time. And in every conversation, whomever I
spoke with, no matter what had happened, whatever regulation Wrightman proposed, we always came to the same conclusion: It's a lot better
than Trump being president.

I'm sure you remember that for several months after the 2020 election, any version of that phrase became our national punch line. No
matter what went wrong, "It's still a lot better than Trump being president!" You got fired and your house burned down? It's still a lot better
than Trump being president. Your spouse cleaned out your life savings
and ran away with their life coach? Well, it's still a lot better than Trump
being president. A building falls on you in Fallujah and you'll never walk
again. It's a lot better than Trump being president. Okay, maybe not a lot
better.

But at this point there remained one nagging question about Wrightman: What was his agenda? Exactly how far was he willing to go to
"Restore Order"? That phrase had always made me nervous; coincidently it had been our announced mission during one of my tours in
the sandbox. And what did he mean by that, anyway? Jeff Greenfield,
the *Pro*'s sports editor, once referred to him as "our first fill-in-the-
blank" president, pointing out how little we knew about him. Everyone
seemed to have a slightly different but acceptable interpretation of his
objectives. Whatever it was, we accepted, it still was better than Trump
being president.

The visible changes seemed minor and rarely interfered with daily life.
Most of the significant changes were structural and were taking place behind the scenes. In my daily walk, everything sort of looked the same—
even with the growing number of empty storefronts. Occasionally I'd see

a member of one of the new militia groups proudly wearing his or her uniform top or unit pin on the street. At times my laptop would freeze or the cursor would move by itself or it would take an unusually long time to load, causing me to wonder if someone was hacking into my work or if it simply was my ingrained distrust of government manifesting itself as paranoia.

The audacity of these three simultaneous attacks changed everything. Regular Army troops in full gear were stationed on almost every corner. I had yet to get comfortable with the sight of heavily armed soldiers guarding our airports, and that had been going on for decades; so seeing troops patrolling the streets of Washington was far more chilling. They had been ordered to protect government buildings, airports and railroad terminals, power stations, and other potential targets. It was as if the city had been transformed overnight into a clichéd scene from an under-budget cold war movie. It didn't feel real. Once I had been one of those soldiers, but far away, in a different city, in a different country.

But there was something else tickling my imagination. It suddenly hit me as I paused to watch a bored soldier standing rigidly at the front door of a Chase bank. There was no logical reason for those soldiers to be there. The attacks were over. They had taken place a few days earlier, and it was unlikely there would be more attacks. So why had soldiers been ordered to blanket the city? The obvious reason was to provide us all with some sense of security, but the result was precisely the opposite. Their presence simply amped up the terror.

Just as we had during the pandemic, all around the country people dug in, stocking up on staples like cheese, water, pet food, toilet paper, and ice cream. Long lines formed at gas stations and ATMs as people filled their tanks and extra cans and put cash in their pocket. When the stock market opened, it immediately crashed and within a half hour, circuit breakers halted trading; maybe not surprisingly among the few stocks that did not drop precipitously were Netflix, Hulu, Facebook, Match.com and Tinder (which rose quickly), and every defense contractor as the country prepared to hunker down.

Wild rumors spread like Covid-19. Stay off the bridges and out of the tunnels; the food supply had been poisoned; two suitcase nukes had been smuggled into the country and would be detonated when the first arrest was made.

Within days, politicians and celebrities were tweeting furiously, reaffirming their patriotism and offering their personal hopes and prayers to everyone affected by the attacks. The Obama family issued a statement expressing their deepest sympathy, reminding Americans that "throughout our history we have always been strongest when we have united to defend our national interests and American values." Senator Lindsey Graham told Jake Tapper in a shaky voice, "It seems to me that right now the right place for all of us to be is somewhere between complacent and panicked." Jay-Z, the Clooneys, and Julia Roberts announced they would be hosting a telethon to raise funds for the victims, and in an unusual tweet, the Kardashian/Jenner family press liaison reported they would be donating all appearance fees to survivor funds.

While the networks eliminated all regular programming and commercials to focus on the search and recovery operations, as well as the continuing investigation, Freedom Caucus leader Jim Jordan (R-Ohio) told Fox News, "While we're burying our dead is not the time to blame the Wrightman administration for this tragedy, but if it wasn't, if it wasn't, I don't have any doubt that the environment that fostered these attacks was created by socialist Democrats, led by Barack Obama."

While most Americans settled in, I was running at super-speed. And I am embarrassed to admit, loving it. When I had come rolling out of the hospital, I'd gone into a pretty deep depression. I thought the best time of my life was done, hasta la vegans, that nothing I was capable of doing could ever approach that feeling of operating in the field, knowing that the enemy was nearby, maybe even watching me, and being so acutely aware of everything around me I could feel a tremble in the air. It was that loss of intensity, of being fully engaged and ready to burst that I missed so desperately.

To my surprise, I'd found an unexpected level of excitement behind my desk, when I caught the scent of a story and began pursuing the hidden truths. That scent was in the air; within hours, a day at most, a journalist was going to identify the terrorists. This was the story of my generation. "Cher," I told her, "turn off the music," and went to work.

Our practice at the *Pro* was to update our home page hourly. Like everybody else in the office I was equal parts exhausted and exhilarated, running on adrenaline and coffee. My phones, both registered and burners, rang incessantly. My email and text message accounts were overflowing. Twitter and Instagram badgered me for my attention. And I read the stories that came across my desk. There were some pretty compelling first sentences:

> Honolulu (AP) July . . . Navy divers continued the gruesome task of recovering bodies trapped beneath the mangled wreckage of the USS *Arizona* and massive slabs of concrete ripped from the memorial platform . . .
>
> New York (AP) July . . . Port Authority engineers estimated it may take as long as five months before the Lincoln Tunnel can resume normal operations, as crews continued to find victims of the Tunnel Massacre in their burned-out vehicles . . .
>
> Outside Morgan City, Louisiana (AP) July . . . Rescue teams believe they have located and rescued a significant number of remaining survivors of the massive flooding that occurred when terrorists gained remote control of the . . .

And, no kidding:

> Washington, D.C. (Special to the Post) July . . . Sources deep within the intelligence agencies refused to confirm reports that evidence has been developed conclusively linking . . .

I read everything, I watched the news reports, but the big question, the only one that really mattered, remained unanswered: Who dun it? Who launched these attacks?

The White House issued statements every few hours in an effort to show they were top of this, but the line they were pitching didn't square with what I was hearing. Supposedly the smarty-pants at the alphabet agencies were making progress and it was only a matter of hours before they identified the terrorist group responsible. The military had been put on full alert; the Fifth Fleet was steaming toward the Persian Gulf, all leaves worldwide had been canceled, and troops in the United States had been ordered to prepare for immediate deployment.

It was an impressive show of force. We were all armed up with nowhere to go.

Okay, I admit it, I am a big fan of Jack Reacher, Easy Rawlins, Dave Robicheaux, Spenser, all the crime-solving tough guys, but as Howie had taught me, real-life investigations rarely involve punching out bad guys or figuring out the meaning of some obscure clue that had evaded even the most astute readers. Good information almost always comes from a reliable source or deep digging into piles of boring paperwork. I Zoomed, Skyped, Duo'ed, and FaceTimed with reporters and continually checked in with my sources. I put Mighty Chair to work too, giving Cher key names, words, and phrases and telling her to scour the internet for them. She reported regularly, "I have not found those words yet, boss."

"Thank you, Cher," I replied, still amused that I couldn't help thanking her.

I activated my Rollie Network, reaching way back to my days in the field. This was the real worldwide net, consisting of many good people with whom I had grown up in the world of guns, guts, and secrets. People I had met on my path whom I knew I could trust. It included men and women I had worked with and fought side by side with in my first life, as well as those I had met and cultivated in my second life—mercs and spooks who were still living on the dark side, chasing bad guys and developing good intel, as well as people who had moved into management positions, often in international or corporate security. They were spread out across the world, my PEWS, my personal early warning system.

I dug deep and came up with a jumble of nothing. Everybody had heard something, but none of it made sense to me. Too many wires were crossing and leading nowhere. A lot of might-be's and could-be's, a few look-at-those-guys. It was a new offshoot of ISIS. It was a resurgent Taliban. It was Al-Qaeda, Hamas, Boko Haram; it was Al-Shabab; it was the homegrown White Legion of Honor; it was a team of mercs employed by North Korea or Russia. It was Colonel Mustard in the parlor with the candlestick. I didn't buy any of it. The most sophisticated watchers in history were using the most sophisticated technology to keep track of these people. If they pooped in Pakistan, we would hear it in Langley.

A guy who didn't exist working at a place with no name that wasn't there, a battle buddy I had pulled out of a burning Humvee in my last life, hinted that an alliance had been formed between two or more terrorist organizations. He had no names—"an all-star team of bad guys," he called them. Maybe, but doubtful; if that had been true, somebody somewhere sometime would have overheard a whisper or droned in on two people together who shouldn't have been together. More than that, though, the competition between these groups for funding, for recruits, for power, for recognition was so extreme it was impossible for me to believe they could work together to plan, coordinate, and carry out attacks of this magnitude. I'd spent almost three years moving in and out of Afghanistan. At times I went to places that don't show up on any maps, meeting with shadows, enlisting cooperation, making payoffs, carrying messages. Some tribal feuds go back generations. These were men who would pull knives arguing over what to have for dinner. No way I believed they could get along well enough for long enough to pull off something like this. And then keep quiet about this success? No, no way. But. But if it was true . . . if they had figured out how to cooperate, now that was a scary thought.

5

By the fifth day I was hearing from sources that people inside the White House were panicking. Immediately following the attacks, the entire nation had gone into shock. By the second day, that shock had given way to a morbid acceptance and even fascination. As the bodies continued to pile up and the funerals began on the third day, the horror turned to white anger. On the fourth day, fear set in.

But for the administration, it was the fifth day that proved to be the most dangerous. That was the day people began deciding who was to blame. A *New York Times* political cartoon by Witte showed a caricature of Wrightman sitting behind a large desk on which sat a small sign reading, "The 63,000,000,000 bucks stop here!" That number being the estimated budget of our intelligence agencies, although in actuality it was considerably more than that. When I was mean and green, we referred to it as the three-step: first, real sorrow for the victim; second, gratitude it wasn't us; and third, the realization the bad guys were still out there.

There was a growing consensus that the administration was fucked. It seemed like every social media post was anti-Wrightman. He was photoshopped water-skiing in the Morgan City flood. His face was superimposed on the classic monkeys seeing nothing, hearing nothing, saying nothing. Another cartoon depicted him being lectured by a furious Uncle Sam, who was berating him, "You had only one job . . ."

"Well," Jenny the eternal optimist said when I reached her mid-morning, "at least there's one little ray of sunshine."

"What's that?"

"I haven't seen one post calling for Trump to come back."

Supposedly Wrightman was on the warpath in the White House, although we weren't allowed to describe it that way, as that phrase was now perceived as being politically incorrect. Instead I wrote that "Sources close to the president apparently are staying as far away as possible from the president . . ."

For the administration this was becoming far worse than an American tragedy, it was becoming a serious political liability. Wrightman had run on the promise that he would restore order—and in exchange we would voluntarily give up a little bit more of our personal freedoms.

The irony was so obvious even a Trump voter could understand it. We had surrendered some constitutionally guaranteed rights to make it easier for the government to protect our constitutionally guaranteed rights. For example, large solidarity marches had been planned for the following weekend in major cities; but citing safety concerns, Homeland Security had prohibited any demonstrations of more than two hundred people. To protect our right of privacy, the government found it necessary to tap into the phone calls and texts of anyone it decided was a risk.

It didn't change the key equation: As long as people had no one to blame, they were going to blame the president. Immediately following the attacks, the president's approval numbers actually went up, as Americans rallied around the flag. But as a day passed, then two, without the terrorists being identified, those polls dropped faster than a politician's promise the day after an election. The president was pissed and getting pissier by the hour. Apparently it was getting ugly at 1600 Pennsylvania Avenue.

I was angry too. I needed so much coffee to keep me going that I'd knocked over my tower at twenty-four. I hadn't even threatened the record. And worse, young reporter Jeannie Lee was at a solid seventeen and looking way too confident. I was working on a feature about people who had narrowly avoided being at one of the sites for some insignificant reason, the standard "fate is the hunter" piece, when Cher interrupted. "Boss, there's a red call for you." Red calls are those people calling on the very private number I give only to my best burrowed sources.

It was a former future brother-in-law currently working on the U.S. Marshals Service New York/New Jersey Joint Fugitive Task Force. I had dated this man's sister when she and I were stationed in Europe. We'd sung a lot of songs together. Deep Quote, as I referred to him, had been Air Force, then signed up with the feds. "Hey, good buddy," I said. "How's the captain?" His sister.

"Big news. She's promoted and pregnant."

"Whoa." That set me back for an instant. Andie was tough and beautiful. She had been sitting by my bed when I'd come out of an induced coma in Landstuhl. She had stayed there through as much of my rehab as her duties allowed. But when shove came to push, literally, my first chair proved too much for her. I couldn't keep up where she intended to go. She was honest about it. No hard feelings. I think her brother has always felt more guilty about it than either one of us, and these occasional calls were his way of expressing that.

"They got something," he said in the requisite whisper, snapping me back.

I turned on Chair's built-in recorder. "Who's got what?"

"The FBI lab. Nobody's saying if it's anything yet. But about twenty minutes ago Justice issued an official warning telling us not to say anything." They had something.

"About?"

"One of our people bagged part of a hand in the tunnel last night. He picked it up a few feet away from an automatic weapon that was used in the attack."

"You guys are fucking amazing," I said, and meant it. These people are incredible. The FBI had broken the Lockerbie bombing after finding a piece of a timer about the size of a thumbnail in a fifty-mile crime scene. As I listened, I sent Howie a text telling him we had a break. I saw him in his office reading the text, then turning and looking at me quizzically. I nodded.

The recovered body part consisted of most of a right palm from the wrist, three complete fingers, and one partial. The partial was the trigger finger. The thumb was gone. It had tested positive for gunshot residue, indicating that this hand had been in close proximity when the gun was fired. They had run prints from the remaining fingers through AFIS, the bureau's Automated Fingerprint Identification System. He paused, waiting for me to ask.

I asked, "And?"

"They got a hit," he said.

A chill ran down my back. Literally, a chill.

Howie came out of his office. He waved his hands to quiet the office, then pointed at me. The place went dead quiet. Until recently, my source continued, that hand had been attached to an American citizen of Middle Eastern descent. "A guy from Michigan. Detroit area. The only thing we know so far is that he traveled to Egypt twice last year."

As I listened, one question plagued me: Would I have to wear a tie to the Pulitzers next year? "What's going on now?"

"Rainbows and lollipops." The opposite of a shitstorm. "Soon as we got the ID, our guys began tracking his phone records. We'll find out who he's been talking to. Some people from the Detroit task force are going out to take a look right now. But they don't want to shake the tree yet."

"So whatta you think?" I actually wasn't surprised. As hard as it was to accept, domestic always made more sense to me than international. Everybody in law enforcement knows there is a layer of bad guys moving undetected around the country, like the cave snakes in Raiders; nobody talks about it because there is nothing they can do about it. The people I know had always believed domestic terrorism was a far greater danger to this country than an away team. And the level of coordination necessary to pull this off without attracting attention required an understanding of this country beyond the capabilities of foreign terrorists.

"I like it," he decided. "We been tracking a thousand leads. Ten thousand. A bunch of them looked good for a while. This is the one that's panned out. This guy was in the tunnel, we know that for sure."

"You got a name?"

I waited through a long silence. *Qui tacet consentit.* Silence gives consent. He had the name, he was just connecting neurons, trying to figure out if it could be traced back to him. Slug that I am sometimes, I debated asking him about his sister again, just slightly ginning up his guilt.

It wasn't necessary. "Be careful how you use this, huh. It could cause me a lot of problems."

"I know that."

"Caleb Hassan." He spelled it for me.

I repeated it letter for letter as if I was writing it down. "Anything else?"

I could tell he was reading Hassan's sheet, probably off a computer, creating a portrait for me. Home address. His birth date making him twenty-nine years old. "Let's just see what we got here. He did thirty months at the Earnest C. Brooks Correctional Center." He hesitated, verbally shaking his head. "Rings no bells. For assault. He must not have been carrying. It would have been a lot longer than that if he'd had a gun. What else? He got his GED while he was in, and it looks like that helped him get an early release."

Deep Quote was a big burly guy in a perennial battle with his weight. I could imagine him sitting at his desk looking over the top of his glasses, scrolling down this guy's record. "Nothing. Nothing. Nothing. Finished parole '20. Current employment unknown. No tax returns last year. Owns a two-year-old BMW 5 Series." An aside, a knowing chuckle. "Wonder where the money for that came from? Nothing. Nothing." Another thoughtful pause, then, "Okay, here's something, there's nine unpaid parking tickets been issued to that car within the last year, all of them on the same block, but a different block from his home address. He got the tickets on Stratford Road. His address is Belmont Circle."

"Which means?"

"Who the fuck knows. Maybe that home address is a phony. Maybe this place is his hangout, gang headquarters, local drop, maybe that's where his squeeze lives, could be anything." I heard a series of puffing sounds as he continued looking over the sheet. "That's pretty much it, bro."

"You hear anything, you know who loves you most, right?"

He chuckled. "Just be smart with this. This'd get me fried."

A few years earlier I would have been taking notes. Instead, soon as he clicked off, I ordered, "Cher, transcribe and print it, please."

"Yes, boss." I hate a wiseass computer.

Howie made a soft landing in my chair. "And?"

I clasped my hands, put them behind my head, and leaned back with a smile. "Who's your favorite reporter?"

"Depends. Downhill, there's nobody can keep up with you."

I told him we had a possible. A name, a background that sounded right. Howie started chewing on one of those green plastic flossers, saving his cigar for the victory. "What do you want to do?"

Before I could respond, Frankie B. Goode shouted, "Listen up, everybody. Something's going on at the White Castle. Lots of smiles. Do some checking, please."

Howie continued, "You ready to go with it?"

"We can't name the guy." The risk of identifying a suspect on such flimsy evidence was much too great. "But we can break it: 'Authorities have identified a person or persons of interest in the 7/11 attack on the Lincoln Tunnel yada, yada, yada . . .' Nothing wrong with that. If we're wrong, so what, we had a solid tip from a trusted source, no one's gonna remember." Besides, truckloads of bullshit were being published. On the other hand, if we were right, if we were right and first, we would attract a lot of attention. Either way, the story was going to get reposted on the major sites, which would have to credit us. Long term, a break like this could even make the difference between the *Pro* suriviving or going belly-up. Even with his ethics, Howie always reminded us there was a reason it was called the news *business*. Too often the bottom line was the bottom line.

"Okay." Howie nodded his approval and pushed himself up. "Okay," he repeated with a little more decisiveness, "let's go with it." He stood in front of the room like a slightly deranged teacher, put two fingers in the corners of his mouth, and whistled the room silent. Everyone paused and gave him their attention. "Listen up, people." He was standing in front of the office, his stomach flowing gently over his belt like the intermediate slope in Vail. He pointed at me. "Big Wheels here just got a heads-up. It looks like the feds got a name out of New York that they're spritzing over. See what you can find out." He scanned the room. "Who's from Michigan again? Anybody?"

Jimmy Klurfeld raised his hand. "I am."

"Right. Our guy is from somewhere around Detroit. See if the Detroit PD knows anything." The noise level in the room started rising, but he raised his voice even louder to shut it down. "People. People, here's the thing. Do. Not. Tell *anyone* what we got. Let me repeat that for the kiddies in the back row. We have a source who we're going to protect. The suspect gets spooked and it's our fault, by next week we'll all be asking people if they want to supersize that." He clapped twice and reminded us what we do. "All right, let's do some journalism."

In a different situation I would have called Eunie Kaufman's office or Danny Ricciardi over at Justice to get an official denial I could quote—"A Justice Department spokesperson told me he would beat the shit out of me if I ran this story," or something like that—to prove that I had tried to investigate further before going with a single-sourced story. But I had no time for that. This was a shape-shifting story. Even in these days of cyber-journalism, breaking a big story in DigiWorld made a difference. Besides, if the White House learned we had this information, it might well try to prevent us from posting it. National security, blah, blah, blah. And the reality was the enlarged eleven-person Supreme Court would probably back them up.

Less than an hour later, after a little editing by Frankie and a quick legal read, I attached the appropriate capital *N* logo to my story, took a deep and satisfied breath, and posted it. "The *Pro* has learned exclusively that a suspect has been identified in the attack on the Lincoln Tunnel." Then I clanged my cowbell. The cowbell was another Howie innovation; to create a team spirit each of us had our own device to ring or bang or shake when we posted an important story. (It also allowed Howie, on those occasions when he was pushing us to dig deeper, to shout out his favorite *SNL* line, "More cowbell!") I got the usual response—several way-to-go's, a couple of hurrahs, and a few lonely claps. Then back to work.

Few things are more exhilarating than a newsroom working at warp speed. There's a physical high you want to grab on to and ride wherever it takes you. Piece by disparate piece, reaching out to sources throughout government and law enforcement, adding reports from other outlets, we began knitting together a scenario. There definitely was serious stirring. The mood inside the White House was described as "borderline euphoric." We learned from a Defense Department source that a combined federal force, consisting of Homeland Security and regular army troops, had been sent to Detroit. A stringer from WWJ, 950 AM on your radio dial, told Klurfeld that the Detroit PD had been ordered to establish a six-block perimeter around a low-income area known to be a center of the drug trade; that area had been quarantined, meaning no one—including police officers, but especially media—was allowed inside that perimeter. The FAA issued a notice temporarily prohibiting helicopters, drones, and probably paper airplanes from being flown in or around that designated area. No pictures, please. Howie had two people researching the suspect, but they came up with nothing more than we had.

I had a pretty good sense of what was going on. I'd been there. I'd been there a lot of times. The procedure was pretty much the same whether it was Fallujah or Detroit. Isolate the neighborhood. Nobody in and nobody out without an escort. I didn't know for sure, but I would have bet undercovers were knocking on doors, quietly moving civilians out of the area. Somewhere, the D-unit, the designated soldiers going in, were saddling up—putting on equipment; testing night vision, cleaning weapons, checking battle buddies, looking at sector maps, reviewing intel, going over their plan, then going over it again. Lock and load, then go to that quiet place in your mind free of all ordinary concerns; then focus, focus so completely on the mission that nothing else exists.

Been there, done that. I knew exactly what those guys were feeling. I could close my eyes and channel those feelings: the anticipation, the excitement, the confidence; that little dash of doubt.

I wondered who they were sending in; and then it hit me. Hello.

Mouth to brain, where have you been? About a year earlier I'd heard scuttlebutt that Homeland Security was positioning small self-contained antiterrorist units in waiting stations at heliports around the country. My contacts in the Special Ops community have always been solid, and became even more so after I went down. We help our own. The story was accurate, I was told; there were thirty-five such units, each of them consisting of twenty-five special operators. They were designed to move fast; they carried light weapons and used troop carriers with remote firing cannon. Their mission was to put boots on the ground on any populated site in the continental US of A within thirty minutes following the identification of a terrorist cell. Of course. I'd wondered how any army unit could have gotten to the Lincoln Tunnel so quickly after the attack had begun. Bing-go!

Detroit, with its large Muslim population, would have been an obvious choice to station one of those units. Who would know, I wondered? I mentally flipped through my contacts, going from *A* to *Z*. I got to *M*. "Cher," I said, "call Oley Masterson." Command Sgt. Major Masterson had been in it with me. He'd retired, but no one I knew was plugged in better than him.

He answered his cell on the second ring. "Oley Masterson." Polite but inquisitive.

"Bucky Dent."

"Fuck you." Oley was a die-hard Red Sox fan; when he was in the soup, he'd carried Carlton Fisk's autographed baseball card in his top hat for good luck. We exchanged the usual affectionate insults until he asked the usual "What can I do you for?"

I told him what I needed. Oley and I had been together when it counted; that was forever trust. He knew I would never use information for my own benefit if it might put people at risk. He didn't know the answer offhand, he said, but he would make some calls. Twenty minutes later he called back, "It's the 8th ATM," Advanced Tactical Mobile unit. On the TOE, the official Table of Organization and Equipment, it was designated as a Quartermaster unit. And yes, the 8th was on the move. It had mounted up three hours earlier. Full gear. "I'll tell Derek Jeter you send your regards," I said, my attempt at a thank-you.

"Fuck Aaron Judge."

By this time my story had splashed down. Within minutes it had spread virally across the country. Almost instantly I had been hit by a social media tsunami that had washed over me and was done within an hour as other outlets added to it with their own reporting. I was still getting the last trickle of response; CNN wanted me to do a Zoom interview, but I turned it down. This was a developing story and we had a piece of it.

We were chasing at least twenty different threads. My story had led to a string of tips; from experience I knew that most of them would be worthless, the usual people next door with iridescent tattoos sitting in the dark playing Gothic rap while they barbecued rats, but we still checked out the most likely. Sitting in Mighty Chair at the front of the office, working my phones and computer, I felt a little like a buccaneer on the bow of his ship, one foot on the bowsprit, cutlass extended defiantly, ready to buckle some swash.

But I was in control. At least I was until Jeannie Lee shouted, "Check out six, everybody."

I swiveled. In all caps, CNN was promising BREAKING NEWS (although in truth this time they might have added, "and this time we mean it!"). I dialed it up. Wolf Blitzer was holding a stack of loose papers. He reported with a tinge of excitement in his voice, "CNN has just learned that at this moment a joint task force of heavily armed state and federal officers have isolated a neighborhood in suburban Detroit. An unknown number of people suspected of having a connection to the recent attacks are believed to be inside a house in that area. No one in the White House will comment for the record, but sources have told CNN's Jim Acosta that President Wrightman ..."—Wolf glanced at the paper in his hands—"appeared to be 'positively gleeful.'

"The entire area has been blockaded, no one is being allowed inside the perimeter, and residents are being escorted out and held for identification. People on the ground there describe the situation as a 'lockdown.' Stay tuned, and as soon as we can get our people near the site, we will take you there ..."

I could visualize the chaos in newsrooms throughout the country as everybody scrambled to keep up. Within minutes, one by one other outlets began reporting their version of the story. Bits of new information leaked out drop by drop. We did our best to keep up. When a Detroit outlet, NewDetroit.org, reported the exact address of the house, 149 Stratford Road, I went on Google Earth to take a look at it.

It was a two-story stucco house. It looked like every other one of the twenty million affordable bungalows built in the 1950s for GIs coming home. This one had deteriorated. It was a chalk-white stucco with a green-shingled roof; several shingles were missing. There were faded red shutters on either side of two large front windows, separated by a two-level brick step. The front windows were partially obscured by bushes. One shutter was hanging askew. The stucco walls appeared pocked and rust-stained in places. A low white picket fence ran the entire length of the front yard, which was mostly dirt and weeds. The gate was closed. What I guessed were two or three motorcycles covered by an oil-stained tarp were parked in the yard. But the money that hadn't been spent on repairs had been invested in security: I counted four surveillance cameras mounted along the front roof gutter. There also were several spotlights. But what caught my attention was the front door.

In contrast to the rest of the house, the front door had been recently painted a high gloss white and was secured with several high-tech locks. (I knew front doors. I'd spent a lot of time staring at front doors in Iraq and Afghanistan. Then I went through a lot of them. It was easy to figure out who most wanted to keep you out.) Oddly, though, a Christmas wreath was still hanging on it. *Well, there's a nice sentimental touch,* I thought.

There also was a steel storm door. The kind with scrolled-steel bars in the frame. I enlarged that door and saw that an additional lock had been added. If I were betting, I'd place my money on the possibility that this door bolted into the frame.

Given those precautions, it did not surprise me that there was no welcome mat.

Frankie was leaning over my shoulder, one arm balanced on Mighty Chair's arm. "It'd take a pretty tough Girl Scout to sell cookies at that house. What do you think?"

Frankie had been a great street reporter at the *Chicago Trib.* He knew how the world worked. I shrugged. "It doesn't shout terrorist to me."

"No," he agreed, shaking his head. He tapped his finger on the door. "See that?"

I enlarged the image and began moving the cursor. I saw what he was talking about, barely visible lines outlining a flap in the front door. I twisted and looked at him. "Isn't that interesting?" It was a drug door; money goes in, drugs come out. Nobody sees nobody.

"Abso-fucking-lutely." He stood up and indicated the house with a nod. "Maybe some of these guys stayed there. But that, that's a drug drop. See what Zillow has to say about it."

I typed the address into Zillow. Zillow told me it was a four-bedroom house with a finished basement. It had been built in 1952, sold in 1985 for $46,500. No transactions after that. It had a current value of $0. I pulled back on the satellite image and the rest of the block came into view, then the several surrounding blocks, several of the homes of equal value. $0. A couple of them, it appeared, had holes in the roof. This was a dying neighborhood.

"Squats," Frankie explained. "That's what happened out there. Middle-class jobs went south with the auto industry. Without the tax base, the whole neighborhood collapsed. People just took midnight moving vans and left the banks holding shit. The banks didn't care, they just packaged them up with decent mortgages and sold them for Christ knows how much. People like these guys . . ."—he nodded at the screen— ". . . squatters, they just moved in. They hooked up to lamp-posts for power. Then the gangs came in and took over the best places. Dave Bing, the basketball player, when he was mayor, he contracted the whole city. He cut off public services to those neighborhoods."

"So nobody knows who's there?"

"Let's say they won't be filling out census forms."

"This is possible, then. It could be outsiders. They'd be under the radar."

Frankie considered that. "Doubtful. I'll bet Detroit PD has eyes in there. They bust a guy carrying a light load, make a deal, give him a few bucks, and he keeps you up-to-date on anything unusual going on."

Suddenly Rod Stewart sang, "You're in my heart, you're in my soooooollll," Jenny's ring. Cher confirmed she was calling. "Cher, tell Jenny I'll call her back, please."

Frankie laughed lightly. "You are something else, Wheels."

I ignored him. "You know what," I decided, tapping the monitor, "I'm going to do a quick piece about the house. About the drugs. The whole shebang."

"The administration isn't going to like that." He turned, then re-minded me, "Make sure you classify it O."

6

believe strongly that America can never sufficiently repay the debt it owes to pizza. It is pizza that almost single-handedly has kept American journalism alive. It is the original fast food; a highly skilled journalist can sniff out a passable pie anywhere in the country at any hour, it is a communal food that can satisfy an entire newsroom, it is filling, it literally can be eaten single-handedly and it is um–um–good. Among the first skills any aspiring TV journalist must master is how to eat a slice without oil or tomato dripping on a shirt or blouse (the famed Diane Sawyer Front-Leaning Technique is favored). And personally, I think the vicious debate between extra cheese and Sicilian is ridiculous.

I was three bites into a slice of pepperoni with extra cheese when the newsroom went silent. I looked at the monitor in front of me. ABC was reporting, "Shots reported fired. Explosions heard."

There were about twenty people still in the office. We sat comfortably, enjoying the four pies Howie had ordered as the horror unfolded on the twelve screens surrounding us. Nothing like pepperoni to accompany a night firefight.

I still sometimes wonder if it is simply a coincidence that I have chosen two careers in which emotion plays zero part. In fact, in soldiers or journalists, emotions are considered an occupational hazard. They tend to get in the way of good fighting and good reporting. So I was able to watch this attack, at least what we could see of it, with a dispassionate fascination. Having been on several similar missions, I found myself far more interested in studying the technical procedures of the attack than in feeling any compassion for the human beings inside that house who were being blown into headlines.

My unit, when we were deployed, was designated AIA: Attack and Infiltration A Team. We lived by the motto "Shoot first. Then shoot second." Literally, that's how we stayed alive and mostly unhurt (well, except for those working legs I used to have). I assumed this unit, the 8th, had a similar philosophy. If the people inside the house did not surrender immediately I had no doubt the 8th was going to light up the whole neighborhood.

The feeds on all the monitors were essentially the same: No cameras or lights were permitted near the scene, so the best the networks could offer was a correspondent standing behind a barricade, seen through the greenish tint of night-vision lenses. Night clouds mostly obscured a half-moon, which periodically became visible through a break in the cover and added an eerie light tint to the picture. I clicked between stations, pausing only long enough to hear correspondents explaining in dramatic whispers that absolutely nothing was happening. The stations all tagged their broadcasts *F.* This was taking place in real time.

I was still savoring that slice of pepperoni when the night lit up. Two quick flashes, like flashbulbs going off, reflected off the cloud cover, followed almost instantly by a series of explosions. I recognized the sound of cannon shells blowing the shit out of a structure. Then came the instantly recognizable tattering of automatic weapons.

"Well," Frankie sighed, "there goes the neighborhood."

A few of my colleagues muttered an impressed "Jesus Christ" or "Holy shit" (no connection intended), but otherwise the office was completely silent. The images reminded me most of those televised pictures from Opening Night in Baghdad when Bush the Lesser launched his invasion of Iraq in 2003. But on a considerably smaller scale, as if this were the Disneyland version.

The firing continued in a cacophony of short bursts for 67 seconds. I timed it. Habit kicking in. I heard at least six distinct explosions. I recognized the strategy; my old squad leader, Sgt. Matt Hill, had called it "The Big Bang Theory," which he defined as "What blows up ain't coming down." We had our own expressions for it: battle porn, shootin' the shit, tickling the Taliban. We used to bet, really, on how high a 105mm howitzer could make a house jump. But the meaning was simple: if you pour overwhelming firepower into a target, all the good guys get to go home safe that night.

No one in that house was going to survive. Which was the intention. The assault ended with a few sporadic shots, as if the last few firecrackers were catching up. Then a cloud of gun smoke rose slowly into the night sky, like the residue of a fireworks display, to the loud silence of ending combat. A few seconds later those clouds got a lot darker and uglier; I recognized that too. Gun smoke was giving way to smoke and flames from the fires that had started. I half anticipated hearing the whines of fire trucks, but instead commentators began telling us loudly and excitedly that they knew absolutely nothing about what had just happened and were going to repeat that in as many different ways as possible for the next few minutes.

"You okay?"

Howie must have sneaked up on me when my mind was in the middle of that battle. "Yeah, 'course. Why?"

He shrugged. "You've been sitting there holding on to that slice with your mouth open for a couple of minutes now."

I looked down. I was frozen in pizza position, a folded slice poised a few inches from my mouth. I laid it down, took a deep breath. "I guess I drifted away," I admitted.

Howie waved it away, no big deal. "You've been a lot of places," he agreed, then walked away.

The media assault began the instant the shooting ended. Whatever actually happened on that block, a heroic portrait was being created. Praise for the troops was showing up on every platform. Wrightman had his team out in force, making certain he was given plaudits for his "leadership in a crisis." Instant poll results reinforced the message that a significant majority of Americans supported this attack. I glanced at several threads and comments, almost all of them lauding our troops and the president for his decisive action. *My, my,* I thought, *it's almost as if the administration is writing these blurbs itself.*

Within minutes, several approved photographs were circulated to the media, among them a blurry image showing a soldier carrying a computer out of a burning structure. If it had been necessary, the government happily would have put the factual *F* on every post or message; I would also have given them the *F,* but mine would have had a very different meaning. A deluge of positive and supportive hype filled Facebook and Twitter, Instagram, Snapchat; people were even creating Pinterest boards and, I was certain, were looking for celebratory companionship on Tinder. It was a masterful performance.

Less than ten minutes later, Press Secretary Kaufman tweeted an official statement: "Earlier this evening elite Special Operations commandos surrounded a house in which an unknown number of suspected terrorists positively associated with the recent attacks were believed to be hiding. Attempts to negotiate a peaceful surrender failed when gunmen inside the house began firing on our troops. In the ensuing battle, an unknown number of persons inside that house were killed. The unit suffered one casualty, which is being described as minor, in the assault. Computers, cell phones, and tablets were recovered and will be sent to the FBI Forensic Laboratory for examination. This is only the first strike in what will be a prolonged campaign to bring the killers of innocent Americans to justice. The president and first lady would like to express their gratitude to our brave men and women who risked their lives to protect this country. God bless them, and God bless America."

I began to work my own sources, trying to confirm or dispute what little was known and add whatever bits I could grab. What I really wanted to know was if the people who died in that house—that's assuming there were people in that house—actually had a connection to the attacks. Call me Mr. Cynic. Here's another fact: You spend eleven years in the military, you develop a highly sensitive bullshit detector. It becomes necessary to navigate that system. My bullshit cowbell was clanking. That house seemed too small, thinking metaphorically, to have played a role in something so big.

Exactly one hour after the shooting ended, President Wrightman spoke to the nation. He spoke from the White House front lawn, with the building lit up artistically in the background. He was not wearing a jacket and his shirtsleeves were rolled up everyman style, obviously to convey the impression that he had been hard at work and was only pausing for a brief time to give these casual, carefully crafted remarks. "I just wanted to take a minute to thank the brave men and women who risked their lives tonight for all of us. I want to make this pledge in front of all of you: my administration will continue to work relentlessly to seek out and kill our enemies. While we don't know for sure yet exactly what role these terrorists played in the attacks, we are confident the information collected at this safe house undoubtedly will provide vital intelligence in our ongoing fight to protect each and every American." He concluded with the usual *God bless*es. Reporters shouted preapproved questions at him (my guess), but he turned, gave an aloof Trumpian wave, and retreated to the White House. The pool camera held on him as he walked alone, head bowed and hands in his pockets, across the perfectly manicured lawn. Ah, the loneliness-of-the-president image.

It was almost midnight; the administration began offering up talking heads to make certain it got full credit for the apparent success of the operation. Among them was Colonel Anthony Ruggerio, who led the attack. His camo unit patch had been covered with tape for security reasons. He was still wearing his battle rattle, including personal armor, with the exception of his helmet, which had been replaced by a baseball cap and sunglasses. The cap had been pulled down over his sunglasses, which I guess was supposed to disguise his appearance from any terrorists who might be watching, but instead made him look like one of the characters from *Mad* magazine's *Spy vs. Spy* comic strip.

The Special Ops community is pretty small, but I couldn't remember crossing paths with a Colonel Ruggerio. But I definitely knew the type. This guy reveled in his tough-guyness. His tone in responding to reporters' questions was a verbal flex: Shots were fired from the house. His men returned with increased intensity. Communications devices had been recovered. No intact bodies had been found yet, but the fires probably ... A beginning, his men will go anywhere, do anything ... Pleased to report his injured man will make a full recovery. Big victory for America over "those who would do us harm." God bless.

Other spokespeople started showing up on other outlets, drilling the message into the American psyche: This was a great victory against international terrorism. America was on the march. The Wrightman administration is protecting you.

Rumors were popping up everywhere, like a digital Whac-A-Mole. Most of them, on the largest sites or feeds, were removed within minutes by the monitors or quickly countered. My favorite came from an anonymous poster on a Facebook Warrior group, which was a hub for active and former combat soldiers. G.I. José claimed that a friend of his on the assault team had told him that the only injury in the attack was one badly wrenched knee, which was caused by a soldier slipping on a pile of dog shit as he was advancing. As his legs went out from under him, he accidently fired his weapon into the air. His squad saw him suddenly fall backward, and hearing shots, assumed he had been hit by fire from the house—and opened up.

No one seemed to know if there had been any firing at all from the house.

The White House released the first official video after one A.M. It was the usual battlefield mess. People advancing, things getting blown up, lots of tracers scratching into the darkness. Then it cut to the aftermath—everything seen through a green night-vision haze. People in hazmat suits were moving cautiously through debris as small fires still popped up, and wisps of smoke curled into the air like geysers, making it look like they were strolling through hell. If anything in the wreckage was recognizable, I sure couldn't pick it out.

I was looking at it for maybe the fifth time, trying to make some sense of it, when Cher interrupted. "The White House is calling, boss." I had placed several calls to administration officials. When I started writing, I wanted to be able to include the fact that I had reached out to various people for comment. But I hadn't really expected any response.

It was the secretary of defense, Rip McCord. That didn't completely surprise me. McCord and I went back to the sandbox. In the desert he was considered a wild man, an officer who never cut corners, just smashed through them, bringing along anyone with enough guts to take the risks and, if necessary, the blame. A lot of people didn't like his methods. But I did. He did whatever was necessary to protect his people, even if sometimes his methods weren't exactly by the book, and that mattered to me. We had done several missions together that remained classified. After he retired, he'd tried to take me with him into his post-military wonderworld. I'd decided to stay in and, as Robert Frost had written, that had made all the difference.

Mostly we'd communicated by rumor and bar tales. But once you spill blood with a guy, that bond never goes away. "How they hangin', my man?" he asked.

"Still rolling along," was always a good answer.

We exchanged the necessary banter for several minutes; then he set the rules. He would be identified in any story as "a knowledgeable White House source" but would not be quoted directly. As he began filling in the gaps, it became obvious to me that I was being fed A#1 superspecial White House bullshit. Everybody was a hero, brilliant work, just the beginning. He gave me a few details, the types of weapons the "terrorists" were firing, the guesstimate that there had been as many as eight people in the house, the fact that license plate numbers of every vehicle in the area were being checked and there had been some "interesting" results. He kept shoveling. Mighty Chair recorded it all. I knew it was all bullshit, McCord knew I knew it was bullshit, and both of us knew I was going to have to write it anyway. I wasn't going to forgo the opportunity to quote "a knowledgeable White House source" even if I knew he was lying. The story would be picked up and reposted nationally, with my byline—good for me, good for the *Pro,* good for the administration.

I was writing the story when Howie showed up again, reading it over my shoulder. "That's good," he acknowledged. "Any of it true?"

I considered that. "Well, the attack did take place tonight."

Howie chuckled wearily. "You know, it almost makes me nostalgic for the days of real fake news."

Three nights later, I had a revelation: If I ever write another book, it is going to be entitled *Thoughts After Sex: A Personal Memoir.* Those postcoital moments might well be when we are the most emotionally vulnerable. Defenses get stripped away and the subconscious sneaks out to play. What you are feeling in those few seconds is as close as you may ever get to touching your soul.

Obviously, that's the problem with it. The safest thing to do, I'd learned, was to sigh in a way that indicates great satisfaction, then mumble something that includes the word *amazing. Best* would also be a good word choice. The problem with turning this idea into a book is that I don't actually remember a lot of those conversations, and it's an awkward time to take notes. I do know those thoughts have ranged from how soon it would be appropriate to get dressed and leave to what I was feeling as I lay there that night next to Jenny—I could stay right here forever.

Sex was the last piece of the puzzle when I started my second life. I had accepted as a general concept that my life was changed forever, but filling in the details was a day-to-day process. The military has a very good rehabilitation program, unfortunately honed through experience, but it stops short of sex. The staff assured me all my parts were working, which to me offered all the security of a test pilot's preflight check.

I had zero-point-zero idea what to expect when I got out of the hospital. I was realistic; I knew there weren't going to be any more moonlit walks on the beach. I did what many people in my situation have done: I compensated. Maybe even overcompensated. I threw myself into new challenges, sometimes literally. When that happened, I picked myself up and tried again. I experimented with new things. I began working out at the gym to strengthen my upper body. My shoulders filled out, I sprouted muscles, but it turned out that the upper body part that most benefited from those workouts was my head. I bought a racing chair and eventually ran three marathons. Just to prove I could do it. I went to work learning how to "do journalism."

And there was that other unmentionable. I wasn't quite back to staring at the phone trying to gin up courage to call a woman, but my confidence had taken several steps backward. I was tentative at first about dating, having no experience in how to act or react. Women surprised me, but that was nothing different—women have always surprised me.

Going through that first time, for the second time in my life, was equally anxiety-provoking, then thrilling, and concluded with the same sense of relief. I'm not going to describe it; I'm not good at writing sex scenes. I've tried in an aborted novel. My problem was I could never get beyond the awareness that my mother was going to be reading it. Nothing kills a passionate sex scene more than that.

In the days following Detroit, Jenny and I had spoken as often as possible between her meetings and my deadlines. Mostly, though, we communicated by brief messages and emojis (mostly hearts, smiley faces, and an occasional "adult pleasure enhancer," which looked more like a wired cucumber) just reminding each other we were breathing. But the story was unfolding quickly. The White House carefully controlled the news cycles, releasing just enough information every few hours to maintain momentum. Wrightman humbly refused to take personal credit for the success of the attack, doing so on every network, cable channel, and social media platform. The people inside the house were identified as members of an Al-Qaeda splinter group whose name translated as Children of the Sword. Nobody I knew had ever heard of them, but hey, terrorism obviously was a growth industry. DNA recovered from the charred remains was matched to that of relatives and friends of missing persons, and it was determined that at least eight people had been killed inside the house, possibly more. Two of them were identified as "illegal Somalian immigrants who had overstayed visas and settled undetected in the Detroit area." The soldier "wounded" in the raid was awarded his Purple Heart in a private ceremony to protect his identity. The administration continued meeting regularly with members of Congress to discuss taking the necessary steps to defend the country while protecting individual rights—which to me sounded about as likely as gift wrapping a cloud.

Jenny Miller had come into my life at the Bernstein bar mitzvah. I had worked up a pretty good sweat doing the hora. When the band struck up the first bars of "Hava Nagila," I was just another guy in a wheelchair; when it ended, I had become a legend at the Riviera catering hall. I had returned to my seat at the Climate Change table (Rachel Bernstein, Howie's daughter, was always precocious; "Preparing for the Future" was her bat mitzvah theme) and was wiping my brow with my napkin when Jenny sat down in the empty chair next to me. The first thing she ever said to me was "Well, don't you give new meaning to rock and roll."

I gave her my practiced "aw, shucks" smile. "Just in case you're wondering," I said, "the only thing I can't do is dance."

Jenny Miller's face was sad and lovely with bright things in it, bright eyes and a bright passionate mouth. Okay, actually that was Jay Gatsby's Daisy Buchanan. The reality is most journalists aren't very good at florid descriptions. That's not what we do. Our focus are the police blotter details: height, weight, hair color, complexion, and distinguishing marks. Honestly, I've always had difficulty visualizing the heroine. I read that she has "an aquiline nose" or "succulent lips" and "piercing blue eyes," and I still can't create an image.

Raymond Chandler did it best when he described his femme fatale as simply "A blonde to make a bishop kick a hole in a stained-glass window."

That wasn't Jenny Miller. Jenny was . . . still is, I suppose, a brunette. That night her hair just brushed her bare shoulders. She was about five-seven, and I never knew her weight. I estimated it as approximately perfect. Her complexion was radiant. (I remember thinking, *No visible tattoos,* which called for further investigation.) She had a mischievous mouth that seemed to be sharing a private joke with her twinkling green eyes. She had applied just enough makeup to show she cared, but not enough to make a statement. What impressed me most was that she wore her confidence as if it had been designed by Saint Laurent. That's style.

"I know who you are," she said. "You're the Rolling Stone."

I nodded. That was the pretty obvious nickname I'd picked up within weeks of starting at the *Pro.* "I know who you are too," I said. There was an old saying that Capitol Hill was the place where money married power and gave birth to politicians. The Hill attracts more bright and ambitious young people than Tinder late on a Saturday night. Most of them come here intending to do good, and many of them end up staying long enough to do very well. Eventually the best of them get noticed, and Jenny Miller was hard to miss, even without a wheelchair. It wasn't just those angular cheekbones; she was the chief of staff for Democratic congresswoman Martha McDonnell, making her at thirty-five (as Cher told me later that night when I asked for her bio) the youngest chief on the Hill. I had spoken with people in that office on many occasions. I believe I might have even spoken with her once. But I took one look at her and realized that she easily could become an important source.

Jenny and I flirted through the night, really savoring the possibilities. There were women for whom my chair was an impediment they couldn't overcome; I got that, I understood it, there were times I wasn't too thrilled about it myself. That question was always in the back of my mind. My "can't dance" line was one of several jokes I could wheel out to cover any discomfort. But I knew it made no difference to Jenny when she asked the band to play "Raindrops Keep Falling on My Head," and to the cheers of the guests rode along of the back of Mighty Chair, waving her napkin through the air with great bravado, à la Katharine Ross on Paul Newman's bicycle handlebars in *Butch Cassidy*.

We approached the possibility of a relationship with the ease of people dipping our toes in peanut butter. I had never been married; she was one-and-done, thank you very much, she told me, determined never to pay psychic alimony again. How can you not love a beautiful woman who tells you, "All I'm looking for is a good meal and a soft pillow"?

We'd finally gotten together in my apartment on the third night after the initial attacks. Here's something else most people don't know; the strongest bond in nature exists between the protein avidin and the ligand biotin. Once they find each other, they cannot be torn apart "by extremes of pH, temperature, organic solvents and other denaturing agents." Or as I like to describe it, tighter even than a rock star and a supermodel. That was us. That was Jenny and me. We weren't officially anything, but we were bonded more tightly than any known noncovalent interaction!

There. A sex scene my mother will love.

All our frustrations, our fears and our anger, our shades of loneliness and sadness, all of it got released in great bursts of passion until we had nothing left inside. If we had been in a 1950s Doris Day/Rock Hudson movie, the director would cut first to a steaming teapot, followed by a nuclear explosion. And then we lay there, Jenny nestled under my right arm, and in those vulnerable moments we openly discussed our feelings—about politics.

That was the second language we spoke. Both of us loved the complexities, the challenges, and the possibilities of politics. We loved trying to decipher the swirling currents and predict the eddies. Jenny working on the inside, me in an aisle seat. So after sex we had some hard-core politics to catch up on. "There's a lot of confusion," she said, brushing back several strands of hair.

"No kidding," agreed Mr. Cynic. "Everybody's trying to figure out how to squeeze something out of this."

She shook her head. "Not everybody. Not Martha, that's for sure. We're already trying to schedule hearings to find out why we were so unprepared."

"Good luck on that. You know that's not gonna happen," I predicted. "The last thing Wrightman wants is somebody suggesting he had some responsibility for this." I kissed her on the top of her head. "Well . . ." and we said together, "at least he's not Trump." Then we laughed, a knowing innocent laughter. She snuggled closer, laying her leg over my groin and settling her breast into my chest. A typically casual, entirely intentional Jenny move.

"So? What?" she wondered, tilting her head and looking up at me through wide-open green eyes.

"The usual," I admitted. "All of recorded history."

"Oh, that." She waved it away.

"Well, you see what's going on."

She lifted the sheet and looked down at my resting passion. "Not much," she reported. Then she said softly, lovingly, "Okay, go ahead and tell me again so everyone reading this book will know that we were in the middle of a crisis that threatened our democracy." So maybe she didn't say that, not exactly. What she did do is kiss me and complain, "Your timing is exquisite." Then she took me in her hand and said seductively, "Hello, little friend."

Rather than going into details of what then transpired (once again), let me cover those few minutes by explaining what Jenny was referring to; and no, I'm not writing this in hindsight. This was the gist of our conversation: I believed completely in the great American experiment. The concept that people of all races and creeds and religions could be bound together in some degree of harmony by a system of laws. That belief was one of several reasons that I had volunteered to fight for this country. It was worth fighting for.

But I also believed that our uniquely American version of democracy had been in decline for decades. That we were slowly morphing into what we had been fighting. This was a discussion that Jenny and I had had several times. (This was us: a small candlelit table at an out-of-the-way family Italian restaurant, a subtle wine, and a lively discussion about the philosophy of George F. Kennan.)

I argued that politicians had been eating away at our core principles like termites chewing on hidden beams. While they distracted us with temporal issues—capital punishment, for example, which in actuality is never going to affect any of us, unless we have a friend on death row—they had been steadily weakening our constitutional foundations.

One night several months earlier we had gone to hear Pulitzer Prize–winning historian David Malinsky lecturing at Georgetown about his new book, *Complexities Made Simple*. What I remember most about that is the great imitation he did of George Carlin's explaining the demise of the American Indian. "Just back up a little, please," he said. "Just a little, little more. One more step. A little bit more, don't worry about it, just a tiny step, a little more, and more . . . Next thing you know you're in North Dakota."

That was what we were doing to our constitutional safeguards. The irony of it is, of course, that the biggest steps have always been taken in response to an event. To keep the nation together during the Civil War, Lincoln had to ignore the constitutional protections that the North was fighting to make the South respect. In 1941 we went to war to fight dictators—and to do so, it became necessary to give FDR dictatorial powers. To deal with the pandemic, first the Trumpers, then the Democrats treated the Constitution as an inconvenience to be acknowledged and respected, but ignored like an irritating older relative.

Essentially, every time there's been a crisis, we've disregarded the

Constitution. And lost just a little more freedom. Just a little more, one more step, a little farther. Vietnam. Wow. Congress voluntarily gave Johnson war powers granted to them in the Constitution. So much for that. 9/11, boom! Next thing you know we're standing in long lines at airports, smiling into surveillance cameras, and giving away our privacy.

What I wondered was how Wrightman was going to use these attacks to consolidate all the small steps he had already taken. I smelled the stink of fascism.

Jenny asked me to pause here and tell you she thinks I am overreacting. She would tell you herself, but she's . . . uh, she's busy right now.

This slow erosion might have continued apace for several more decades if the internet hadn't burst into our lives and changed everything. The internet allowed people to find their tribes, to locate people who believed as they did—no matter how sensible or wacko. It allowed small, highly motivated groups to organize and take power away from much larger but complaisant or distracted groups. The result of that was Trump.

Voltaire wrote: "To learn who rules over you, simply find out who you are not allowed to criticize." But this was exactly the type of warning Wrightman would have erased if it had been possible. Several weeks after Wrightman's inauguration a group of students at Vermont's John Rogers University occupied the administration building to protest an announced tuition increase. In response, the chancellor said that while he admired their spunk, he abhorred their tactics, and to "crush dissent" he sent in the cops. The kids were carried out and charged with disturbing the peace.

Trump was a proud pussy-grabber, Wrightman turned out to be a quiet power-grabber. He turned this minor incident at Rogers U. into a federal case. "To protect the constitutional right to protest, one of our core freedoms," he issued a presidential directive allowing the federal government to issue a cease and desist order to any person, business, or institution that attempted or appeared to attempt to take away or limit First Amendment rights. It was a beautiful bit of legalese, giving the government cover to use First Amendment powers to curtail First Amendment rights.

That same type of twisted logic was being applied to the most important freedoms. To guarantee the right to safely demonstrate, for example, Wrightman had limited the size of demonstrations. We were leaking civil liberties like oil from an old Dodge Dart. What bothered me was that as long as their Xbox was working, people didn't seem to mind.

"You're exaggerating again," Jenny said with the usual tolerance in her voice.

She had popped up beside me. "You really think so?"

I frustrated her. Intellectually, I mean. Always did. I used to complain she was much too smart to be such an optimist. She described me as the only person she knew who worried that the sky was falling and my insurance had expired yesterday.

I reminded her about that actual building that did fall on me.

Jenny wasn't naive. She didn't necessarily trust Wrightman much more than I did, but at times she was willing to defend him. That was the whole "the country's in desperate trouble" argument. She wasn't the lone ranger: a lot of people bought into that. The country was facing potentially catastrophic economic, social, and geopolitical problems. Trump had alienated our allies and surrendered ground to our enemies, and we couldn't even agree on whether to permit a right turn on red. What we really needed was a human superglue. "If Wrightman can bring us together," she posited, "then I'll accept some temporary limitations. I just don't want to see anybody get hurt."

We never argued about it; we defended our beliefs, we discussed, we disagreed, we cajoled, but we never argued. We also never reached any conclusions. I wondered, where do you draw the line before you end up in North Dakota? To satisfy my fears she promised that if it ever came to that, she would move there with me—but insisted we have two Franklin stoves in our cabin.

What was true was that immediately after the attacks, the country had rallied to support Wrightman. So it was not surprising that instant polls showed strong support for the Detroit raid, even if no one was quite sure what was accomplished. We sure got 'em! Got who? Them! Way to go!

The administration spent the following few days doing everything possible to link the people who died in that house to the July eleventh attacks. But that just didn't ring true to me. Their activities were like trying to fit together pieces taken from several jigsaw puzzles: no matter how hard they tried, it just didn't add up to the picture on the cover of the box. I collected sourced stories, rumors, even obvious fabrications. I read several foreign newspapers on the web and put them together to try to figure out which organization was pushing what story line, and from that determine what the administration wanted people to believe. Whatever was going on, what the administration wanted us to believe it was wasn't it. They clearly wanted Americans to believe 'twas a famous victory.

In late July a sidebar in the *Detroit Free Press* caught my attention. The mother of one of the people reportedly killed in the raid, a man who had been identified as Mustafa Haddad, had hired an attorney to initiate a wrongful death suit against the government of the United States. If that wasn't weird, it definitely was unusual. Families of terrorists rarely sued their assailants.

On a whim I decided to call her. It had the potential to be a good story. A friend in my battle buddy network had a contact at FedEx, who got me her phone number. She answered on the second ring. I introduced myself and started speaking without waiting for a response. To catch her attention, I said a few words in Arabic, basically a noncommittal commiseration: I share your sorrows. I am a big believer in the five-sentence rule: If I could get five sentences into an introduction without the other person hanging up, I'd get my interview. One: My name is . . . Two: I'm a reporter (always a reporter, never a journalist). Three: I am sorry about . . . (Or, when appropriate, I was happy to hear that . . .) Four: I understand you . . . (whatever action I was calling about). Five, the clincher: Would you tell me about . . . (your husband, wife, daughter, amazing animal)?

She wanted to talk. There wasn't a comma of hesitation in her voice.

She spoke firmly and clearly with a lilting accent I couldn't quite pinpoint but recognized as from someplace in North Africa. Too many reporters had banged on her door and shouted nasty questions at her, she said. They had no respect, they had scared her. "Ghouls," she said, "ghouls."

"I'm sorry to hear that," I said somberly, while actually pleased that she considered me sympathetic.

Her lawyer, the cousin who had been born in America and worked very hard, a good man, had helped her file the lawsuit. "They killed my son, mister, they killed my son." And then she wailed, a long primitive expression of a mother's pain that instantly transported me to another life, in another place, at another time. "They killed my son."

The one thing of which she was very certain was that her son was not a terrorist. She repeated that twice, three times. I sat at my desk, eyes closed, absorbing her emotion rather than hearing her cries. Unfortunately, I'd heard similar protests before, and then I'd found weapons hidden under floorboards. That didn't make her pain any less real. But what was clear is that she wanted me to tell her story to the world. When finally she quieted, I said, with the sensitivity of a fisherman sensing a tug on his reel, "I'm so sorry, Mrs. Haddad, but other people don't believe this. If you want me to tell them about your son, I need your help. I need to know how you can be so certain."

"My son, he was born in America," she said, pausing at times to take a calming breath. "He was American. He didn't care nothing about those people. Crazy people, he said they were. He didn't go to the mosque or say his prayers. He played the games on the television, that was his love. And his motorcycle. And the girls. All the time I tell him, Mustafa, stop with the girls. He is a handsome boy, my son."

I let her ramble, let her pour her memories into Mighty Chair's taping system. The portrait she painted of her son did not resemble the typical terrorist profile. If he had been radicalized, she swore, it was to be against killing innocent people. The Boston Marathon bombing had enraged him. "He screamed at the stupid people who had done it. They make it . . ."—she fumbled for the right word, *easy* or *nice,* remembering his fury—"nice for people to hate us." He would get angry when others called the bombers martyrs. She lowered her voice and almost whispered, "One time he heard about people planning something and he made a phone call without telling no one his name to stop it."

She certainly sounded convincing. But in my experience few sons have admitted to their mothers, *Yeah, Ma, you're right. I'm a terrorist.* True or not, she certainly believed he was innocent. And as our conversation wound down, I finally found out why: "Here is the truth, mister," she said. "My son, Mustafa, he was a drug man. What could I do, that's how he worked. What could I do?" Her son had gotten into the drug business as a fourteen-year-old, making deliveries on his bicycle. Then he started dealing. "But not to children. No time, never. He promised me, never to children. My son was a good boy." He was making a lot of money, she continued, offering to show me Mustafa's "money pad," his notebook. He had bought beautiful things, a beautiful car, a motorcycle. He had bought the house for her. None of it was in his name, though, because the police would know where the money had come from.

I took notes as I listened to her. Not to rely on when I wrote my story, but to remind me of the questions I wanted to ask. The kid was living a big life; he was making money and he had no overt religious beliefs to get in his way. In the background I heard a baby crying. Twice the mother had asked someone to pick up the child. Then it suddenly dawned on me. "Do you need to take care of the baby?" I asked. I figured that was the best way to ask the question.

She responded with a massive sob as her emotions again overflowed. "My grandson . . ." she started. "Mustafa lived for his son. His boy, his whole life is that boy."

After I'd thanked her for her time, given her my contact information in case she thought of anything else, and left open the possibility I would call her again, I leaned back and asked Cher to play *Night on Bald Mountain*. It seemed like the appropriate background music for my thoughts; it was soft and dramatic, loud and threatening. Her words settled in my mind. On balance, I decided, who the fuck knows? To me, it seemed pretty unlikely this guy was a terrorist, but stranger connections had been made. Was it possible? It definitely wasn't impossible. "Cher,"

I said, "transcribe and print, please." The transcription wouldn't be perfect, but it would be good enough for me. *F* or *O,* I wondered?

One thing for certain: The administration was not going to love this story. If the mother was right, the government of the United States essentially had assassinated her son and everyone else in that house. I could imagine the phone call I was going to get from harmless, lovable Eunie. And who knows, maybe even an in-person scolding from one of her boys.

It could be worse, I thought. *I could still be walking down dark streets in Fallujah.*

(And within the flick of a Bic I remembered that in actuality that was not possible. So I guess it couldn't be worse.)

7

When I was fifteen years old, I received first place at my high school science fair for an experiment showing the effect of X-rays on memory. I timed ten mice going through a home-made maze several times; then I exposed half of them to X-rays at my dentist's office and ran them through the maze again. My prize was an invitation to a VFW dinner honoring astronaut Pete Conrad. The original Mercury and Apollo astronauts were my childhood heroes. These were American men risking their lives aboard American technology for the greater good of America. That was several years before Nixon turned patriotism into a political statement.

At that dinner Conrad told one of my favorite stories. "The night before they put you on top of a billion-dollar candle and light it up," he admitted, "no matter how much confidence you have in the men and equipment, you still don't sleep very well. I was scheduled to be awakened at four A.M. to suit up. I finally fell into a restless sleep about two o'clock. When I woke up, the sun was shining and the birds were singing. Great, and then I realized that the sun is not supposed to be shining at four A.M. I looked at my clock; it was after six. I'd spent years as part of the most complex engineering program in history; I'd been chosen from thousands of applicants and been in training for a decade. None of that mattered as I looked out into the morning sunshine and thought, *Oh my god, they've left without me.*"

That feeling of discombobulation in the pit of your stomach, of being late for something important, was exactly what I felt when my phone rang at eight-fifteen several mornings later. Jenny had worked late and stayed in her apartment. Shit, I'd completely missed my workout. "Thanks a lot, Cher," I said sarcastically. "You were supposed to wake me. What is wrong with you?"

Cher did not respond. "Cher, remind me to call Y." He'd figure out her problem.

Frankie B. was on the phone. "Working from home this morning, are we?"

"That's how I earn those big bucks."

"Then you don't know?"

"What don't I know?"

"Turn on the TV."

I clicked on the big screen and lay in bed. I was pretty sure I knew what was going on. I'd posted my interview with Mustafa's mother a day earlier: *The mother of one of the alleged terrorists killed in Detroit by an elite antiterrorism unit claimed that her son, 23-year-old Mustafa Haddad, had no connection to the recent attacks. While admitting that Haddad was involved in the local drug trade, as police had reported, she insisted . . .* My assumption was that my story had caused a ripple.

I was wrong. I couldn't have been more wrong. During the night three known terrorist groups had released a joint statement claiming credit for "the first unified attack on the American homeland." What made it believable was the inclusion of the names and photographs of the "martyrs of New York," as well as previously undisclosed details about the bombing at Pearl Harbor and the cyber-destruction of the Old River Control Structure.

The fact that this statement did not praise the so-called terrorists killed in the Detroit raid was a strong indication they were not involved. Kaufman had made some vague statement that American intelligence agencies had not confirmed these claims, but I could just imagine the panic inside the White House as they searched for a link, any link, between these terrorists and Detroit.

This had the makings of a supersize colonoscopy for Wrightman. A lot of people were going to be looking way up the administration's derriere to see if it had committed convenient killings. Blowing up that house in Detroit might be blowing up in their face. If it could be proved that the president had acted to turn down the political heat, he was cooked.

"Cher," I commanded, "come here, please." Mighty Chair rolled over to the side of my bed. I maneuvered myself into it, then felt a need to apologize. "Cher, I'm sorry I snapped at you. I guess I forgot to give you a wake-up time."

Cher did not respond. But I felt better.

A large Dunkin' was sitting in my place when I walked into the conference room about an hour later. "Come on in, Rollie, take a seat," Howie said pleasantly, our little joke. "Cher, good morning to you."

Cher recognized his voice. "Good morning, Howie," she replied.

Stephanie Ruhle was reporting soundlessly on the monitor in the front of the room. The chyron running at the bottom of the screen summed it up: MULTIPLE TERRORIST GROUPS CLAIM ALLIANCE FOR ATTACKS: NO INDICATION DETROIT INVOLVEMENT.

"So what do you think?" Howie asked.

Nodding toward me, Frankie B. said, "I think I'd like to be that mother's lawyer right now."

Howie ignored him. "The president is lying to the American people. *Quel* surprise."

I sipped my cold coffee. "Why bother this time?" I wondered. "What's the gain?"

"You're the reporter," Howie pointed out. "I'm the boss. You figure it out."

Throughout the day additional reports from foreign intelligence services confirmed the initial claims. Three different terrorist organizations, under the banner Brotherhood United for Freedom, had planned and financed the operations and put their people in the field. Not surprisingly, several previously unknown terrorist organizations also tried to grab some credit. Whether or not they actually were involved, this was an attention-getting, fundraising, volunteer-building opportunity. Which of course is precisely what our politicians would have done.

Kaufman issued another vague statement. Standing on Conway's

Corner, the same spot on the White House front lawn where several years earlier Kellyanne Conway had given us the Orwellian concept of "alternative facts," she said, "We need to show these terrorists that they can't terrorize us. The president urges all Americans to show their courage by doing the normal things." (Historical aside: A reporter named Tom Robbins had dubbed that place Conway's Corner. It was an expansive grass-covered area. Referring to it as a corner, Robbins had explained, was simply "an example of an alternative fact.")

The problem was that America had been terrorized. Weeks after the attacks, body parts were still being dug out of the Louisiana mud. New York hadn't cleared all the burnt hulks out of the tunnel. In Hawaii, forensic anthropologists were collecting DNA samples from the descendants of sailors who had died on the *Arizona* eight decades ago to enable them to identify the recovered bones.

Unless you were living in one of the repurposed cold war bomb shelters featured on *Flip This House,* the fact that the government apparently had mistaken a minor-league drug dealer for the people who had launched the most successful terrorist attack in our history had to shake your confidence in any claims.

The first antigovernment demonstration consisted of an estimated twenty people. (Only the *Times* would "estimate" twenty people.) On a gorgeous Saturday afternoon, New Yorkers began venturing out to Central Park. Most of them were happy to just be outside, but typically those estimated twenty people were carrying hand-drawn political signs attacking the administration. The roads were a mess. Traffic patterns throughout the city had been changed to deal with the massive problems caused by the loss of the tunnel. Wooden barriers had been set up to funnel all downtown traffic onto Broadway. It worked for vehicles, but less so for pedestrians. Mounted cops tried to stop the jaywalkers from interfering with the flow of traffic, which resulted in a big crowd backed up behind the wooden horses. Additional NYPD officers rushed to the scene to maintain control.

Imagine this scene: Traffic is at a total standstill. A large crowd has been herded into a small area, and more people are showing up with essentially no place to go. Did anybody really think New Yorkers were going to stand there? It took less than a minute for the barriers to be pushed over. With one great cheer pedestrians took over the streets, bringing traffic to a complete stop. Making a confusing situation even worse, an Uber attempting to make a right turn off Central Park West onto 83rd Street collided with a Lubavitch Mitzvah Tank (I can't make this stuff up!), adding to the gridlock. Emergency vehicles and ambulances from every hospital in the city were trapped racing to get to the accident, their endlessly bleating sirens creating even more panic.

New Yorkers being New Yorkers, the wailing and whooping sirens drew even more curious pedestrians into the area. With fire department and EMS vehicles stalled in traffic, mounted cops began weaving through the cars. They attempted to use their horses to gently force people back onto the sidewalk or into the park, opening a traffic lane for the emergency vehicles. Unfortunately one of the twenty protesters, later identified as an NYU sociology professor, was caught between a horse and a wooden barrier and panicked. He slashed at the animal with his poster, a caricature of Wrightman gleefully blowing up a birdhouse, captioned "Bird Brains!" The horse, being a horse, responded by backing up, unintentionally knocking over the professor. An unidentified person, seeing this, shouted, "Watch out! The cops!"

The fear, the anxiety, the frustration that had been pent up for more than two weeks was suddenly let loose. People trying to get out of the area knocked down other people moving into the area. Fights broke out, forcing NYPD officers to wade into the crowd, waving their batons, to restore order. Dozens of people were arrested and hundreds more were temporarily detained.

The first photographs of the "West Side Uprising!" to spread virally showed a man holding an anti-Wrightman sign falling under the hooves of a large police horse. Videos posted on YouTube were equally confusing; it was impossible to determine if the cops were attacking or protecting people. Within hours, demonstrations in support of the "New York Twenty" had popped up in more than a dozen cities. Other rallies were planned. The general anxiety people were feeling was suddenly channeled into an anti-Wrightman fervor.

Somebody inside the White House decided that these demonstrations had to be stopped while they were still small. Having learned the lessons taught by the Trump administration during the Black Lives Matter protests, the administration set out its legal case. Two nights later, the president made the first of what were to become regular fireside chats. It was broadcast from his suitably rustic cabin. He was sitting in a rocking chair in front of a gray-stone walk-in fireplace, a portrait of a rippling tattered flag hanging above the mantel. Although it was late July, a fire was crackling in the hearth and Wrightman was wearing a friendly sweater. It was a beautiful setting, obviously carefully planned to reinforce those basic American values designed by Ralph Lauren. I had no doubt there had been long discussions in the press office whether he should rock or sit still.

He sat still. After the patriotic introductions he asked patriotic Americans for their understanding, pointing out, "It would be a grave injustice to the sacred memories of those brave Americans who perished in the attacks if we allowed a small number of rabble-rousers to desecrate their sacrifice to further their own political agenda."

Of course not, thought your humble Mr. Cynic. What type of man would use dead Americans for political gain? Wait a second . . . I was with several staff members watching this speech at Lucille's Ballroom. Lucille, all of her, was sitting directly across from me.

Wrightman continued: "In previous administrations we saw the terrible damage that could be done by dividing us. On Inauguration Day I gave you my solemn word that I would bring us together as the truly . . ."

Here he paused for dramatic effect, then enunciated carefully: ". . . *United* States of America. In this, our most vulnerable hour, we must prevent our enemies from ripping us asunder. To prevent that from happening, I have asked the Justice Department to issue a directive to all state and local law enforcement reminding them that they are our first defenders and asking them to continue playing a vital role in protecting and preserving our freedoms."

"Uh-oh," Lucille said. She was so rattled that she had actually sprung for drinks for the whole table. This was, I realized, the first direct benefit I'd received from the Wrightman administration.

After the boilerplate *God bless*es, and as the first strains of the

Mormon Tabernacle Choir's a cappella version of "America the Beautiful" rose softly in the background, President Wrightman turned and stared meaningfully into the fire as the camera slowly faded out.

A legal directive was issued to all law enforcement agencies by Attorney General Langsam several minutes later, while the talking heads were still marveling over Wrightman's "courageous effort to unite the country." It read:

> Under our constitutional obligation to promote and ensure
> the general welfare, we are hereby requiring that all public
> assemblies involving or likely to bring together a substantial
> number of people who have not applied for and received a
> permit be temporarily suspended. While this administration
> will fiercely defend the fundamental First Amendment
> right of every American to gather peacefully to petition the
> government, under the existing circumstances these so-
> called pop-up rallies constitute a clear and present danger
> to the public safety. We do not want to repeat the errors
> made during the BLM protests. To enable law enforcement
> to continue to protect the lives and property of the American
> people, we request you take action to prevent such large
> or uncontrollable gatherings. We strongly urge you to do so
> without the use of force, but should such actions become
> necessary, the Justice Department will provide appropriate
> legal support.

The response was immediate and predictable. Led by the American Civil Liberties Union, numerous organizations protested this directive. The ACLU filed a legal challenge, causing Louisiana senator John Kennedy to refer to it as "the pro-riot organization."

The administration was considerably less forgiving, suggesting that any "person, institution, or organization who opposed defending American lives at this crucial moment in our nation's history is providing aid and comfort to the enemy."

A massive social media campaign supporting the president erupted instantly. Almost as if it had been planned, prepared, and ready to launch as soon as he finished his speech. There's nothing wrong with that, I guess; in some form every president—indeed, every politician—makes an effort to shape public opinion. One man's propaganda is another man's Fox News. A significant difference between this situation and the escalating violence of the BLM protests was that while Trump had already lost the trust of a majority of Americans, Wrightman remained popular and people still supported him. It worked; this strategy was as effective as it was heavy-handed: I'll bet you knew that at some point in this book I was going to dig up that appropriate H. L. Mencken quote, "No one ever went broke underestimating the intelligence of the American public."

Twitter reported a record-shattering 10 million tweets and retweets had been sent within a day, the majority of them from accounts including *#IsupportAmerica, #stopterroristrallies, #Istandwiththepresident;* even the old saw *#Americaloveitorleaveit.* Videos showing riots intercut with funerals of Americans killed in the initial attacks, as well as American flags being burned, were posted on Facebook, YouTube, TikTok, and Instagram. Hundreds of patriotic-themed boards popped up on Pinterest.

Several rallies were announced for the following weekend to test this policy. Law enforcement (and local militias) responded by issuing riot gear (with shields), tear gas canisters, and rubber bullets. Joseph Heller would have loved the administration's logic: In an effort to prevent people from being hurt, the police were going to have to hurt people.

Rather than trying to calm the situation, the broadcast media was promoting it. Instead of urging people to let the legal process proceed, they treated it like Wrestlemania, promising complete coverage of the confrontation: (*Theme music up, then*) "Watch what happens when determined protesters go head-to-head with America's fiercest defenders!"

The whole thing was mind-bogglingly insane, and there was absolutely nothing that would stop it. As I look back, this was the first time I seriously began to wonder if American democracy could survive. Even during the Trump riots I was comforted by my belief that Trump simply was reacting to events, that his response was not part of a plan. He didn't use that uprising as part of a long-term strategy to fundamentally change the country. I had real faith that he wasn't smart enough to pull that off.

But Wrightman? It was sort of like looking at a bruise on the skin of an apple and wondering how deep it went. How far was Wrightman willing to go to "restore order"? I had been brought up to believe this type of government takeover happened in the old eastern bloc or in banana republics. Not here. Not in America.

One thing I do know, I wanted to get out and cover the Washington rally myself. Howie refused, insisting I work the desk. He wanted me to write the national story. I never found out for certain, but I was pretty confident Jenny had talked him into it.

Instead of riots, Wrightman got incredibly lucky. Several years ago I'd done a story with a Boulder, Colorado, district attorney who'd had to prosecute a highly incendiary race case. A group of white kids had chased two Black kids onto a highway, where one of them had been hit by a car and killed. Whichever side won, the other side was threatening to riot. He prevented that from happening by scheduling the case for the following February. "Nobody riots in February," he told me. "It's much too cold."

Instead of frigid temperatures, just about the entire country was blanketed by an oppressive heat wave. In many cities, temperatures soared above 100 degrees, which combined with an inversion that resulted in unusually poor air quality created unsafe conditions that forced people to stay safely inside. Rather than tempers boiling over, they were air-conditioned. The rallies fizzled out, forcing the organizers to reschedule the demonstrations for September.

The administration was also fortunate that millions of Americans were distracted by the historic three-day *The Voice vs. American Idol: Battle of the Champions* competition. The newly legalized betting on reality TV outcomes, which had just been approved by several states, turned this into a huge attraction—further dissipating a lot of the anger. The "final showdown" pitted a nine-year-old suffering from a collapsed immune system that forced her to compete from inside a sealed-plastic bubble against an eighty-seven-year-old man with Alzheimer's who could re-member only the words to love songs he'd crooned to his recently de-ceased wife. Okay, maybe I'm exaggerating. (The man was lying about

his age.) But the combination of climate change and wagering on entertainment greatly reduced the level of anger.

Members of Congress expressed outrage on every TV show that
would invite them, and within days both the Senate and the House, by
voice vote, approved a "Sense of the Congress" resolution calling on
President Wrightman "to respect all rights granted by the Constitution
upon which this great nation was founded and has long endured," and
warning him that if the administration insisted on following "this dangerous course it would face the possibility of congressional censure!"

Leaders of both parties promised additional votes, threatening "even
harsher language" if this policy was implemented.

I couldn't blame them for their cowardice. As Republican senators
had demonstrated during the Trump impeachment, the first job of an
American politician is to get reelected. Standing up to a popular president
preaching security is a direct path to spending more time with your family. The polls continued to show that Americans were willing to "compromise" on constitutional protections in exchange for an increased sense
of personal safety. It was not surprising that Wrightman's approval numbers, which had wavered, finally stabilized and even began rising again.

In mid-August the president made a surprise appearance at the annual
convention of the National Association of Chiefs of Police being held at
the Georgia International Convention Center in Atlanta. Without any
introduction he dramatically walked out of the wings onto the giant bare
stage, as an American flag waved proudly in 3-D on the screen behind
him. Apparently, his appearance was no surprise to the cable networks
that covered the event. I was having a quick burger at the ballroom with
Jenny, and we watched it on the row of TVs over the bar.

When the cheering subsided, an appropriately subdued Wrightman
began his brief remarks by thanking the gathered chiefs for their service to America, as well as their individual "cities, towns, villages and
hamlets." Calling their departments "our first line of defense against
those who would do this nation harm," he specifically cited the work
of the several police officers who had distinguished themselves on
7/11, as well as "Lieutenant Martin Shaw, Detroit PD, and the men of

his anti-crime unit." During the raid on the safe house, he continued, "Working side by side with elite Special Operators, Lt. Shaw and his men identified, located, and eventually disrupted this terrorist network."

That's interesting, I thought. *He's doubling down on that lie.*

The president shaded his eyes from the spotlights as he looked out upon a sea of uniformed police officers. "Is Marty here? You here, Marty? Please stand up." Marty did not stand up. Marty was not there. The problem with having an active curiosity is that you're always curious. I wondered why he was singling out a Detroit cop involved in that raid rather than the military.

The president finished to raucous cheers, promising that his administration would continue to provide law enforcement with all the tools needed to meet "both small and large threats, today or in the future. We have your backs!" he shouted as the arena erupted, almost drowning him out. "We will defend you! We will protect you! We will honor you!" The walls rocked from the ovation. "And together, together! We will make this nation a safe place for democracy to flourish and grow!"

Eighteen thousand police officers from all around the country leaped to their feet, shouting in unison, "Wright-man! Wright-man! Wright-man . . ."

The man knew how to work a crowd, that was obvious. After quieting the audience, he announced that congressional leaders were ready to assist local law enforcement in purchasing technologically advanced bulletproof vests, strong enough to deflect even the powerful steel-jacketed bullets recently made legal by Congress. He took a moment to thank the manufacturer of both those bullets and the bulletproof vests that could safely absorb them, the Khyber Munitions Corporation, for its generous offer to provide both ammunition and those vests to the departments at a significant reduction.

I actually smiled when he said that. I had read about Khyber; it was the first company to sell advertising space on the jackets of its bullets.

Admittedly, it was a bravura performance, a masterpiece of political theater. It locked down the support of every law enforcement officer in the country, while at the same time reassuring anxious Americans that he was taking the steps necessary to keep them safe.

"He's good," I said to Jenny as the cheering faded and the networks returned to their anchors. "You know, he reminds me of something Will Rogers said." Will Rogers was a major star of vaudeville and early movies, a comedian who appeared onstage twirling a lasso while he lamented about current events. Jenny knew all about him. I raised my index finger in the air and said, in a voice I made up that might have sounded like him, "The single most important trait any politician can possess is sincerity." Then I slipped into my best Groucho, tapped my imaginary cigar with my fingers, and concluded, "And if he can fake that . . ."

She frowned. She was so cute when she frowned. She looked like my first-grade teacher disapproving my lurid finger painting. "Maybe you should give the guy a little break," she said, raising her beer stein toward the TVs. "C'mon, Rol, look what the guy inherited. It's going to take a long time to clean up this mess. So far he's doing all right."

There was a time I thought of people as diamonds, whose facets changed with reflected light. But Jenny was more like a Rubik's Cube, a complex array of vivid colors spinning on an axis that I could never quite figure out. Maybe that was her appeal, that and her great figure. "How about your boss?" I asked. "What does she think?" Officially McDonnell was a liberal Democrat; in reality she was a hard-nosed realist who had become adroit at tweaking the system to benefit her constituents. A lot of people gave her credit for saving those shards of Obamacare that had eluded the Trumpsters' efforts to wipe it out completely.

"Oh, you know Martha," she responded. "She always wants more for . . ."—here she did her own impersonation of McDonnell's raspy voice—"real Americans who go to work every morning to keep this country running."

I raised my glass and clinked it against her empty stein. "To sincerity."

"Skoal!" she agreed, clinking back, her smile brightening the room.

I stared at her.

"What?" she wondered.

"Nothing," I said, shaking my head in wonder. In this case, of course, *nothing* meant everything.

She blushed.

I was smitten. If you've been really lucky, you know what I was feeling. You might even be able to close your eyes and re-create it. If you haven't experienced it, all I can say is, I hope it happens for you. There had been a good run of women in my life since I rolled off the reassembly line, but not one of them had shown any staying power. Maybe that was my fault. It didn't really matter, because that's what it had taken me to get to this place. I didn't know where we were going, neither of us did, so we lived happily in the present. Occasionally she would refer to her ex, "perfectly proper Peter," without expressing any anger or regret. I was naturally curious why their marriage had failed, amazed that any man could let her go, but whatever had happened, she didn't want to talk about it or repeat it. Unlike a lot of people, she was perfectly happy simply being perfectly happy.

I was still basking in her smile as I was on my way to the gym the next morning. An early morning rainstorm had temporarily broken the heat wave. Along the way I stopped at all my regulars, and after a few mumbled words dropped my usual buck in a cup.

There was no place I felt more at home than in a gym; the clacking of weights, the occasional grunts, the friendly banter had been the background music of my life. The smell of sweat was my perfume. Obviously, I couldn't do everything I'd once done, so I compensated by doing more of what I could do. The Light Brigade had been with me the whole trip.

Wrightman's speech was the only thing anybody wanted to talk about. There was a general uneasiness about his over-the-top patriotism. Wayne Chang, a D.C. detective, compared it to Dubya's use of 9/11 to launch the war against Saddam Hussein. Everybody had an opinion about exactly what it meant, about how far he might be willing to go. No one could figure out his real intentions. He wasn't banging the war drums, there was no screaming about political enemies, there weren't even any obvious legislative goals. For me, I piped up, it was like an itch on your back that was just out of your reach; it was real and it wasn't going away.

What was clear was that the White House was struggling to regain its solid footing. The doubts about the administration's competence had provided an opening for us to publish Inside the Beltway stories that otherwise would have attracted little interest. I had published two additional stories pretty much demolishing the links between the attacks and the Detroit raid. *The Hill* ran a piece revealing that the Department of Labor had quietly changed the method used to compile economic statistics, making the economy appear significantly more resilient than it actually was performing. A *Politico* piece exposed the confusion inside the Defense Department about how to respond to the attacks. A *Washington Post* feature criticized the National Security Council for not taking stronger steps to restore the nation's intelligence capabilities, which had been decimated by Trump and obviously insufficiently repaired by the Dems.

All of those stories, including mine, had required information from "knowledgeable" sources. The White House had sprung a leak, and steps were being taken to prevent it from sinking. Which is why the phone call I received didn't much surprise me.

"Mr. Stone?" She had a pleasantly officious voice. "Secretary McCord would ..."

"Rollie!" Rip interrupted, picking up the phone. "Thank you, Michele, I got it." He waited a beat as his assistant hung up. "I've been reading your stories this week."

I couldn't tell if that was supposed to be a compliment or a threat.

"You guys are doing a great job there." I was waiting for some kind of busting-balls comment, but it didn't come. "So I was hoping you might be able to help me out."

Here's another dirty secret from the wonderful world of journalism. We respected quid pro quos even before Trump made them popular. If we owe favors and we can repay them without compromising ethics or personal integrity, we do. Rip was somewhere on my list.

"If I can. What do you need?" I heard a soft whir as Mighty Chair began recording.

"A little patriotism, actually. Off the record, I need you to help us protect America." I looked at the phone and grimaced. That was not the McCord I'd known. Even *he* had to be embarrassed hearing those words coming out of his mouth. I had no doubt he was taking one for the team.

I didn't say a word. I waited for him to fill the uncomfortable silence.

"Listen, man," he finally said in a whispered, conspiratorial tone. "There are things going on here that I can't tell you about. But you'd be doing both of us a big favor if you believed us on this one."

There. I finally figured it out. My stories about the Detroit debacle had touched some Very Important President's nerve. "I'd be happy to quote you, Rip," I offered. "Just put this conversation on record."

McCord laughed. "Right. C'mon, Stoney, gimme a break here. You know I can't do that."

Stoney? *Stoney?* Are you frigging kidding me? He'd been spending far too much time with the same glad-handers we used to laugh at. "Just between you and me and the NSA, Rip, give me a hint. What's really going on here? We both know Detroit is bullshit. Those people didn't have dick to do with 7/11."

For the first time I heard a hint of desperation in his voice. "If I could tell you, I would. You know I've always been straight with you. I can tell you that there are a lot of moving pieces, but I promise you, if you stick with us on this one, I'll make it up to you big-time." *Ping* went one of the strings of my heart. I actually felt a little sorry for him, at least until he added, "And by the way, you're wrong. We've got money transfers, plane tickets." His voice actually got strained as he lied, "It was no coincidence Hassan was in the tunnel, I promise you that. Just do us both a favor and get on board this train. You really don't want it leaving the station without you."

I could almost taste the desert grit in my mouth when I hung up. McCord had always been a stand-up guy; he was a legitimate hero. It hurt a little seeing him made small. Whatever was taking place inside the White House, they were getting ready to play rough.

Howie had plunked down in my dining room chair. "Well, that was weird," I said. "That was McCord trying to get me off the story. They're trying to protect something."

"Or someone," Howie corrected. "It's all the same. This is the eighth administration I've covered, starting with Reagan. I've been flattered and promised and threatened and lied to, I've been offered bribes, I've been accused of treason. Once I was even seduced." He smiled at that memory and tapped his index finger on his chest. "Yeah, that's right, I was seduced."

"Hey," I agreed, tossing my hands palms up, "why not?"

"Damn straight. But I always knew what they wanted. This one . . ." He frowned. "The first thing any reporter wants to know is why have I earned this attention? What does this person want from me?"

"Except the sex," I pointed out.

"Except the sex," he agreed. "You've written some good pieces about this, but we both know there have been more damaging stories out there. What is it about your stories that's got the White House so upset?"

My incredible insight, perhaps? "No idea," I said. And at that moment I didn't.

Howie pushed himself up and adjusted his glasses. "Keep pecking away," he said.

8

pecked.

I downloaded my laundry list: my running compilation of notes, story ideas, little things that bothered me, all those passing thoughts that I'd told Cher to remember. I was looking for anything that might relate to Detroit. McCord's phone call had rung my cowbell. Detroit was old news. Both Snopes and PolitiFact had ruled the story *Incomplete*. The rumors were still floating in cyberspace, but every big story spawned rumors. Six decades later, millions of people still believed the moon landing had been faked, the government was going to invade Texas, Barack Obama had been born in Kenya, and Melania Trump had been known in L.A. as Melvin Knauss before her sex change operation. No one paid too much attention to any of them. To me, at least, it looked like the Detroit story was in the rearview mirror. Whatever truth there was to it, the administration had successfully fended it off. So what was McCord afraid of?

Near the bottom of my list I found the name Martin Shaw, Detroit PD. It took me a few seconds to remember who he was; Shaw was the police officer Wrightman had singled out in his speech. I thought it was a little odd that there had been no follow-up story. Usually when the president mentions someone, the media rushes to tell that person's story. It's like the Wheel of Fortune landing on your name. Especially in this context. But this time, nada. There hadn't been any follow-up stories.

Putting my legendary investigative reporting skills to work, I googled the main number for the Detroit Police Department and told Cher to dial it. When Sergeant Someone answered, I asked in my best good-old-pal voice, "Hey, hi. Marty Shaw around?"

"Hold on," the obviously distracted sergeant said.

A few rings later, in a voice that resonated command presence: "Lieutenant Shaw."

"Lieutenant Shaw, this is Rollie Stone. I'm an editor at *The Promethean*. I just—"

"I know who you are," he responded evenly. "I've seen you on TV. Look, I'm sorry, Mr. Stone, but I can't talk to you. This is a legal matter and the lawyers—"

He was talking to me. I just had to keep him talking. "If you want," I interrupted, "we can make this completely off the record. I've been writing a series . . ."

Shaw chuckled. "Oh, c'mon. Do you know a single cop who hasn't been burned by that line? I've read a couple of your stories, I'd like—"

I mirrored his friendly tone. "Well, sometimes it works." I was three-plus sentences in and he hadn't hung up. A good sign. Rather than asking questions he wasn't going to answer, I looked for common ground. A high percentage of law enforcement officers have military backgrounds. I took a shot. "Can you at least fill in a couple of blanks for me, Lieutenant? I think I read that you were army?"

"Marty," he corrected; I knew I had him when he told me he had been in the desert. He had commanded an MP platoon attached to an Urban Affairs unit. Over there, that wasn't just directing traffic or collecting Saturday-night drunks. The MPs provided security for the do-gooders, going into the villages and cities with them, sometimes while the fires were still burning. Marty Shaw had ridden the danger trail. I didn't offer much about my experience, allowing him to drag it out of me. Special Ops, advance scouting, and mission targeting. In addition to providing boots-on-the-ground intelligence, painting targets for laser-guided weapons.

Shaw had been there after me but knew about our work. Having seen Mighty Chair on TV, he asked how it happened. This isn't a story

I tell often or easily, but this was guy to guy, soldier to soldier, journalist to source. "We had intel that several tribal chiefs were meeting to collect payment for planting IEDs." As I told the story, I was there. I could see the glare of the day. "The going rate back then was $50 for each successfully planted device."

"That didn't change much when I was there."

I took a deep breath and just kept going. "We ID'ed the building. My job was to drop sensors, then stand back. Problem was that about three minutes before bingo the chiefs left the building. Maybe they got a warning, who knows, but I watched them scramble. They got into their vehicles and out of Dodge. Thing was, soon as they were gone, a bunch of kids ran into the building to see if they'd left anything behind."

Shaw didn't say a word. Those kids were still running through my mind.

"I went in right behind them. I got them out just before the missiles hit, but I didn't make it. The whole fucking building collapsed on top of me. The locals didn't know I'd painted the target, they just saw me go in and get their kids. They dug me out by hand and kept me breathing until our people got there. That was it."

"Sorry," he said in a tone that carried his own experiences there. In a far more upbeat voice he wondered, "So how'd you get there?"

"There" being the *Pro*. "Friends in low places, I guess." We both laughed. Subject changed. I gave him the pitch. In contrast to the denizens of Trumpworld, a place in which beliefs trumped truth, we took great pride in what we were doing. We believed journalism mattered. Rah, rah for the good guys.

Sha . . . Marty told me he'd heard of the *Pro* but hadn't read it until a friend forwarded the article I'd written about the mother. "You did a nice job," he said. His response told me a lot about what he wasn't saying. After an uncomfortable pause he continued. "Listen, you understand I'm not allowed to talk to you about any of this. I doubt that's going to change, but if it does, I promise I'll get in contact with you."

Some stories have to be developed slowly, like old-fashioned negatives coming to life in a darkroom, before you know exactly what they're going to look like. When I hung up, I thought, *That's a good start*. Whether it would lead anywhere or not, who knew? I gave him my contact information. No different from dozens of similar conversations. But now, sitting here, knowing what it led to, I do wonder sometimes that if I could go back to that night, would I have made that phone call?

I hope so.

Seconds after I'd hung up Cher told me in her lilting electronic voice that my sister was calling. It's called timing, a *ticka-ticka-ticka.* Just when I'd finished exposing my emotions. "Cher, tell her I'll call her back, please." I liked my sister; I even loved her in a familial way, but we weren't especially close. Before, when traveling was easier and the Army cooperated, I'd get home at least once a year to see my mother as well as my sister and her kids. She was six years older than me, so our lives just brushed at the edges while we were growing up. Bea was a settler, always was, living happily in a gated village with her accountant husband, a good guy, and their two girls. My nieces were repeating Bea's life, but with more TVs.

We spoke around holidays or when there was a family problem or a decision had to be made or there was a payment due on our father's headstone or when she saw me on air; often enough to know the broad strokes of each other's lives.

Maybe I'm being a little bit of a downer. Our relationship was actually better than I portray it. I never doubted that she was always proud of her little bro. In fact, she's already brought the girls up here to visit Uncle Big Mouth. But whatever it was she was calling about, it just wasn't the right time. By the time I went back to work, I had already forgotten about my conversation with Marty Shaw.

Apparently I'd made much more of an impression on him than I had imagined. Three nights later, I got the biggest surprise of my career. It was almost nine o'clock. I was still at my desk, trying to piece together a story about those seemingly innocent places in the budget where Congress hides billions of dollars for intelligence operations. Specialized Educational Benefits, $2.3 billion? Transportation in Developing Nations, $1.4 billion?

I was just finishing a Google Duo talk with Jenny, who was reviewing proposed legislation for political traps, to figure out where we would meet for a late dinner, when I received an anonymous chat request. The caller's sign-in name was NFA, the reporter's catchall meaning "not for attribution." No reporter in history has ever rejected a mysterious anonymous call. "Hold on a second," I told Jenny. "Let me see who this is."

A few seconds later a grainy video popped up on my monitor. It was black and white, very dark, and for several seconds I couldn't figure out what it was. Whatever it was, it was framed, and I realized someone using a handheld device, a cell phone most likely, was recording a scene from a different source. That's one way of protecting your identity. As my eyes focused, I saw a soldier in full gear standing about two feet away. That's when I figured out this was night-vision footage from a body cam.

"Holy shit," I whispered. Thank you, oh great father Thomas Alva Edison.

I remembered that Jenny was on hold, but I was afraid to switch back, afraid this might have been sent to me by mistake and I might lose it. Without taking my eyes off the screen for an instant I said, "Cher, send a message to Jenny. Tell her I'll call her back." I grabbed a cell phone, tapped the video camera icon, and aimed it at the screen. I paused the video. I rewound it.

Two years ago I was invited to speak about journalism at the VA's career fair. During the Q and A, I was asked where story ideas come from. "Everywhere," I'd said. "Everything you read, everything you see, every conversation. You're always looking for something that sparks your curiosity. Then you start digging. And you dig and dig and dig, and then sometimes while you're digging, a story drops on your head." Like this one. I added one more tidbit. When you're working on a story, it takes over your life, it's always on your mind, and when that happens, you realize this isn't your story, it's the story that owns you. David Marash, the legendary *Nightline* correspondent, once described it to me as "going into the trance." While you're working on it, that story becomes the most important thing in your life. The only thing that matters. *Well,* I thought, *here we go again.* I pressed play.

The soldier's face was barely visible. He had covered his tag with a strip of black tape. But he was wearing an embroidered black star. A colonel. "Son," he said in that assholey condescending tone adopted by assholey officers. "What we have here is called a situation. You do know what a situation is, right?"

The audio was clear, although slightly out of sync.

"Yes, sir," the man wearing the camera snapped, his voice crisper than an officer's dress pants. "A situation is something between a shitstorm and a snafu. Sir!" I recognized that tone almost instantly. Marty fucking Shaw. *Son of a bitch,* I thought. *He's been holding on to this since the night of the raid.*

I remembered watching the colonel being interviewed. I didn't remember his name but it would be easy to find. Shaw continued, "Sir, obviously nobody wants me to know what's going on here, but if anybody is crazy enough to believe the people in that house are terrorists, they are out of their friggin' minds. Sir!"

Jesus.

Shaw must have taken a step backward, because the body cam suddenly showed the colonel's face—just in time to capture that don't-fuck-with-me look that I knew so well. "Lieutenant, right?"

"Yes, sir. Sir, please, I'm telling you—"

"You are telling me nothing, Lieutenant." The colonel took two steps closer, limiting the image to a square of uniform. "Let me tell you sumthin', hotshot. As of right now, this area is quarantined. Locked down. Your people are going to perimeter. This isn't any picture show and I do not want any pictures, so order your people to turn off those fancy-schmancy body cameras . . ." As he said that, he literally poked Shaw's camera, but didn't seem to realize it was still taping. I actually had to laugh. I've been there: Sir, I was told to order my men to turn off their body cameras, which I did. I was not instructed to turn off my own cam.

The colonel continued with that same nasty, officious *Platoon* attitude. "Then I want your people doing a house-to-house to shut down any surveillance cameras. Rip 'em the fuck down if you have to. No civilians within a six-block radius. I don't give a rat's fuck if Grandma needs oxygen, I want every swinging dick and dickess out of this area within one hour, and I do not care how you get it done. I want these shit-boxes emptied, and the only people I want to see anywhere near this house will be wearing this patch." I assumed he indicated his camouflaged unit patch. "Do you understand?"

Shaw did not respond. Nodding, I guess.

The colonel stepped back again and eased off his aggressive tone, "We may take some casualties, so I want wagons standing by and a clear path to the highway. One final thing, unless you want to find yourself picking your toes in Poughkeepsie, I don't want any reporters getting close enough for me to smell them." He leaned his face closer and added, "And, son, believe me, I smell like a son of a bitch."

"Yes, sir!" Shaw agreed fervently. I was laughing so hard I almost missed his last few words: "If you say so, sir."

The video went black for a second, and when it resumed, I was looking at a completely different scene. Someone had edited at least two segments together. This second one also was taped from another source; this original source appeared to be a monitor. This image had been recorded by a night-vision camera, so it washed out green with some hint of other colors. It was in a fixed position, and I had no idea where it was set up. I was looking at a circa 1950s suburban house. Locked up tight. Foliage in front partially covered the front windows. It looked like there might be lights on inside, but I couldn't be certain; it could just as easily have been a reflection. There was no movement outside.

There was no sound. I checked the sound level to confirm that. No sound.

I recognized the house. I'd seen it on Zillow. Stratford Road. For several more seconds nothing happened. It could have been a photograph. Suddenly wisps of smoke burst from the front and side of the house. It took me another few seconds to realize bullets were smashing into brick and stucco. It had been more than a decade since I'd seen this same thing for myself, but I had no doubt that's what it was. The rate of fire increased. All the windows were shattered, and a shutter fell off.

It was tough to watch. I looked around the office. Several people were working at desks, a small group was in conversation around the Keurig, and Howie was in his office, feet up on his desk, talking on the phone.

Just a normal evening. And I was sitting there watching a house being blown to bits, knowing the eight people inside were being murdered.

The gunfire grew in intensity, reaching a crescendo; an explosion blew the front porch and door off the house. I didn't see any indication of return fire, although it would have had the impact of a snowflake in a blizzard. In a corner of the screen I saw two men pouring fire into the house as they moved toward it.

Another explosion. Then another. Most of the house lifted off the ground, then slammed into a cloud of smoke. When that smoke dissipated, all that was left was debris. I couldn't tell what type of munition had been fired, but it had to be more powerful than a mortar. Had to be. It could have been fired from a chopper, but it felt like ground fire. A Bradley, I guessed. I shook my head in wonder. A Bradley firing at a house on American soil. Wow.

Two more shells ripped into the pyre, taking out the remnants of a wall and the base of the chimney. The firing ebbed and gradually ended. Flames and black smoke rose from the rubble. No one was visible near the house. For several more seconds everything was quiet. Then boom! A secondary explosion sent bits of house hurtling toward the camera. It might have been caused by a stored pile of ammunition or a ruptured gas line. Whatever it was sent a towering needle of flame and thick smoke into the sky.

The video ended. I sat there, staring at the blank screen. Then I clicked off the phone camera, rested my elbow on Mighty Chair's arm, and covered my mouth with my palm. Staring, thinking, trying to absorb what I had seen. And hadn't seen. If a shot or shots had been fired from inside the house, as the government claimed, I would have seen flashes. There were no flashes. Maybe I would have seen a puff of smoke from a window. Nothing. No troops had gone near that flaming wreckage; there was no conceivable way anything inside—a computer, phone, or tablet—could have been recovered. This was a massacre. And now I had the evidence, evidence that the government was killing Americans and lying about it.

I just stared at my monitor. I took several deep, controlled breaths, trying to find my equilibrium.

The real question was what to do with this footage. It obviously put

Shaw in jeopardy. My guess was he had saved it to cover his own ass if push came to indictment. He had tried to prevent it. He was only following orders. That first segment made it simple to trace it back to him; he could admit he'd made it but deny he sent it. "I gave it to the military." No one was going to believe that. But it had to go public. When the American people saw it, they would . . . what? What would they do? Turn off Netflix? Send a tweet?

Suddenly the grainy video began running a second time. Marty was making sure I was able to make my own copy. I watched it again, this time looking more carefully to see if any shots came from the house.

It was no better the second time.

There was one thing I knew for certain: whatever I did with this tape, my life was going to change. For better, which admittedly was unlikely, or worse, I was in it. I did the smart thing: "Howie!" I screamed across the newsroom. "You'd better come over here and take a look at this."

There was considerable debate inside the *Pro* about how to proceed. Billy Garvey, our tech whiz, had put my copy on all twelve of our monitors so we could watch the murders in SurroundVision. We reran it several times. Responses varied colorfully from "Holy shit!" to "What the fuck?" but everyone grasped its significance. We were all involved. Once seen, it couldn't be unseen. An intern, Lauren Curtis-Bachman, wondered aloud if this was how Woodward and Bernstein felt when they met Mr. Throat.

The first and most important question was simple: Is it real? If we posted it and it was proved to have been edited or photoshopped, we'd have to close the doors. It also would force me to explore other career options. "It's good," I insisted, although I wouldn't reveal the source, not even to Howie. "That's your rule, Howie," I told him. "Journalism 101." Then I added the two words no reporter wants to hear: "Trust me."

Second, do we inform the administration that this tape exists and ask for a response? I was against that, fearful they would claim some national security bullshit and prevent us from posting it. Besides, Frankie B. pointed out, once people saw this, the government would have plenty of opportunities to respond. Frank Biondo, our often-beleaguered advertising genius, expressed concern that the sure-to-ensue controversy might drive away timid advertisers, then responded defensively to the derisive staff comments, "Hey, I'm not advocating anything. I'm just explaining the facts of life."

The fear that the government would prevent us from going public eventually outweighed all our other concerns. At my request—okay, insistence—we cut the first portion of the video, making it more difficult to trace it back to Shaw. Howie decided to post it exclusively on our site for four hours, then repost it to YouTube with our logo embedded. I wrote the introduction: "This video was forwarded to my attention on a social media platform. It was sent anonymously. I do not know its provenance, but I believe it was sent to me because of the interview I conducted with the mother of one of the men who died in the Stratford Road attack. (Link attached) While I have no way of confirming that this is an accurate recording of the events that took place that night, technical experts have examined the video and concluded to the best of their ability that it has not been doctored or photoshopped in any way."

Frankie slapped a title on it, "Three Minutes That Shook Our World," and posted it. Within an hour it had gone viral. Two hours later the FBI walked into the office and asked to speak with me. They handed me expensively embossed cards—he was O'Reilly, she was Pfiser. O'Reilly was older than Pfiser. His hair was cut close but in a stylish rather than a political manner; her blond hair was pinned in a bun. Her suit was nicer than his. They were both professional and polite. Howie and I sat with them in the glass-enclosed conference room while everyone else pretended not to be watching. "We're simply trying to learn as much as possible about this video," Pfiser said.

"Am I under oath?"

She wiggled her hands. "Not exactly. But lying to a federal agent during an investigation, whether or not you take an oath, can be prosecuted."

"The penalties can be pretty tough," O'Reilly added.

I told them the same thing I had written; the video had shown up and I didn't know its source. And technically that was absolutely true.

O'Reilly asked pleasantly, "You have any idea who might have sent it?"

Howie started to respond, but I put a restraining hand on his arm.

"I have a lot of sources, and even if I did know who sent it to me, I wouldn't tell you. That's the way the First Amendment works." Why couldn't I just shut up sometimes?

Agent Pfiser smiled with closed lips. "So you're not actually denying you might know who sent it to you?"

I agreed with that. "I think I can say pretty confidently that I either do or do not know the source." I glanced at Howie. "Howie?"

"Yeah," he said, nodding firmly, "that's a good way of putting it."

Pfiser dutifully wrote down my answer. Each of us in that room knew this whole interview was a charade. We were playing our roles. They knew they had to ask the questions; we all knew Howie and I weren't going to answer them. I actually was a little embarrassed for them. After all, they probably had been yanked out of bed to come in and play this game. When they were done, we shook hands with both of them and I got ready to go home. I didn't delude myself, though, I knew that wasn't the end of it. Not even close.

By the following afternoon we had been overwhelmed by the avalanche of technology. This was as close as social media could come to the excitement of stopping the presses. The video became a front-page story in both the print and digital worlds. It was viewed more than 4 million times within a day. Our site crashed; new servers were added, and it crashed again. We still had some landlines in the office, which rang incessantly. Online, a roughly equal number of congratulatory and threatening comments were posted. Several current advertisers canceled existing contracts, while about the same number of new companies requested a rate sheet. Our IT guys strengthened the firewalls to fend off the hackers we knew would be coming after us. I couldn't tell you how many requests I got from TV outlets and other media for an interview, but I turned down everything. There was nothing of importance I could add to those three minutes.

Among the people who called me was Miss Jenny Miller, calling in her capacity as congress member McDonnell's chief of staff. Chairman McDonnell's Homeland Security subcommittee was officially requesting a copy of the video and would like Roland Stone to appear voluntarily to answer a few questions. Rather than responding, in my capacity as a journalist I dutifully forwarded the request to the *Pro*'s attorney, Jon Lindsey, who politely turned it down, citing First Amendment protections.

Jenny was especially careful not to cross the line between her professional and personal worlds. That was our agreement, and we both stuck to it. It wasn't exactly bedroom conversation; she never said, "Oh, I love how you touch me there, and by the way, where did you get that video?" And in response I never said, "Oooh, go ahead and subpoena me, baby."

We did talk around it, though. At dinner several nights later, she asked me why I hadn't tried to get a comment from the administration before running with it. Her tone suggested disapproval, but I didn't want to get into it. I just said, "Sometimes we're gonna find ourselves in a tricky spot. It's just inevitable. The best thing we can do is avoid talking about it. Are you really gonna eat all those fries?"

The governing philosophy of the Wrightman administration appeared to be, What the American public doesn't know can't hurt us. In that, it was no different from any previous administration. The public remained remarkably loyal to the president until it found out about a transgression, be it a blow job or a mass murder. Then a sense of betrayal kicked in.

This video did significant damage. After the endless lies and duplicity of Trump/Pence, Americans had latched onto Wrightman's boring integrity. They liked him because they trusted him, and they trusted him because they liked him.

Real video versus fake video reignited the battles that had been fought throughout Trump/Pence. Polling showed that overall support for the administration was declining substantially, but the intensity among those people who continued to support Wrightman increased significantly as those people doubled down on their beliefs.

In an effort to position Ian Wrightman as more user-friendly, his pollster, Nolan Noyes, arranged an appearance on Jimmy Fallon's late-night show. Charisma dressed him to convey the desired image: a suede jacket without a tie, a just-one-of-the-great-outdoors-guys look. The purported reason was to discuss his daughter America's upcoming nuptials. "You're darn right, Jimmy, that I'll have tears in my eyes when I kiss my baby on the altar."

Later in this interview, when pushed by Jimmy, the president admitted sheepishly that he had never really wanted to be president. His years in the Senate were the happiest of his life. "But let me tell you, when I was asked to serve the American people by bridging the gap between Democrats and Republicans . . ."—he chuckled at the memory—"well, no man who loves this country could have turned it down."

Jenny and I were in bed. I started humming "God Bless America." She slapped my hand.

Yes, the job was even more difficult than he had imagined it would be, he admitted. Yes, there had been many sleepless nights. No, he hadn't lost his enthusiasm for improving the lives of every American. Yes, now that his team was finally in place, he would soon be announcing a series of additional measures that will make the country stronger and safer.

When the show returned after a brief commercial break, Wrightman took the opportunity to address "the growing concern" about "that strange unsourced video" that was circulating. "Frankly, Jimmy," he said, looking directly into the camera, shaking his head and tossing open his hands in bewilderment, "we don't know where it came from. But I can tell you with all my heart . . ."—he tapped his chest twice with his right hand to emphasize his sincerity—"that it doesn't reflect accurately the reality on the ground that night. And I have to tell you, it really gets my dander up to see people impugning the integrity of those brave Americans who literally put their lives on the line for all of us."

The audience burst into cheers. To me, at least, the guy had all the sincerity of a love letter from a lonely Russian beauty. It surprised me that anyone would believe any of this, but then I remembered, at least he isn't Trump. Of course, all of this was the setup for the real reason for this appearance.

Jimmy leaned closer to the president and asked him, man to man, "Where do you think the video came from? What do you think about those stories it was produced by Russians to cause dissension?"

Wrightman grimaced; darn, that was a painful thought. With obvious reluctance he finally agreed, "Truthfully, Jimmy, we haven't been able to rule that out."

The administration followed up that appearance with the strongest tried and true political strategy: Promise them money. The next afternoon the secretary of the treasury, Penelope Farber, announced "a reverse tax credit." To further stimulate the economy, a $1,000 tax credit was being granted to all Americans earning $40,000 annually or less. For people counting at home, this was the twelfth attempt to use tax credits to convince people to begin spending at pre-pandemic levels. "This stimulus will pay for itself by the increased economic activity it creates," the secretary explained. "So we're confident this new benefit will not increase the deficit one penny. Consider it an early Christmas present." It was late August.

Even that diversion didn't stop the decline in Wrightman's approval numbers. The growing acceptance that he had mistakenly authorized the raid in which innocent people had been killed and then tried to cover it up fueled the furor. Mistakes were acceptable; cover-ups were not. We saw the anger at the *Pro* every day. We became sort of a central clearinghouse for people to vent their frustration. Among the obvious changes, a security guard was stationed at the door and Howie was forced to rent an expensive X-ray system to scan every piece of mail.

Ambitious politicians from both parties seized the opportunity to come out strongly and bravely in support of the truth. Several members of the House angrily demanded that a congressional committee be formed to investigate why no congressional committee had been formed to investigate this raid.

Millions of Americans had voted for Wrightman demanding only one thing from him: That he tell the truth. That tenuous belief they had placed in his administration was suddenly shaky. The lie was like a dab of toothpaste stuck to your finger: no matter what Wrightman did, he couldn't shake it off.

I watched all this happening with the growing sense of dread that I was right about my fears. The American people don't like to be told what to do. Rather, they like to be manipulated into being told what to do. They had been told not to hold large demonstrations. Exactly nobody was surprised when pro- and antiadministration demonstrations erupted into brawls. Law enforcement did as much as possible to keep the two sides apart, but they were outnumbered. Street fights broke out in a dozen cities. Cars were set on fire. Rioters in several cities crashed through the downtown area, breaking windows and looting stores. It was difficult to watch this without thinking of the chorus from We're Your Children's 2021 "smash" hit, "Welcome to Portland," "It ain't pretty, burning a city; it ain't no fun, but it gotta be done . . ."

Video from Detroit, where it had all started, showed police officers in full riot gear spread across a street, clear plexiglass shields protecting them from rocks and glass bottles, inexorably pushing the mob backward.

I was incredulous, knowing I had at least some responsibility for this. But even as I watched this happening, I couldn't keep myself from wondering, Where the heck are people getting glass bottles from these days?

The White House continued testing different strategies to change the narrative. Initially Wrightman had halted the Trumpist efforts to elevate the alternative media into respectability, ignoring unregulated sites like QAnon, TTT3, and 4chan. These conspiracy sites allowed anyone to anonymously post stories, but during the Trump years, on occasion these bizarre claims slithered into legitimate media, like sludge seeping out of grease traps. Initially when that happened, the government editor gave them the *O* for opinion, although in fact they deserved a *B* for bullshit. But Munchmeyer's propaganda office understood the value of these sites in getting out stories that supported the administration agenda to gullible people. While they still published an abundance of the usual *Zombies Are Real and Voting Illegally in Wisconsin* and *Proof Found That Hillary Is an Extraterrestrial*, more stories supporting administration initiatives began appearing: for example, *Administration Adding Safeguards as China's 100-Year Plan to Conquer America Enters Final Decade*. Several stories about the Detroit raid appeared on these sites; what was chilling is that the editor gave them an *N*, news, which made them more believable.

The administration also continued its efforts to distract and distort. The Defense Department announced that three more people involved in planning the 7/11 attacks had been killed in a missile attack outside Mogadishu. The raid was a joint exercise of American and Somalian Special Operators, acting on information supplied by unnamed allies.

"For those people keeping score at home," Chris Wallace reported, "that brings the number of terrorist leaders killed in the last six weeks to seventeen, although at least two of them purportedly have been killed multiple times."

I did note that the administration had completely given up trying to tie any retribution to information taken from the house on Stratford Road. That effort had ended.

I was watching Wallace losing the fight to prevent himself from smirking as he read this report when Jenny called. In a voice infused with an odd mix of resignation and anxiety, she said, "Two guys from Homeland Security just left my office. They were asking all about you."

Homeland Security? That was interesting. "Not FBI?"

"That's what they said. They were . . ." She paused and obviously read from a note or card: "Jackson and Devine."

Jackson and Devine? "They sound like they should be on late-night TV advertising for people who slipped on fruit in a supermarket."

"This isn't funny, Rollie." I was Rollie when she wanted to make a point. "They asked me a lot of questions about our relationship."

"What'd you tell them?"

She sighed. "Basically, that you're a rotten dancer." She knew it was a cute line, but there were no smiles in her tone. This visit had shaken her up. "I mean, what could I tell them? I don't even know how to describe it."

"So the government of the United States knows we're dating," I said, trying to lighten the conversation. "I hope they don't tell Europe."

She completely ignored the fact that I'd ignored her comment. "It was more than that. They're investigating you. They didn't even ask about the video. They asked me if you gambled or drank, if you owed anybody money. They even asked me if I thought you were mad at the government because, you know . . ."—she hesitated here, not certain how I would react—". . . because of what happened to you."

I literally could feel my anger rising, my face flushed. I pressed down hard on my emotions. My index finger, I noticed, was thumping away. Well, that was an interesting outlet for them.

"Rollie?"

"I'm here. It's okay."

She misread my silence. "I had to talk to them. It wouldn't be appropriate for me not to cooperate with Homeland Security in an invest—"

"It's okay," I interrupted. "It doesn't matter. Here's what's happening, I think." I was as curious as Jenny was to hear what came out of my mouth, so I would know what my subconscious thought about this. "They know there's no way I would give up my source, so they're trying to intimidate me. Or us. They know how I feel about you, so questioning you is their way of warning me."

"They do? Really? Sometimes I'm not even sure how you feel about me. Maybe I should be the one asking questions."

"Jenny," I said, lowering my voice to demonstrate that I was serious, "there is no one in this world I would rather roll with than you." Sometimes being corny will suffice.

It was her failure to come back with some sort of snappy retort that made me uneasy. Instead she said she had to go back to work and would call later. After we hung up, I sat there trying to decide what was more difficult: understanding this woman or saving American democracy.

I focused on what I could handle. What the hell was Homeland Security's objective? Maybe I was right, maybe they were firing a warning shot. Well, I definitely got that message, fuck you very much.

The Washington curfew was still in force; soldiers patrolled the mostly empty streets. Truck-mounted spotlights cast long angular shadows across the avenues and up the sides of buildings. I was stopped twice while walking to the garage to get Van. I produced identification without giving them the usual hard time. I just didn't have the energy.

By the time I got home, I'd managed to compartmentalize my thoughts. I had to reassure Jenny. A comfortable night at home would help. We'd order in, I'd let her choose the restaurant. Even Mexican if she wanted. *Okay,* I thought, *it's time to have that conversation, time to take the next step.*

Then I opened my front door.

9

Whoever they were, they were efficient. There was nothing obvious that caught my attention. They hadn't tossed underwear on the floor or washed the dirty dishes in the sink, but someone had broken into my apartment and conducted a pretty careful search. People like me, active people with a disability, share the everyday world with other people, but we live entirely different lives. For convenience, I'd made some adjustments in the apartment, but unless you are living with restrictions, you wouldn't notice them. The glass that I always left near the edge of the kitchen counter so I could reach it easily had been moved back several inches. The bottom drawer of my desk, which I leave a tiny bit open because it tends to catch and it's hard to get leverage to pull it out, had been closed. The chair next to my desk had been moved, probably because whoever had gone through my computer needed it to sit on, but when they put it back they failed to leave sufficient space between the side of the desk and the wall for Mighty Chair to slide past. The lids on my pain pill bottles, which I always leave partially opened, had been tightened. The search had been thorough, and unlike those agents who had visited Jenny, these people did not want me to know they had been there.

Jenny was the only other person who had a key, which she used when she got home before me, but she would have told me if she had stopped by. And she wouldn't have tightened pill bottle lids.

I knew they were looking for anything that would lead them to the source of the video. In an odd way this was exciting. I'd never thought I would be involved in something so vital to national security that the government would break into my apartment. Not only was there no link to the video there, there was nothing that could compromise me or embarrass me. As boring as it makes me appear, I literally had nothing to hide—I mean, unless someone was really desperate to know what I'd bought my mother for her sixty-fifth birthday. The most interesting things on my desktop were what I laughingly referred to as "my business records" and my tax returns, courtesy of H&R Block.

I clicked through my computer, although I had no idea what I was looking for. It just seemed like a smart thing to do. It's what every TV detective would have done. I assumed they copied my address book and maybe my emails. I smiled at that thought: Some poor schmuck was going to have to waste a day looking through several thousand emails I hadn't gotten around to erasing. I suspected they had planted a listening device somewhere, but I didn't bother looking for it. Unless it actually looked like a bug, I wouldn't be able to spot it.

"Cher, call Howie," I said.

My apartment had been "tossed," I told him. I smiled as I said it. "They 'tossed' it, Howie!" I loved speaking noir. "You believe that? Do they really think I'm stupid enough to leave evidence like that on my computer?"

Silence.

"Oh, come on, Howie. That's not funny." If there were listeners on the line, as I had to assume, I hoped they got a laugh out of it.

Howie had a guy who had some kind of whoop-de-do device that detected electronic bugs. He'd get him over to my apartment first thing. "I never thought I'd say this in real life," he told me, "but be careful. There're a lot of crazies out there, and you've made some enemies."

"That's okay," I responded, "I never thought I'd get to tell someone my apartment had been tossed."

Jenny was in an Uber on her way over when I reached her. "Guess what," I said, "they tossed my apartment."

"They what? Who did what?"

Jeez, some women can take all the fun out of a home invasion. Rather than meeting at the apartment, we met at Uri's Portable Chef, a restaurant and delivery service known for its deliciously healthy home-style cooking. (And no, this is not a paid testimonial, although if Uri wants to send some of his Filipino chicken adobo up here no one would turn it down. Wink, wink.) She was carving our initials into the construction timber tabletop with a knife provided for that purpose when I got there. She greeted me by blowing wood chips onto my lap. "Very mature," I said.

Over the organic chicken I told her about my visitors. Yes, I was sure. No, I wasn't going to call the police. "What am I going to tell them? Somebody moved my cheese?" And finally, it probably wasn't a great idea for her to stay there with me that night. "Bedbugs," I said, admiring my own cleverness. If the place had been wired, I didn't want her on tape.

I had Van, so I dropped her off. When I got settled, I called to make sure she was okay. Actually, to make sure *we* were okay. As we started to hang up, I blurted, "Hey, Jen . . ."

"What?" I was silent. "What?" she repeated with a hint of irritation.

"I mean, you were kidding, right? You know how I feel about you, don't you?"

She wasn't going to make it easy for me. "Honestly, sometimes I'm not so sure."

I took a deep breath and almost went for it: "I really care a lot about you. I mean, a whole lot."

That probably wasn't what she was hoping to hear, but it was a step. "Me too," she responded.

When I went to bed that night, I left a lamp on in the living room. I also took the shade off my bedside lamp; if someone came into the bedroom, I could turn it on and the bare bulb would briefly blind them. And then I took my pistol from its secure place, checked to make sure it was loaded, the safety was on, and a bullet was chambered. I slipped it under my pillow.

I lay in bed with my eyes closed, but there was no way I was going to sleep. It wasn't fear—I still could handle whatever came my way. But man, it had been a long time since I'd been so lonely. Why couldn't I tell her that I loved her? I wondered. What the fuck was wrong with me?

I thought about one of my first stories. I had interviewed an Indian shaman who was making a nice living predicting the future at parties. "Parlor games," he called them. Everyone goes home optimistic about their future. But he told me a story I've never forgotten. He was lying in bed with his wife; the lights were on, but his eyes were closed. In that brightness behind his eyes he saw blackbirds flying around her. But when he opened his eyes, the birds were gone. He knew then that she was an evil woman. And as he later discovered, after she'd emptied their joint accounts, she was. That's when he understood he could see reality with his mind far more clearly than with his eyes.

However, he complained, he had once traveled too deeply into his mind, all the way to the end of his subconscious, to the dressing rooms in which his dreams were putting on their makeup and costumes. In his opinion, that journey was too dangerous for the unenlightened to make.

He also had given me a gift, a mantra. I'm not going to tell you what it was, but to my surprise it often proved valuable. When my mind was churning with unsettling thoughts, the demons still lived there, I used it to calm down. It often helped me relax into sleep. Not this night, though. There was nothing calming about what I saw that night. I was confronted with the true objective of the Wrightman government. The future in my mind was far more ominous. I was seeing a repressive government that clamped down on individual rights—with the tacit approval of the distracted majority. It wasn't the historic fascism that we had fought and defeated. It was the irrational buffoonery of the Trumpsters. In this form of fascism, people weren't being lined up against walls and shot; rather, they were being restricted in what they could say or write or post. Or by extension, think. Anyone who broke those rules was silenced, shunned, or in the extreme, "separated."

And here was the most chilling part: Few people objected to it. Instead, they appeared to embrace it. They continued to proudly profess a strong belief in democracy, but a democracy in which the rights of the individual had to be sacrificed for the good of the many. This wasn't a nightmare. It didn't spark my fears. I didn't start sweating. I'd left most of those fears behind years earlier. This just seemed so patently obvious that I was astonished my eyes hadn't seen it.

Whoever had broken into my apartment did not return that night or the nights that followed. I eventually put my gun back in its place. The overwhelming police—and militia—presence eventually defused the protests. Several governors declared state emergencies and temporarily suspended habeas corpus, arresting and holding hundreds of people without charging them or granting them their right to representation. In defending this action, those state's attorneys cited Article One, section 9, clause 2 of the Constitution: "The Privilege of the Writ of Habeas Corpus shall not be suspended, unless when in Cases of Rebellion or Invasion the public Safety may require it." The attorneys claimed that out-of-control antigovernment demonstrations qualified as acts of rebellion and constituted a direct threat to the public safety.

Numerous lawsuits were filed, but before they could be adjudicated, all the prisoners were released without any charges being filed, making those lawsuits moot. I had to admit, it was a clever strategy. Most of the same lawyers then filed civil lawsuits claiming their clients' constitutional rights had been violated, demanding multimillion-dollar damages. Those cases immediately got bogged down on the badly overwhelmed calendars of local courts.

More troubling, an embargo was declared prohibiting any print or electronic platform from publishing any information about scheduled demonstrations. When *The New York Times* challenged that directive, its site was suspended for a day, and its distributors, both brick-and-mortar and online, were threatened with expensive legal action that might shut them down if they circulated the paper.

This time no demonstrations were held to protest the crackdown on demonstrations.

Not surprisingly, Wrightman was given credit for doing exactly what he had promised during his campaign: he had restored order. Once again, his approval ratings stabilized, then began rising. A submissive Congress began granting every White House request without holding public hearings or full disclosure. Essentially, they handed him a blank check.

At the *Pro* we worked through the turmoil with a growing sense of frustration. The administration's relentless effort to change the subject had finally taken hold. The nation had moved on. Stories about the terrorists no longer dominated the front page, replaced by events like a sex scandal on the PGA tour, which allowed a delirious media to use words like *balls* and *strokes* in suggestive headlines. The contest to design the most attractive memorial for each terrorist site had practically become a national obsession. At Pearl Harbor, there was strong support for building a new bridge-like visitor center over the now-sacred wreckage of the old bridge-like visitor center. In Louisiana a recirculating river two feet wide by one foot deep along which lighted candles would float following the path of the flood past the ruins of Morgan City had been approved by the state legislature. In New York, a tastefully subdued pattern of lights that would change throughout the entire length of the Lincoln Tunnel was the favorite.

International tensions also had wound way down. Most nations were so pleased at the restored predictability in relationships and trade that they avoided provocations.

This passive acquiescence gnawed at my soul. It became a sore spot between Jenny and me. One night, after we'd finished watching the final episode of the *The Crown*'s eighth season (Queen Elizabeth II had survived!), I asked, "When did we become this nation of spectators?"

"Oh, it's not that bad," she said dismissively. "Please pass the remote."

In my best Joe Pesci, "You think I'm funny?"

Eyes closed, face scrunched up, she gave me that "do we have to go through this again?" look. "What do you expect people to do? Go fight the terrorists themselves?"

"Isn't that what we have those 300 million guns for? All that militia stuff?" I hadn't told anyone about my night visit to the shaman's world. But I sure hadn't forgotten it, either. "Don't you get it, Jen? We're seeing exactly what the government wants us all to see: peace, security, and great television. But that's not what's really going on. That's not the real story."

"You know what, Rollie, sometimes you just need to take one deep breath and relax. Really, Wheels, it's okay to enjoy *Schitt's Creek*." She leaned over and kissed me, a really sweet patronizing kiss. "Life goes on, you know. As painful as it is sometimes, life goes on."

Well, except for the victims, I thought. For the victims, this is a bitch. Jenny was right, though. I have to admit that most often Jenny was right, the world had moved on. By late September, Detroit had become last summer's news. Or "olds," as Howie referred to it. "If it isn't new, it's no longer news." Within a period of a few weeks, a Belgian submarine had disappeared in the Adriatic and a joint naval force that we had formed with the Chinese had located the damaged vessel and made a daring rescue of its crew. A North Korean defector claimed the food crisis inside that country had become so bad that farmers in rural areas had resorted to cannibalism, while Kim Jong Un had suddenly begun promoting tourism. Putin was hinting that he planned to annex Ukraine unless American sanctions were removed while still bemoaning the loss of his "good friend President Trump."

I'd made changes to deal with this new reality. I installed surveillance cameras in my apartment and linked them to Mighty Chair. I set up a bright red dye-pack trap that would paint any intruder with indelible ink. And at night I felt myself holding on to Jenny just a little more tightly.

I'd moved on, although there remained an unfinished pang in my heart. It appeared no one was going to pay for what happened in Detroit. I wrote several good stories and came within one coffee cup of topping the tower record. 7/11 was taking its place as another sad day on America's calendar to memorialize each year. My involvement in it might have ended there for me, and I might have let it go and gone on to a long and semi-distinguished career in journalism, at the end of which I would write a fine and unpublished memoir. That might have happened. But then my phone rang.

It was a dreary December day. There was light snow in the forecast. The early afternoon light was the pale yellow of faded newsprint. The landline on my desk rang only occasionally, most often with an announcement that my excellent credit score had earned me the right to go deeper into debt. So when it did ring, I expected to hear a recorded woman's voice gleefully informing me that there was no problem with my credit. Instead a man asked in a mildly accented voice, "Is this Stone?"

There was a tremble in that voice. Whoever it was, he was hesitant about making this call. "It is."

"I need help, man." It came in a rush. "Please, you help me."

The voice of a stranger reaching out for help was a siren song no journalist could resist. Of course, it was also the opening line of an infinite number of bad detective novels. In various forms I'd heard the same plea several times before; they had ended up being about as exciting as the early bird special at IHOP. "Okay, if I can," I said. "But I can't guarantee this call isn't being tapped, so be careful what you say."

"They're after me," he said urgently. "You need to help me."

And that is the second greatest line a journalist might hear. "Who's after you?"

"Everybody." There was an urgency in his voice. "They all looking for me."

"Everybody is a lot of people." He was beginning to sound like another one of the crazies.

Then he explained, "They killed my friends. You know, in that house. In Detroit, that house there."

I pressed the mute button, then ordered, "Cher, record." I took a deep breath and pressed the mute button a second time. "Go slow," I said. My heart was playing a rumba. I knew who this guy was; two men had driven from Detroit to New York to complete a drug deal. The remains of one of them had been scraped up in the tunnel. It had been assumed that the second man had died in the tunnel with him; the fact that his remains hadn't been identified wasn't surprising. Not after the explosions and fires.

"Look, you got to help me, man. I'm not no terrorist. It was just drugs that we was doing. That's all. That terrorist shit, that's fucked up."

I had learned how to handle panic on some very distant streets. Without having to think about it, I switched into calm mode. "How can I help you?"

In a tone somewhere between desperation and frustration, the man pleaded, "I don't know. You the reporter. Get me out of this shit."

Elijah Amram, I remembered, that was the name. "Does anyone know where you are? Are you sure people are looking for you?"

"Fuck yeah, mon. They been crawling over my peeps. They all scared. Nobody wants a help me."

"I know who you are," I said, with a coolness that even surprised me. "Do you know exactly who is searching for you?"

"I tole you man, everybody. They all fucking looking for me. I gots to keep moving."

It wasn't much of an answer. "Okay. All right. Listen to me. I want to help you, but I need to know more. Do you know where I am?"

"Shit, yeah, you in Washington."

"Can you get here?"

He laughed at that question, the lilting laugh of an immigrant. "I already here, mon."

"Okay, here's what I want you to do." In most situations the best protection for someone with knowledge of a dangerous secret is to go as public as possible. Then it is no longer a secret. This is my advice to you: If you are privy to a potentially blockbusting secret, call a reporter immediately. In fact, call me. I still can be reached. I thought about asking Amram to come to my office, but instead I suggested we meet close by. We were still receiving the occasional threat and I didn't want to invite someone I didn't know into the office. After I had confirmed he was legit, I could bring him inside.

I picked that location because it was easily accessible and it fulfilled my journalistic fantasy: In homage to Woodstein and Deep Throat, we would meet in a parking garage. There was a public garage a block away from the *Pro*; I parked Van there when I drove to work. I told Amram to meet me on the fourth level in an hour. Among the many lessons the military had drilled into me was that before meeting someone you didn't know, stake out the territory.

I turned down Howie's offer to send someone with me. We agreed if this was legit, I would bring him back with me and we would try to talk him into surrendering to law enforcement. Howie said he would speak to Lindsey the lawyer to protect the *Pro* from any potential claims of harboring or cooperating with a fugitive—although we couldn't figure out how a supposedly dead man who had not been indicted could be considered a fugitive.

The promised snow was just beginning to fall as I walked over to the garage. I pulled up the collar of my trench coat; not as homage, I was just cold! The vibrancy that once activated Washington's afternoon streets was gone. Instead it felt like the whole country had been lulled into the same kind of complaisant stupor as a hive of yellow jackets in the hard days of winter.

The garage had the architectural elegance of every municipal parking garage in every city in every state. Its cement ramp spiraled up six stories. The outer walls on each level were slightly more than four feet high. There was a roadway about two cars in width between parked cars. A folding billboard out front advertised the early bird special: $25 for all day if entering before six A.M. I usually got there about an hour early on my way to the gym. Van was parked where I'd left it, in a handicapped spot on the first level. I took the elevator to the fourth floor, then rolled slowly and carefully down the wide ramp, braking often until I reached the third floor. The light mist snaking in over the half walls made the visibility uneven. Certain areas were illuminated by caged industrial lighting, while others lay in deep shadows. I found a spot in the shadow of a inside retaining wall and waited there. I was out of the flow of traffic but still able to look over the wall to spot anyone driving up the ramp.

The garage was quiet. It was used mostly by people who worked in the area, people like me who parked there in the morning and departed at the end of the day. The shops in the area served mostly the locals— office workers; employees of a coffee shop, a florist, a CVS—so there was limited in-and-out activity. A couple of cars wound up the ramp to the upper floors and drifted slowly past me. Occasionally I heard the mechanical banging of the elevator rising or descending. An intermittent gust tickled me with a touch of wetness.

I waited, my emotions coiled, ready to spring. Okay, that is so completely not true. What I actually did was sit there trying to deal with my boredom. You rarely see that part of police work or investigative journalism in movies or on TV. That's because boredom is, well, boring.

I'd learned different tricks to keep my mind occupied while waiting. At times the toughest challenge is staying awake. I read an old James Lee Burke book I had on my phone; I responded to emails, checked the news, and sent a funny meme to Jenny.

Several minutes after the scheduled meeting time I heard someone walking up the ramp. He came around the corner into the light. He was a thin, dark man, his skin the color of old asphalt. He was wearing an open green military coat and khaki pants that sagged below his waist. A black nylon shirt hugged his sinewy upper body. He had on white high-top sneakers with no socks. I wondered if that was a drug-world fashion statement. His hair was close-cropped, and he had a short beard. He paused and looked around. "Stone?"

I stayed in the shadows. "Yeah." He turned toward my voice and saw me. "Who are you?"

"Amram. I'm Amram."

I kept my hand on Mighty Chair's control module. I had several options available if needed. I moved a few feet closer. "What do you need from me?"

He waved his empty hands. "I need you to help me." It was as much a demand as a plea.

"Tell me who's after you."

His tongue ran across his lips. He moved closer, walking in the center of the ramp. Cars were parked diagonally on either side of him. He was about twenty feet away. "The drug guys. They want their money. The government people too. The FBI come to my sister's house. They tell her they lookin' for me."

I heard a car winding slowly up the ramp. "Were you living there?"

"That was my house," Amram said loudly and defiantly, angrily pointing his index finger toward me. "My house. But we weren't no terrorists in there. No fucking way. Those are crazy fuckers, those terrorists. I heard them when they call me a terrorist, and I think, *What the fuck, man?* you know. I'm Muslim, right?" He sneered at the insult. "So I gotta be a terrorist. I'm telling you the truth, Stone, we had the drugs. We come to New York . . ."

The squeal of tires twisting on damp cement caught our attention.

We both turned. A black SUV careened around the corner, its engine roaring. Amram turned. The SUV accelerated. "Run!" I screamed. By the time he understood what was happening, it was too late. The SUV plowed into him, flinging him into the air. With a horrific thud, his body slammed into the rear of a parked white van. The back of his head smashed against its rear window, his blood spattering across the rear gate. His body dropped to the cement floor. He lay there faceup, eyes open, mouth open. Rivulets of blood winding down the gate dripped onto his face like melting red icicles.

The SUV raced past me, the parked cars preventing the killer from angling into me. The SUV's windows were deeply tinted, so I couldn't see the driver. It skidded to a stop at the end of the fourth-floor ramp, its rear end rising like a bucking horse. Smoke churned from the spinning wheels. I smelled the burning rubber. The driver jammed it in reverse, slammed it into the rear wall, bouncing off it as he turned.

I ran. I punched the control lever. Mighty Chair's wheels spun briefly before gaining traction. Then I burst forward. I started racing down the curving ramp. As I reached the first corner, I hunched my shoulders and shifted my weight, leaning into the turn as if I were cutting through packed snow on the slopes. I could hear the SUV turning. There was no room for it to turn without shifting back and forth, so the driver was making his own room, banging and smashing cars out of his way, pushing them into the retaining walls.

Mighty Chair wasn't aerodynamic, but it did hold a line and cornered well, for a wheelchair. Y's imagination was paying off. When he'd built it, he'd been playing mad inventor, envisioning video-game scenarios, James Bond escapes, neither of us believing any of that would become necessary. Or that one winter afternoon it might save my life. I had just reached the third level when I heard the SUV crashing down behind me. Its wheels shrieked as the driver drifted into the corners, bouncing off walls like a pinball bouncing off bumpers, but it kept coming.

Incredibly, I heard Cher's stern voice warning me, "Rollie, Mighty Chair wants me to tell you this speed is not safe."

Sorry, Cher. Y had added an auxiliary motor to Mighty Chair, but I wasn't going to outrun an SUV. I twisted to see where he was, and as I did, I had the odd thought that Y should add a rearview camera. There were several nifty tools already built into the chair that might have helped, like spewing silicone, but I had dismissed that as another one of Y's Bond jokes and hadn't bothered to memorize the program code. I could slow down and ask Cher to find it, but the one thing I could not afford to do was slow down.

I whirled around the next bend, trying to hug the inside wall. I'd run several wheelchair races, so I had some idea how to maximize and control my speed. But racing chairs were designed for speed. Mighty Chair was the real thing. Gravitational forces buffeted me from side to side and I was struggling to stay in the seat. I slipped my left arm under the armrest and curled my fingers over the front of it, holding tight.

The SUV was gaining; I heard metal crunching and glass shattering as it bounced off parked cars and slammed into a wall, then a long shriek as a metal piece sliced into the cement. It must have dropped the muffler because suddenly the engine got a lot louder. And a lot closer. A beast was hunting me.

When you're running for your life, you don't think, you react. Everything I did was pure instinct. I'd never ridden a wheelchair downhill at maximum speed—in fact I had never heard of anybody who had—but turn by turn I was figuring out how to survive. I was careening from side to side, shifting my weight from side to side to maintain my balance as if I were slaloming downhill. Cher was making all types of warning sounds. This was Chair to the max. I guessed I had two turns, about 250 feet, and a tollgate to get through before the SUV hit me. In that instant my mind flashed back to the last time I'd been sprinting to save my life. I could see that open door in front of me. I could see kids racing in front of me. I could see that bright sunlight framed in that doorway. I never got there. The house had collapsed around me. Somehow, though, I'd gotten a second chance. Make it or die.

The SUV was getting close. I could hear it, smell it. The crunching, scraping, ripping sounds echoing through the garage got louder. I went for speed, pushing the lever all the way forward, turning into the last straightaway with every bit of speed Chair could generate.

The scene in front of me was not promising: The ramp split into entrance and exit lanes separated by the ticket kiosk. Black-and-white-striped gates blocked both lanes. The gates were about four feet high, I estimated, not nearly high enough for the back of Chair to slip under. I leaned way to my left, hoping there was sufficient room between the end of the gate and the wall for me to squeeze past.

Just as I did, a dark blue SUV entering the garage stopped at the ticket kiosk and a woman reached out to take a ticket.

I leaned all the way to my right. Several years earlier, when I was learning how to navigate the world in a wheelchair, I had to fill out an insurance form. It required all the basic information. Two questions stumped me: height and weight. Months earlier, that had been an easy question, six-two, 215 pounds. But on this form I responded five-five, 550 pounds. It was at that moment I accepted how completely my world had changed.

Five-five goes into four feet only with great damage. I had one chance, I figured. I pulled up on the seatback control and Chair's back started dropping. I grasped both arms and pushed back on it as hard as I could, willing it to move faster. It was going to be tight; if I hit the gate with my body or my head, I was a dead man rolling. Even if the gate just clipped the top of the chair, it would flip backward and I was still a dead man.

Every inch, every tenth of an inch, would make the difference between life and death. The SUV swung around the final turn. In that instant the driver must have realized he had run out of ramp. He slammed down hard on his brakes, which caused the rear end to spin slowly around until the front and rear wheels were parallel and the side of the SUV had become a metal wall sliding toward the kiosks—and still gaining on me.

Bad for me. I faced even worse problems than he did. My brakes might be able to stop Chair—but not me. The science about that was pretty simple: A body in really fast motion tends to fly through the air in really fast motion when the Chair in which he is riding stops suddenly.

The woman in the SUV got her ticket and straightened up in her seat, then looked straight at me as the gate went up to let her enter. While it sounds like something you'd read in a book, our eyes met. She saw me sliding directly toward her and, I'm guessing, she also saw the black wall of sheet metal a few feet behind me. Rather than thinking, she reacted. How she did it, I swear to God I will never understand, but somehow she slammed that SUV into reverse and gunned it. The SUV rocketed back, slamming into the side of a cement mixer stopped in a long line at a traffic signal.

The gate began closing. I went for it, twisting my body as far to the left as possible. Chair's right wheel lifted off the ground. It moved an inch. Making it required the kind of perfect timing, and magic, that it took to race through a moving revolving door without touching it. I slipped under the gate. I was barely in control, my seatback still partially reclined, heading directly for the spinning cement mixer.

Admittedly, the fact that I'm telling this story does eliminate the suspense. Once again, I got lucky.

The whine of jagged metal scraping along concrete had alerted pedestrians. They were running for safety even before I came hurtling out of the garage into the street. I heard screams and saw them scrambling as I tried desperately to regain some balance. Chair's right wheel hit something and bounced into the air like a racing car hitting a speed bump.

I didn't know what the SUV was doing. Later I learned that it had slowed when its tires went flat, and finally skidded sideways into the kiosk.

I held on. There was nothing else I could do. My fingers dug into Chair's arms. I had slowed down, but not enough. I saw the cement mixer directly in front of me. I closed my eyes.

Suddenly, something slammed into my side, like a tackle hitting a running back. Mighty Chair was jolted, then whipped sideways. Stuff was falling all over me. Chair slowed, bounced, tilted, then regained its wheels, finally spinning to a stop. My heart was blasting. I forced out a huge puff of air. I was alive. Alive. It was a surprise to me too.

I had no idea what had happened. "Y'okay, Rollie?" I heard a man asking with concern. "You 'live in there?" I heard sirens, a lot of them, loud and insistent. I opened my eyes. Everything was black.

I reached up toward my eyes. I pulled a flannel shirt off my face. I was covered with clothing. I picked off some of it, while other pieces fell off. People were standing around me, looking down at me with curiosity. I heard a distant voice ask, "What happened to him?"

I kept looking around, trying to figure that out. The blue SUV and the cement mixer were blocking the street. They were entangled. In the garage entrance the SUV was wrapped around the kiosk, smoke pouring from its undercarriage. The broken kiosk was dutifully spewing tickets. Firemen were rushing toward the wreckage, pushing spectators out of the way. Nothing was making sense to me. People were shouting, trying to shake me back into the moment with questions; their voices were jumbled. I had no answers.

Then I saw a supermarket shopping cart, a small one, lying on its side. A lot of clothing had fallen out of it and scattered on the street.

Reality slowly came into focus.

I figured it out. As I came flying out of the garage, an instant before I'd kissed that mixer, I'd been hit by something, or I hit something and got pushed to the side. Amazing. It was one of the people leaning over me, one of my street guys, one of my buck-in-a-cup people. Another veteran. I couldn't remember his name. He'd been wounded too, but his wounds were storm clouds in his mind.

Son of . . . Jesus, this was the man who'd saved my life. When I burst out of the garage, everybody else was running away, but he came running to help. He either pushed his cart into me or maybe abandoned it, but Chair had hit it. It had gotten caught up in the wheel enough to turn Chair a few inches and slow it down. Then somebody had grabbed hold to bring it to a stop. Maybe this guy. It didn't matter.

I looked up at him, shook some confusion out of my head, took a deep and delicious breath, and said, "Yeah, I'm okay."

And then the tears came.

10

I was running. I was maintaining a steady pace. I was in the desert; there was nothing around me but sand. The ground was hard, though, and I had no difficulty running. I could feel each breath as it was pushed out of my lungs, then traveled down my body, splitting into two at my waist then coursing through both legs until it escaped from the bottom of my feet. Then I took another breath and the process started again. I had found my rhythm and knew that I would run forever.

It was the old dream.

I knew it was a dream, even when I was in the middle of it. I didn't care. I considered it a gift from my subconscious. For those seconds or minutes, I had no idea how long it actually lasted, it was real and that was all that mattered. I was running. I could feel my legs working hard. I could feel the cooling breeze against my skin and I ran until sweat dappled my body.

When I woke up, I was sweating.

I spent five days in the hospital. Incredibly, I'd suffered no serious injuries. I was battered and bruised and scraped, but other than ten stitches, some serious painkillers, and substantial loving care from Miss Jennifer Miller, I required only basic medical care. The hardest part were the memories it dredged up. I thought I had buried them. It was a different hospital, in a different place, with different doctors and nurses, but the sounds and the smells were the same. Emotions that I had once fought hard to contain, that I had finally managed to put away a long time ago suddenly reappeared in my mind, bringing with them the familiar fears, the night sweats, the reality of what I had lost.

Mighty Chair had been banged up too, but Y went to work repairing and replacing parts. Originally Chair had been designed to enable me to overcome my new limitations; I called it Viagra for my legs. Most of the work had been done by my nephew, Noah Glenn, a former mechanical engineering student who'd dropped out of Cooper Union to invent in my sister's garage. I dubbed him Y in deference to James Bond's Q, as in, "Why aren't you in school?" But with parts readily available off the shelf, he'd transformered an upscale wheelchair into a mobile environment. He was constantly experimenting and adding features, until only the two of us knew all Mighty Chair's capabilities. Given this opportunity, he upgraded its technology, adding among other enhancements a rearview camera. Chair was ready to roll when I was ready to leave the hospital. Y did wrap an elastic bandage around one arm, though, just as a reminder.

I learned that Jenny had come to the hospital three times during the day and a half I was sedated, but when the drugs finally wore off and I opened my eyes, it was Frankie B. sitting next to my bed. He put down the newspaper he was reading. "Welcome back," he boomed. "Have a nice trip?"

"Nice place to visit," I managed to get out. The words coming out of my mouth didn't sound too much like the words I was forming in my mind.

Frankie filled in the details: The man murdered in the garage had been identified as Elijah Amram. His cause of death was officially blunt trauma, unofficially the rear gate of a Chevy Tahoe. Amram had been linked to the Detroit house, but law enforcement was describing him as a "facilitator" rather than a participant in the Lincoln Tunnel attack. They were hinting that evidence existed connecting him to Terror Inc., as Homeland Security was now referring to the murky coalition of terrorist organizations, but for "security reasons" that would affect "ongoing investigations," they could not release it.

It hurt when I smiled. How could I have injured my cheekbones? "Total bullshit," I said.

Frankie B. threw up his hands defensively. "Hey, don't blame me. I only know what I write in the papers." The driver of the van was a man named José Peña Moncada, a Mexican national. After surviving the crash, Moncada had limped back up to the sixth level, leaving a trail of blood. The door to the roof had been locked, trapping him there. Rather than surrendering, he had elected to shoot it out with D.C. cops, which, as Frankie B. colorfully pointed out, proved to be a poor decision. "He ended up with more holes in him than the plot of *Godfather 3.*" His motive hadn't been determined . . .

"Drugs," I said. "That's what he told me. The cartel was looking for him."

Frankie B. shrugged. "Says you." His motive hadn't been determined, he repeated, then continued, nor was it known how Moncada had tracked Amram to that garage. "That's why they want to talk to you," he said casually. "Howie said for me to tell you not to talk to anybody without a lawyer sitting on your lap."

That made sense. I asked him to hand me my tablet. I wanted to start making notes as soon as the symphony playing in my head quieted down.

He didn't move. "That's probably not the best idea," he said. "Don't put anything down on paper. And don't say anything to anybody, even Jenny." He hesitated there and avoided my eyes.

"What?" It was a passive question, as in, *What's the problem?*

"It's not all good news," he joked. "They've been asking us a lot of questions about you too. They want to know what you were doing meeting a terrorist."

"What?" An active question, as in, *Are you fucking kidding me?* "I told you, he wasn't . . ."

Frankie held up his hands as a barrier. "Hey! Hey! I'm one of the good guys, remember. I'm just telling you, that's the way they're selling it." He scribbled a headline in the air: "Most Wanted Terrorist Killed Meeting Secretly with Sympathetic Journalist."

I settled back into a clump of soft pillows, disbelieving. "No way they're getting away with that. No fucking way." I was a suspect? I didn't know what I was suspected of being. An accomplice? But I definitely was a suspect. "Is there a cop outside the door? They going to arrest me?"

He shook his head. "No cops. Well, there's a few of them out in the parking lot."

A half hour ago I had been in a wonderful dream. Now I was awake in a nightmare. That's not the way life is supposed to be. "What's going on at the shop? How are we covering all this?"

Frankie B. refused to look at me. "There're two guys been waiting to talk to you. They've been coming around the office too." He picked up the juice box from my tray, punched the straw into it, and handed it to me. "Here. Look, Rol, do yourself a favor, don't even think out loud. Remember, they're from the government of the United States. They are *not* your friends."

My room filled up pretty quickly with people who *were* my friends when word got out I was my usual semi-charming self. Jenny was crying. Howie and several people from the *Pro* showed up. Hack Wilson and Wayne Chang from Light Brigade came in, Hack complaining that I really wasn't pulling my own weights. It got so noisy in there that when my mother called, she asked if I was having a party.

The first interview took place that night. Rather than Lindsey the Lawyer, Howie had brought in an experienced criminal attorney, Barton Reich. Reich was tall, thin, and proudly bald. He wore humorless thin-wire glasses. Before allowing the agents into my hospital room, Reich preached the defense lawyer's mantra: *You are not under arrest. You don't have to answer any questions. If you decide to answer, respond as succinctly as possible. Do not volunteer any information. When I interrupt, be quiet.*

I smiled, painfully, at this, asking, "Am I really a suspect?"

Reich did not smile. In fact, it looked like he hadn't smiled within this decade. "At this point they are referring to you as a person of interest. What that means in reality is that they are interested in fucking you over. Mr. Stone, please listen to my suggestions. If you provide the rope for these people, I promise you, they will hang you with it."

Three men showed up at seven o'clock: two agents from Homeland Security and a D.C. detective. I know I've told you that physical descriptions rarely provide an accurate impression of what people look like, but after everything that happened, I think I owe it to these characters to at least make the effort. Generally, these two agents looked like men who had missed the last cut for the FBI. They wore slightly different shades of gray suits, matching white shirts, and monochromatic ties. Both of them were thin. Agent Richard Corbin, who was substantially shorter than his partner, looked amazingly like my vision of a walking inferiority complex. Everything about him was taut, as if he were holding in a feral temper; his face was pockmarked, his receding hairline was cut into a defiant crew cut, and he had an unfortunate habit of punctuating almost every question by scratching the side of his nose with his thumbnail. Let me put it to you this way: he looked like the type of guy you wouldn't want to have to tell first thing in the morning that you'd just run out of coffee.

This tells you everything you need to know about me: if a string had been protruding from him, I would have pulled it.

If Corbin was all sharp angles, his partner, Agent Francis Russell, was given to latent puffiness, like a half-deflated pale white balloon. I could see instantly that if he held his breath, his whole face would swell up and his chestnut-round cheeks would turn a bright red, which would then match his moussed-down, sharply parted hair. (How about that for a description?)

D.C. detective Harry Markopolos, who was glum and plump, was wearing blue slacks, brown shoes, and a black baseball jacket. "Coach" was stitched in cursive letters over his left breast. He stood several feet away from the agents, as if their attitude might be catching. As we were introduced, he thumbed a Tums from a roll and popped it in his mouth.

The agents handed Reich their business card. Reich stood protectively next to my bed and laid out his rules: I had volunteered to answer their questions. As my attorney, if he didn't like the tone of those questions or if he believed they potentially might put me or my employer in jeopardy, he would advise me not to answer them, and if they continued that line of questioning, we would end the interview. "Gentlemen," he finally said, forcing up the two sides of his mouth in a truly pathetic attempt at a sardonic smile.

The agents stood on either side of my bed. They didn't precisely alternate questions, but it was close: How did I know Amram? How many times had I met him previously? Did I record my conversations with him? Reich's warning had been accurate, these guys weren't there to gather background information. This was an active investigation. Did I know anyone else in Amram's organization? Did he give me anything? It went on for more than a half hour. Did I give him money or any other items of value? Did Amram discuss other people?

Detective Markopolos stood silently near the door. It suddenly dawned on me why he had been invited. Under district law, he was the only one empowered to make an arrest.

Agent Russell handed a copy of the story I'd written about Hassan's mother to Reich, who glanced at it, then gave it to me and asked me to confirm that I had written it. Jenny would have been very proud of me for resisting the urge to say what I was thinking. I simply said, "Yeah."

As instructed by Reich, I answered most of their questions with short declarative sentences. Amram had contacted me. I did not know where he had gotten my phone number; perhaps from the *Pro* site where it was listed. He told me he was involved in drugs. I had no information or reason to believe Amram was a terrorist or was involved in any way in the 7/11 attacks.

"Jeez," Corbin mused, without looking at me, "I guess you don't read the papers."

"Actually, Dick," I responded, emphasizing the Dick (sorry, Jen, I just couldn't help myself), "I write them."

I told them as much as I remembered about the murder. The SUV came out of nowhere. It whirled around the corner and aimed right at Amram. It definitely was intentional. I was waiting in a corner, by parked cars, making it impossible for the SUV to hit me without plowing into those cars. The SUV pursued me but I outraced it down the ramp. That's how I ended up lying in a hospital bed.

Corbin looked at me skeptically. "You're telling us you outran that SUV down the whole garage? In a wheelchair?"

"Yes, Dick," I said, "that's what I'm telling you."

"Hoo-kay," he said somewhat dubiously, scraping his thumbnail along the side of his nose, then writing down my answer.

This interview continued considerably longer than I had expected.

When they were done with their questions, Russell said, "Thank you for your time, Mr. Stone. I have to inform you that until we complete our investigation you need to let us know before you leave the area. Just in case we have a few more questions."

Dick added, "One more thing. You are familiar with the new National Secrets Act, aren't you?"

I glanced at Reich. He shrugged. "I'm not," I said.

"Officially it's a presidential directive rather than a congressional act." He handed Reich another sheet. "Here, this outlines it. What it does is give the government the right to limit communications when national security is invoked. We are now officially informing you that due to the sensitive nature of these events and legitimate national security concerns, writing or communicating in any format information about this event will be considered a violation of this act and subject you to its penalties."

"What are you talking about?" I looked at Reich. "What's he talking about? This is total bullshit." I turned back to Corbin. "How come I've never heard anything about this?"

With a smile that reeked of official power he explained, "The existence of this act is covered by the National Secrets Act."

I was incredulous. "You're telling me the Secrets Act is a secret?"

Russell waved a cautionary finger. "That means you can't discuss it and you can't write about it. With anyone."

"Really? Wow." I considered that, then wondered, "Then how come you're talking about it?"

"Look, you . . ." Dick snarled, taking a step forward.

"Stop!" Reich warned him, shocking him back to reality.

"I know the whole thing sounds strange," Russell said, trying to defuse the situation. "But there are times the government has to take steps to protect the public. This is one of those times."

I couldn't believe this. I couldn't write about the fact that I was almost murdered. "What about the fucking First Amendment? You people just going to ignore that?"

"It isn't up to us," Corbin said. "We're just following orders. And that's what you need to do."

I wondered, is calling Dick a dickhead redundant?

"Look, Rollie," Russell said, taking a friendly step closer. Obviously he was playing good cop. "I can tell you that you're not the first person to ask that question. And the proper courts have already affirmed its legality. Let me explain. During both World Wars and in Vietnam, the government imposed strict censorship regulations. The American people understood and accepted the need for them and went along. Whether you want to believe it or not, we're in a similar situation right now. There are some very bad people out there, people who would just as easily slit your throat as whistle Dixie. Our job is to prevent that from happening. So right now the government has decided that if the information you possess should become public, it might cause serious harm. This is a national security issue now, and that gives us a lot of leeway. Do your country a big favor and don't write about this, don't discuss it with anybody, don't . . ."

I just couldn't resist. I'm sorry, Jen. "Can I whistle Dixie?" I interrupted. "Would that be legal?"

Detective Markopolos pushed himself off the wall and spoke for the first time. "Listen up, pally. For all I care you can shove that whistle up your ass and fart 'The Star-Spangled Banner.' But like these guys said, you go ahead and write about this, talk about it, or even hint to anyone that you're not allowed to hint about it to, you'll see me again." He closed his eyes and shook at the prospect. "Trust me, you don't want to see me again."

In an earlier life I must have been in vaudeville. On a second-rate circuit. But be honest, if someone served you a straight line like that one, you wouldn't be able to resist, either. "Have you made that offer to your wife?" I asked.

Reich winced, then put a restraining hand on my shoulder.

Markopolos started to respond, then caught himself. With a dramatic tilt of his head he told the agents, "Let's get outta here." He shot one final look at me, which I assumed was meant to be a warning, and left.

When they were gone, I asked Reich if he knew what the penalty was for violating that Secrets Act. He inhaled and shook his head, and we said simultaneously, "It's a secret."

He plopped himself down in the chair next to my bed. It seemed obvious that this threat had stunned him too. His demeanor had been stripped away and he was trying to process what he had just been told through the filter of a life spent inside the legal system. In a shaken voice he admitted, "I don't have the slightest idea. This whole thing, it would require secret courts, enforcement mechanisms, confining people in places that we don't even know exist." He was thinking out loud. "Maybe that's what they're using Guantánamo for. But look, those guys were serious. As your lawyer I've got to advise to be really careful about what you do." He picked up the now half-empty juice box and sipped from it. "You don't mind, right?"

"Go ahead, live it up."

"Here's the other thing," he continued. "Whatever happened in that garage, the government obviously is trying to build a case against you for who knows what. Aiding and abetting, maybe? Collaborating with the enemy? It's bullshit, I know that, but those are serious charges, so you need to pay attention to it. Far as the American public knows, this guy was a terrorist, and rather than turning him in, you were meeting secretly with him."

When you put it that way . . . Shit! I turned to Reich and took one long and very deep breath. Then I asked, "You finish all the juice?"

I called Howie first thing the following morning. I'd spent a long restless night trying to decide how to proceed. I'd made a difficult decision: I'd fought for my country on distant battlefields and I wasn't about to stop fighting for those same values at home. The existence of a secret law passed in secret flouting the First Amendment was something every American had to know about. I didn't care what they said, it couldn't possibly withstand a legal challenge. When I got Howie on the phone I began, "You aren't going to believe this . . ."

I told him about the visit, the warning, and my decision. "Soon as I get out of here, I'm writing it. Fuck the consequences. Let 'em bring charges against me. Imagine what that's going to look like, Wrightman throws a handicapped veteran in prison for telling the truth."

Howie listened as I rambled on. When I finally asked him what he thought, he told me in a voice so soft I had to strain to hear him. "There's no easy way for me to tell you this, Rol. But we can't run it."

That certainly was not what I expected to hear. "What are you talking about? Of course we can."

"No," he insisted in a voice mellowed with frustration, embarrassment, and probably some pain. "We can't." I could almost hear him swallowing his pride. "We had some visitors here too," he continued. "Long story short, if we run anything about it, they're going to shut us down." I tried to interrupt, but he spoke right over me. "The reality is, they can do it. You know damned well what I'd do if it was just you and me, but it isn't. There's a bunch of other people here that I'm responsible for. So I'm asking you, as a friend, give it a little time till the pressure eases up. This is just one story. I promise you, we'll find other ways of making the point . . ."

"One story?" I exploded. "Are you fucking me? The government of the United States is fucking with the First Amendment and you, you're going to let them do it? What happened to that journalistic integrity you're always telling—"

"Don't do this, Rollie. Don't make it harder than it already is."

"What happened to you, Howie? When did you become a fucking coward?" By the time I caught myself, I had already blurted it out. I shut up. He didn't deserve that. But even as I was venting, on some visceral level I understood Howie's decision. And truthfully, I wasn't sure he was wrong. For the *Pro*. But not for me. I knew the next words out of my mouth might determine the fate of our friendship.

"You done?" he asked.

"Yeah."

"I'm not gonna fight with you, Rollie. I can't defend myself, and believe me, it's killing me. But here's what I know—fights aren't won or lost in the first round. Sometimes it makes sense to take a few punches before hitting back. Then when you hit back, you hit him with everything you've got, because you're not getting a second chance. You're right, this is fucked up big-time. You want to make your stand here, go ahead. I can't stop you. Write your story and put it up on the net."

His anger was building as he continued. I could picture his face wrinkling up.

"But what do you think's going to happen if you do, Rollie? C'mon, tell me. You think you're going to spark some massive uprising to overthrow the government? You think Wrightman's worried about that? You saw the response we got to the mother's story. It lasted what, two days? Three days? Let me tell you what's actually going to happen. Your new pals are going to find some evidence linking you to Amram. They're going to arrest you and destroy your reputation. Even if you win the case, three or four years from now, it's going to cost you every penny you've got.

"So if you are so damn certain you want to go ahead, good luck. Be my guest, I'll be rooting for you. I'll admit you've got a lot more guts than I do. But I can't let you take the rest of us down with you."

Well, that was a sobering response. The real problem was how much sense he made; I felt like someone had pulled the plug and all my bravado had drained out of me. In a conciliatory tone, I asked, "What do you expect me to do, Howie? Just be a good boy?"

After a long, contemplative silence, almost as if he was deciding how much to reveal, he said plaintively, "There are ways to fight back, Rollie. Trust me. We will."

As difficult as that conversation was, it was little more than a warm-up for what was to come. Jenny arrived at the hospital midmorning, bringing chocolate and Jelly Bellys. As I was telling her about the visit, I sensed a stiffness come over her, and suddenly it dawned on me. "You knew all about this crap, this Secrets Act?"

She couldn't even look at me. "Martha did everything she could to fight it. There was nothing . . ." Her voice drifted off. Then she explained, "You know what we agreed. I couldn't tell you."

She was right. We were both constrained by legal boundaries, and at the beginning of our relationship, we had agreed to respect them. We had shaken hands in agreement. Then we did other things to make it a binding agreement. Respect legal boundaries. No questions asked. I understood she wasn't allowed to tell me, so why was I feeling betrayed? It wasn't rational—but I had to strike out at someone. And she was the person I trusted most not to tell me to go fuck myself. (Which, admittedly, I probably deserved.) "I'll get over it," I said coldly.

She stayed a half hour. As she left, she gave me a perfunctory peck on the cheek. "I'll see you later," she promised.

"Take the chocolates," I told her, making a desperate attempt to alleviate the tension. "Leave the Jelly Bellys."

She snapped a smile at me and was gone.

It took me several weeks to ease back into work. As before, I turned down numerous requests for interviews or appearances, explaining this remained an open case and prosecutors had advised me against making any public comments. I wrote a long and loose story about what happened in the garage, offering few details beyond what was already publicly known: I had met a potential informant and somehow been caught up in a murder. It was not an easy piece to write, as I had to weave a duplicitous path through a maze of half-truths. I flirted with hinting at the existence of the Secrets Act, but Howie reminded me the *Pro* couldn't print it and Reich warned me of the consequences.

Still, my column, "A Murder in the Garage," was widely republished. I let other media outlets link it to the "raid on the Detroit safe house" articles; the implication was obvious. Somehow this brutal killing was involved with Detroit. My involvement in this second violent episode raised my public profile to the edge of celebrity. The media embraced the Rolling Stone image, highlighting my military record and my "futuristically enhanced wheelchair." Within the disabled community I was hailed as a role model, or as TMZ described me, "a roll model," although I was careful not to let anyone know the full extent of Mighty Chair's capabilities. In fact, the only scheduled public appearance I did make was tossing up the first ball at the National Wheelchair Basketball Association championship tournament, which was being held in Washington. For several weeks I was stopped regularly on my way to work by people asking for an autograph, a selfie, or—and this was a new one on me—Mighty Chair's treadmark: people would place a sheet of white paper under a wheel and I would roll over it, then sign it. Other people wanted to shake my hand and thank me for my service. Several pleasant strangers trying to find common ground with me told me they loved watching old episodes of *Ironside* on TV Land. The interruptions got so time consuming, most often I drove the van to work, although I no longer parked in that garage.

There was one significant disappointment. The homeless veteran who had saved my life was a man named Jerry Stern. I intended to find a way of repaying the debt I owed to him. I vowed to find him a safe place to live, get him the medical assistance he needed, make sure he had money in his pocket. He wasn't interested; he refused all offers for assistance, from me as well as others, explaining he was already scheduled to fly on the first flight to Mars and thus had to remain within the boarding area until his flight was called.

I also received inquiries from book publishers and movie producers about optioning the rights to my story. I didn't respond to any of them. Nor did I accept offers from manufacturers of wheelchairs and other medical devices to act as a spokesperson or simply endorse their products. Y, however, was practically deluged by people wanting him to customize their chairs, which I encouraged him to accept.

Gradually Jenny and I got back on track, although sometimes it seemed like that track was running straight up the side of a mountain and we couldn't pick up any speed. One night, as we ate pizza by candlelight, I watched with appreciation as she moved around the room, setting the table, pouring the wine, picking the music, unexpectedly kissing the top of my head. She was barefoot, wearing bell-bottomed jeans and a man-tailored white shirt that hugged her contours. Her hair was pulled back in a no-nonsense bun. As with everything else she did, she seemed completely confident and utterly at ease. I marveled at her ability to so easily make the transformation from powerful political insider to loving partner, but even at that moment, even as I felt overwhelmed with comfort, I couldn't help wondering, what else isn't she telling me?

No matter how hard I tried, I just couldn't get rid of that feeling. Rather than slowly disappearing, it had taken root in my mind and was growing. And it caused damage.

As I feared, the National Secrets Act proved its value. The Wrightman people were able to contain and shape the story. Investigators told friendly media outlets they were tracing the complex relationship between

Amram and his killer, Moncada. Moncada turned out to be an honorably discharged Marine who had several minor convictions, the worst being a road-rage incident during which he'd threatened another driver with a crowbar, but no clear ties to terrorism. "Informed sources leaked" to administration-friendly outlets that during Moncada's military service he'd done tours in Afghanistan and Yemen and suggested he may have been radicalized at that time. There were casual mentions of time spent off the "civilized grid." On *Meet the Press,* Homeland Security secretary Rocky Penceal stated that the government was successfully "rolling up Terror Inc. one body at a time," predicting it would cease to exist within the next year. Asked about rumors that Amram may have been targeted by terrorists because he had extensive knowledge of future plans, Penceal said that "sadly, I'm not able to comment on that at this moment."

Moderator Chuck Todd pressed him, asking, "So are we talking here about the man who knew too much?"

I would have fallen off the couch if I had been able to sit on the couch.

Penceal smiled noncommittally, repeating his answer that he was unable to comment on that. Although this time he added a knowing smile to that lie.

After six weeks, the only reminder that a brutal murder and an incredible chase had taken place in downtown D.C. were the hop-on, hop-off tour buses that stopped regularly outside the garage so tourists could take selfies in front of the early bird special sign.

11

When I look back on that period, which admittedly is not very often—the pain is still there—I refer to it as the American Autostereogram. (Don't worry, I had to look it up too.) Surprise! Believe it or not, you already know what that means. An autostereogram is popularly known as a Magic Eye. It is one of those colorful images that at a glance appears to be one thing, but if you stare at it long enough or close enough, you see the hidden image. It was right in front of you all the time.

This was the most unsettling Christmas season of my life. Almost 250 years ago, when the colonies were busy forming a nation, the powerful Russian statesman Grigory Potemkin supposedly created elaborate stage-like sets to convince his sometime lover, Catherine the Great, that great towns and villages were flourishing in the Crimea. The term, a Potemkin village, has come to mean a shiny facade being used to conceal decaying conditions secreted behind it. That was the United States. On the surface, there were signs of stabilization and the roots of real recovery. The Christmas lights and joyful Santas were hung, happy holiday jingles were bursting from every platform, the Salvation Army pots were out on every corner, the smell of Christmas pine was in the air, and people moved with holiday determination in and out of stores burdened with gaily wrapped packages. If you were just plopped down in the city, it would look like normality was returning, finally. But it wasn't—not even close.

While the Labor Department continued to report booming economic numbers, the reality was far different. Doctored employment figures issued monthly by the administration couldn't hide the ugly reality that millions of jobs no longer existed. The economy had essentially been destroyed by Trump's tariff tantrums and the pandemic, and the Democrats' attempts to breathe life into it had been smothered by the multitrillion-dollar debt they had inherited, complicated by the drought and famine that devastated the third world. International supply chains were about as reliable as the colorful paper chains third graders made out of construction paper. Wrightman's efforts to repair the damage by lowering or even eliminating tariffs had resulted in an upturn in exports his first few months in office. The passage of the multitrillion-dollar Rebuild America infrastructure bill had buoyed markets and led to the creation of good-paying jobs, but it didn't last. It couldn't; those markets wrecked by Trump's trade wars were gone forever, and the bureaucracy and environmental lawsuits stalled the largest infrastructure projects.

The healthcare system had been devastated by Trump/Pence in collaboration with the right-wing Congress, leaving too many families without health insurance or the funds to pay for medical attention when they needed it. The Biden Band-Aid, as the Democrats' healthcare plan became known, temporarily stopped the bleeding but did little long-term to cure the problem. As a result, there was a steadily increasing number of violent attacks on healthcare facilities by people unable to afford lifesaving care for themselves or their family.

Desperate people were forced to take desperate measures, and the crime rate was soaring, aided in some cases by Uber's new gun-rental division, which rented weapons by the hour.

To combat this crime wave while keeping unemployed workers from rebelling, volunteer militias had been transformed into paid neighborhood watch organizations under the direction of Vice President Hunter. Local merchants contracted with them for protection from predators. To encourage pride and professionalism, these militias designed their own outfits. While these uniforms were generally similar to those of state troopers, featuring gray or brown pants and shirts, high-gloss black boots, and "cowboy" hats, set off by de rigueur fake Oakley sunglasses, several militias selected clothing of a deep burgundy, supposedly paying homage to the blood spilt by American patriots in defense of our liberties. Each militia took a local name, from Olympia, Washington's Apple Corps to Texas's Ted Cruzers, but in general they became known as Wrightman's Watchers. According to Breitbart, these neighborhood watch teams consisted of "patriotic Americans on the watch for those who would put our freedom in jeopardy."

What was most stunning to me was the lack of outrage. Jackbooted bastards were patrolling American streets and nobody was screaming about it. The general attitude seemed to be that Wrightman hadn't fooled anyone; after all, he had run promising to "Restore Order," and that was exactly what he was doing. What did people expect him to do? As Eunice Kaufman said, dismissing the protests, "Americans should be proud to have a president who doesn't lie to them."

There were some objections. But when a local newspaper in Erie, Pennsylvania, referred to the Pennsylvania Brakemen as "a pseudo-military organization reminiscent of the worst days of fascism," that militia broke into their office and destroyed their computers and workstations. Other media outlets critical of the administration, including the *Pro,* received anonymous warnings that the same thing might happen to them. Watching this happen, I was reminded of a story I'd read years earlier: The respected community activist Saul Alinsky had completely rejected the use of violence to achieve his political objective; when asked why, he explained logically, "Because they have all the guns."

The fears and frustrations plaguing Americans more and more were being transformed into anger, which too often exploded into rage. Trivial encounters escalated into fights. In the recently incorporated town of Trump, Mississippi, for example, a long-simmering feud between neighbors over ownership of a two-foot-wide strip of land between their houses erupted into a furious gun battle. Family members shooting across the contested strip from windows, like defenders of a besieged fort, fired into their neighbor's house. Three people were killed and four more were wounded, but the survivors came together and copyrighted the concept. The resulting cable program, *Neighbor Wars,* roughly an action version of *Family Feud,* which taped episodes in suburbs throughout the country substituting paintballs for bullets, became a major hit show.

There were at least a few people brave enough to stand up to Wrightman. Illinois senator Tammy Duckworth, the former Army helicopter pilot who had lost both legs when her UH-60 Black Hawk was hit by a rocket-propelled grenade, led a futile effort to force the administration to reinstate all constitutional guarantees. *New York Times* columnist Carole Cooper created a furor when she claimed to have evidence that monthly job creation and unemployment numbers had been falsified under direct orders from the White House, although her reputation was severely damaged when she was indicted for tax fraud and subsequently fired before the release of those documents was blocked under the Secrets Act.

There were others too, but to my shame, the *Pro* was not among them. As much as I pushed Howie to join what we laughingly referred to around the office as the "flaccid resistance," he refused. "Trust me on this," he said. "We're keeping our powder dry. Now's not the right time," he said. I trusted him to keep our powder dry until the right time, even if I had no idea what he was referring to. He was Howie, and that was enough for me. I wasn't wrong.

The administration fought back with its best weapon, other than guns—patriotism. Members of the administration took every opportunity to define "real Americans" as those people who supported the president of the United States while dismissing the opposition as "misguided people who may not even understand how their attempts to undermine confidence in the government are assisting the enemies of democracy."

The highlight of this "America first, last, and always in our hearts" campaign was the introduction of the New American Pledge. Standing directly in front of the Statue of Liberty on New York's Liberty Island, the president asked several hundred children invited there for this ceremony to place their right hands over their heart and repeat these fifty-four words with him: "I am an American. I am born of the sacrifices of heroic men and women. I was shaped in the cauldron of liberty and justice for all. I accept my solemn duty to preserve and protect the rights of all

Americans to live without fear wherever our flag might wave. I am an American."

I have to admit on some level I admired the political skill that had enabled Wrightman to seize control of the narrative. As I'm certain it was intended to do, this pledge created a furor. Or as I referred to it in a column—to Jenny's dismay; "Why do you always need to start trouble?"—"a führer." It solidified Wrightman's support among people who self-identified as patriots while painting those of us who opposed it as anti-American or even terrorist sympathizers.

When possible, I fought back with my keyboard. As long as I didn't directly attack the Wrightman government, Howie ran what I wrote, although we noticed that *Pro* pieces were getting less pickup and re-posting than previously. Of all the columns I wrote, it was my Christmas column that attracted the most interest. Admittedly it was controversial: I attacked Santa Claus. I wrote:

Since the 1949 publication of George Orwell's dystopian novel *1984,* we have remained diligently alert for the appearance of Big Brother, the Stalin-like dictator who would destroy American society and impose a totalitarian structure on us. As it turns out, we have been looking in the wrong direction for all these decades. It wasn't Big Brother we should have been watching out for. In actuality, it was Santa Claus.

We built the finest military in history to keep out the would-be Big Brothers; meanwhile we invited this jolly old man into our homes. Why not? He had a friendly smile, a delightful ho-ho-ho of a laugh, and best of all, he came bearing gifts for us all. What could be wrong with that? Not only did we welcome him, we set out milk and cookies for him!

But as we discovered too late, behind that jolly old facade lived a very different man. He wasn't at all what he seemed to be. The warning signs were there. He moved only in the darkness and was known by an alias. While we were welcoming him, he was taking advantage of

our hospitality. He learned all about us. He spied on us,
compiling detailed lists. He determined who was "good" and
who was "bad," and he rewarded those people who fulfilled
his expectations and punished those who took actions he
didn't approve. Without our knowledge he managed to install
an extraordinary surveillance system that enabled him to
determine when people were sleeping or when they were
awake. He knew how to ensure our cooperation, bribing
us with promises of gifts that we had already told him we
wanted. It was an amazing scam . . .

It continued for several more paragraphs. It generated an unusual
number of responses. I thought my satire was perhaps too obvious, but to
my surprise, many people believed I was writing about Mark Zuckerberg.

Throughout this period, Jenny helped me maintain my equilibrium. Difficult times drive people closer, and no matter how frustrated
I became, she was there almost every night to calm me down. Naturally I didn't discuss marriage, but only because she had made it clear:
one-and-done. Naturally. We did, however, visit my mother during the
Christmas holidays. Let me tell you about that. It actually was a pretty
big deal, because Jenny was the first woman I'd brought home in my
second life.

My mother was warm and welcoming, which was not surprising.
But her hearing had gotten considerably worse since the last time I'd
been home. On the phone she had been able to hide it. At dinner that
first night she had asked Jen how we'd met. "I was doing a hora," Jenny
had replied.

My mother was shocked. "You were a what?"

Jenny laughed. "The dance. The hora. We were dancing."

She shook her head. "Oh no," she said. "My Rollie can't dance."

Jenny agreed. "I know."

"But he's very good at other things," Mom responded confidently,
defending me.

That was one of the few times I saw Jenny get embarrassed. She
looked at me and told my mother, "I know."

We were lying in bed several weeks later, still laughing about it. My bruises had pretty much healed and my stitches were scarring into a facsimile *J* (if you had a vivid imagination). Jenny was poking me playfully, teasing me about "those other things," when Cher interrupted us. "Rollie, there is a major event taking place," she informed us, as she had been programmed to do.

"Cher, turn on the TV," I said. We both sat up. CNN was showing a still image of an airplane, a Boeing 777 I thought. My first thought was that a passenger plane must have crashed. But the chyron below the image was frighteningly different: REMOTE HIJACKERS TAKE CONTROL OF PASSENGER JET.

"Oh my god," Jenny said.

The details, as much as were known, got filled in quickly. Northern Airlines Flight 342, a red-eye from New York's JFK to LAX, had been flying into the night at 36,000 feet when the cockpit warning system alerted the pilots that they had a problem. The plane, it was a 777, which had been cruising on autopilot, was inexplicably descending and veering off course. When the pilots attempted to regain control, they discovered that none of the flight systems were responding. That's when they had called for help. CNN replayed the conversation between the first officer, a man named Mark Stein, and the control tower in Albuquerque. In an amazingly calm, professional voice he reported, "This is Northern Airlines flight 3-4-2 declaring an emergency. We have a complete loss of control. I repeat, this is . . ."

I took Jenny's hand.

A voice had responded with equal dispassion. "Reading you clearly Northern Airlines 3-4-2. This is Albuquerque. Are you declaring an avionics failure?"

"Negative, Albuquerque," the pilot said. "All systems A-OK. But we've lost the ability to control any of them. Seems like the only thing we can operate is this com system."

CNN's aviation expert Pete Sawyer was on the phone with Anderson Cooper. "Obviously we don't know for sure, Anderson, but this appears to be the scenario that a lot of people have been concerned about for a long time. It looks like, and believe me I'm just speculating here, we certainly don't know with any certainty, but it looks like someone has hacked into the flight computer and taken control of this airplane."

Cooper handled it well. "Are you saying a hacker is flying this airplane?"

"I don't know. But that appears to be one of the possible scenarios."

Cooper paused to regain his composure. He coughed the tension out of his voice. "Can the pilots regain control?"

Sawyer hesitated, then answered as sensitively as he could, "There is no procedure for this." He was silent for several seconds, then said almost as an afterthought, "I'm sure that's what they're trying to figure out right now."

It was as if we had walked right into the middle of a horror film. "This can't be real," Jenny said, laying her hand on mine. "It can't be."

I began channel surfing. It was real, terrifuckingly real. Someone, somewhere, was playing with the lives of more than three hundred people. On Fox, Bill Hemmer asked their aviation expert, I didn't hear his name, "So who is flying this airplane?"

In a soft and respectful voice, the expert responded, "God." After letting that thought hang in the air for a few seconds, the expert caught himself, cleared his throat, and said, "Or hackers."

One of the flight attendants, ignoring protocol, had begun texting her husband. He in turn was passing her texts along to CNN. The pilot, Captain Sanchez, had briefed the flight crew. He had laid out the situation. Then the first officer, Stein, had told them, and she quoted him, "This is really fucked up. We're doing everything humanly possible to regain control. But what happens aboard this aircraft is up to you. You want to start a panic, go ahead, but that isn't going to help anybody. Just do your best."

Sanchez had then alerted his passengers, waking them to explain the aircraft was experiencing "unexpected navigational difficulties." He had assured them this was not a serious problem and asked them to remain calm, to stay in their seats with their seat belts fastened and follow whatever instructions they were given. He promised to keep them updated but warned them they probably would be late getting into Los Angeles.

Jenny and I listened silently, doing the same thing everyone else watching was doing, fighting with our imagination, which was trying really hard to put us on that airplane.

My mind clicked into journalism. I tried to reassure her. "Look, if whoever is doing this wanted to kill those people, they could have done it already. Whatever is going on, that's not it."

"They still can, any time they want," she said.

"They still can," I agreed.

The networks began referring to this as a cyber-hijacking, which immediately was shortened to cyjacking. It appeared the entire country was being awakened by people calling friends and family to turn on their TV. The White House told reporters that the president was at his cabin and that he and the first lady were monitoring the event and joined all Americans in praying for a safe outcome.

The networks had all made the same decision not to run any commercials. That decision was pretty easy to make, seeing as how not too many companies want to be associated with an out-of-control aircraft flying at 36,000 feet. With few new facts to report, they began focusing on the pilots, Sanchez and Stein, providing as much background as possible. MSNBC got the president of the Air Line Pilots Association to say, "If you're going to be caught in this situation, Steve Sanchez is the guy you want in the cockpit." Sanchez had been flying for three decades and had flown every type of aircraft from carrier-based fighters to jumbo jets.

According to reports, the plane was flying in great circles, as if it had no particular destination, slowly descending. The flight crew was in direct communication with Boeing engineers, who were reviewing all procedures to try to figure out how to regain control of the computer system. A Boeing spokesperson said chief engineer Pete Schaeffer was working with Sanchez and Stein to decide on a strategy and that Boeing remained "supremely confident" in its products and its people.

I suddenly realized Jenny and I had been transfixed for almost forty-five minutes; neither of us had moved. "You okay?" I asked her.

She shook her head as she took a deep, calming breath. She couldn't speak.

This must be driving the intel people nuts, I thought. I had absolutely no doubt they were desperately trying to get their hooks into whoever was doing this, sort of a cyber version of catching robbers in the bank. But I also figured they had no chance of identifying the hackers. Anyone skillful enough to carry this out certainly had the ability to obscure their tracks behind them.

On ABC, David Muir was reporting that Sanchez and Schaeffer were trying various techniques to work around the plane's electronics system, but thus far nothing had worked. "There is no manual for this," he said. "This is literally seat-of-the-pants flying. They are making it up on the spot." He paused dramatically. "And it appears they are running out of time."

He started his next thought but stopped suddenly and raised a just-a-minute finger. He looked down at his desk, cleared his throat to maintain his composure, and said, "We're just getting word that they've made a decision. It appears that they are going to attempt to reboot the computer system." The ABC expert was a former naval aviator and NASA astronaut, Steve Peters. "Steve, what exactly does that mean?"

Steve Peters was sitting at the anchor desk, a model of the plane in front of him. "It means just what it says, David. Just like you do at home when your computer locks up. You kick it a few times, and when that doesn't work you turn off everything, count to ten, and turn it on again."

Both Jenny and I had checked in with our offices. There didn't seem to be any need for us to show up there—certainly we would be fairly useless—but we needed to confirm that. We had each received several calls. This was one of those unnerving events that made you need to reach out to other people.

"Will that work?" Muir wondered.

Peters frowned. "It's dicey," he admitted. "But I've seen it work on simulators." After the still-unsolved 2014 loss of Malaysia Airlines Flight 370, also a Boeing triple 7, he continued, engineers had gamed every conceivable problem and solution in an attempt to figure out what had happened to that aircraft. This was one of the scenarios they'd run.

"So we know it does work?" Muir asked.

Peters clearly did not want to be nailed down. "It has been successful in regaining control, yes."

"Right," I said to Jenny. "There's a lie of omission. I guarantee you. He isn't telling us about the times it didn't work."

"So what do you want him to say? That they're all gonna die?"

For one of the few times in my life, I didn't have an answer.

Muir asked, "About how long does the reboot take?"

Peters hedged, "With luck, about a minute."

Whoa, that took my breath away. It meant that for about a minute one of the largest airplanes ever built—an extraordinary complex jumble of steel and aluminum, fabric and wires, and 330 human beings—was going to have to remain airborne without enough power to flush the toilets.

Muir asked the only question that mattered: "How long can this airplane stay in the air without power?"

"With luck, about a minute."

The long pause that followed was broken by Muir, looking for some cause for optimism. "Sully kept his plane in the air longer than that, didn't he?"

"That's right," Jenny agreed.

I had written about that. "Little more than four minutes," I said.

CNN was still receiving texts from the plane. An incredibly subdued Anderson Cooper reported that Steve Sanchez had finally informed his passengers about their situation. "He spoke very calmly." He shook his head in some combination of awe and admiration. "I'm reading the text here. He told them that, this is a quote, 'I've got a lot of confidence in this bucket of bolts, but we need your help too. We're all pretty nervous . . .'"

Cooper paused again and pursed his lips, then appeared to wipe away a tear.

"'. . . but we need you to stay as calm as you can. This airplane was built to fly, not be on the ground. So just sit tight and work with me, and we're all gonna have a hell of a story to tell our grandkids.'" Cooper just sat there for several seconds. What else was there to say?

Finally he looked directly into the camera and said, "You want the definition of courage, that's Captain Sanchez."

He turned to that station's aviation reporter, Charles Modica, and asked what to expect. Modica scratched his head. "It's going to be the longest minute of their lives," he said. Captain Sanchez was going to shut down that plane. During that time, they would be flying blind and deaf, "as out of touch with the rest of the world during those seconds as Apollo 13 was when it went behind the moon to slingshot home."

Completely unexpectedly, Cooper read something, shook his head in admiration, and laughed. "This is unbelievable," he said, holding on to a sheet of paper. "We just got this text that they're getting ready to shut down and Sanchez told the passengers he would see them on the ground . . ."—he laid down that sheet of paper—"and while they were waiting, they might focus on who they'd like to play them in the movie."

Jenny sobbed.

Anderson Cooper had his hands clasped in front of him. "Captain Sanchez has just reported to ATC that he is shutting down all systems. It is exactly 2:45 A.M. here on the East Coast." He paused, then whispered, "Godspeed flight 342."

We held hands tightly. Neither one of us could speak.

I don't know how Cooper did it. "We estimate that at this point Northern American flight 3-4-2, en route to Los Angeles, has been in the air without power for fifteen seconds." Then, "Thirty seconds . . ."

Modica said, "It would be completely silent on board. They probably can hear the wind whistling outside the fuselage. The plane is slowing. I can't begin to imagine what those people are thinking."

"Forty-five seconds," Cooper said.

"The nose has dipped by this time," Modica said, sounding as if he was speaking to himself. "The downward descent has begun. They have no way of determining their altitude. Low and getting lower."

"Fifty-five seconds."

"Right about now they're powering up." A brief pause. Then, "The systems should be coming back online. We're going to hear from them in a few seconds."

Silence. Silence. Silence. "Please," Jenny said. "Please."

Silence. Silen . . . Cooper broke into a huge smile. A breath of relief exploded from his mouth as he said, "Albuquerque air traffic control is reporting that they are in contact with Northern American flight 3-4-2. Pilots Sanchez and Stein report they have regained control of their aircraft. Everyone aboard A-OK." He paused once again and took a huge breath. "They're coming home." He actually laughed. "They're safe and they're coming home. Although Captain Sanchez told the air traffic controllers that if they didn't mind, he'd like to put down in Albuquerque for a cup of coffee."

Through her tears Jenny laughed. I admit it, I wiped away my own tears.

I flicked around the stations. On ABC David Muir was shaking his fist to express his joy. CBS somehow had gotten a several-second video from Boeing, showing unidentified people hugging and high-fiving each other in a control room somewhere.

I could hear people cheering in the background, although it was impossible to determine if those cheers were coming from Albuquerque air traffic control, the network studio, or, to be honest, my apartment. Most likely all three.

Sanchez and Stein landed as heroes. The entire nation rejoiced. Really, I'm not being sarcastic. Millions of Americans had been awakened in the night and lived through almost two desperate hours together. We had shared a compelling, heart-wrenching emotionally draining experience. We had held our collective breath, many had prayed, and we had cried together at the joyous conclusion.

It was an extraordinary night; one of those I'll-never-forget-where-I-was events. For most Americans, though, where they were was in bed, which is why that blip in baby births nine months later was not a surprise. No one could get back to sleep, so like Jenny and me, we all celebrated.

On that night, America came together. (Figuratively.)

For President Wrightman, this was the victory he needed. For a brief semi-shining moment all of the economic, political, and international challenges disappeared. The United Nations passed a resolution praising the two pilots for their courage. The president invited the flight crew "and any passengers who want to join us" to the White House. Every journalist wanted a piece of the story. I got lucky; a friend of my cousin Jon's brother-in-law worked in Albuquerque air traffic control and spoke with me about what it was like in the tower that night. I described it in a widely reposted piece:

> The three air traffic controllers had an out-of-their-control airplane in their skies. They had less control over it than a drifting leaf in a storm. Within minutes they had cleared their screens of other aircraft for hundreds of miles while maintaining an unnatural calm. For the next 98 minutes they were the only communication between Northern Airlines flight . . .

The euphoria lasted three days, until all the feel-good stories had been published, all the crew and passengers had been interviewed. Then reality intruded: Cyberterrorists had successfully hacked into the computer system of a sophisticated passenger aircraft and taken control. It clearly was meant to be a demonstration of their capability; they could have crashed the aircraft at any point but for whatever reasons elected not to.

The world's commercial and cargo aviation fleet was grounded. For a story I tried to figure out how many flights that included, but even Google didn't provide that answer. I guesstimated 125,000 planes take off and land every day worldwide. It was a shaky figure, but I'm a good researcher, and if I couldn't find a better number, no one could question it. Whatever that number, it was a scary day. Arguably it was the greatest terrorist success in history, impacting the most people, even though not a single person was killed. It reminded every American how completely vulnerable we are.

The fix was relatively simple. A second, entirely independent computer control system was added; experts compared it to loading a personal computer with both Windows and Foxfire. If a hacker compromised either one of them, the pilot could shut it down and activate the redundant system. Hacking into one system required tremendous skill and a great deal of luck; hacking into two independent systems on the same aircraft was calculated to be one in the multitrillions.

Nine days after the cyjacking, President Wrightman asked the networks for a half hour in prime time to address the nation. I'd heard rumors that this was in the works, but even I—cynic, skeptic, and wiseass that I am—didn't believe he'd have the guts to do it.

Rather than from the casual setting of the cabin, he spoke from the Oval Office, with a bust of Lincoln and a painting of FDR visible over either shoulder, and instead of a sweater he wore a somber dark suit offset by a blue shirt and a tie speckled with red, white, and blue. "Good evening, my fellow Americans. Tonight I'm going to discuss with you a matter of the greatest importance to all of us . . ."

"Uh-oh, this is serious," I said to Jenny. "He's using his deep I'm-a-serious-guy voice." We were at Lucille's Ballroom. The place was completely filled and absolutely silent. Even Tommy O'Neil behind the bar had paused and was watching Wrightman's reflection in the mirrors on the far wall.

As the Miracle of Flight 342 had proved, the president continued, the ability of our enemies to reach into our lives from vast distances had continued to improve, and unfortunately, our defenses hadn't kept up with them. Skillfully deflecting responsibility, he continued: "The substantial damage done to our intelligence services by previous administrations has taken a terrible toll, and repairing that has been a priority of mine since the day I took office. But we are still fighting a determined enemy with an undermanned, underfunded, and somewhat inexperienced capability." He leaned forward and clasped his hands on his desk, an action any body language coach would recommend when you want listeners to believe you're being candid with them. "Let me be completely honest, my friends. As much as it pains me to admit this, and I have sufficient faith in each of you to know that you will understand and appreciate what I'm about to say, unless we make significant changes, we are not going to defeat these people."

He let that warning sink in. I drained the last drops of my one glass of wine. I was beginning to see where he was going. "Holy shit," I said to Jenny. "I think he's really going to do it."

He went on: "We have seen too many instances in which our enemies have used the very freedoms they have vowed to destroy to protect
themselves and hide their hideous plans. Yes, thanks to brave men and
women like Steve Sanchez and Mark Stein we'll stop them most of the
time, and we'll kill a lot of them . . ." He paused dramatically, looked
directly into the camera, and vowed, "We will kill many of them, but
variations of what we've just experienced are going to continue taking
place until this enemy is destroyed. And I'm afraid this puts all of our
lives in danger. To prevent that from happening, to provide the safety
that we want, I need your support." He cleared his throat. "And I need
your trust."

A buzz rose in the bar as people realized what was about to happen.
Lucille hushed the room.

In his earnest manner the president explained that it was time to
either commit this nation to wiping out the scourge of terrorism or
accept the reality that we will be fighting these people without resolution for the rest of our lifetimes "and our children's lifetimes. We are
at war with these terrorists in every way except officially. For too long
we have been fighting this war with one hand tied behind our back. To
rectify that, to take the fight to our enemy as we have never before been
able to do, tomorrow I will be submitting to Congress a request for an
official declaration of war against terrorism."

The Ballroom exploded with a burst of noise. Lucille screamed, "Shut
up! Just shut up, everybody. C'mon." As the noise subsided, I glanced
at Jenny. Her bottom lip was quivering, her way of releasing pent-up
emotion. A dubious look crossed her face. "I don't know about this."

Wrightman turned in his seat to look into a second camera, a director's
interlude. "Many of you will wonder what that means and how it will
affect you. The easy answer is, not very much. In most ways this is simply a legal declaration that allows your government to take greater steps
in pursuit of those who wake up every morning plotting to destroy
everything this nation stands for. In real terms, it will have very little
impact . . ."

The president continued for several more minutes. It was a deeply
emotional speech, delivered in a carefully rehearsed heartfelt tone. The

guy could sell a Yankee cap to a Red Sox fan, I had to give him that. As he wound into his big finish, he said, "You gave me the greatest honor any American can receive when you cast your votes for me, and now I am asking you for your trust. I give you my solemn word . . ." He thumped on his chest to show how much he meant that. "Every step I take will be done with your personal safety and the welfare of our great nation at the forefront. This declaration will enable our fighting men and women to seek out and destroy terrorists wherever they may be hiding."

He turned and faced camera one again. The stagecraft was really well done. "At crucial times in our history our forefathers were called upon to move boldly with courage and confidence into an uncertain future. Now it is our turn to prove the sacrifices they made for you . . ."—pointing directly into the camera at us—". . . were not in vain." After asking every American to call, write, email, and tweet their member of Congress to demand that he or she stand up proudly for America and the future of all of our beautiful children, he closed with an abundance of *God bless*es.

While he was speaking, the White House had long-tweeted to the media the official request the administration would be submitting to Congress. In it, Wrightman quoted President Woodrow Wilson's stirring 1917 demand to Congress that it declare war on Germany: "[T]his is a war against all nations . . . American lives have been taken in ways which have stirred us very deeply . . . Our motive will not be revenge or the victorious assertion of the physical might of the nation, but only the vindication of human right, of which we are only a single champion."

An instant after the speech ended, Lucille's exploded in a cacophony of rings—a postmodern symphony, a clinging, clanging cry for immediate attention. Everybody sprang into action. It had occurred to me once that if babies learned to ring rather than cry, they would be a lot more successful at getting attention.

Lucille did not suffer people talking on cell phones in her place (in fact, in a pique she had been known to drown a ringing iPhone in a wineglass), but this time she didn't say a word. This was our siren call:

We were a roomful of newspeople watching news taking place that in some way was going to involve all of us.

I told Cher to call the office. Jenny and I had agreed we would never respond to a call while in a public place unless it clearly was an emergency. This qualified. Around the room people were settling their bills, giving Lucille a quick peck on her cheek as they raced back to work.

"I got this," I told Jen, handing over my credit card. She believed paying her own bills maintained her independence. Who was I to dissuade her of that notion?

She was as wound up about the speech as I was. "What do you think this means?" she asked.

I shrugged. "Maybe everything? How about Martha? She's not going to go for something like this, is she?"

Jenny frowned. "I don't know. Wrightman did a great job scaring people. There's going to be a lot of pressure on Congress to give him what he wants. I don't know who's strong enough to face those winds."

The waiter, John, returned with the credit slip. As I signed it, I asked her, "What do you think you'd do?"

Jenny had the politician's gift of physical prevarication; whatever was going on in her mind, her body language didn't give it away. When fully dressed, I mean. "Depends," she said finally. "There's a political calculation, obviously." The left side of her mouth frowned, while the other side stayed level; it was a neat trick, a perfect way of expressing her indecision. "Lincoln and FDR had that power and they did okay with it. Maybe. I mean, I guess it depends how he uses it."

"That's a pretty long leash to give a guy like this, don't you think? Doesn't it bother you at all that he's using the cyjacking to consolidate his power?"

"Of course it does," she said sharply. No equivocation there. But then came her thought check. "Sometimes it's necessary." She stood over me, not ready to leave the question alone. "We've never faced an enemy like this. You . . . you as much as anybody knows that. I had a pre-law professor who loved to quote the Greeks to show us how smart he was; one of them was Hippocrates . . ."

I backed Mighty Chair away from the table and spun neatly around. "The medical oath guy."

"The oath guy," she agreed. "But he also said that for extreme diseases, extreme methods of cure are the most suitable."

"Desperate times," I began as we walked out.

"Call for desperate measures," she concluded.

I stopped and looked at her. "You believe that?" It was a question, not a challenge. After all the time we had spent together, I really didn't know how she would answer.

"Probably not tonight," she decided. "We'll see about tomorrow."

Lucille was at her table by the door. I stopped and gave her the usual peck on the cheek. "You write that that fucker should go to hell," she said, waving angrily at the TVs. Then she offered Jenny a cheek and Jenny planted the obligatory kiss.

It was a lovely spring night. When we were outside, Jenny laughed, "Well, certainly no equivocation there."

"If she ever gets over her shyness . . ."

Jen leaned over and kissed me, holding it for a second. "I'll call you later," she said. I watched her walk away. She knew exactly what I was doing, and without looking back gave me a single wanton twerk.

As I walked to the parking lot, I began considering the potential consequences of Wrightman's request. There was nothing especially threatening about Ian Wrightman, nothing he'd done in his political career that caused my warning lights to start flashing. He'd staked a claim to the political middle, and as far as I knew, he had held on to that position as tightly as a sailor hugging a mast in a hurricane. There was nothing he'd done in his career that struck me as being inherently evil. But still.

Evil is real. I'd seen it close up. I laughed as easily and as often as I did because if I let those horrors live in my head, I'd never have another good day. Spend as much time as I did in the places I've been, and if you don't come back as a cynic, then there's really something wrong with you. I'd seen the things human beings are capable of doing. I'd watched passively evil people like Trump, whose own psychological problems allowed him to hurt people without regret or even understanding of the damage he was doing. I'd watched the religious fanatics, the people in the desert plotting against civilization and the Mike Pences of the first world, all of whom justified their actions by claiming allegiance to a greater good, anointing themselves vessels carrying out their Lord's will rather than accepting responsibility for their actions.

Ian Wrightman didn't strike me as any of them. There was a certain unctuous smoothness in his manner; but he wasn't an irrational zealot. He was as radical as the latest polls, as religious as American politics demanded. Rather than passion, he had calculation. That made him a wild card.

I wasn't sure it made him dangerous, but it definitely made me nervous. Being granted the powers that went with a declaration of war would essentially make him king. The powers of the president had expanded almost continuously for decades as Congress ceded more and more of their constitutional responsibilities to the executive branch. But war powers were the keys to the kingdom. He would be unchecked by traditional checks and balances. He could pretty much take whatever steps he decided were necessary. He could use the Constitution as a road map or as toilet paper. The dictatorial powers that Trump had dreamed about and reached for, he would have in his grasp. Maybe that wasn't the level of power you wanted to hand to a wild card.

The question that rattled in my mind like a can of oil bouncing around in a trunk on a dirt road was *why?* Why did he need more power than he already possessed? The why had always intrigued me: Why did a billionaire need a second billion dollars? Why did dictators risk what they already controlled to gain more? I couldn't wait to get to the office to start sorting out these thoughts. This is what we did best at the *Pro*: take a complex situation and run it through the mind grinder to make it easy to understand and digest. It was going to be a long night, and I expected to love every minute of it.

And then I got to the parking lot.

12

I did not have the emotional attachment to Van that I had to Mighty Chair or Cher. I liked Van; he was reliable and dependable. He was always there when I needed him and required little maintenance. But to my mind, Van lacked the panache of Mighty Chair or the warmth of Cher.

I had parked Van at a diagonal to the curb in the last handicapped spot on the right. There were several feet of empty space next to me, painted with blue crisscrossed lines prohibiting parking. That was pretty much a necessity when I was driving alone. It left me sufficient room to remotely slide open the side panel and extend the ramp. Van's single front seat was on tracks that enabled it to slide back and forth between the driver's slot and the passenger side, which enabled someone else to drive. If Jenny or someone else was with me, I didn't need that extra room on my right; I could park anywhere. The other person could back Van out of a spot and lower the ramp for me. But if I was alone, that space was essential.

Jenny had met me at Lucille's and we were planning on going home together. Instead, she had taken an Uber back to the Hill. But some jerk had wedged an expensive sports car in the restricted space on Van's right. In their quest to protect that car, they had not left enough room for me to extend and lower the ramp.

Yes, I was pissed. I had spent considerable thought and the necessary time and money to create a world in which I could live a life that was as close to normal as possible. Most things just required a little extra planning and anticipating the hurdles I might encounter. The important people in my life had become so used to Chair that they rarely even thought about it. At times they had even won bar bets, usually a free round, wagering that Chair and I could complete some esoteric task. But this one, this was tough. If I had one of the new self-driving vans, I could have backed it out, but I didn't. And I couldn't materialize the extra few feet I needed.

It was a big deal. This wasn't the first time it had happened. It actually was a pretty common problem in my community. We talked about it at rehab. One friend had been forced to spend a cold night shivering outside when his spot had been blocked. Another time he had gotten so angry when people without need had taken the handicapped spots at a restaurant that he had parked his van lengthwise behind them, blocking them in. About an hour later, the manager had asked him to move his van so the other people could get out. He would be delighted to do so, he said, as soon as he was finished with his dinner. When the other drivers complained, he suggested they call the police, who might wonder why they had parked illegally in those handicapped spots.

I had options. I could ride Mighty Chair the seven blocks to the office or call a Lyft van, but you know what, I didn't want to. This thoughtlessness, this sense of entitlement, made me furious. Wrightman's speech had put me in a rotten mood and this only added to it. "Cher," said the devil inside me, "open the panel door, please."

The door slid open. "Cher, extend the ramp." In response the ridged metal ramp eased out of Van, a sharp corner digging into the sports car's door. "Cher, lower the ramp, please." The ramp descended, gouging a perfectly vertical slice in the sports car's metallic paint job. After the ramp settled on the pavement, I instructed, "Cher, raise the ramp." The ramp retraced the cut into the door with a deeper growl than I'd expected, but still satisfying. It then retreated back into Van, disappearing innocently as the panel door slid closed behind it.

I turned on Mighty Chair's blinking night-lights, which were powered by stored electricity generated by the wheels, and took off for the office, whistling a ragged version of "Satisfaction."

It took me about twenty minutes to get there. During the trip I was surprised to see several seemingly handmade signs supporting Wright-man's request already posted in windows. Three themes appeared re-peatedly: 1. It's U.S. or the terrorists. 2. Tell Congress now or it will be never. 3. I [heart] America and I [poop] on terrorism. The fact that these three slogans had popped up almost immediately in several dif-ferent places made it obvious the administration was rolling out a pre-planned PR campaign.

On my way there, I made a point of stopping by Jerry Stern's night doorway. He was lying on a cardboard slab made from boxes, covered by a dirty blanket. He was asleep and I didn't wake him, but I put ten bucks in his cup and slid it under the corner of his blanket. Maybe it would be there when he woke up.

There was a growing pile of research neatly piled on my desk when I got to the office. Some of the information I already knew; some of it was a surprise. Franklin Roosevelt was the last president to ask Congress for an official declaration of war, his "Day of Infamy" speech. Since then, the country had been involved in the "police action" in Korea (I wondered who came up with that label) and "conflicts" or "extended military en-gagements" or "advisory or training roles" in Vietnam, the Persian Gulf, Afghanistan, and Iraq, in addition to Reagan's 1983 "foray" or "incursion" against Cuban Communists on the island of Grenada. We had also fought the undeclared cold war against communism and the drug wars in Cen-tral and South America—but no president since Roosevelt, responding to the attack on Pearl Harbor, had requested a formal war declaration.

Not surprisingly, former elected officials were speaking out force-fully, most of them happy to get the exposure, while current senators and members of Congress appeared to be in political hibernation. On the walls around me men and women were doing nighttime stand-ups in front of the brightly lit White House. There was a minor flare-up when CBS correspondent Major Garrett accidently wandered into ABC's Jonathan Karl's space as he was discussing this threat to peace. After a little pushing, the two men had to be separated by producers.

Wrightman sent a barrage of tweets intended to shape and reinforce public opinion, trying to harden support before the media could raise doubts:

Confidential briefings from top intelligence analysts after
cyjacking of Flt 342 persuade me this is essential . . .

Time to take the handcuffs off our brave fighting men and
women. Our enemy is getting bolder and more resourceful.
American lives are at stake . . .

Well-meaning people seem to be more concerned about
protecting the rights of terrorists than lives of Americans . . .

This is a temporary measure. You have my promise, as
leader of the free world, I will not abuse this grant of power.
By trusting me, you are trusting yourself . . .

And if there still was any doubt, first lady Charisma tweeted:

Wonderful news! Our daughter, America, is pregnant. We
should be grateful the president is doing what is necessary
to ensure our grandchild lives in a safe and secure country.

He was good, I had to give him that. He was raising all the usual
fears, calling out the familiar demons.

Several times in the next few hours I tried to reach Jenny. I wanted to
tell her about the Van incident as well as get a read on Martha McDonnell's attitude. Would she support the president? I assumed things were
even crazier on the Hill than they were in every news bureau, as people
scrambled to figure out what this might mean to the country and to
their careers, then determine how to react. As much as I hated to admit
it, I was feeling guilty about scribing that deep slice in the car door.
Even if the guy was a selfish jerk. Telling Jenny about it would get it off
my mind. Although I was pretty sure she would tell me what I already
knew, I'd have to find the guy and pay for the repair.

I found myself completely unexpectedly smiling. Life sure was simpler before I fell in love with a walking conscience. With great legs.

Love? The real *L* word? I remember sitting there amidst the confusion of that night and finally admitting it to myself. For the time being, I
decided, I would keep it a secret. Why risk ruining a good relationship?

As the coffee cups began piling up (fourteen) throughout the night, bits
of information supposedly leaked from the White House. They weren't

leaks, the administration was watering its plants—growing the story. The challenge for us was to figure out what was public relations and what was real information. According to these so-called sources, Wrightman's request was going to be delivered to Congress that afternoon. Supposedly there had been considerable debate about doing this at the "highest levels." The initiative was reported to have been led by Charisma Wrightman, while Attorney General Langsam planned to resign in protest.

One report I was certain had been planted was a rumor that the president's first action under these powers would be to declare a weeklong tax holiday to stimulate the economy, the third time that rumor had surfaced at a convenient moment. But this time it might prove true. Throughout American political history, bribery has always proved to be an effective strategy. Money is a good argument.

I read and reread the research and the stories being posted by other outlets and listened to the instant analysis. Howie and I discussed it. Then I sat down to stake out the editorial position for the *Pro*. As always happened, when I was ready, the ideas that had been born, nurtured, and developed deep in my subconscious suddenly popped onto my screen to be honed into a coherent column. The writing process has always been beyond my understanding. Maybe other people work differently, but for me the keys seem to form a bridge between my subconscious and the finished page, passing completely over most conscious thought. To be honest, there are times I'm surprised and delighted (or dismayed) to read what I was thinking.

I wrote:

> Like millions of Americans on election day, I voted for Ian Wrightman to become president of the United States. I did so because I believed this country was locked in an untenable political gridlock. It was my hope that a moderate, independent leader might find a way to bring us together. But I was wrong. President Wrightman's request for a congressional declaration of war against international terrorism is the most dangerous reach for dictatorial powers in my lifetime. If we truly value those principles on which this nation was founded, Congress must reject this effort . . .

The words just poured out of me, flowing onto the screen. At times I felt like Lucy and Ethel on that assembly line, the words coming so fast I barely had time to discard the bad ones. Whatever trust or hopes I once had in the administration had disappeared one bloody night in Detroit, I wrote. "It is my firm belief that legalized murder was committed that night and the administration has lied blatantly about it." I wanted to reveal my hospital visit from Dick and Francis and the existence of the National Secrets Act, but Howie talked me down. Live to fight and all that rah-rah.

The remainder of the column outlined the consequences of a declaration of war. Short form: It would allow the president to unilaterally suspend the Bill of Rights. I concluded:

> This declaration would grant to the president emergency powers to enforce his desires on all of our lives, stripping from us the protections of our basic freedoms. Would you have granted those powers to Trump? Not me. So why would we grant them to anyone in this situation? These powers would give to the federal government the right to compel federal and local law enforcement agencies and the military to enforce any and all of its decrees, no matter how outrageous they might be. This is how dictatorships are born.
>
> Sinclair Lewis warned us in his pre–World War II classic novel, *It Can't Happen Here,* that if we are to survive as a great nation, we must zealously protect our fundamental rights. It is with great sadness that all these years later it is necessary to repeat that warning, and to sound the alarm: It *can* happen here.

The debate in Congress was spirited. A lot of bright people said a lot of smart words. They definitely sounded defiant. Watching it was a waste of time, but intellectually stimulating. After almost two days, citing Article One, section eight of the Constitution, a joint session of Congress voted to declare that a state of war existed between the United States of America and International Terrorism.

This marked the first time a sovereign nation had declared war on an amorphous enemy, an enemy consisting of small groups, individuals, and essentially any person or entity Wrightman decided was the enemy. It was an enemy with many names, different objectives, and no central command, an enemy that avoided fixed battles and waged war against civilians and soft targets.

A substantial majority of Congress supported the declaration. The White House had successfully ginned up so much fear that it was the politically expedient vote. Only those few secure in their office or planning retirement dared buck the winds of blind patriotism. Martha was one of them, to her credit. On the floor of the house she said she refused to hand unlimited power to any one person, no matter how noble the purpose. "In their wisdom our founding fathers gave us an ingenious system of checks and balances. It has been the bedrock of our government for almost 250 years, and I'll be damned if I'll be frightened into abandoning it."

Martha was great. So were a few others. She created a stir when she demanded the roll be called rather than accepting a voice vote. That meant that the vote of each senator and member had to be publicly recorded, a parliamentary move she defended because "years from now I want Americans to know who voted to give away our democracy." While there was some grumbling, it didn't change a vote; none of her colleagues were willing to risk being blamed when the next terrorist attack took place.

Which also was a memorable threat from the administration. The White House media manipulation campaign was hugely successful. Every published poll showed that more than 91 percent of all Americans were strongly opposed to terrorist attacks.

The day after the vote protesters were out in the streets once again. Police and militia successfully prevented large groups from gathering, but the opposition stayed together in groups of four or less. There still was no law against carrying signs, and homemade signs criticizing this as a "legal coup!" were everywhere. At the same time anti-administration leaders were emerging, among them Indiana "Senator Pete" Buttigieg, who strolled down Mulberry Street in his hometown of South Bend, Indiana, the sleeves of his work shirt rolled up. When he was arrested for disturbing the peace, he went with the South Bend officers peacefully.

The photograph of Senator Buttigieg being led away, hands cuffed behind him, chin defiantly thrust upward, was published around the country by the underground newspapers that were beginning to emerge. News organizations like the *Pro* were urged to report his arrest, which we did, presumably to serve as a warning. But that photograph of his perp walk was not allowed to be circulated under the new regulations.

Not that it makes any difference now, but I still sometimes wonder if people knew then what was about to happen, would they have responded differently? Obviously we'll never know. I like to believe they would have, but then I remember what America had transformed into by that point. Even if people had wanted to react, what could they have done? And when I do, it makes me ... it makes me so very sad that young people will never understand or appreciate what was lost.

Wrightman waited only a few days before utilizing these new wartime powers. It was Trump who had initially attacked social media—Facebook, Twitter, Instagram, TikTok, WeChat, and Pinterest—claiming they were being used against him by his political enemies. Without evidence he accused them of censoring right-wing posts—and naturally his followers believed him. In fact, the evidence is just the opposite: members of right-wing fringe groups actually had found each other on Facebook.

Wrightman understood the capabilities of media hubs to bring together people, reinforce their anger, and allow them to coordinate events. In this case, people who might oppose him. To prevent that from happening, with minimal public disclosure, Homeland Security alerted each of the social media platforms that the anti-American activities being planned on their sites constituted "a clear and present danger to public safety" and ordered them to "take any and all steps necessary" to prevent those activities. It was not a subtle threat: You censor your site or we will. There was no public announcement, but suddenly protest organizers saw posts removed or rejected.

I had long been active on all of those platforms; to me they were just as essential as reading the daily newspapers. RollingStone467@writerman—that's me. More accurately, it *was* me. I didn't post very often, although I did share funny animal videos when I thought people needed to see goats and giraffes bonding or a bear pushing a man in a wheelchair. I sent birthday and celebratory wishes and participated in Nats player debates, but as a journalist I kept my political opinions to myself. Well, actually myself and the almost million regular readers of the *Pro*. I barely noticed several "cyber-friends" disappearing. These were people I had been silently following because their opinions, whether or not I agreed with them, allowed me to get a sense of the public pulse. Suddenly they weren't posting anymore. At the time I didn't think much about it, but now I realize this was the first cyber-roundup.

(The good news was that, at least judging by the posts I did continue to receive, that the government did not think additional credit cards, Wrightman bobblehead dolls, or generic little blue pills posed a threat to the general order.)

As protests were successfully defused, White House surrogates continually reassured Americans that this "purely technical legislation" would not impact their daily lives—but would make them considerably safer. Proud grandmother-to-be Charisma Wrightman went on *The View* and told a dubious Whoopi that most Americans wouldn't notice any differences, describing it as that kind of great deal in which you trade something you never use, "something that was up in the attic that you even forgot was there," for a brand-new toaster oven. Then the panel bantered pleasantly about her first grandchild.

During a rare *Fox & Friends* appearance, a genial Vice President Hunter reminded his hosts that the Constitution had been written centuries earlier, "long before we had electric lights and flight seemed like an impossible dream," so even men as brilliant as the founding fathers could not have foreseen the complexities of the modern world. "Which is why," he explained in his guise as a constitutional expert, "in the very first article of that hallowed document they provided the mechanism we are using today, right now, to modernize and protect it to make certain [index-finger-pointing certain] that the principles it enumerates endure exactly as they were given to us, with only a few necessary changes, for at least another quarter-millennium!"

On *Saturday Night Live*'s Weekend Update the following Saturday, Thomas Jefferson, played in a surprise guest appearance by Will Ferrell, demanded that the "revised and updated" constitution include such articles as "freedom from Kardashian selfies" and an official price list for lobbyists interested in purchasing their own senator.

The administration's first public action was to divide the country into twelve military districts. This was done purely for administrative and budgetary purposes, Secretary of Defense McCord explained, and would not have any effect on daily life. People should just go about their normal business. No one would even notice it, other than noticing new patches appearing on the uniforms of the active military and militia they might encounter. The greater Washington area was designated District 1 and Marine major general Michael "Steel Mike" Herman was named military governor.

Someday I intend to write an essay entitled "The Role of Coffee in Fomenting a Revolution." Voltaire, for example, supposedly drank as many as fifty-two cups of coffee a day (demitasse, I am assuming) while laying the philosophical groundwork for the French Revolution. We definitely had the coffee; it was the revolution we were lacking. There didn't seem to be any great interest in fighting the government.

That became apparent to me at the gym a few mornings later. The Light Brigade had edged a little deeper into politics, and we were debating the potential ramifications of this war declaration. To my surprise, people were pretty evenly divided about it, and unlike most issues, those feelings did not necessarily follow party loyalty. Maybe it's accurate to say they were independently passive. The two lawyers were split, the detective wanted to see how it was utilized before he reached any conclusion, and the TV producer praised it for the stability it promised. The Georgetown professor, while admitting some uneasiness about it, took comfort in McCord's contention that it shouldn't affect any law-abiding citizen.

"I wonder if you guys really get this!" I shouted. My shouting got their attention. I was lying on my back, doing reps with 125 pounds. I was sweating, but my anger at this response had pushed me to another five reps. "It means some government bureaucrat is now free to listen to your phone calls, read your emails, and hack into your computer without a search warrant."

Charlie Fitzgerald was doing leg lifts (no, I didn't take that personally) and responded, "You know what, Rol, I have to tell you, if I have to give up a little privacy if it means all of us are a little safer, then as long as they don't tell my wife anything I don't want her to know, then it's okay with me. I mean, c'mon, what do I have to hide?"

I rested the weight bar on the stand and looked at him with disbelief. "Charlie, you're a lobbyist."

His mouth fell open with feigned astonishment. "Oh, oh yeah. Wait a second, I take that back. I never said what I said. What I'm really in favor of is an invasion of everybody else's privacy!" He thoroughly enjoyed the laughter he got. "You got to lighten up, Rollie. You're making more out of this than it's worth. This is just turning de facto into de facts."

That whole discussion was still resonating in my mind when I walked into the office and discovered Dick and Francis waiting for me. They were sitting comfortably in Howie's office, looking as smug as a Homeland Security bug in a Persian carpet. They were wearing, as far as I could determine, the same nondescript gray suits. Maybe that was a new uniform. They clearly had established their authority over the space.

Howie was actively ignoring them, overdoing his "I don't want to talk to you" paper-shuffling act. As I approached, Little Dick stood and asked me to come inside.

"Can't," I said, spreading my hands to indicate that Mighty Chair was wider than the doorway. "Sorry." That wasn't true, obviously—all I had to do was flip up Chair's arms—but they didn't know that. Howie flashed me his oh-you-naughty-guy semi-smile.

"Is there a place we can speak in private?" Francis asked.

"Absolutely," Howie said with enthusiasm. He stood and commanded, "Let's go to the executive suite. Follow me!"

As we walked single file through the office, down a short corridor, I began softly whistling the "Colonel Bogey March" from *The Bridge on the River Kwai*. We all squeezed into the men's room. A toilet flushed and we waited patiently as a man washed his hands and left with nary a curious glance. To demonstrate my respect for these agents, I backed Mighty Chair into the extra-wide handicapped stall and waited there with the door wide open. "Thank you for coming to my office, gentle-men," I said.

"Mr. Stone," Dick began, "you've been identified by Homeland Se-curity as an opinion maker, and . . ."

"Wow. Gentlemen, thank you. Seriously, thank you. Hear that, Howie, just like I've been telling you. About that raise . . ."

Dick did not appreciate my attitude. "Hey, let's stop shitting around here, okay?"

It was impossible not to laugh. I mean, literally impossible.

"Okay, I get it," Dick said, letting his anger seep through. "You're the smart one and we're the bad guys. Know something else, smart guy? I don't give a fuck what you think. Things have changed a whole lot in the last few days and people like you better get used to it. We're legally at war now and there are serious penalties for subversion. None of us want—"

"Go fuck yourself," I said. I hadn't left my legs in the desert to be lec-tured by an asshole. Are you kidding me? "Seriously?" I asked. "You're actually threatening me?" I would have stepped toward him, but honestly, rolling close to someone lacked the inherent threat of closing that gap.

Howie saw what was coming. "Rollie, c'mon."

"Just hold on a second," Francis said in the least threatening tone he could muster. "Don't get us wrong. We're not trying to tell you what you can write or post. We'd just like you to show a little loyalty to your country."

"Show some loyalty?" I questioned. "Show some fucking loyalty?" My voice rose. "How the fuck do you think I got into this chair?"

Howie stepped between us like a fight referee. "Stop! Just stop!" He looked at them. "You guys have made your point. We get it." He faced me. "Right, Rollie?" I was too angry to answer, so he repeated with a little more insistence, "Right, Rollie?"

Dick didn't wait for an answer. "Look, Stone," he said, "we're not your enemy—"

"Yes," I told him, "you are."

"That's it," he said, turning, "I'm outta here." When he reached the door, he stopped and waved a cautionary finger at me. "You've been warned."

The door closed slowly behind them. I looked at Howie and shook my head with disappointment. "Well, you sure were a big help. You still don't get it, do you? You still don't see it?"

Howie leaned backward, bracing himself against a sink. "I need you to come with me later," he told me. There was a firmness in his voice that made it clear this wasn't optional. "Don't ask me any questions." As we were leaving the men's room, he added, "And don't mention this to anyone." He paused and then repeated for emphasis: "And I mean *anyone.*"

I have to admit that Little Dick was right about one thing: My increased visibility had made me a go-to person for anyone who believed they had evidence of government malfeasance. Since the garage, I had been regularly receiving emails from people describing every type of plot from CIA agents implanting transmitters in their teeth to a secret agreement with China to take control of the world. I dutifully printed them all out and stored them in a folder. Eventually it would make a good story. That turned out to have been a smart thing to do; when I checked my in-box later that afternoon, many of them had simply disappeared.

I got the message.

There were a measly eight empty coffee cups piled on my desk when I took a late-afternoon meditation break. Usually I was able to dismiss my thoughts and flow easily and briefly into a deep state of relaxation. Not today, though. My mind was churning, and when I lowered my conscious defenses, a cavalry of disturbing thoughts came charging into my mind. The theft of American democracy was taking place in plain sight and nobody was doing anything to stop it. When I was in the hospital, government agents had ordered me not to report a story, and this morning they had returned to warn me against sharing my opinions. That wasn't America. That was an alternative America, a place where the president openly used the Justice Department to pursue a political enemy. That was *1984.* That was a Trump/Barr wet dream. There were no realistic limits to a president's power; citing national security, he or she could simply ignore the Constitution, and the secret Homeland Security courts would support that.

The worst part of my meditation is that I had to listen to myself whining.

As Howie had instructed, I met him at eight o'clock, in the parking lot of a twenty-four-hour CVS in Arlington. It was raining lightly. I'd told Jenny I was meeting a potential source, knowing she wouldn't ask questions about that. *I'm not really lying to her,* I lied to myself. But I had given Howie my word. I was sitting in Van, the heater fogging the windows, singing along with Muddy Waters's version of "Mannish Boy" from the Band's *Last Waltz,* when Howie climbed into the passenger seat. He ran his hand through the last remaining strands of his hair to brush off the droplets. He was wearing the same ragged jeans and sports coat he'd been wearing earlier in the day. "So what's this all about?" I asked.

Howie was as serious as I had ever seen him, and that covered a lot of ground. I'd been there when his second child had been born prematurely and had struggled to stay alive. He had the same type of grim look on his face. Rather than turning down the music, he turned up the volume, then leaned across the center console. "I need your word that you're never going to talk about anything you see tonight." He pursed his lips, took a considered breath, and added, "And that includes to Jenny."

I felt like I had walked into a John le Carré story. "Wait now, what's going on, Howe? What does Jenny have to do with this?"

Our faces were no more than eight inches apart. "Your word, Rol, or we'll say good night and forget about this."

Sure, walk away and spend the rest of my life wondering what this was all about. Walk away with the understanding that my relationship with Howie was changed forever. Some chance. He had grabbed hold of me right where he intended, right in my curiosity. "Okay, yeah." I swiped my hand across my body like I was cleaning an invisible counter. "Nobody."

He leaned back in his seat, turning down the music. "Okay, let's go. Just follow what I tell you."

"You want me to give Cher the address?"

"No, absolutely not. And turn your phone off too."

"Cher, turn off your GPS, please."

I followed Howie's instructions through Arlington, got on and off the 495, and ended up in a residential neighborhood in Annandale. We parked on a quiet block of well-maintained brick-bottomed split-levels. We sat in the car for a few minutes as Howie checked the mirrors. I assumed he was confirming we weren't followed. We definitely weren't followed. "Let's go," he said.

The rain had mostly stopped, but the night was crisp. The sky was black and pocked with stars. We walked about four blocks through a lovely, quiet neighborhood. Each of the houses had the same bones, but upper floors and dormers, garages and porticoes, porches and decks, walks and landscaping had been added as the development settled. A couple of cars passed us; a woman was dutifully picking up her dog's poop and two kids were riding their bicycles. Howie ignored them. "Where are we going?" I asked. I knew it was a stupid question, but I wanted the comfort of hearing my own voice.

"You'll see."

We finally stopped across the street from a lovely red brick and white-washed wood church. A sign in front announced in white plastic letters that there were services Sunday at 9:00 and 11:00, and suggested provocatively, "Say your prayers, you never know Who's listening!" There were only a few cars in its side parking lot. We followed a gravel path around to a rear entrance. In addition to a stairway, a wooden ramp abutted the building, the type that had been hastily added to satisfy the Americans with Disabilities Act. Howie walked alongside me as we went up that ramp. The rear windows were covered with curtains, but lights were on in the rear of the church. When we reached the landing, I grabbed Howie's arm before he could open the door. "Okay, now tell me."

He nodded. "Welcome to the resistance, Rollie."

13

I f this was the resistance, it was time to start boning up on my Canadian. Most of the people gathered there looked like members of the losing team at a Sunday picnic sack race.

We were in a small room behind the sanctuary. Its paneled wooden walls had been painted white. A large cork bulletin board was covered with overlapping messages affixed to it with bright-colored tacks. A trestle table covered with white paper from a long commercial roll had been pushed against a far wall, just under a colorful lithograph of a benevolent Christ. The Lord appeared to be staring down at a tray of cheese and crackers, bottles of soda and specialty waters, and, fittingly, white wine.

There were about forty people standing in small groups. Several of them looked vaguely familiar, but there was one person I recognized instantly. "We're glad you're here," Congresswoman Martha McDonnell said to me as she grasped my hand with both of hers. After a brief exchange, Howie wandered away, leaving us alone. The congresswoman sat down right next to me and leaned over, making it impossible for anyone else to hear her. "I know this is hard for you to hear, Rollie. We would have invited you to join us a while ago, but to be perfectly honest, we're not a hundred percent certain about Jenny."

"What? What are you talking about?" I gave it a few seconds to sink in; instead it floated on the surface of my mind. "That's total bullshit, Martha. C'mon, are you kidding me?"

"I wish I was," she said heavily. There was just enough pain in her voice to convince me she was serious. "And believe me, even more than you, I hope I'm wrong. I love Jenny too. At least as much as you do. But things have happened around the office that have forced me to wonder. So until we're sure, the stakes are just too high."

How do you respond to an absurd accusation made about the most important person in your life? Maybe I should have walked out right then, but I didn't. I wanted to hear what McDonnell had to say. I had remained outwardly calm, and to demonstrate that, I closed my eyes and asked in a restrained voice, "What are you talking about?"

McDonnell took hold of Mighty Chair's arm with both hands, using it for leverage as she leaned closer. "No one loves this country more than Jenny," she said. "No one. I get that. That's why she went into govern-ment service. Did she tell you her uncle was killed on 9/11?"

I nodded. "Of course."

"He sat at his desk waiting to die, Rollie. He called her aunt to say goodbye. That family has made a big investment in this country." She actually tapped me gently on my arm as she added, "As you well know. But maybe that's why it's so hard for her to see what's really happening."

I still didn't believe her. "Oh, please," I said, waving away the thought. "Give me an example."

She hesitated, which I took as a small victory. "It isn't that easy. There isn't any one thing. But when I ask her opinion about something the president proposes or has done, her response has always been, 'Go slow, he's the president, give him a chance.'"

That struck home. I heard her telling me, "Sometimes it's necessary."

"Rollie, I don't know where she stands right now. Today. But we can't take any chances. She'll . . ."

"She would never betray—"

"Absolutely not," she snapped, not letting me finish. "Of course not. Not in a million years. Jenny is someone who tries to see the good in everyone. So getting to where we are isn't going to be easy for her. You know that.

"Rollie," Martha continued, "we'll understand if you can't stay."

I stayed. We had a much longer discussion than I'm reporting here, but that was the heart of it. My feelings were all jumbled—my loyalty, my love for Jenny crashing headlong into my love for the idea of America. Not only was I being asked to join a semi-organized resistance to the government that I hadn't known existed, I also was being warned that the woman I loved might not be exactly that person I held so tightly in bed. What was racing through my mind wasn't just thoughts; the whole damn Indianapolis 500 was thundering in there.

Could I really have been that oblivious? I scoured my memory, trying to pinpoint one moment, one word that might make me question Jenny. The military had trained me to pay attention to small cues that created a large picture: a sudden increase in the frequency with which a soldier left the office for a smoke or bathroom break; unexplained wear on the heels of combat boots; any change in an established pattern or habitual behavior. That awareness had become ingrained in me, but Jenny?

Maybe she didn't rail against Wrightman as strongly as I did, but that was her nature, her inherent kindness. Remember, Jenny the optimist meets Rollie the pessimist? La-la-la and all that, why can't we all be friends? I didn't know how to react to all this. Maybe I should have walked out. That certainly would have changed everything, but whether that would have been for better or for worse, I will never know.

I stayed, but I couldn't decide if that was an act of courage or cowardice.

Before the program started, several people made a point of introducing themselves to me. First names only for security purposes. Who knew if even those names were real? Among those people was a sparkling young woman with unusually round blue eyes that stood out boldly against her flowing jet-black hair. She looked vaguely familiar but I couldn't place her. Her name tag identified her as Laura, so at least for that night she was Laura. She greeted Howie, who was still Howie, who introduced her to me. I remained Rollie; I was too well known in Washington to be anyone else. (Although I did flirt briefly with being

Biff for the night; I've had an odd affection for that name since I played Biff Loman in a college production of *Death of a Salesman*.) My mind was much too caught up with Jenny to pay attention to Laura, but I advise you to remember her name. She'll show up again.

This organization, I learned that night, had sprung up several months earlier. Similar local groups were spreading across the country. It had no name; the consensus being a lack of identity would make it difficult to identify: How could anyone be a member of a group that didn't consider itself a group? There were no leaders, no central communications, and its financial resources seemed limited to a collection bowl sitting on the table. There wasn't even a secret handshake. But everyone was asked never to talk about it and certainly never to write about it. It didn't exist except when it did.

The local groups were linked together loosely by a chain of men and women called "two-staters." These were people who carried information back and forth between their home state and one neighboring state. The whole operation was essentially a national game of telephone. It was arguably the least efficient means of communications short of smoke signals, but at this stage of development the organization without a name or leadership was still small and contained enough for it to be sufficient. And it provided extraordinary secrecy.

There was no formal program. No schedule of events. No one was urging anyone else to take specific actions. It became clear very quickly this was little more than a like-minded group of people getting together to air their grievances against the government. People stood up and told their stories. I'd attended several AA and NA meetings because I thought it was important to understand addiction, and in structure, this meeting was vaguely similar. An older potbellied man described the growing sense of mistrust in his once-harmonious insurance office as people became reluctant to talk about much other than TV programs, movies, and sports. A woman who described herself as a soccer mom complained that her child was required to recite the New American Pledge in his second-grade class every morning.

The two-stater from Virginia had some disquieting news. The movement was growing so rapidly that the government had become aware of its existence and was beginning to gather intelligence about it. A member of the group had been detained in Springfield, Illinois. Under the new regulations no charges had been filed against him, so it was unclear if his detention had anything to do with his participation in the meetings. War regs allowed law enforcement and, under certain conditions, militia groups, to hold people in custody for an extended period without officially filing charges. Supposedly this allowed the government sufficient time to question potential terrorists before his or her collaborators became aware of that arrest.

My attention kept shifting focus; I'd be listening when suddenly all I could think about was Jenny. Then after a few minutes I'd find myself back in the discussion. As one speaker was outlining the various ways Wrightman might legally use the hundreds of special powers given to the president through the decades by Congress, I found myself wondering if the men who came together in the churches and taverns of Boston 250 years ago to protest the injustices of the king might have felt as impotent and inconsequential as I did at that moment. Did those men, Sam Adams and Hancock and Revere among them, truly believe they could be more than a mosquito bite on the ass of the greatest empire in history? When they started meeting, I remembered from my history courses at Michigan, they had no intention of founding a nation. They didn't threaten war. They simply wanted their government in England to extend to the colonies the same rights given to its other possessions.

I looked around the room. As much as I tried, I couldn't imagine Adams and Jefferson in a sack race. (And the name Biff Jefferson did seem to lack the necessary gravitas.) But I was struck by the sincerity of the people there. These were people who understood what was slipping away and wanted to prevent it from happening. During that sweep I caught Laura-for-the-night looking at me quizzically. Too late, she averted her eyes, and then made a show of rubbing them, jutting out her chin and turning toward the speaker.

This particular speaker was advocating the publication of cyber-pamphlets on pop-up pirate sites. The administration had successfully cowed major media outlets into self-censoring content. Broadcast "news" had become so bland, in fact, that at the *Pro* we laughingly had begun referring to Chuck Todd's once-incisive Sunday morning show as *Meet the Presbyterians.*

There was some support in the room for using these pirate sites just as the founding fathers had circulated anonymous pamphlets, to spread information and sow dissent. I started to raise my hand; I wanted to discuss where sites like the *Pro* fit in, but Howie put a restraining hand on my shoulder. "Not yet," he mouthed.

Martha McDonnell was the final speaker. She described in general terms what was going on in Congress, admitting surprise that so many smart, decent people had rolled over so quickly and quietly. Their lack of moral courage had been a great disappointment, she said. In response she had organized a small group of people she trusted, they were calling themselves the Congressional Knitting Society, although thus far they hadn't settled on any course of action, or for that matter, any knitting pattern.

Martha was a gifted speaker. She was a small woman, but her voice projected an oversize load of candor and intelligence. The whole room was leaning forward to catch every word. The most visible change on the Hill, she explained, had been the emergence of lobbyists as middlemen. The administration had designated certain lobbyists to carry its demands—and its rewards to those who publicly supported Wrightman. A woman raised her hand and asked, "Is that ethical?"

The whole room erupted in laughter. When it quieted, McDonnell responded, "It's Congress."

Martha the teacher then gave a brief lesson on the presidential use of special powers. I knew a bit about it, having done background research when Trump claimed his emergency powers allowed him to build his wall. "The powers of POTUS to take affirmative actions during a crisis have never been completely defined or expressively limited, either by constitutional law or congressional action." She was standing in the middle of the room, turning slowly so we all could hear her. "In fact, no one has been able to even define what constitutes a crisis. Congress and the judiciary have invariably permitted the executive branch to take whatever actions unilaterally deemed necessary to meet existing conditions . . ." She coughed, a dramatic tool, then added, ". . . without restraint. In fact, those powers might be viewed as elastic, as they have been stretched by various administrations to meet a variety of real and imagined challenges.

"Let me also remind you that in addition to government cooperation the exercise of these powers has required the acquiescence of a supportive public, which accepts the actions to be both necessary and appropriate to protect this country." She made one full turn to make sure she had the attention of every person in that room. "If we're going to stop Wrightman, this is where we need to start."

Her lesson continued; the application of these special powers actually predated the founding of the republic. The Continental Congress passed acts and resolutions that permitted the nascent government to successfully prosecute the Revolutionary War. President Washington took actions not granted or proscribed when he raised a militia to combat antitax protestors. It actually was quite similar to the way Wrightman had done it. "Whoever is advising him," she said, nodding with admiration, "they know what they're doing."

Martha was no slouch, either. She knew her stuff. When Lincoln had utilized his presidential powers to quash dissent during the Civil War, the Supreme Court had decided that "the government, within the Constitution has all the powers granted to it which are necessary to preserve its existence."

The list was much longer than I had realized. Woody Wilson had used these powers to raise and equip an expeditionary force to fight the Germans in World War I. FDR had discovered unexpressed powers to impose economic controls during the Depression and later intern American citizens of Japanese descent after the attack on Pearl Harbor. Harry Truman sent troops to Korea; Kennedy and Johnson sent them to Vietnam. Ronald Reagan gave permission to the National Security Agency to conduct domestic surveillance. And Wrightman had already begun, updating existing Executive Orders 12333 and 10990, which gave the president the power to seize control of modes of transportation, including "railroads, waterways, and public storage facilities" to include "driverless vehicles and all modes of transportation known now or to be invented in the future."

There was hardly a sound in the room as she told us what was possible. And when these actions had been taken in the past, most Americans, just as was happening now, accepted them without complaint. "A nation of squeakless mice," she called them. Martha concluded her lecture with an especially apropos quote from Richard Nixon's White House lawyer, John Dean. "'Democracy works best in times of peace, where there is debate, compromise, and deliberation informing government rules, regulations and policies. When confronted with a major crisis—particularly one that is, like terrorism, of an unfamiliar nature—the nation will turn to the president for initiative and resolute leadership.'" She raised her voice to make sure everybody heard the last few words. "'If our very existence and way of life are threatened, Americans will want their president to do whatever is necessary.' Just think about that." Martha certainly had mastered the political skill of holding an audience. "'To do whatever is necessary.'"

She stood silent, letting her last few words sink in. Essentially, she warned, there were no limits on presidential power. And Wrightman had exceeded them.

As Howie and I were driving back to Arlington I felt a long-dormant surge of excitement. If I didn't know it was impossible, I could have sworn I felt it in my legs. But that, I knew, was my mind playing jokes on my body. I was feeling the same type of exhilaration I'd chased during my operational days, when I was applying camouflage or putting on a disguise or winding down. Overcover or undercover, I was going into the mix, I was in the game. I'd gotten a whiff of that tonight. For a long time I'd been pounding out copy that didn't seem to make any difference. I didn't have the slightest idea whether this was just revolutionary masturbation or the beginning of something important. I just knew it felt great to get off my ass and do something.

Before Howie hopped out, I apologized for my outburst earlier that morning, when I'd watched him fold in front of the Homeland Security agents. There was a stew of emotions roiling his voice as he took one really deep breath and responded, "I didn't have a choice. Those guys were as serious as the pandemic. If this thing keeps going south, we're going to need each other."

My apartment felt emptier than usual that night. Jenny had worked late and had decided to go to her place. I gave her my usual chipper Rollie when we spoke, telling her my meeting with a potential source had gone okay. She knew not to ask any more questions. Boy, I hated lying to her. There was a part of me that wanted to set a small trap that would allow me to dig into her psyche and find out what was really going on; another part just wanted to ask the question out loud, rather than letting it hang there. It was like trying to grab a fistful of cotton candy.

Instead, when we said good night, I just told her flat out, "You know I love you." And as I said it, I realized that I meant it.

Her response was the ultimate payback: a long thoughtful silence. Maybe she was wondering where those words had come from, and why so suddenly? "Yeah?" she said finally. "Okay, then I love you too."

Did her response lack conviction? I wondered. It sure sounded to me like it did. Maybe she didn't really mean it. Maybe she just didn't want to hurt my feelings? My mind wasn't playing tricks; instead, it seemed to be playing the bongos in my chest.

"Say good night to Cher for me, please." And she was gone.

Not gone actually, just moved into my dreams. In those dreams she was lying next to me. Her body was warm and willing. I licked my index finger and drew small circles around her nipple. It hardened to my touch. Then I slowly moved my fingers down the contours of her body, resting finally on her firm inner thigh. She drew her legs together and made a small sound of pleasure.

I was kissing her gently, just brushing her lips with mine. Then using my elbow to balance myself, I had pushed over on top of her. For a moment we just lay there, staring into each other's eyes.

Later, as we lay satisfied in the flickering candlelight, she asked the lover's question: "Do I really make you happy?"

To which I responded with the bachelor's answer: "How can you even ask that?"

She wiggled a few inches away and propped herself and looked at me. "I don't know. Lately you just seem so . . ."—she frowned, unable to find the right word—". . . so preoccupied."

I mumbled my confusion. I'd invested my life in this country, in both its real and symbolic presence, and I couldn't ignore what was happening. I'd seen the faces of young people in Iraq and Yemen and Afghanistan as I told them about a place where people lived in safety and . . .

She placed a slender index finger over my lips, and as her hair cascaded on the pillow, she reassured me, "Oh my darling Rollie, you don't have to worry about any of that anymore. The American people are happy. We have a leader who cares so much about us watching over us, protecting us. People have jobs and homes and large-screen television sets. Children are being taught the right values. Why don't you just let yourself accept this? Why do you have to fight . . ."

I sat up. I shook my head clear of that dream. My pillow was drenched with sweat. It was as if I had survived my own *Invasion of the Body Snatchers*. This wasn't fair to Jenny, to convict her on the basis of some vague suggestion of unease. There were many parts to Jenny, which of course is what most men want in a woman. What I was doing wasn't fair, demanding she answer a question she hadn't been asked.

"Cher, come here, please." Cher woke Mighty Chair and directed him to the side of my bed. I muscled myself into it and we went into the bathroom. I threw cold water on my face, as cold as I could stand it, getting even with my subconscious. Until now I hadn't been personally affected by the political bitterness that had split families and ended friendships. During Trump/Pence I'd watched from a distance as insults replaced ideas and cursing substituted for commenting; as positions hardened and righteous anger split relationships as permanently as Lincoln had once split logs. When the Democrats regained power, I'd rooted for them, but from a safe journalist's distance.

I watched it unfold dispassionately. And with equal doses of wonder and amusement. As a journalist, I saw myself as an observer of a fascinating social experiment. I'd written several stories about the changing dynamics. One of them that got a lot of pickup was the story of a man who had tracked down someone who had insulted his intelligence on Facebook and shot him three times—apparently to prove he wasn't dumb. Until now, though, I had been a spectator, firm in my belief that these tectonic shifts didn't affect me personally.

Now I found myself staring at my reflection in a bathroom mirror at three o'clock in the morning. "This is crazy," I said aloud. "What am I doing? I *know* who she is. And even if . . ."

Even if? Even if?

"Stop it!" Whoa. The sound of my voice startled me. Yelling at my reflection was something I had never done before, and it was so outlandish I couldn't help smiling. This definitely was an interesting and unexpected turn in my life, and surprisingly, I sort of liked the feeling. "You talkin' to me?" I De Niroed, pointing to myself. "This is bullshit and you know it. Calm down. Be cool, man." And then I winked.

I had hung a gold-framed sampler crocheted by my sister on the wall opposite my bed. It supposedly was an old Chinese curse: "May you live in interesting times." It was the last thing I saw before I closed my eyes.

Jenny was still there, she'd been waiting in my mind. Either I trusted her or I didn't. There was no middle ground. The military was big on trust. They drilled it into us day after day, in the mud and in the sunshine. It was all-or-nothing, and yeah, your life might depend on that decision. And once trust was gone, it was almost impossible to restore.

To succeed, a dictator has to turn people against one another. He has to destroy trust. I made a decision that night: I was going to trust Jenny until the day, the moment, she gave me a reason not to. But after that, admittedly I found myself listening more closely to her words and weighing the meaning. And I was more careful when I responded.

If the next few weeks were a test, she passed. She was becoming more outspoken in her anger or perhaps frustration. When she began referring derisively to the Wrightman administration as "the regime," I appealed to Howie to invite her to a meeting. "It's time," I insisted. "I'll vouch for her."

"It's up to Martha," he told me.

"I thought there were no leaders?"

"There aren't, but some non-leaders are more equal than others."

This was arguably the most disorganized organization with which I had ever been involved. In the following weeks there was one more meeting, this one held in the rear of a hardware store. At least they told me where it was being held, which I considered progress. I admit it, the whole thing seemed like a colossal waste of time to me. When I complained to Howie, he quoted Lao Tzu: "The journey of a thousand miles begins with a single step."

"Yeah, well, that's probably going to be a problem for me," I responded.

Howie pointed out my hypocrisy. "Love it. Situational handicap."

Jenny was right, though: the administration had evolved into a regime. It had continued to consolidate its control over the media, reducing if not completely eliminating opposition voices. Some minor opposition was necessary to maintain the illusion of a free press. In addition, the existence of media outlets like the *Pro* provided a convenient target for Wrightman's supporters to speak out against: Either you supported the president or you supported the enemy. Fortunately, the *Pro*'s location on the sixth floor of a downtown building provided substantial security. Mobs and elevators are not a good mix.

Much more significantly, the FCC regulation that had prevented corporations from controlling multiple outlets in the same region had been lifted, allowing administration-friendly mergers and purchases to further erode free speech.

As a result, the news from Washington was unfailingly upbeat. The war against terrorism was going extremely well; McCord's Defense Department reported that American troops, finally let loose to fight the enemy, were rooting them out and killing them in increasingly fantastic numbers. The president had awarded the newly created American Freedom Medal to seven patriots who had informed local law enforcement about their neighbor's suspicious activities.

According to the administration, the economy was booming; it was growing so rapidly, according to Labor secretary Sean Kelly, that the numbers were "unbelievable!" Naturally I quoted him on that, suggesting we take him at his word. In reality, people were continuing to struggle. Automation continued to devour jobs; rising manufacturing and agricultural costs had resulted in higher retail prices; loosened institutional lending regulations combined with increased interest rates had sent millions more Americans into debt; and changed behavior had devastated the travel and energy sectors. Through all this, the Treasury Department continued to issue upbeat reports.

The good news for us was that the *Pro* was too inconsequential to be considered an immediate problem. I continued to post my stories, getting in subversive digs whenever possible, even if on occasion I was the only person who knew the dig was subversive. For example, when citing those rosy job creation numbers, I referred to them as "a novel approach to economic statistics." We knew the rules: We were permitted to criticize the administration whenever we wanted to; first the administration informed us when we wanted to, and then we did it.

I had to give Wrightman credit: not everything he did was suppressive. Or, as I referred to it, the Santa Claus factor. For example, over the following few months being able to impose wartime policy without having to bother negotiating with Congress allowed the administration to reinforce the shaky foundation the Democrats had laid down for an affordable healthcare system. The administration also imposed gun control regulations that limited certain types of gun ownership to militia members. The immigration problem was solved by informing the media it was not permitted to write about the immigration problem (and to be fair, employing cutting-edge technology on the borders). Crime too was reduced measurably when Wrightman issued an executive order authorizing pre-facto search warrants, giving law enforcement and militias the ability to prevent potential terrorist acts at the earliest possible time—thus allowing them to detain suspected criminals before they had even planned any crimes.

International relations were a bit more dicey. European governments, watching the increasingly repressive steps taken by the Wrightman administration, were wary of strengthening treaty and trade relationships. Far more alarming, State Department officials supposedly were in discussion with China, Russia, and the Saudis to forge a joint self-defense pact, a commitment that if any of the signatories were attacked by terrorists we would act jointly in response.

Here's the way I summed it up: "You have to hand it to the administration," I wrote, "otherwise they simply are going to take it." (Ba-dum-bump!) The Wrightman people did an incredible job of diverting public attention from reality. It was like ancient Rome, where the emperors distracted the populace with great entertainments, highlighted by sword-carrying midgets pursuing obese people in the Coliseum until they caught and killed them; instead we had TV shows like *Survivor: Chicago* and *Neighbor Wars*, we had legalized betting on murder trials, and most of all we had readily available drugs. Whoever thought that the opiate of the people actually would turn out to be opiates?

This country hadn't been transformed into North Korean or Syrian type dictatorships, I accepted that, and I also was aware that if you minded your own business, kept a reasonably low profile, and didn't complain about the government, you had little to worry about. For many people, in fact, life was easier and better than it had been. I hated having to admit that, even to myself, but it was true. People now had access to semi-affordable healthcare while keeping all their earned benefits. On the local level, the legal system still sputtered along to the benefit of the wealthy. Kids still went to school every day, and state college tuition remained reasonable. If you worked hard and got a little lucky, you could afford a house or a car. Big-screen HDTVs, video games with intense graphics, cable hook-ups and an array of gizmos providing access to 500 channels were available and affordable. The sex doll industry was booming. There were no restrictions on travel, although for many destinations, it had once again become necessary to obtain a visa. But it was no longer Norman Rockwell's bucolic America, either. It was more like Dalí's America.

Rather than the system that had more or less governed the nation for centuries, a system in which three reasonably co-equal branches of government were forced to work somewhat in concert by a constitutionally mandated system of checks and balances, meaningful power was now vested entirely in the executive branch. More than that, in the executive himself. While Trump had governed mostly by whim, while the Democrats had stuffed thumbs in the leaks, Wrightman's objective now seemed obvious: Consolidate power.

I suppose I could have gone along with it. I thought about it. Believe me, I thought about it. It would have made my life so much easier. I was living a wonderful life; I had a job I truly enjoyed; I had loyal friends and a woman I loved; with my salary and military disability payments I was financially sound; and I knew where to find the best quesadillas, Chinese food, and everything bagels in Washington. I had mine. So why couldn't I just go along to get along?

I certainly wouldn't be where I am today if I had been able to do that. Eh! I couldn't, though. I've always been honest about placing blame where it belongs. I accept responsibility. So I will admit the truth—it was all my mother's fault.

Another diversion. My mother. I suspect you're familiar with the evil Cruella de Vil, the flamboyantly long-nailed villain from *101 Dalmatians*. Well, my mother was the opposite. (Fooled you there.) She was the person who would have taken me and all my friends to see that movie. And then bought popcorn for all of us. Just my luck to have decent, supportive parents. Back in the barracks I had to listen to other people complaining about their colorfully terrible families. What could I say: My parents made me study! My parents taught me ethics and values, honesty and integrity, that there was a definable right and wrong and that I had been given so much, I had an obligation to stand up and cry out when I saw injustice. So it's her fault that I'm sitting here.

Any chance I might have been able to figure out a way to live in Wrightman's America and fight back from inside the system ended on an early spring morning. After that, the decision was made for me. I was walking into the *Pro*'s building when I was attacked by Richard Rodgers.

The stirring main theme from the composer's *Victory at Sea* symphony suddenly and without warning began blasting through Mighty Chair's Y-enhanced speakers. I looked at the touch pad, trying to figure out what in the world I could have done and how to turn it off. "Cher," I said over the music, "stop the music."

Instead, the music got louder. And then Mighty Chair reversed direction and began rolling backward into the street. I tried to put on the brakes, but it did no good. I started punching codes into the keyboard, whatever I could remember. I again ordered Cher to stop. Nothing worked. The system had been overridden. I was out of control again—exposed, vulnerable, caught in the open. For me, who was so confidently in control, having lost control was terrifying.

Rodgers's naval theme stopped abruptly. Seconds later I heard the voice of Ian Wrightman explaining why it was necessary to curtail free speech in order to protect free speech.

A wave of panic passed over me, then was gone as my training kicked in. If I couldn't regain control of Chair, I had to abandon seat. As I got ready to hit the ground, I reached into the seat pocket for my weapon. As I did, I saw him. Smiling.

Waiting on the sidewalk, a huge grin on his face as he played with me, tapping numbers into a remote, was a pear of a teenager. He was small and round, covered by a blanket, sitting in his own wheelchair.

14

Mighty Chair came to an abrupt halt. The kid had surrendered control. I whirled the chair around and powered toward him. He held up his hands in surrender. "I'm sorry," he shouted before I got there.

"How'd you do that?"

His hands remained in defense mode. "I'm really sorry, Mr. Stone. I had to get your attention."

"It worked. You got my attention." The kid looked shook up. Probably like I looked the day I met Barack Obama. I offered him my hand. "Rollie Stone."

"I know," the young man responded, shaking it with teenage enthusiasm, "I know."

"Now it's your turn. Who are you?"

"Me?" The question seemed to surprise him. "I'm just Brain—Brain McLane."

"Brain?"

He nodded. "That's what they call me—my friends. I mean. It's Brian, really."

McLane was so small he almost disappeared beneath his coat and blanket, but he had a broad, somewhat reticent smile that was pretty much overwhelmed by extra-large round wireless Harry Potter specs, as if he was wearing magnifying glasses. It was his chair that caught my attention. If Mighty Chair was my office on wheels, this kid's chair was a mobile teenager's room. It was festooned with stickers and signs promoting political causes and metal bands; a variety of tools and toys dangled from hooks. It actually reminded me of an old western Conestoga wagon, with pots and pans dangling along its sides. "I really need to talk to you," he said with an earnestness in his voice. "It's really important, really."

"As long as you can tell me how you did that." And how to stop anyone else from doing it again. "C'mon, I'll buy you a cup of coffee." I caught myself. "Or a Coke or orange juice or something."

We formed our own mini-wagon train as he trailed me down the street and up the metal ramp into Nonna's. As was typical at that hour, the coffee shop was warm and noisy. "There's one in the back," George yelled to me. As we maneuvered down the narrow aisle between the counter stools and the row of tables, several people greeted me. Coats were hung on the back of most chairs, so several people had to pull in closer to the table as we went by. One well-dressed woman made a show of ignoring us for several seconds as she buried herself in the menu, then expressed her disdain at being disturbed with an overdramatic sigh. I flashed her my winningest smile and whispered in her ear, "Whoosh!"

George deftly removed two chairs from a small corner table, and Brain and I slid in across from each other. I handed him a menu. "Okay, let's hear it."

Before responding, he took off those huge glasses. "It's a disguise," he said sheepishly. Then he filled me in. Brain was a sixteen-year-old high school junior from New York City. He had taken Amtrak, not the Acela, from the city that morning and needed to be back by early evening.

"I'm assuming your parents know you're in Washington?"

He rolled his head from side to side. "Sort of," he said, then looked around suspiciously.

"It's okay," I said reassuringly. "Spies only do takeout."

He leaned closer to me and said urgently, "I'm not kidding, Mr. Stone. You have to listen to me."

"Okay, all right, I said I will. First, though, tell me how you did that."

Brain dismissed it with a wave of his hand. "That was nothing." Mc-Lane explained that he was vice-president of his high school hacker club. Hacking, it turned out, was an extracurricular activity, for college credits, and his team had finished second in the state championship. He'd like an onion bagel and an orange juice, please. With a schmear. I got an everything with coffee.

Brain McLane spoke in great bursts, his excitement causing him to race through each sentence, pausing only at commas and breathing at the period. After reading about me following Detroit, he continued, he had decided to put his own chair online. "The Beast," he called it, tapping it proudly. But to do that he'd had to learn the generic operating system. "I found out who made Mighty Chair . . ." He said it with hesitation, as if perhaps he was crossing a personal line, and raised his eyebrows questioningly.

I tapped Mighty Chair. "I'm sure Mighty Chair is happy to meet you. Cher, say hello to Brain."

"Hello, Brain," Cher said. "I'm pleased to meet you."

Brain's entire face split into a huge smile, and his cheeks reddened. "Hello, Cher," he said, and laughed.

"So you found out who made Mighty Chair . . ."

His head bobbled. "You know, the original. Before, you know, all that extra stuff." After the attack in the garage, Chair had become pretty well known himself within the community. "From a photograph," he continued. "Then I hacked into their database. It wasn't hard at all—they probably didn't think somebody was going to bother hacking into a wheelchair. Once I had the code, all I had to do was find a back door into the operating system. That back door let me bypass all the upgrades you've made."

I was impressed. "That's why Cher didn't see you looking up her skirt?"

He covered his guffaw with his palm. "Don't worry, I sealed it for you. Nobody else can get in, I promise. But if you want to, you can tell the manufacturer."

Y really was going to be impressed when I told him about this. Or highly pissed. "Thank you," I said, meaning it. Sometimes you forget to lock the door and you don't want the burglar reminding you. "Now you go ahead. What do you need to tell me?"

I was curious. This kid had come a long way to tell me something that obviously was very important to him. I couldn't imagine what it might be. But whatever it was, I intended to treat him with respect. Brain obviously was a smart kid with great potential. I was going to take him seriously and send him home feeling good. I made a show of listening intently.

He leaned forward in the Beast as far as he could, made sure there was no one within hearing distance, and told me, "I know who cyjacked that plane."

Brain continued, "I mean, I don't know exactly *who* it was, but I know *where* he was. Or, or, or maybe where *she* was. Sorry."

George suddenly was standing at our table. Brain sat back as he put down our breakfast. "Anything else?" George asked as he wiped his hands on his white apron.

"No, that's great, George, thank you." We waited until he was gone. Then as I poured half-and-half into my coffee, I told him, "Okay, you got my attention. Tell me."

More than three months had passed since NA342 had been cyber-jacked. The administration had twice claimed to be close to unraveling the cyber-knot, but eventually admitted those leads had not panned out. It was very hard for me to believe that a sixteen-year-old high school junior had succeeded when the best hackers at the NSA, the CIA, and all the alphabet agencies had failed. But Brain was wearing a big, confident "ha, I got you" smile that said at least he believed it.

"It started as a challenge," McLane explained. "We knew that every intelligence agency in the world was trying to identify the hackers, so we thought wouldn't it be really cool if we could beat them to it. If we could, we figured, we could use that on our college applications. That's a lot better than math club or building houses in Guatemala, right?"

"Right."

"We knew we couldn't really compete with those guys." He threw his arms up in the air. "Like, our whole budget was $45, which was all we'd been able to raise with this terrible bake sale." He closed his eyes and smiled at that memory. "Boy, that was awful. But we didn't have any of the tools they have and we didn't have their experience, so we had to find a completely different path to follow."

Brain was eating his bagel as he continued, and even that didn't slow him down. All his club had to work with, he said, was the snippet of the code the cyjackers had used to take control of the plane, which the Defense Department had released to the hacker community when asking for assistance. "So we had this code." His voice was infused with confidence. "See, Mr. Stone, most people don't know this. Well, I'm sure you do, but most regular people don't. Every coder leaves a cyber-footprint. Like, you know, a pattern." He flipped his hands up in the air. His enthusiasm seemed to activate his body. "Everybody does it one way or another. Like every time people go online, they always go to the same few sites. Usually in the same order. That's a trackable habit. An identifiable footprint."

I thought about that. Brain was absolutely right; when I went onto the internet I always went to the same sites, generally in the same order.

"I read in this book that the feds use that to find fugitives. They work with the person's provider, and as soon as anyone goes online and hits those sites, they get an alert." With a chaw of bagel puffing out his cheek, he waved the other half in warning. "So you should be careful about that."

Next time I'm a fugitive, I thought, *I'll remember that.* Life sure is strange sometimes.

Kanye interrupted us. Brain glanced at his clearly jerry-rigged pop-up monitor to see who was calling, then ignored it. He was on a roll. "We started dissecting the code they released, seeing if we could find a foot-print. It was really hard. But then Judy, Judy McElnea, she's secretary of the club, anyway, she also plays the guitar. She's in a real band . . ." He frowned, then admitted, "They're not that great. Anyway, Judy told us that music has footprints too. She was doing a project, trying to figure out why some groups get popular when their songs don't really sound that different. So she converted their music into code, trying to find the repetitive elements. You should see what she came up with, Mr. Stone. It's really good, I mean really. You could look at a code and figure out what band it came from."

As he dived into this explanation, Brain was transformed from a teenager huddled in a chair to a confident young man, swimming easily in his element. His whole being had come alive as he explained this to me. The chair seemed to disappear. There was a twinkle in his eyes, a brightness to his spirit. And suddenly, enjoying my bagel and very impressed by Brain, I suddenly realized why I couldn't keep my big mouth shut. Why I felt compelled to stand up against the Wrightmans of the world. I wanted to make sure the America this kid and his friends inherited provided for them the same opportunities I'd enjoyed. I wanted them to know what it meant to be proud to be an American.

I caught up with him mid-sentence. "... treat the segment of code they released as a piece of music instead of digits. We graphed the repetitive elements and we were able to figure out its rhythm. Listen." He hummed about fifteen seconds of seemingly atonal bars, moving his hand up and down as if conducting it. I have to admit it sounded a lot like progressive rap to me, which I don't appreciate. He ended his demonstration and looked at me somewhat sympathetically. "You understand what I'm saying?"

"Oh yeah, sure. Absolutely." I did get the general concept. "That music you were humming is the code."

"Exactly. Anyway, we named it 'Judy's Screaming Cat.' That was 'cause Judy has this cat that just wouldn't be quiet. But we took that rhythm and backtracked, trying to find the composer, the hacker. We had to go backward, find another code that had the same rhythm. If we could do that, we would know who wrote the cyjack code."

He paused as George refilled my cup.

"That was tough. Honestly." He looked down, into the past, as he remembered that. "It took weeks and we tried everything we could think of. We got code from all over, from any source we could think of." He confided to me, "If you want to know how Barbie is programmed to answer questions, just ask me. And this was all going on while we were prepping for the SATs. It was totally crazy." Then he sat back and smiled with self-assurance. "Then we found it."

I didn't say a word. I didn't move, not wanting to interrupt this narrative. It wasn't possible that a bunch of high school kids could do this, I knew that. But it did make sense.

"A long time ago, three or four years at least, there was this big international teenage hackers' competition. We were just kids then, none of us even were in high school, and we didn't win anything. They gave everybody samples of code to hack. We went back and looked at all of those samples." He looked at me.

I waited. Then wound my hand in the keep-going gesture.

"One of them had exactly the same rhythm. We couldn't believe it. We couldn't believe it really worked. But we tested and retested it." He hummed a few bars that sounded equally awful as the first one. "So we could say with a high degree of confidence that whoever wrote that code for the competition was the same person who hacked into the airplane." He nodded toward Mighty Chair's arm. "Go ahead, check your screen. I sent it to you."

I glanced at Mighty's pop-up monitor. I was looking at a graph showing two roughly parallel lines. While the baselines were different, both lines spiked at about the same points. While not duplicates, the similarities between the two were obvious. I nodded. "Okay, I get it." I have to admit, the kid had me at "I know who cyjacked the airplane." I looked at him. "Go ahead. Who wrote these?"

McLane squeezed every bit of enjoyment out of this moment. He sat perched on his chair like a peacock on a perch. "You know how cool this is?" he marveled. "I mean me, sitting here with you. You know, Mr. Stone, you're like my idol. I've read everything they wrote about you and Mighty Chair."

I imitated his surreptitious glances around Nonna's to make sure no one else could hear me. Then I whispered, "Don't forget Cher. She's very sensitive."

Brain laughed with the delight of a sixteen-year old Spider-Man discovering his web-slinging powers.

"Now, tell me, who do you think it is?"

"It's not exactly who." He shook his head, then admitted, "We don't know exactly who it is. Just where it comes from."

Several months earlier I had played the guessing game with just about every journalist in the country. I had pored through all the available information and decided that the cyjackers had to be Eastern Europeans, or possibly Iranian. Iranian hackers were good. In 2012 they had wiped the servers of Saudi Aramco, Arabia's state-owned oil company, successfully attacked a Las Vegas casino, dug into numerous American banks, and—this was key to me—they had attempted to take control of a small dam in upstate New York. But the Russians were good too. And so were the Chinese. I thought the cyjacking was a demonstration of capabilities and would soon be followed up with a demand for a billion dollars. But that hadn't happened; in fact, no one had claimed credit for it, which had made it even more of a mystery. "I give up. Where did it come from?"

"You're really not gonna believe this, Mr. Stone. It came from Fort Meade, Maryland." With a slight nod to reassure me he was serious, he added, "You know what's there, right?"

I closed my eyes and laughed. Of course. Of course. It was so fucking obvious. How could I of all people, me, how could I have missed it? The NSA, spy central, the nation's top intelligence agency, was headquartered at Fort George G. Meade. It made perfect sense. Wrightman needed a fresh terrorist attack to scare Congress into supporting his request for war powers. And what could be better than this scenario? Unlike an attack on some distant city or even two cities, this one hit home with every American who ever got on an airplane. It sucked them into the middle of a real-life survival drama more exciting than a Jordan Peele movie, then left them feeling vulnerable. And no human beings were hurt in the making of this entertainment.

It had achieved the ultimate goal of all terrorism: it made people terrified that the next time, it . . . could . . . be . . . me.

Brain continued: After the hackers' challenge was done, all the code providers had been identified and thanked. This sample was "courtesy NSA."

"Brain, listen to me." I made sure there wasn't a quiver in my voice. "Have you told anybody else about this?"

He thought about that. He pursed his lips. "Just our faculty adviser, Mr. Calandros. And he warned us not to tell anybody else."

"He's a smart guy, Brain. Listen to me." I lowered my chin and locked eyes with him. This was no joke. I wanted him to hear my urgency. "You and your friends, you can't tell anybody about this. I mean it, no-body. If you're right . . ."

"We're right," he insisted.

"Okay, whatever. But I'm completely serious. Do you understand? You can't tell anybody, even your parents." I waited until he nodded accep-tance. I tapped the screen. "Have you got anything else to back this up?"

Brain responded with an "are you kidding me?" shrug. "Are you kid-ding me? We got all kinds of stuff. We compared them about twenty different ways. We got probability charts, formulas . . ." He smiled at the next thought. "We even made a tape of Judy's band playing both of them. We overlaid them on the tape, so you can hear the two codes together."

"Did you tell the band what they were?"

"Those guys?" He laughed at that thought. "Those guys wouldn't understand it anyway."

"Good." I rested my left elbow on Mighty Chair's arm and dug my chin into the well between my thumb and index finger on my left hand as I figured this out. "Okay, here's what I want you to do. Go home. Send me everything you've got. Tell all your other people, tell them not to say a word about this to anybody. Tell them not to talk about it; don't hum it, don't even think about it if you can help it. I'm going to give you my email address and a good phone number. Give it to everybody and tell them to contact me right away if anybody comes to talk to any of you, or even if you get any weird messages."

I just stared at him, hoping he understood the danger. If there was any truth at all to this, the NSA would take every necessary step to protect the administration. "You got it, Brain? I'm serious. This infor-mation could be dangerous." I hesitated to say out loud what I was thinking: This is Wrightman's America. No one knows how far they might go to protect themselves.

His smile was gone. He nodded tentatively.

"And don't you give that number to anybody except the club. If that number rings, I'll know it's one of you."

Brain tilted his head and asked, "What are you going to do with this, Mr. Stone?"

"Rollie. From now on, I'm Rollie."

"Rollie." He smiled broadly, then repeated more firmly, "Rollie."

"I don't know yet. I'll need to check it out first, you know, just to make sure it's accurate. Then I'll have to make some decisions. But I promise you, if this is what you guys say it is . . ."—tap, tap on Chair's pop-up screen—"I'll protect you. And if anybody ever gets credit for it, I'll make sure you guys get all of it."

"Do you think we were right about it helping us get into college?"

I wet my unexpectedly dry lips. "Maybe. But for now you can't use it." I chuckled. "Somehow I don't think you're going to have any trouble getting into a good school. You and me, we're diversity on wheels." I was about to suggest I go with him to Union Station, but it occurred to me that he would be better off not being seen with me. Just in case. "You gonna be okay getting home?"

He reached into a pocket and held up a train ticket. "Shit, yeah," he said.

"Do me a favor. Call that number when you get home so I know you're safe. And one more thing: I want you to give Cher your contact information."

"Really?" His face lit up brighter than the national Christmas tree.

"Cher, record and file this, please." Brain gave Cher his phone numbers, his email, and his social media contact information. I paid the check and one more time told him how important it was that he not tell anyone about the club's discovery. I didn't want to freak him out, but I also did not want to pretend there was no danger. "All right, time to go to work. You're gonna be careful, right?"

"I will. But can I ask you one favor?"

"Sure."

"Can we take a selfie?" After he promised not to show it to anyone but the club, we bumped chairs like "walkies" might fist-bump. Then I went to work, wondering if a high school hacking club had handed me the evidence I needed to take down the Wrightman administration.

I have a terrible memory. (Did I tell you that already?) I can remember general details about the meaningful events of my life. But it is rare that I can remember every moment, every word, everything I was thinking and feeling during an event. This is one of those exceptions. Even today, when I close my eyes and think about it, it becomes a physical reality and I can reproduce my feelings.

Walking to the office from that meeting, I was confused, excited, exhilarated, doubtful; I was resolute and fearful. The question I was wrestling with was what to do with this information. If it was true—and boy, was that a big if—but if it was true and if we could prove it beyond any doubt, it would completely undermine the credibility of the administration. I didn't kid myself, it wasn't going to spark a great uprising. And this wasn't Europe, it wouldn't cause the government to collapse; our system isn't structured that way, but it would inflict damage on the administration and give the opposition an issue around which we could make a stand. And it might cause our allies to take a good long look before reengaging with America.

The first decision I made was not to involve Howie. If the *Pro* published it, Homeland Security would declare us a "threat to national security" and close us down. They might even arrest Howie under the new sedition laws. That decision was easy. Whether or not to tell Jenny was the tough one. It was possible to view this as a test of my trust in her. To avoid having to make that decision, I reasoned it through and finally came up with a good enough excuse not to involve her: There was nothing she could do other than bring it to McDonnell, and just knowing about it and not alerting the government might put her in legal jeopardy. So for her own safety I did not tell her about it. Really.

Really, really.

Martha McDonnell was my only option. She had emerged as a leader of the dwindling opposition in Congress. That fact that there was little she could accomplish against the large majority from both parties who supported Wrightman actually provided her with a level of protection. The administration needed opposition in Congress to continue the charade that this country was still a functioning democracy.

"How do you know it's accurate?" she asked, holding out her open bag of Cheetos to me. We were huddled in a quiet corner in an elementary school classroom waiting for the meeting to begin.

I waved it off. This was, I think, three, maybe four days after my meeting with Brain. That secret had been growing inside me and I was ready to burst. The same rationale I had used for not telling Jenny was applicable to members of the resistance: what they didn't know couldn't hurt them. But Martha could provide the outlet I needed. She had a reputation as a good listener and her previous career as a prosecutor had made her a deft questioner. But mostly she was a great politician. She had several gears and could shift effortlessly into whichever was needed to get to her destination. She could transition from a warm friend flattering a constituent to an incisive inquisitor in the time it took to exchange glances. She was respected in the House for being a loyal supporter or an honest enemy, and her harmless opposition to Wrightman was tolerated as Martha being Martha.

I'd spent a reasonable amount of time with her as Jenny's plus-one at events and liked and respected her, but Jenny's continued absence at these meetings stood between us. In this case, though, I needed her. As I started to answer her question as to how I knew it was accurate, I suddenly felt incredibly foolish telling her that a high school kid gave it to me. It didn't get any better as I filled in the details. Even I had to admit, the possibility that some high school kids doing their club project had solved the problem that had stymied the leading intelligence agencies in the Western world did not sound particularly credible. When I told her that a kid named Brain riding the Beast had cyjacked Cher to get my attention, she looked at me with great sympathy.

And it didn't get any better when I hummed a few bars.

She savored one Cheeto as she considered her response. "This is the kind of information that changes lives, Rollie," she said as she slid my printouts back to me, "especially yours and mine. I'm willing to take that risk, but only if you can prove to me without any doubt this is legitimate. I can't take that chance until we're one hundred percent certain this isn't complete bullshit."

"Any suggestions?"

She held one long slim Cheeto between her teeth as she considered that. Then she crunched down on it. "I guess you could call the NSA and ask them if somebody around there had cyjacked an airliner. But other than that . . ." She shrugged.

The rest of the meeting that night is sort of a blur. As I listened to a litany of scary news, I just couldn't help wondering how I could prove the kid's claims. And there was a lot of bad news. The situation was getting worse. The administration was getting more active. The thin line between docile opposition, which the White House encouraged, and an effective movement was close to being crossed. The rapidly growing resistance had finally forced Wrightman to react. More people were being questioned and detained. A two-stater passed along a rumor that the White House was producing and posting antigovernment social material, then working with providers to identify people who passed them along. Those names were added to a secret watch list.

That night, for the first time, I heard people threatening violence. A squat, balding professor from American University was waving his arms furiously as he complained, "This is bullshit! When is enough going to be enough? We keep meeting here to tell one another how bad things are, but we're not doing anything to stop it. It's time we stopped talking and start to take some action." He reminded me most of a burly union organizer from a 1950s black-and-white B movie, maybe played by Broderick Crawford, exhorting workers to march on the bosses.

I bit down hard on the inside of my cheek to keep myself from saying anything. These big talkers infuriated me. I'd seen the damage they could do. Obviously we were a long way from planting IEDs along the 495, but stuff like that begins with blowhards like this professor planting those seeds.

It was Laura—she still went by Laura, so I guessed that was her real name—who responded. "I get it." There was a resignation in her voice. "We all get it. What are we going to do to stop these people? How do we take back our country? Believe me, I get it. We all get it, that's why we're here. Here's the reality; we can't do it with violence; trust me, like every one of you there have been times I get so angry I wish we could. But it's insane. That's what they want us to do. We'd be playing right into their hands. We have to fight them with ideas."

Several people snickered. I heard a frustrated sigh. Then someone said softly, "Here we go again."

Laura heard it too and whirled around. "Are you kidding me?" She was furious. "You think we have a choice? You see what's out there? We have one weapon. One." She shook her index finger. I have to admit, it was an impressive performance. "We have got to prove to Americans that Wrightman is lying to them. That he is spitting in their face. We have to confront them with it so they can't pretend . . ."

Somebody shouted from the other side of the room, "That sure didn't matter with Trump."

Laura whirled to face the voice. "You're right, and you saw the result of that. Just maybe people learned a lesson." She turned slowly, speaking to the entire room as she continued, "Here's one thing I guarantee you: if Patrick Henry was standing here today, right here in this classroom in the Michelle Obama Elementary School, and he demanded 'Give me liberty or give me death,' they'd disappear him. Big threats aren't going to do anybody any good. We need to organize and take actions that make sense."

She sat down moments later to a smattering of polite applause. A Maryland dairy farmer who called himself Chuck spoke next. He began by complimenting her, then said, "You know, I've been sitting here for a while, and until tonight I never said one word. I didn't think I needed to, listening to smart people saying smart things. But here's one thing I've figured out, years from now when people ask how this happened . . ." He shook his head. "Well, this is the beginning and I already hear people saying we should have stopped them yesterday. I gotta agree with that professor, I've had enough. I don't know what I can do, but I want to do it."

In response to Chuck the dairy farmer, Mike the dentist warned, "This is exactly what they want us to do, so they can crack down on us."

It went on like that into the evening. I got their frustration, but while it makes great movies, the Bad News Bears are not going to beat the Yankees. As Mighty Chair was being lifted into Van, Laura's words stuck in my head: We have to throw the truth in their face. For less than the instant it takes a neuron to jump a synapse I considered telling her what I had, but by the time it became a thought, I had already dismissed it.

In my first life I had been a runner. I'd stick a folded piece of paper in my waistband, hook a pen to my T-shirt, and let my mind wander as I ran. When an idea worth remembering wiggled into my mind, I'd stop and scribble it down. I'd started using my time alone in Van for the same purpose, turning off Mighty Chair's sound system and letting my thoughts fill the silence. Instead of a pen and paper, though, I had Cher.

I considered my options. I had to prove that McLane was right: a cyber-footprint could be used to positively identify the source of computer code, and in this instance, that footprint could be traced directly to the NSA. And I had to do it without the government learning I had this information.

That meant trusting someone else. There were several men I'd served with who probably had this level of computer expertise, people who once had trusted me with their life. But those people had been trained by the government, had risked their lives for the government, were receiving benefits from the government, and maybe still worked in some capacity for the government, so they probably weren't safe bets. I whittled down my list until I realized that the person who might be able to answer this question had been right under my nose for the past two years.

15

As part of my recuperation I had become a gym rat. What I could no longer do with my legs, I intended to do with my upper body. At first I sort of felt my way around the circuit, staying away from certain pieces of equipment, figuring out my own modifications on others. But as I gained confidence, I went back into attack mode, figuring out ways to push, pull, lift, and stretch without the use of my legs. My problem was that I couldn't find a spotter. While people were polite and encouraging, they gave me a pass on spotting, probably more for their own safety than mine. I couldn't blame them. But I kept showing up, doing my workout by myself. At times I'd catch one of them watching me, then turning away when caught. Who knows what they were thinking or feeling—sympathy, empathy, maybe relief it wasn't them? Gradually, though, I earned their respect.

Hack Wilson had been the first person to trust me. One morning he shouted across the gym, "Stone! Get over here and spot me. It's your turn."

He was standing by the weight rack, chalking his gloves. The gym got silent. Lifting was serious and dangerous. People got hurt. Spotters had to be alert, strong and stronger. "You sure?" I asked.

"Hell yeah!" he boomed back. "Damn straight. You been hanging around here too long without doing your part. Nobody gets a free ride."

It was a pretty dramatic moment. When they make the movie, this will be one of the highlights. People stopped to watch, no longer pretending they didn't see me. It was a little tricky, and even with all his bravado, Hack knew he was taking a chance. But we worked at it; we figured it out and became gym buddies. We made the necessary accommodations, and at least three mornings a week, we were separated only by a few inches and a hundred pounds. To the accompaniment of moans and groans, we got into each other's lives.

Hack wasn't a big man, but he was as solid as a three-story building. With a roof of blond hair. And arguably harder to move. More than anything else, though, he was a good guy. His bulked-up appearance belied his gentle nature and seemed more fitting for an NFL lineman than for some kind of computer geek. He also was a settled man; he and his wife, known to the entire brigade as Wake Up Maggie because her name was Margaret and they'd met at a Rod Stewart concert, had two young children and lived in Alexandria.

He was former military too, but never a grunt like me. He knew I had worked in the field, so it became a joke between us. "*Mud* spelled backwards is *dum*!" he liked to point out, "and my mama didn't raise no dummy." He was always vague about his MOS, his military specialty: "You know, stuff." He actually didn't go to college, taking great pride in the fact that he was educated by the Army. "They gave me a full scholarship to Can U," he bragged. "As in, Wilson, can you do this? Wilson, can you do that?"

Supposedly he was the IT guy at a successful cybersecurity start-up, something to do with cargo containers, but he was vague about that too. I believed that one about as much as I believed that Mother Teresa had actually wanted to direct movies. "Cybersecurity start-up" was a popular catchall for men and women who needed to hide their actual employment. I never pressed him for details and he never offered any, which is proper etiquette in Washington, so I was reasonably certain he worked somewhere in Spooktown.

Could I trust him? Tough question. Maybe he did work for the government—okay, he probably worked for the government—but I knew his politics. He'd enthusiastically joined in my condemnation of

Trump/Pence, laughing at the jokes and shaking his head in disbelief in all the right places. Long before the full extent of Trump's relationship with Russian oligarchs was known, he was pointing out angrily that every move Trump made concerning Russia, even concerning our allies, "coincidentally" benefited Putin. As I drove home from the meeting I tried to remember if we'd had any conversations about the last election. This was where it would have been nice to have had a better memory. I did remember him cheering Biden's election, but I couldn't recall him voicing any support for Wrightman. One time, this I did remember, one time when he was pumping iron he started complaining about Wrightman's gutting the capabilities of our intelligence agencies. He channeled his anger at that into five more reps. That was the closest he'd ever come to disclosing his real employer.

Could I trust him? A government man? I couldn't overlook the risk he had taken in trusting Rollie 2.0, as he sometimes called me. Somewhere along the line I had to take a shot with this. And I was pretty sure he had the expertise to determine if the whole scenario was plausible. I didn't have a lot of options.

Our noses were about fifteen inches apart when I asked him in a low voice, "What are you doing later?" I was lying on a bench on my back, pressing 175 pounds.

Hack was hovering over me, ready to grab the bar. "Oh, c'mon, Rol," he said with a smirk, "I didn't know you cared."

I strained to do another rep. "I'm serious, Hack. This is important."

"Keep your back straight," he cautioned. "You can't talk about it here?"

I lifted the bar onto the stand and rested the weights, then took two restorative breaths. "It's got to be private."

He shrugged. "Fine. Your call."

We met at sunset at the base of the ramp along the left side of the Lincoln Memorial. It had been an unusually warm day, and as the Old Professor, Charles Dillon "Casey" Stengel, might have said, the city held the heat well. The twilight sky was streaked with the whispered rose of cherry blossoms in full bloom. The ramp led up to a door that opened onto an elevator, which took us up to the central hall. I have never been much for Washington's tourist attractions, but the Lincoln Memorial was different. Lincoln had always affected me, with his imposing eyes and the tragic nobility that burst out of the marble. I had been there for the first time on a seventh-grade trip and again on my last day in the city before leaving for deployment. I had wanted to remind myself why I was going.

Hack and I stood in silence for a few minutes, watching with appreciation as the shadows of the evening crept slowly across the reflecting pool and the lights of the Capitol twinkled into life. Around us everything seemed so perfectly normal it was difficult for me to accept that we were living in the shell of American democracy.

"Pretty impressive," Hack said with admiration. "So? What's going on?"

I glanced around before replying. A young couple, the boy's arm around the girl's waist, stood transfixed in front of the statue, looking up into his face. A little boy made the moment special by reading aloud the words of the Gettysburg Address inscribed on the near wall; he struggled with several words and his mother helped him sound them out. In contrast, three soldiers in protective gear, carrying automatic weapons, stood guard in front of the columns.

I laid out the scenario to Hack. Since the Detroit massacre, I explained, I'd become the repository for every crackpot conspiracy theory. "I've ignored most of them, and the few that I've followed up fell apart pretty quick," I explained. I told him about the warning from Homeland Security. I told him how Chair had been cyjacked by a kid. I wanted him to know what was going on before he made his decision. "I hate to sound overly dramatic about it, but these days a little too much information can cause you some real problems. If you don't want to get involved, I get it. Truthfully, Hack, that's probably the smart thing to do. I'll just see you at the place tomorrow morning and pretend this didn't happen."

Wilson laughed lightly. "Right. You're telling me some high school kid took control of this baby here . . ."—he tapped Mighty Chair's arm—"then told you some story you obviously believe is so important you reached out to me, and you really think my curiosity is going to let me walk away? You kidding me? C'mon, man, you're the Rolling Stone. Let's rock and roll!"

I nodded my appreciation. Without thinking about it, I lowered my voice. "The first thing I want to know is if what this kid told me is plausible. It seems like a stretch to me." Rather than revealing the specifics, I asked him about Mozart. Was it possible to identify repetitive patterns in his composition, in a symphony, for example, and use that data to determine if he had written a different piece of music?

Hack considered that. "You mean, does an artist have a signature? I guess in theory—sure, why not? Art experts match brushstrokes and paint composition to identify the artist, so I guess it could be done. There would have to be a bunch of known factors and it would require more than just a sampling to be certain, but most coders have their own styles." He nodded decisively. "Yeah, it could work."

The more he thought about it, the more he convinced himself it was possible. The concept clearly intrigued him. He went into a lengthy and somewhat technical explanation of what constitutes a discernible pattern and how often people confused it with simple repetition, copying, or even chance. "There's a measurable element of chance in every comparison. Even the legal system recognizes that." For example, he continued, every fingerprint consists of a unique array of arches, loops, and whorls, but given several billion possibilities, certain elements of two different people's prints will look very similar, which is why the FBI requires at least twelve points of comparison before accepting a match. He circled back to my question. "Is it possible? Yeah, sure. So what've you got?"

"Okay, okay. Here's the deal, Hack. These kids think they've ID'd the Flight 342 cyjackers."

Whatever reaction I might have been expecting didn't happen. His expression gave nothing away. He wet his lips, cleared his throat, and said, "Boy, that's something. So what do you need me for?"

"I want you to take a look at these charts," I said, twisting around and pulling a manila envelope containing the code samples, the graph, and several other documents Brain had sent me from my backpack. I'd removed all the identifying information, just leaving the bare bones. It was possible Hack would recognize the hacker's coding the government had released to the cyber-community. But even if he did, he'd have no way of knowing where the original code had come from. "I just want your opinion. Are they from the same source or not?"

He slipped a fingernail under the clasp to pry it open. I stopped him. "Not here, not now. Take a really good look at them, Hack. Just tell me this isn't crazy."

He grinned. "And don't talk to anybody else about this, right?"

I nodded. "Right." That young boy finished reading the Gettysburg Address. "Thanks for this, Hack. Thanks for everything."

As I drove home that night, I regularly checked my mirrors to see if I was being followed. This had become another new habit. When I first started doing it, I'd felt foolish, but then I discovered that other people at the meetings were doing the same thing. As a man who called himself Troy told me one day, "Just because you're paranoid doesn't mean somebody isn't following you."

I made the proscribed four right turns to confirm that no one was tracking me, then headed home. Okay, I admit it, I still felt at least a little foolish. And when I was in a hurry I ignored it. But I had just handed over documents that could shake up the government, so at least I had a reason for it.

As was usual now, I didn't ask Cher to find a radio station, preferring to muck around in my own thoughts. In the previous few months I'd begun reading about totalitarian regimes, fiction and nonfiction, from *Animal Farm* to *The Rise and Fall of the Third Reich*. Talk about paranoid, I did not take these books out of the library or order them online under my own name; there were rumors the FBI was compiling lists of people who had shown a sudden interest in this topic.

So I got the books wherever I could. Then when I was done, I passed them along at the next meeting. I'd found a tattered paperback copy of *1984* on a used book table for $2 on U Street, for instance. I'd read it in high school and had forgotten most of the details beyond Big Brother was watching me. The irony of it was, I made an effort to hide my copy of the book from the ubiquitous security cameras on every building, on every floor of every building. Big Tech was watching me.

It did not surprise me that new copies of Orwell's classic were "temporarily out of stock" from Amazon, or for that matter, from almost any source in America. Supposedly this was at the request of the executors of Orwell's estate, who had suspended printing new copies because the book required "a major update to stay relevant." (I could just imagine: Big Brother becomes Big Non-Gender-Specific Person or, more likely, Big Facebook Friend.)

I was still searching for the why. Why was Wrightman continuing to accumulate power when he already had operational control? Did he really believe this was necessary to save the American economy and restore the country to its international standing? Or was it megalomania, a psychological need to fill the void in his soul? These books provided an array of possibilities but no satisfying answers. What did Big Brother have in common with Pol Pot? What did Napoleon the pig share with Hitler? Was it simply human nature? Was Robert Browning offering an explanation when he wrote: "Ah, but a man's reach should exceed his grasp, / Or what's a heaven for?" Maybe short and stubby Henry Kissinger understood this when he said, trying to explain his personal appeal, "Power is the ultimate aphrodisiac." But I kept coming back to the simplicity of mountaineer George Mallory's response when asked why he so desperately wanted to summit Mount Everest: "Because it's there."

Whatever Wrightman's reasons, the impact had now touched the most basic aspects of life in new America. I now stopped at yellow lights, for example, in an effort to avoid attracting any unnecessary attention to myself. Me, who had always believed the yellow simply meant hurry up and beat the red. Boy, plotting to overthrow the government of the United States was a hard job! But as I'd learned from all my reading, strict adherence to the civil laws, even as those laws were adjusted and improved, was a hallmark of most totalitarian regimes.

The one common thread I found in all of those books, fiction and nonfiction, was that in each instance the dear and glorious leader established a law enforcement organization directly responsible to him. A quasi-Gestapo, whose bootsteps could be heard coming in the night. Obviously Wrightman had nothing like that. But what he did have was far more insidious: He had won the loyalty of law enforcement by giving officers almost free rein, granting them legal protection from any responsibility for overly aggressive actions taken to enforce existing laws. *Existing laws* were of course left open to a broad interpretation.

The message he'd sent by his appearance at the convention of police chiefs had been embraced: Those officers who didn't get with his program were either given dead-end assignments or asked to submit their resignations. "Unable to fulfill the duties of a law enforcement officer" was the general catchall given to explain those dismissals.

Regular law enforcement had also learned to work with the militias. It was literally a shotgun marriage. There were some confrontations when legal jurisdiction and macho pride overlapped, but overall, they had figured out how to distribute authority. I have to admit the administration did a good job selling this program, using a wholesome young mixed-race couple sitting at the kitchen table with their two beautiful young children, preaching happily, "The law is the most powerful weapon we've got. Following the law makes us all safer. So remember . . ." They paused and looked sweetly at their children, who singsonged together, "When you see something, say something." All of which had resulted in my now stopping at yellow lights.

Jenny was hard at work when I got home. She was sitting cross-legged on the couch in front of the TV, dressed in satin pajamas, her glasses perched on the end of her nose, her laptop appropriately on top of her lap. Loose pages and open books were strewn around her, as if she were a college student working late on a paper. She took off her glasses and smiled at me. "Hey!"

"Hey back." I savored the moment. This was the way my life was supposed to be. Her coral satin pajamas resting casually on her curves said sex, the computer said intelligence, and her dazzling smile said everything else I needed to know. Home and hearth. It continued to amaze me how often I refell in love with her.

In that instant I decided to tell her the whole story. If I trusted Hack Wilson, my gym buddy, then I damn well better trust the woman I might marry. Someday. Sometime. In the future. It was time.

She was watching the revised CNN, the Citizens News Network. While it had not yet gone full Fox, the once left-leaning channel was bending with the winds. They were doing a segment on the justice system. She rose off the couch and gave me a kiss. "You eat?"

"No. The meeting with Howie went longer than I expected." The lie rolled out of me as smoothly as a Sade song. "I don't know how much longer we're going to be able to keep going. We're hemorrhaging advertisers. There's a lot of pressure on them."

"Oh, you'll think of something," she said confidently. "That's what you do, reinvent yourself. Want me to make you something?"

The mail was lying on the burnished metal table in the foyer. As I flipped through it, I told her: "No, that's all right. What are you working on?"

"Just the usual constituent stuff," she said with a dismissive sigh. "A lot of people are angry and they're letting her know it. I mean, every single day with Martha it's the same thing: the president did this, he did that. And a lot of people don't like it." She looked at me and smiled. "She's even worse than you sometimes."

The snail mail consisted of bills and department store offers. There was nothing of importance, but I continued staring at it, trying to process Jenny's flippant complaint.

She interrupted my silence, continuing, "Well, you have to be honest— not every single thing the guy has done has been terrible."

I deftly turned Chair to face her. "Really? You mean, like, 'Other than that, Jackie, how was your trip to Dallas?' You've got to be kidding me, Jen. This scumbag is taking away our rights. Your rights." I honestly don't know how it got there, but my index finger was at the end of my extended arm, pointing accusingly at her.

Well, I figured this probably wasn't the best time to tell her. She was wound up, though, which truthfully I didn't think was fair. This was my time to be angry. "You know what, Rollie, my uncle John was on the eighty-ninth floor of the World Trade Center on 9/11. He had to sit there, just waiting to die. He had time to call my aunt and tell her how much he loved her." Tears followed the path around her cheekbones.

"I know. Look, Jen . . ."

"I think about it, I think about it a lot. What it must have been like for him. Can you imagine?" She tried to shake the thought out of her head. "I don't want anyone else to have to go through that. That's what real terrorism is. And if it takes a little compromising to keep people safe, well, yes, I am in favor of that."

"A little compromise? That's what you think this is? A little compromise?" You know that feeling of rolling downhill out of control? And not being able to stop? Like in a parking garage? Well, you don't, not really. I heard the words coming out of my mouth and there was nothing I could do to stop them. My anger and my frustration had been festering too long, waiting for the right time, the right person. "Believe me, oh please believe me, Jen, I am so terribly sorry about your uncle. I'm sorry about every single one of those people. I'm sorry for what it did to you and to me and to this whole country. But do you really think giving up your rights is 'a little compromise'?" I went over to her and reached out. "Listen to me, Jen, please. Please don't use your uncle, don't use those people who were murdered, to let Wrightman scare you into turning this country into something mean and ugly." I emphasized that by scrunching up my face in a mean and ugly way, which probably wasn't the smartest thing I could have done. The smartest thing I could have done was the one thing I couldn't do: Shut the fuck up.

She pulled away. She opened and closed her mouth wordlessly, searching for the right response. When she found them, they dripped with bitterness. "Maybe if you took a good look around you might not be so sure. People have jobs, Rollie; their kids are going to school. The borders are protected. The shelves are stocked again. The streets are safe. People have access to healthcare. So you tell me, what's so terrible about all of that? After all the damage, what's so bad about having a decent person in the White House? He's not Hitler, you know that."

"No," I agreed as calmly as I could manage, "no, he isn't Hitler. Hitler told the Germans exactly what he intended to do. Then he did it. And they supported him. He was obvious. Wrightman . . ." I took a deep breath. I shook my head. "Wrightman is devious. He . . . he . . ." If I was going to tell her, this would have been the time. And if I had, maybe everything would have been different. But I couldn't. I stopped.

"He what?" she snapped.

I closed my eyes as I spoke, my voice suddenly calm. "You're right, Jen, he isn't Hitler or Mussolini . . . he isn't any of them. He's the Pied

Piper and he's leading the parade with a happy tune. And people are just following him, singing along. They're happy, all the way to the end.

"And I am so sorry you can't see that."

She sat down on the carpet directly in front of Chair, as implacable as the anonymous protester blocking a row of tanks in Tiananmen Square. "Just listen to me, please." She sobbed, caught herself. She wouldn't look at me as she continued, instead focusing on her interwoven hands in her lap. "The essence of democracy means sacrificing some of your own rights for the greater good. That's all Wrightman is doing. Why can't you see that? What difference does it make if you can't go online and call the president rotten names if you don't have to worry about suicide bombers?" She wiped away her tears with the back of her hand. "I love you, Roland Stone, and I love Martha, and I would do anything for either one of you, but I don't understand why you have to be so rigid. Can't you just give him a chance?" She looked up at me, her expression a plea for understanding. "Please."

I picked my next words carefully. All of those mysterious forces that had shaped our lives and led to us being together were breaking us apart. We are, all of us, the sum total of our heritage, our experience, and every teacher we've ever had, and Jenny and I could be no less. We saw the world through different filters; we processed the same facts very differently. Those things that seemed so clear and obvious to Jenny were equally foreign and dangerous to me.

She leaned against my leg. I felt nothing, no sensation at all, but I laid my hand on her head and gently kneaded my fingers through her hair. *This is what they do,* I thought. *They turn people against each other. They create mistrust.* We sat there like that for several minutes, trying to figure out where to go from here. I heard a siren screaming somewhere in the distance. In the street below my window someone was drunk-singing. Life goes on. I couldn't identify what I was feeling. A witches' brew, I guess: a dose of loss, two bits of fear, a snippet of anger, a handful of regret, and a caldron of emptiness. All the words in the world, no matter how cleverly strung together, would not be enough to put us back together whole. It was amazing to me that she couldn't see the steep cliff waiting at the end of this road, a road rutted with compromise.

She finally looked up at me. She started to speak, her mouth opening and closing several times wordlessly. And when finally she spoke, it was in measured words, searching for common ground. "You know who I am. You know we care about the same things. We both know what this country should be. There is no way I could have worked with Martha all these years if we didn't share the same values. Can't you see that?"

"I wish I could," I said. "More than anything." What was I doing?

She stood, wiping away the last of her tears, regaining her composure. "Do you want me to go?"

"No. Absolutely not." I took hold of her hand. "We'll figure this out." I was fumbling for the right words, but there was no going back. We had staked out our positions. "Listen to me. I love you, Jen. You're the best thing that has ever happened to me. And we're not going to let this drive us apart." I caught her eyes. "You understand?"

She nodded. She inhaled deeply and forced a wan smile. "Yes."

Later that night, as we watched an old episode of *Curb,* she rested her head on my shoulder. I slipped my hand under her pajama top and began rubbing her back; then I reached around and began stroking her breast. She sighed and cuddled deeper. We were trying desperately to hold together a cracked relationship, turning back to what had always worked, but I think each of us knew the truth.

For the next few weeks we held it together as best we could, like a favorite old rocking chair held together with duct tape and love. And maybe, just maybe, we could have made it work. But we never really got the chance.

It took three shots.

The president, first lady, and members of his cabinet were safely ensconced in an enclosed reviewing stand, waving happily to marchers on Pennsylvania Avenue as America celebrated our first Military Appreciation Day. It was a magnificent spring morning; puffy white clouds were playfully creating bizarre animals in a sky the color of watered-down ink. The long parade of troops, tanks, and brightly shining missiles had almost reached the end of the route and the Marine Corps band was playing the introductory notes of "America the Beautiful" when the shots were fired.

Three shots. Each one followed by a brief pause. Boom. Echo. Pause. Boom. Echo. Pause. Boom. Echo. Pause.

At first I thought someone had dropped a coffee cup. Reality clicked in when I looked up at the monitors and saw people running. "Aw, jeez," somebody said. "Here we go again."

Seconds later Cher alerted me, "Rollie, there has been an important event."

Howie had come out of his office and was looking up at the wall-mounted monitors. His sleeves were rolled up and his hands stuck in his back pockets. His time-to-do-journalism pose. He was chewing on one of those green plastic flossers, but his mind was already at work planning coverage.

We had the details within minutes. The first shot had cracked the double-paneled bulletproof glass protecting Wrightman and his family, then ricocheted into the exposed VIP section below the booth. It struck Senator Grace Lindsey in her right shoulder, breaking her collarbone. The second shot hit and killed Treasury Secretary Penelope Farber, who had just left the president's box hoping to beat at least some of the traffic. The third shot grazed Army master sergeant Glenn Deutsch, who was standing guard at the entrance to the reviewing stand.

The panic had erupted even before the echoes had faded. Spectators scattered like a blob of paint struck by a hammer. Marchers either hit the street or scrambled for shelter. They had no way of responding; while the parade had been the most impressive display of military hardware in one place ever seen in this country, for safety reasons, none of the participants had been issued live ammunition.

More shots were fired. A later investigation revealed that a female Secret Service agent had fired two shots at a figure standing in the window of a building across the street; she testified she was certain she had seen that person aiming a rifle. Her shots missed the target but did incite additional chaos. An estimated one million spectators began pushing back from the wooden barriers, trying to get to safety. Many people fell, including children. Network cameras covered the entire event. One handheld was dropped as the cameraperson had been knocked down, and ABC switched to the ground-level shot of countless legs fleeing.

The announcers were doing a lot of shouting, but no one was making a lot of sense.

I heard another shot. That probably was the moment a bank officer named Anthony Eldridge, who had pulled out his legally concealed weapon to protect his wife and two children from being trampled, was shot dead by a D.C. police officer who mistook him for the gunman.

The final toll was fourteen dead, including Farber and Eldridge, a four-year-old who was crushed by the mob, and two men who died of heart attacks, while an additional hundred and thirty people required hospitalization. The president and his entourage were led to armored limousines behind the reviewing stand and taken to a secure location in the subbasement of the White House.

Martha had refused an invitation to the parade, so I knew Jenny was safe. As I went to work, I remembered the angry voices at the last anti-government meeting. *This has been coming for a long time,* I thought. *A long time.* And then I was struck by another, darker realization: this was what Wrightman had been waiting for.

Three hours after the assassination attempt the president appeared on television and social media. It was obvious he had been carefully made up to appear as if he hadn't been made up, that the strain on his face was natural. But whoever had done it had stopped halfway between his jawline and his neck, and a completely different shade of skin was visible. Some makeup artist had forgotten the lessons of Trump and his sprayed-on orange tan. It was a half-chinned job. "Neither Carrie nor I were injured in this despicably evil attack," he began, oozing sincerity, "and the first lady and I truly appreciate the literally millions of good wishes we have received. But unfortunately, many people were hurt, and we want to send our condolences and sympathy to all the victims of this act. We know how you feel . . ." A pause of three beats here. "The entire White House family is mourning the death of Treasury Secretary Farber, a deeply loved person. Out of respect for all of the people killed and wounded today I have ordered American flags flown at half-mast."

The president was sitting behind the Resolute desk. Occasionally he looked down at notes. "We don't know yet who is responsible for this cowardly act. Forensic evidence recovered at the scene will help us identify the perpetrators and, I'm confident, catch them. But this was the last straw."

Here we go, I thought. It's never good to run out of straws.

"To prevent these kinds of horrendous attacks on innocent Americans I have asked the appropriate law enforcement agencies, under the direction of Vice President Hunter, to begin detaining well-documented and confessed dissidents who by their words and deeds have created this hate-filled atmosphere that drives people to take such actions."

I tried to breathe. Behind me I heard gasps and muttering.

"As I speak to you this has begun." Wrightman emphasized that these people were not being arrested, and in most cases, they faced no criminal charges, but instead they were being "temporarily removed from the public debate until this crisis was over," so their "harsh tones and inflammatory rhetoric" could cause no further harm.

As the camera slowly dollied in for the sincere close-up, he stated firmly that no one in his administration was accusing these people of being terrorists or even sympathizing with terrorists. "I can say without hesitation that many of them are good people and loyal Americans. They are well-meaning, no matter what so many of you might believe. But their misguided words and actions are hindering the efforts of your government to prevent . . ."

To prevent potentially dangerous rumors from spreading, to provide access to truthful information, he announced the creation of the dedicated White House network. It would be broadcasting to the American people twenty-four hours a day on local cable networks and social media platforms, rather than being filtered by the mainstream and small pond media.

The president spoke with appropriate solemnity for several more minutes before his closing *God bless*es. He gave his personal word that everyone taken into temporary custody would be treated with respect, would be well-fed, would be safely housed, and would receive all necessary medical treatment. Army bases would be used where possible, but in major cities centrally located office buildings would be used to house detainees. Occupied buildings would be emptied and converted into dormitory-style housing. Corporate tenants in designated buildings were being urged to vacate their office space immediately, and replacement space was being made available to them. I noted that he avoided referring to those people as prisoners.

As he finished, the camera held on his grim face, which slowly faded into an animated American flag blowing straight in a stiff wind. I just sat there looking at it, transfixed, stuck in place by the enormity of this announcement. Obviously the whole thing forced me to wonder if we had witnessed an actual assassination attempt or another administration ploy. *It doesn't matter, really,* I thought bitterly. *The end result is the same.*

The roundups had begun.

16

owie broke the silence. Without turning around, he said loudly,
"Okay, everybody. Go home."

After an instant of silence as we all absorbed that, the room
erupted into a mishmash of disbelief, refusal, and complaints. We were
journalists, reporters. Our job was to inform. This was one of the most
significant stories in American history. Go home? I had never before seen
any quit in Howie.

He stood there, letting it play out. Finally he turned. His hands were
still stuffed in his back pockets, but now tears were running down his face.
"Lock it up," he ordered in a tone that left no room for compromise. "Go
home. Now." Then he went into his office, closing the door behind him.

In retrospect, that probably was the right decision. There was no
book entitled *What to Do Till the Police Come for You*. We lacked all protocol. Nothing prepared any of us for this; there were no instructions in
the employee handbook. There was a lot of grumbling, but the office
emptied quickly.

Jenny and I exchanged texts. "Going home," I wrote. "See you there?"

"Crazed," she responded. "The Hill is in chaos. No idea what's going
on. I'll call later. Love you."

"Okay. Love you too." What else could I say? I decided to stop at
Lucille's, I wanted to be with people, but when I got in front of the place,
I saw that the steel gate had been pulled down and all the lights were off.

My memories of that night are hazy. I do remember sitting in front of my TV watching the networks reporting the story. Truthfully, it was more announcing than reporting. I was not surprised that reactions ranged from mildly supportive to wildly supportive. There was literally no criticism. None. (Some media outlets knew how to retain their license.) It suddenly seemed obvious the administration had been laying the groundwork for this since the day Wrightman moved into the White House. I sat in my living room, sipping a beer, then a second and a third, speaking with different people and exchanging texts with others. Bottom line, no one had any idea what was going on, what was going to happen, or how to react.

Jenny didn't call. She sent several more texts, all of them telling me in different ways that the Hill was in an uproar. People were running from meeting to meeting, trying to figure out how to stop this. Reactions there ranged from satisfaction and support to anger and tears.

Satisfaction to tears? That was a pretty wide spread and an accurate appraisal. Me? Mostly, I think, I felt lost. I felt like I was floating, waiting to see which way the winds would blow me. For someone like me, a person used to charging through the days with a plan, a direction, and an objective to guide me, this rootlessness was terrifying. Having absolutely no idea what to do, I fell back on the security of routine.

The gym was nearly empty the following morning. The scent of antiseptic from the overnight cleaning was still hanging in the air when I got there. A teenager was punishing the heavy bag, a dream in every punch. A ponytailed woman in a gray T-shirt was standing over a weighted bar, practicing the new psycholifting technique in which she visualized lifting it. It must have been a hard visualization, because a single dark gray line of sweat ran crookedly down the front of her shirt. But Hack wasn't there. I needed to get an answer from him, nothing got started until I had that. He didn't show. That wasn't surprising. After Wrightman's speech, I imagined it had to be a pretty hectic day inside those nonexistent agencies. But still, the fact that he hadn't responded to my texts was disconcerting. I hesitated to call him. At that moment I probably wasn't the most desirable phone pal for a government agent.

I went through an abbreviated workout, possibilities running through my mind like a slot machine searching for matching cherries. Wrightman had made the move to consolidate his power, and obviously done so with the backing of law enforcement and the military. I didn't think he would have risked it without that assurance. So there was no going back; even if it could be proved the NSA had nearly murdered a planeload of innocent people, it would make little difference. The administration was sewing up the country tighter than a body bag. But that evidence still might make a significant difference.

The presidential election was scheduled to take place in fifteen months. Wrightman needed an election to maintain the illusion that America was still a functioning democracy. But he was such an overwhelming favorite to win reelection that for the first time in electoral history British bookmakers had stopped taking action; they couldn't find enough opposition money to balance the bets. As it turned out, they couldn't even find an opposition.

The president was considered such a sure thing that neither party had thus far been able to find a suitable candidate willing to risk his or her career, and now perhaps their freedom, by running against him. Those few people who had stepped forward were from the unelectable fringes of both parties; running would provide them with a glimmer of attention in exchange for becoming political fodder. Those billionaire businesspeople who might have opposed him had been scared off by the probable loss of government contracts. The media was no longer a factor: the FCC's "equal time" regulations had been rescinded in the crisis regulations. The remaining media outlets had been consolidated through approved mergers into four major corporations, none of them willing to risk losing advertisers or their license by providing time or exposure to those fringe candidates.

I had a slim hope that the American people would react with horror when confronted with real evidence that Wrightman had instigated terror attacks to grab power and take their anger with them to the ballot box. If there was any chance of beating him other candidates would emerge. But time was running out for them to file in each of the fifty states.

Perhaps more important were the international ramifications. The

administration initially had been welcomed by our allies for its commitment to respect new agreements reached with the Bidens in an
attempt to return to international norms. The president had pledged
to support our friends and stand with the Western democracies against
our enemies. As a show of good faith, foreign aid grants had been restored. Ties with NATO continued to be strengthened. Many of our
traditional allies, countries that had lost faith in America as the "arsenal of democracy" and the enduring symbol of freedom for oppressed
people around the world during Trump, believed sanity had returned to
the United States. In the previous few years they relaxed their vigilance.
Whatever they really believed happened in Detroit, they accepted the
administration's explanation.

But as our government took increasingly bold steps to limit individual rights, some of those same governments had become alarmed.
British prime minister Bix Dickens had expressed the concern of the
UK when he publicly asked Wrightman to consider the consequences
before taking actions to curtail civil liberties. Vice President Hunter had
reassured Europe that these measures were temporary and would be removed once the threat had diminished. That all might change if I could
get this evidence out. And if it raised doubt, the UN might be compelled to take some action. It could shatter these still-fragile alliances
and might lead to censure, political isolation, even economic sanctions.

Once I started imagining the possibilities, I started to feel a little better. The weight of the entire Western world might be brought against
Wrightman to force him to release all the political prisoners. Who
knows, with enough support maybe Congress would show some balls. I
could see it happening. Sure, it was only a glimmer, a flea on the labradoodle of life, but it was real. Well, it was possible. It was something. My
mind transformed hope into excitement, which my body turned into
adrenaline that my heart pumped through my body. My parts were all
in on this one. I started sweating.

For any of that to happen, though, the evidence had to be irrefutable,
it had to be conclusive, and I had to make it public. I was working it all
out; I'd have to find out where Hack was. Get an answer from him. If

he verified the graph . . . I was trying to figure out who had his address. I could go over . . .

"You okay there, Rol?" Charlie Fitzgerald asked loudly. I caught myself. I had gotten so into my fantasy that without realizing it I'd broken my personal speed record for lat pulldowns. The rapidly clanking weights had attracted Charlie's attention.

"Yeah, yeah, I'm fine. I was just thinking . . ."

"Be careful with that," he joked. He rolled his eyes back and forth as if warning me to keep my thinking down.

"Right." I eased back into a rhythm. I can close my eyes right this minute and be back in that gym. I can hear it, smell it. That was the first time I'd worked through the possibilities. Did I believe it? Probably not. But at that moment I needed it. Hope was the only weapon I had.

I didn't kid myself. Big rewards require big risks. A government willing to kill its citizens to gain power, as I was certain Wrightman had done in Detroit, would do whatever was necessary to hold on to that power. Was I willing to take those risks? I considered myself a risk-taker but not a gambler—an odd combination. If I believed I could control the narrative by making my own decisions, I didn't hold back. I had run into that building believing I was quick enough to get out. But if success depended on the roll of the dice or turning over a card, I was much less gung ho. I was the kind of guy who sat on 16 in blackjack and never put more than three hotels on Park Place.

I went to the office. Habit, mostly. I had no place else to go. The early morning streets were unnaturally quiet. A massive street cleaner moved like a square metal animal down the block, its circulating brushes spinning curb debris into the air. There were more soldiers and militia than people, looking bored. I walked past Jerry Stern's spot over the grating. All traces of him—his shopping cart, blankets, cardboard signs—were gone; there was nothing to indicate he ever existed. He had been wiped away, "cleaned up," in the new vernacular.

As I walked along, I was wary but not overly concerned. Mighty Chair was my all-access pass, its bulk making me invisible. No threat to anyone. I considered my options. Whatever steps I took had to be carefully planned. I couldn't involve anyone else. Anyone specifically meaning Jenny. First thing I had to do . . . Cher interrupted my reverie: "Rollie, your mother is calling."

Perfect. I have always admired my mother's intuition. It seemed like every time I was busy trying to save the world, she would interrupt me. "Hi, Ma," I said as cheerfully as I could manage.

"I'm worried about you. Are you okay?"

"I'm fine."

"You don't sound fine."

How many times had we had this same conversation? Oddly, her voice was reassuring. The country might be collapsing, we might be on the verge of becoming a police state, but all that mattered to her was that I was okay. "Honest, Mom, I'm fine."

She hesitated, trying to decide if I meant it. Apparently I was fine, because she changed the subject. "Did you see what he did last night? Have you ever seen anything like that? Oh my god."

I needed that laugh more than she would ever know.

The office was mostly empty when I got there. Frankie B. greeted me. He was standing at his own desk, putting his Trump-on-his-haunches pencil holder into an already overstuffed backpack. "Hey, Rol," he said. "You okay?"

"Yeah," I said. Apparently my health was the question of the day.

He stopped packing. "So what are you going to do?"

I'd thought about that. I was going to work as long as possible. "I'm going to start with a reaction piece, I think. See how people . . ."

Frankie looked at me as if I were an alien. "You're kidding, right?" He shook his head in disbelief. "Rollie, we're done here. This . . ." He indicated the office. "We're done. These fuckers aren't going to let us publish anymore. I just came in to collect my stuff before they lock the doors."

Back in the sandbox, when I was getting shit together to meet the fan, I was always calm. I knew the risks, I knew my skills. I had learned how to channel anxiety into positive energy. That was in my Rollie 1.0 days. But as I looked at Frankie, I could feel the fear in the air. This time fear had control. "What are *you* doing, Frank?"

He scratched his neck. "Whatever I have to, I guess. All that crap

I wrote about Wrightman? Maybe that wasn't such a great idea." He looked up and yelled at the ceiling, "If anybody's listening, as of right now I have always loved my president!"

We shared a hollow laugh. Then he continued: "Working here, you and me, we've got to be on one of those lists. So Amy and I, we're just gonna ... we're taking a little vacation and seeing how it all shakes out. Who knows, Rol, maybe we're overreacting." And then he broke into a big Frankie B. Goode smile. "Maybe those soldiers in the street really are there to protect us." He cleared his throat, then pointed at his desk. "I gotta ... you know." He threw a few final items into his backpack and zipped it closed. He looked around at the mostly empty desks. "Well ..." he started, inhaling deeply, his shoulders rising as if the breath had filled them. Then he caught his emotion and brought it under control. Unable to speak, he shrugged, waved, and started toward the door. Then stopped. He had one more thought. He walked over to me, leaned down, and kissed me on my cheek. "It's been great, Rollie. I'm proud of us. We did some really good stuff here. Be careful, huh?"

He stood tall and forced himself to smile. The last thing he did was pick up an empty Dunkin' cup and add it to the tower. A dribble of cold coffee snaked down the tower and pooled on my desk. I didn't bother cleaning it up. The tower was eight cups tall, and we both knew it would never get any higher. "You too, Frankie," I said, forcing a smile even I didn't believe. "Give Amy a kiss for me, please."

As I packed, several other people trickled in and out, but the background music of a newsroom at work was gone, replaced by a muffled silence interrupted occasionally by whispered conversations as people said goodbye or made last-minute phone calls. I shook hands, kissed back, said goodbye, made vague promises to maintain contact, and offered optimistic predictions, but even as I did, I couldn't help feeling like I was in the middle of one of those overly dramatic movie scenes in which government personnel are racing to clean up files as the enemy reaches the gates of the city. The *Pro* was done.

I finally ran out of things to do. The truth is, I had been stalling, waiting, hoping that Howie would come in. He would have been there if it was possible. "Cher," I said, dreading this, "call Howie's home phone." It rang several times and I was ready to hang up when Karen answered. "Are you okay?" I asked.

I liked and admired Karen, but she had never struck me as an especially tough person. So the resolve in her voice surprised me. "Yeah, I am."

"Where is he?"

I heard her take one deep breath. "We don't know." There were three cops, she said. Howie asked to see their warrant, and they laughed at him. "They were polite, Rollie. It wasn't any tough guy stuff. One of them even apologized to me and said he felt really bad about this, but he had to follow orders. They let him pack a bag."

"They didn't say anything about where they were taking him?" It was a silly question, but I couldn't help asking it.

"I'll be notified, they said." I imagined Howie being shoved into the back seat of a dark late-model sedan, probably making some kind of "can we stop at McDonald's for detention?" joke to the cops. "I don't know what to do, Rollie. Isn't there somebody you can call?"

I hesitated. How many times had I been asked that question? And often there was someone I knew who knew somebody who had a friend. But the new answer was, not anymore. Calling somebody with enough juice to help? I almost laughed at that thought. That was so eight hours ago. It was difficult to accept the fact that the laws Americans had lived by for nearly 250 years no longer applied. "Temporarily suspended." Right. The traditional ways of dealing with the system were done, finished. Realistically there was nothing I could do, but I wanted to hold out hope. "I'll make some calls," I said with as much conviction as I could manage. "You never know."

"I've tried to get hold of Jenny to see if Martha could do anything. I called and I texted, but I've haven't heard from her. You know where she is?"

"No." Calmly, dispassionately, no. "I got some texts from her telling me things were crazy up there. Soon as we hang up, I'll try again." I shifted into the most positive tone I could manage. It actually was so good even I almost believed it. "Look, Karen, if you hear anything call me right away, okay? There's got to be something we can do."

While Cher was dialing Jenny's cell, I glanced at the mess covering my desk: the scattered piles of printed pages; the cryptic notes and phone numbers I'd jotted down on torn slips of paper and yellow and blue Post-its; the rubber bands wound around pencils; the loose paper clips and promotional pens that long ago had dried up; the twisted charging cords from discarded devices; a dull scissors and a rusting stapler that I don't think I'd ever used. It was a snapshot of a hectic life, my second life, when the story on which I was working mattered more than anything else in my world. It was residue from the hundreds of stories I had written or edited, notes for stories I was reporting, ideas for stories I intended to develop "when I had time." It was all clutter, but it was my clutter: half a roll of clear Scotch tape, a collection of newspaper stories clipped together, a strip of undeveloped negatives from my sister, seven lucky pennies I'd found lying heads-up and I'd taped to the desk, my Rangers challenge coin in a corner where it was the first thing I'd see every morning, and my tower of cups. I tried to freeze the sight in my mind, inscribe it in my memory so deeply I would never forget it. Rollie 2.0 was over. I would never be in this office again. The record would stand forever at twenty-eight Dunkin' cups.

I think even Cher was surprised when Jenny answered after three rings. Her heavy breathing and the background noise made it obvious she was moving in a crowd. "It's crazy here," she told me. "I haven't had a second. Are you okay?" There was a wisp of fear in her voice.

"I'm good. They picked up Howie. Karen's been trying to call you. You think Martha can do something?"

"Excuse me," she said to somebody. Then she was back. "Oh god, no. Not Howie. Yeah, I'll call Karen. But nobody knows what any of this means yet. There're all these people carrying guns walking around. We're on our way over to the Capitol for a special session. Wrightman wants some kind of Conscience of Congress resolution supporting him."

Fuckers. Of course they would. It was a loyalty test. A way of rooting out the opposition. "What's she going to do?" I asked. Then before Jenny could respond, I said firmly, "Tell her she has to vote for it." This wasn't the place to make a stand.

Jenny laughed at the thought. "Right. I'm going to tell Martha what to do. Not in this world. Look, sweetheart, I'm sorry, but I have to go. Where will you be later?"

Where was I going to be later? I had no answer to that question. "Home, I guess," I said. Then added, "I guess."

I stuffed as much as possible in my backpack and Mighty Chair's various pockets and carry bags, including my burner phones, tapes, and the original materials Brain had given me. Using my fingernail to scrape away the tape, I lifted my challenge coin, tapped it twice on the desk—once for my fellows and once for those who didn't make it home—and dropped it in my breast pocket. I wondered if I should take the time to erase the data and emails from my computer, then smiled at the thought. By now they had all the information they needed. But just in case, I picked up the stapler and finally put it to use, slamming it as hard as I could into my computer's hard drive—three times, four, five, slamming it again and again, until the whole side of the tower was caved in.

There were still two people in the office, cleaning up and closing down, when I was ready to leave. I wished them well and meant it, then picked up my cowbell and rang it one last time, slowly and mournfully. I put it in my backpack and left. I didn't look back.

It was still early afternoon, but the building was late-night quiet. No one was waiting at the elevator bank. I reached out to press the call button, then stopped; I left my index finger hanging in midair as I thought about it. In this new world it made sense to pause and consider the possible consequences before taking even the most ordinary action. My paranoia kicked in.

In that instant, Rollie 3.0 was born. It was as if my brain suddenly kicked into a new gear.

Was I really in any danger? Let's put it this way: I wouldn't sell a life insurance policy to myself. I had to be on somebody's naughty list. I'd earned it. Dick and Frannie were probably salivating. My guess was they hadn't picked me up in the first sweep because they believed being stuck in a chair limited my options. To them, I was a permanently sitting fuck. Where was I going to roll? So after collecting all the people who might scatter, they would come back for the easy pickings. I had to smile at that thought. Being underestimated definitely had its advantages.

Instead of pressing that elevator button, I walked around the corner and took the freight elevator to the subbasement. It was surprisingly brightly lit. Cardboard boxes of cleaning supplies, toilet paper, and fluorescent bulbs—whatever was needed to keep an office building humming— were piled neatly against the walls. As the doors opened, I heard voices. Then I saw two young women; they jumped when I emerged from the elevator. "You scared me," one of them said, the hand holding her cigarette pressed against her chest. Clearly they had sneaked down there to have a smoke and were relieved to see who I wasn't.

"Ladies," I said, smiling pleasantly as I moved past them. They stepped back to make room for me, then resumed their conversation. The basement was well-organized and surprisingly immaculate. Management was taking good care of it. It smelled of slightly damp cement, cardboard, and cigarettes. I made a note to myself that if I ever needed a place to hide, this would work. The last place anyone would look for me was . . .

Wow. That was quick. It had been only hours since Wrightman's announcement, and already I was compiling a list of safe places.

The custodial door opened onto a rear alley that stretched the entire length of the block. Rather than steps, a cement ramp sloped very gently up to street level, obviously to make it easy access for maintenance to dolly supplies in and garbage out. That didn't surprise me. Most large buildings have rear ramps, but those people who don't need them don't think about it. In particular the Dicks and Frannies.

The alley was wide enough to allow small trucks and vans to make deliveries. It was lined with green metal dumpsters bursting with small mountains of black and clear plastic garbage bags. I followed it for about forty yards until I reached a narrow passage between buildings, just wide enough for Mighty Chair to squeeze through onto the street.

I eased out, as if I were a car nosing into a busy intersection. I looked to my left and sat there for several minutes. There were several soldiers on the block, but no one seemed to be paying any special attention to my building. I took a hard right and picked up speed, leaving the *Pro* in Mighty Chair's rearview screen.

In those few hours, the sidewalks had come alive; in fact they seemed even more crowded than a typical downtown weekday lunch hour. But instead of the usual businesspeople, it was an odd juxtaposition of armed troops wearing modified combat gear, D.C. cops in their formal riot gear, members of different militias wearing colorful uniforms and matching armbands, and casually dressed spectators who had come downtown to see the show for themselves. The spectacle of a young couple wheeling a stroller past militia members with automatic weapons strapped on their backs was startling. Rather than Washington, D.C., on a glorious early summer day, it felt about as gay and carefree as the Unter den Linden in 1938.

It served my needs, though. Chair disappeared into the mix like a green pea in mashed potatoes.

I moved slowly and steadily, trying not to draw attention to myself. I couldn't afford that, not with Brain's evidence in my backpack. Most people focused in front of them, safely preventing any type of human connection. Those few people who met my eyes smiled sympathetically or nodded condescendingly, then stepped out of the way, as if doing me a favor. Occasionally someone recognized me from TV; I wasn't especially memorable, but Mighty Chair had his own fan club. He was by far the most famous wheelchair in America. (Well, to be fair, also the only famous wheelchair.) When that happened, I smiled and nodded, and before they could stop me, I raised my eyebrows in frustration and pointed ahead as if I were late to an appointment and couldn't stop.

There didn't seem to be much interaction between the troops and civilians, although if four or five people stood together for more than a few seconds, a cop or militia would ask them to move on. It all seemed casually organized; some of the militia were posing proudly for photographs or selfies on certain streets, positioning themselves so the Capitol was visible in the background, while others sternly ordered people not to take pictures. But all of them shared a common mission: There would be no demonstrations on the streets of the Capitol.

I suspected similar scenes were taking place on the streets of every major American city. I couldn't confirm it, because media coverage of demonstrations had been specifically forbidden to prevent protests from spreading.

While I waited on a corner for the light to change, an army corporal stopped next to me. We glanced at each other and smiled in acknowledgment. As he turned away, he said out of the side of his mouth, "This is total bullshit. What the fuck are we doing here?"

Rather than saying anything, I reached into my shirt pocket and showed him my challenge coin.

The soldier looked at it and rattled a supportive fist. "Hooah!" he said, then walked away.

Look, I admit it, I was being way overly cautious. I wasn't even a small fish in a big pond. In reality I was probably more like one of those plastic deep-sea divers blowing air bubbles out of a helmet at the bottom of an aquarium. I wasn't especially valuable, I'd served a minor purpose, and I wasn't going anywhere. The reality was that having to deal with Chair probably made detaining me more of a hassle than I was worth. But the government didn't know what I had, or more accurately what I *might* have. Being me, though, just in case I looped around the parking garage before going inside. I always paid attention to my paranoia; it probably had saved my life on patrol several times.

Van was parked on the first level. The once comfortable whir of the van's panel door sliding open and the ramp extending now seemed unusually loud and threatening; I climbed inside and got locked down as quickly and quietly as possible.

Van had been outfitted to allow me to live in it for at least a couple of days, more if I conserved resources. I wanted to be free to travel, and with the spotty availability of accessible hotel and motel rooms, I needed a bedroom (and bathroom) I could take with me. Y had designed and built it. It had all the comforts of home, if home was a space slightly smaller than a cargo container but with less charm. The decor was American rudimentary: On one side panel I had hung a print of Munch's *The Scream,* and directly across from that, a poster of a kitten dressed as a ballerina. The facilities could run on batteries for a full day, which could be at least partially recharged through two solar panels on the roof, but also could be hooked up to water and waste lines at campsites.

I used one of my burners to call Hack. I couldn't put it off any longer. "What's happening?" I said with exaggerated bonhomie, not identifying myself. "Missed you this morning. Just checking that with everything going on, you still want to work out tomorrow morning?"

He didn't miss a beat. "Sure, why not? Be there or be square."

"Great." Then, as if an afterthought, "Oh hey, do me a favor. Don't forget to bring those insurance papers you wanted to show me."

After ending the call, I took the Sim card out of the phone to prevent the law from pinpointing my location. *This is really weird,* I thought. *I'm on the run.* Me, on the run. How absurd is that? Other than the techniques I'd been taught in Special Ops training, none of which had been conducted from a permanent sitting position, everything I knew about escape and evasion had come from novels and movies. An entire entertainment industry had been built around that concept. I had taken out the battery because that's what Jason Bourne would have done to "stay off the grid."

Stay off the grid? That's how my go-to experts, Robert Ludlum and Lee Child, might have referred to it. I was about to find out how much they actually knew about it. As long as it didn't include jumping out of helicopters or beating up six tattooed guys, I probably could handle it. Mostly I had to operate on common sense. "Adapt and adjust" to changing conditions, my instructors at Bragg had drilled into us, "adapt and adjust" being military speak for "make it up as you go along." "Think out of the box," they had told us, although more accurately in my case, it was think out of Mighty Chair. I moved to the back of Van for several hours, watching the battery-powered TV. Most of the coverage included footage of ordinary people doing ordinary things. *See, these new laws aren't a big deal. Just go ahead with your life. Your newly safer normal life.*

When I was finally ready to move, I put the card back in the phone and called Jen. She was still operating at NASCAR speed. An emergency session of Congress had been scheduled for later that evening, she told me. All kinds of rumors were floating around. She was going to spend the night on a cot in the office; the Hill was sort of locked down. She did not say whether or not she had a choice. "Listen," I told her, adopting my new default position, the assumption that the phone had ears, "there's a problem with the air-conditioning in the apartment." Meaning don't go there. "I'm getting ready to park Chair for the night." Meaning I was going to stay in Van.

Our conversation was mostly smoke, hiding any real information. We ended with "love you" and a promise to keep in touch.

It was dark outside when I finally left the garage. What rush hour there was had ended, and traffic had thinned. One lane in either direction was closed for military traffic. Every few minutes a Humvee ferrying troops would speed by. Cher cautioned me when I went more than five miles over the listed speed limit. When I got outside the city, feeling very Bournish, I tossed the burner out the window into the brush.

I drove to a McDonald's in Bethesda, about two miles down Rockville Pike from Walter Reed, one that no one in my phone book knew about. Well, it was a McDonald's, everybody knew that, but not my connection to it. This was one of the first places I'd gone on my own during my recuperation. There had been no Mighty Chair, my chair was the manual Rollie-wheel drive, so just getting there represented significant progress for me. I went there often enough to get to know the manager, a Mexican immigrant named César Hernández. I walked in one night as three guys were giving a double amputee from the hospital a hard time, grabbing his food and tossing it back and forth. When César tried to stop them, two of them turned on him, knocking him to the floor and holding him down. The third guy went for the cash registers, their real purpose in starting the fight.

There were six people in the restaurant, but none of them made any move to help. Then a pretty amazing thing happened. My instincts kicked in and I reacted. Picking up as much speed as I could (it was a confined space, so it wasn't much), I slammed the chair into one of them from behind. That sent him tripping forward headfirst into the soda dispenser. I spun the chair around and leveled a Bruce Lee arm block right into the second thug's midsection. He doubled over and I hammered down on the back of his head. He hit the ground; I must've hit some nerve because he started flopping around like a landed fish.

By then, the other customers had jumped in and grabbed the third guy before he could get away. Sirens blasting, the gendarmes arrived a few minutes later.

Everything had happened so quickly it took my thoughts several minutes to catch up to my actions. It was the complete battlefield experience: act first, think later. Depend on your training. I had no idea where that reaction had come from. But in those few moments I had glimpsed the possibilities of my new life.

To show his appreciation César had made his store the most accessible McDonald's in the country, good enough to earn a cover story in *Franchise Times* magazine. But he went even further, installing power, water, internet access, and waste hookups in the back of his parking lot for two vans or properly equipped SUVs, then limiting its use to wounded vets and their families. Both spots were open when I got there. I backed in, safe for the night.

Van wasn't especially comfortable, but it would suffice. Once I was settled in, I opened up my tablet. Remembering Brain's warning about browsing patterns being detectable, I went first to *Bustle,* the leading site for young women, then to *Popular Science,* thereby fitting no known demographic. I didn't bother looking at the most prominent news sites. At this point, they wouldn't be helpful; if they were still up, they had made the necessary compromises. They would be spewing bullshit. Instead I began searching for the myriad pirate broadcasting sites. All it took to go live was a handheld camera and big cojones. With some luck I'd be able to find one of these picture pirates.

While I was searching, a text message popped up on the screen. It had been sent by Diogenes, someone from the meeting reaching out to the others. It read: *PopUpCongress.org.* Several seconds later this message disappeared. The resistance was starting to figure out how to communicate safely under the new restrictions.

That site opened quickly. I was looking at the floor of the House of Representatives. Someone up in the gallery was livestreaming the emergency session. A whispered voice explained that the speaker had introduced the resolution of support for Wrightman. The camera obviously was hidden from view; they had gotten so small, it could have been disguised as a brooch or even a pen. It scanned the entire chamber: Law enforcement officers stood against the wall both on the floor and in the gallery. Whoever was narrating this whispered they were Capitol Police, U.S. Marshals, and Homeland Security agents. I leaned as close to the screen as I could trying to pick out Jenny; she had to be there, but I didn't spot her.

The roll was being called. Other than several pages moving in the aisles, it could have been a still photograph. Although roll call votes normally were recorded and tallied electronically, in this instance the Clerk of the House was conducting it in a far more dramatic fashion. As each member's name was called, he or she stood and verbally cast their vote. Members who voted yea followed that vote with a few words expressing their loyalty to America and the president, then sat down. But two members loudly voted nay. One of them, Representative Amy Bowers (D–New Mexico), told the House that this was the single most shameful moment in the history of the United States Congress. That was met with several boos; one unidentified person shouted she was a "terrorist sympathizer" and she should "sit down and shut up." After casting their no votes, both members remained standing as two Capitol Police officers came down the aisle and took them into custody. They went silently, although as Bowers was escorted off the floor, she defiantly raised her right clenched fist high in the air.

The clerk got to Mrs. McDonnell. Martha stood to her full height and turned slowly around the entire room. Oh no, I thought, please, please don't do it. Her voice resonated through history as she said, "The stain that is on this House will never be erased. Shame on all of you." She faced the podium. "Mr. Speaker, I vote no. Never."

The House was absolutely silent. Then someone coughed. As two officers walked down the aisle, I heard what sounded like a sob. The officers stopped at Martha's row. Several members stepped back to allow them to reach her. One of those officers put his hand on her elbow to guide her, but she angrily shook it off and glared at him. She said something inaudible to him. She was going on her own terms. She reached the aisle and without waiting for the officers turned to her right and walked to the top.

It was an act of courage equal to anything I had ever seen on the battlefield.

As she did, a spectator shouted from the gallery, "Cowards!" Everyone on the floor turned and looked up. Several members pointed at someone, eerily reminiscent of those men on the balcony with Martin Luther King pointing in the direction of the shooter. Then I heard what sounded like a brief scuffle and some shouting, although whatever was taking place was not shown.

The roll call resumed. There was one more nay vote before the stream wobbled, then abruptly ended. There was no way of knowing if it had been intentionally shut down or the streamer had been discovered. It disappeared without any explanation.

I spent the next hour searching the net for any believable reports, while enjoying a bologna sandwich I had defrosted in the microwave. The news sites were still reporting the details of the assassination attempt and the frantic search for whoever was responsible, the tragic backstories of the victims, and the "surprisingly widespread support" for the government's temporary crackdown on dissidents. One effervescent young woman earnestly told a reporter, "We're either going to be America or we're not. This has to stop."

All the sites repeatedly ran footage of staffers cheering the clearly shaken president as he returned to the White House.

I didn't sleep. For some reason I started thinking about the last dog I'd owned, or who had owned me, depending on whose point of view you believed. Chuck Waggin' was a mixed breed with a visible abundance of retriever. Old Chuck had been a loyal wing-dog through college and grad school, as well as after Fort Bragg, dying in my arms soon after we celebrated our fourteenth year together. I loved that dog. He'd been my anchor—the grinning, tail-wagging friend waiting for me at the front door whether I'd gone to the store or to the desert, making every place we stayed together our home. On nights like this one, when I was getting ready to hit the road, I was glad there was no Chuck. I wasn't certain I would have been able to leave him behind, even knowing they were looking for me.

Jenny would understand. I opened my eyes and lay in the dark thinking about her. She knew those few possessions that mattered to me and would go to the apartment and pack them away. I desperately wanted to call her to find out how she was coping and what she knew about Martha, but I couldn't do it from a stationary location. I'll call her in the morning, I decided, soon as I got what I needed from Hack, when I was on the road.

Jenny would understand.

17

onfucius said, "Never give a sword to a man who can't dance . . .
a blade of death in his hands is a dangerous man to be around; be
he friend or not." Really, he said that. I don't know why I was
thinking about that as I drove to the gym the next morning. The report
was going to be my weapon. It was not as sharp as I might want it to
be, but I had been taught to fight with the weapons I had. You can
kill a person with a pen, for example, literally and figuratively. Martha
McDonnell's weapon was her integrity. She shamed those people and
they were going to have to live with their moral failure for the rest of
their lives.

It would plague those of them with a conscience. The rest of them,
unfortunately like so many of their fellow Americans, were afraid or
unwilling to take a stand. Maybe they convinced themselves it was acceptable or for them it served some purpose, or maybe they had been
bought out, but it still amazes me today that so many seemingly decent
people could have watched this unfolding and done nothing to oppose it.

Wrightman's so-called peacekeeping force had done its job. The city
seemed amazingly calm as I sat patiently in the shadow of a Staples
awning, watching the entrance to the gym. It was pretty much impossible
to disguise a wheelchair, even one as versatile as Mighty Chair. When
I was awarded my Silver Star, I'd ridden into that ceremony dressed as
a farmer astride his John Deere, and two years ago I'd shown up at the

Pro's Halloween party as a vendor inside a hot dog stand, but slipping into the gym to meet Hack was far more complicated. There was little I could do but surveil the place carefully before going inside and hope my name hadn't reached the top of someone's list.

I'd found a parking spot on the street several blocks away. I used a second burner to call Jenny, but I'd hung up when it went directly to voice mail. I called her office, hoping a staffer might know where she was, but again it went to voice mail. Finally I'd sent her a text, asking her to "get back to me on this when you can." When you can. I guessed she was in an office somewhere, fighting to get Martha released; that was a whole lot better than the darker possibility, that she too had been "detained." It didn't matter, really; whatever her situation, I couldn't do anything about it. My mission training kicked in; those efforts made by my instructors to distract me from my assigned mission paid off as I put all those thoughts and fears in my pocket and focused entirely on my objective.

I got there early. Soldiers and police officers were patrolling the streets, but in the dull sunlight of the early morning, they somehow seemed less ominous. As I waited, I checked my devices. In only a few hours what already had been dubbed Resin, the Resisters' Network, had gone totally social. It had moved like a shark through social media, never pausing in one place long enough to be tracked and killed. It had just showed up on my phone. I didn't have any idea who sent it and who else was receiving these updates. I didn't know how extensive Resin was, how information was being gathered, or even whether it was sending from America. But it was welcome evidence that an active resistance movement was probing at the system, figuring out how to fight back.

The instructions were explained in a text message. Our phones or tablet would start vibrating to alert us that a new message was being posted. Nine quick dots, a long dash, a dot: Morse code for Resin. A text message would direct us to the specific platform: Twitter or email, Snapchat, Facebook, Instagram, Pinterest, Tinder, or another easily accessible site. The message would provide a onetime-use password. Ninety seconds after it was opened, this invitation would disappear.

Invited members could then go to the designated site and open it with that password. After it had been read and closed, it would be deleted, leaving no history of having ever existed. It could not be saved, printed, copied, or forwarded.

And right on cue, my tablet started vibrating. A new message had been posted. A text message directed me to YouTube and provided a password. The password opened a cartoon: Bugs Bunny's mouth was moving but it was entirely out of sync with the report. A woman's voice delivered the latest updates: The sweep had continued through the night. Among those people supposedly detained were Alec Baldwin, Lorne Michaels, and several *Saturday Night Live* performers and writers, Barbra Streisand, Colin Kaepernick, basketball coaches Steve Kerr and Gregg Popovich, Bono, Liam Neeson, Jimmy Kimmel, and Stephen Colbert. Justice Sonia Sotomayor had been marched out of her home in handcuffs. It was rumored but had not been confirmed that the entire Kardashian family had been swept up, although a convoy of black government vehicles was seen leaving their family compound.

(Apparently the fact that Bono and Neeson weren't American citizens made no difference. As people were being "detained" under emergency regulations, rather than arrested, immigration law did not apply.)

The report continued. Many people had managed to escape. A large group had been flown out of the country by John Travolta; among those people believed to have been on his private jet were George and Amit Clooney, Arnold Schwarzenegger, Jennifer Lawrence, Jay-Z and Beyoncé and their children, Stephen King, Morgan Freeman, and George Lucas with their families. Travolta had not filed a flight plan, but it was believed his destination was Montreal. The Obama family had made it across the border into Canada secreted behind stacks of packages in a FedEx truck. Soon after his safe arrival, the former president had announced the formation of the American Resistance Movement, Barack's Battalions. He vowed to use every means possible, other than force, to pressure President Wrightman into restoring complete democracy to the United States.

All of that actually was a good thing, I decided. When those Americans who had avoided learning about that coup thing turned on their

favorite shows or went to the movies and discovered that their favorite actors had been replaced, they were going to be furious. And then,
when they found out what had happened in this country, they were
going to demand those characters return. It wasn't going to be pretty.

Bugs Bunny continued her report without coloring it with emotion: This is reality. She might just as easily have been delivering the
weather: Rain with a chance of revolution. She spoke with a slight
European accent that added an unusual solemnity to the antics of the
cartoon characters. Bugs was getting ready to clobber Yosemite Sam
with a sledgehammer when she reported that Wrightman had ordered
the army to fortify both America's southern and northern borders, "although rather than keeping immigrants out, his objective appears to be
preventing Americans from fleeing." She added that according to the
BBC, Russian president for life Vladimir Putin had announced his support for the "long overdue crackdown."

After slightly less than five minutes an illustration of a nuclear weapon
detonating into a mushroom cloud appeared and the video ended. As
promised, all traces of it disappeared. I was now officially a member of
the active resistance. I wondered if they had a health plan.

As I continued watching the gym entrance from a safe distance, about
half the Light Brigade showed up. Hack was one of the last to arrive; he
paused at the entrance and looked around, then, satisfied, went inside.
Handicapped people have our own way of thinking: before taking an
action, we run through the entire chain of steps in case there is a step
we can't manage or bypass. Adapting that to life on the run was relatively simple. Getting into the gym was easy. The problem was getting
out. If it became necessary, was there an escape route?

There had to be a rear exit. D.C. fire regulations would have mandated it. I circled around to the rear of the building. Back entrances and
overlooked doors had taken on a new importance for me. The rear door
to the gym was a faded blue steel, the color of well-used tools. Someone had scratched a heart into the door, apparently *DJF loved LMF.* And
a good time might be had by calling Violet, at the given number. An
overlapping metal flap prevented anyone from jiggering the lock. (Not
that I knew how to do that anyway; in the military, when a lock got in

our way we blew the shit out of it. While not neat or secret, it definitely was effective.) I knocked on the door several times until I heard someone pressing down the interior bar. The door was pushed open by a chubby man wearing basketball shorts and a white T-shirt. A towel was wrapped around his neck. "Hey, Rol," he said, holding open the door and stepping back against it to let me in.

Chair did a little wheelie over a two-inch-high sill. "They're doing some work out front. They told me to come around."

"Need some help?"

"Nah, thanks."

The door opened into the corridor between the men's and ladies' locker rooms. I found Hack sitting on the narrow bench in front of his locker, changing into his workout clothes. When he saw me, his shoulders sagged and there was genuine relief in his smile. "You okay?"

"So far. But there's going to be a lot fewer people at my birthday party this year. Whatta you got?"

He reached into his locker and took the manila envelope off the top shelf. "If you told me what this is all about, you'd have to kill me, right?"

I shook my head. "Not me. I'm sorry to be a jerk about this, Hack, but believe me, if you knew any more about this, you'd wish you didn't."

"Okay." He heard the gravity in my voice. He held up the envelope. "Whoever did this is pretty clever. You know, lots of times when I'm watching a basketball game, I'll turn off the sound and put on some classical music. It's pretty amazing; more often than you'd think, it looks like the players are choreographed. They're completely in concert with the music. It shouldn't work, but it does.

"That's what your friend did here." He tapped the envelope. "Whoever it was created their own measuring system. It shouldn't work, but it does. I ran a whole bunch of challenges, I ran it against other samples, I changed a few things and ran it again, but it makes sense." He brushed his hand through his long hair, and as he continued, he began nodding his head, reminding me of one of those perfectly balanced wooden birds that peck into a trough with the pull of a string. "I'd say both of these codes probably were written by the same person. I can't say it's unique the way a forensic examiner can, not without running it against a few hundred million samples, but if I had to testify, I'd say, 'Yeah, odds are pretty good that these came from the same place.'"

He handed the envelope to me. "I never saw this, right?"

I wasn't sure if that was for my protection or his. But the answer was the same. I slid it under my seat. "I owe you, Hack. For everything."

Wilson rattled a supportive fist. He knew where I was coming from, and more important, he knew who was coming for me. "Gather no moss, my friend," he said, turning away. He slung a towel over his shoulder and headed toward the gym.

There was an expression we used in Goat Country when we had to fix or correct an error: we would try to unfuck it. What I was trying to accomplish was maybe the single greatest unfuck in history. I was sitting on the story of the century. Literally, I mean, sitting on it. Evidence that the government of the United States had cyjacked Flight 342 would cause a political earthquake. It was impossible to guess who might be left standing when the ground settled. Once again, the question was what to do with it? The Trumpazines had destroyed the lines between truth and complete right-wing bullshit with the creation of "fake news." If I posted it online, Wrightman would flood the media with experts who would ridicule the concept, laughingly deride it as fake news, muddying the waters enough to dilute its impact. For this to be taken seriously, it had to be vetted, approved, and finally released by a universally respected entity. A source that could not be doubted.

That pretty much narrowed it down to Oprah or the Canadian government. I had to deal with reality: I couldn't get to Oprah. Actually, the Canadian government made sense on so many levels. The rifts between America and Canada caused by Trump had been stitched, but those wounds hadn't completely healed. All I had to do was put this evidence in the hands of the proper Canadian government official.

O Canada, here I come! Getting there would be difficult, especially with the new restrictions, but not impossible. The administration had no idea this evidence even existed, much less that I had it in my possession. If they were aware of it, they would have to do pretty much everything possible to prevent me from getting over the border. But I wasn't overly concerned; I couldn't think of any way they could find out about it. All I was to them was another name on an official list. Just another runner.

At least that's what I believed at that time. And if it had been you, and you were in the same situation, you would have thought the same thing. I guarantee it. Thanks, Confucius.

I had just put Mighty Chair in gear when Hack came rushing back into the locker room. "There's two suits out front looking for you. Jake told them he hadn't seen you come in." Jake was the manager of the gym; he didn't know I was there. The man who'd opened the door for me was in the shower, loudly singing Dylan off-key, a feat in itself. "Want me to do anything?"

There is a moment in every classic monster film in which a character rushes into the lab to inform the protagonist, "It's reached the edge of the city!" This was my official it's-reached-the-edge-of-the-city moment. I was surprisingly calm. I guess I'd been preparing for this for longer than I'd thought. "Stall 'em for a few minutes if you can." I needed to get to the rear door and skedaddle.

"I'll try." He was gone.

Seconds later I heard him in the hallway, asking loudly, "Can I help you guys?"

So much for the rear door. I looked around the locker room, trying to figure out WWBD? (What would Bourne do?) There was only one place to hide. I went for it.

I had just closed the door when I heard Hack's voice booming through the locker room, "See, I told you guys he wasn't in here. It's pretty hard to miss a big guy in a wheelchair. If he shows up, you want me to give him a message?"

"Thank you, but we're just going to look around." It was impossible to miss the derision in Dickie's voice. I heard the metallic clank of lockers being opened and slammed shut. Could they possibly be that stupid? Did they really think I was hiding in a locker? But then they came into the bathroom.

"Well, well, well," Agent Richard Corbin said with satisfaction from his position on the tiled floor. "What do we have here? It appears that someone is back in a handicapped stall. I wonder who that might be." Then in a sarcastic twang he singsonged, "Oh, Mr. Stone, come out, come out, we know where you are." Then he rattled the locked stall door. He pulled it several times as if it might suddenly spring open. "Open up, Stone," he ordered. "You're not going anywhere."

I could see his shoes under the door. He stood there in silence for a few seconds, obviously trying to figure out what to do. His partner, Francis Russell, said to Hack, "Thank you. We'll take it from here."

Well, they didn't want any witnesses. "I'll be right outside," Hack said. I didn't know if that was intended to be a warning to the agents or a message to me. I heard the door brushing closed. Corbin cleared his throat. Then in his most officious voice he said to the closed bathroom stall door, "Roland Stone, we have an order from the Department of Homeland Security to take you into protective custody. Resisting a lawful order is a felony and will be prosecuted to the full extent of the law. You will be entitled to all of the protections granted under these regulations." He jiggled the door again. "C'mon, Stone, this only has one ending. Open the damn door."

It was time and I was ready. I positioned Mighty Chair directly in front of the door, then withdrew the bolt. "It's open."

"That's a good boy," Dickie said as the door swung open. He filled the doorway, a smug look on his face. His jacket was unbuttoned, his feet spaced widely apart. I moved Chair forward a few inches, lining it up.

"I told you we'd be back," Russell said, looking over his smaller partner's shoulder, gloating. "Now come on out . . ."

Even I was surprised at how calm I was. "Cher," I said, "arm bar, please." I pushed the control lever forward. Chair's retractable arm, its metal fingers balled into a fist, shot straight out of the armrest. It slammed directly into Dick's honkers. It must have been a direct hit because he responded with a deep nasal "*Hooooonck*" as he looked down in utter surprise, put his hands over his balls, much too late, then folded over from his waist like a jewelry box being shut. My hand pressed against the top of his head and I shoved him backward hard, sending him reeling directly into Russell. Russell bounced off a sink on the far wall. Both of them sprawled to the ground in a tangle.

Corbin was curled into a fetal position on the bathroom floor, his hands between his legs, moaning in pain. Russell managed to free himself and was trying to regain his footing. "Stop!" he screamed at me, reaching under his jacket, clearly going for his weapon.

I grabbed hold of his leg just behind his knee and yanked it. Russell went sprawling backward, his head clunking off the edge of the sink. He went down as if Iron Mike had nailed him.

Both agents were writhing on the floor as I headed out the door. I couldn't resist one final statement. The last they saw of me was Chair's extendible arm pointing straight up in the air, its middle "finger" held high.

Hack was in the corridor. "Go," he said, pushing open the rear door for me. As the door closed slowly, I heard him shouting, "Hey! What's going on in ...What the hell! Where'd he go?"

For several seconds I savored that thought—until I realized I was now officially a federal fugitive, subject to prosecution "to the full extent of the law." That part wasn't so funny. This wasn't a sitcom. I had assaulted two federal officers. There were serious consequences for my actions. It was time to start adapting and adjusting. First, I had to get back to Van. I remembered a primary rule from the E&E course at Bragg: when on the run, don't run. Running attracts attention, and that is precisely what you don't want. Move slowly, move steadily, use whatever natural cover exists.

When possible, I stuck to alleys and lanes; when I had to be on the sidewalk, I took my time, stopping regularly in front of store windows to check the reflection. There didn't seem to be any immediate reaction to my escape. No police cars or military vehicles came racing through the streets with sirens blaring, and I didn't see troops fanning out to find me. When I thought about it, that made sense. There was no reason for me to be considered a high-value target; I was just another name on the list. In fact, the more I thought about it, I doubted Dick and Frannie would even report my escape. They would look pretty inept being taken out by a cripple in a wheelchair. Jokes would follow. More likely they would report they hadn't been able to locate me, then keep after me without additional support. For the next few weeks Corbin would be cursing me every time he took a piss, but a sore Dick wasn't enough to make me an agency priority. My name would be added to whatever lists were being circulated among law enforcement and military personnel in case I was stopped at a street check or for a minor violation. But if I was smart, careful, and lucky, I should be able to make it to the Canadian border.

I would need help. I hated asking for help, just hated it. Always did, even when I was upright and even more so after the event. It's just the way I am. But I had to deal with reality: no matter how independent I was, even with Mighty Chair, Cher, and Van, I would struggle to make that trip by myself. There were going to be situations in which having someone with me could make all the difference. It wasn't going to be Jenny, wherever she was. At a meeting six weeks earlier, we had been given emergency contact information; it was one use only, only for real emergencies, and don't be surprised if there was no response.

Trying to save American democracy, I decided, definitely qualified as an emergency.

After reaching Van without incident, I opened my tablet to eBay and thumbed through to the designated page. It was an array of old baseball cards for sale. I searched until I found the wildly overpriced Ted Williams 1954 Topps card being offered for $18.95. I ordered it, using a fictitious name and a made-up address and credit card information, but included the phone number of one of my remaining burners.

While waiting for a response, I drove to Tysons Corner Center, one of the largest malls in the region, and parked outdoors roughly equidistant between two exits. Hiding in plain sight. The lot was about a third full. I backed into a space between two black SUVs; I didn't need room on the passenger side because I had no intention of getting out. Homeland Security could easily trace my plate number, but I doubted anyone would be looking for it. The space was as safe as anywhere else; no one would notice me sitting there.

The sun finally had come out; I checked Y's electric gauge and noted the solar panels were working. I opened up my devices. There had been a continual flow of posts from all over the country. Many of them, presumably, were part of the government propaganda campaign. But among the cat videos, birthdays, recipes, opportunities to earn $2,000 a week working from home, photographs of unusually large-breasted women at supermarkets, and other clickbait, I found some information that might have been valid. *Might* being the operative term. According to several Facebook posts, there had been a minor uprising at the Mexican border just south of San Diego as thousands of Californians tried to cross the border, but it had been quickly quelled. In Northern California a significant number of people were fleeing into the hills. A group of renegade Apple employees supposedly had founded their own nation; they announced it would be governed on Groucho Marxist principles and named it Freedonia. True or not, I liked it. There were no other posts indicating resistance in other military districts.

The rest of the news was disheartening. In Military District 4, the Upper Midwest, district military governor Damon Burns had announced the creation of a Junior G-Person organization for children twelve and under; the goal was to enlist boys and girls in "the fight against terrorism" by teaching these "young patriots" how to recognize and report anything suspicious. The first Young Patriot's Medal had been awarded to Chicago sixth grader Tommy Fenton for alerting law enforcement when he discovered his science teacher was spending nights in the school's science laboratory.

The story seemed too absurd to believe; on the other hand, I was sitting in a van in a parking lot, waiting for a return call from an embryonic resistance organization, planning an escape from America.

I was especially interested in information from District 2, the Northeast. I figured that would be the best route for me. I'd drive through upstate New York, crossing into Canada at the very busy Niagara Falls checkpoint. I wondered if it might make sense to go through New York City. The city was an easy place to get lost in and I still had a lot of friends living there who would be willing to help me. But it looked like it might be too big a risk; the self-declared Sanctuary cities, in particular New York and Boston, had been designated for enhanced security. According to the district military governor, Peter Poopé (pronounced *Poop-A,* the French way, he proudly pointed out), international flights had been temporarily suspended to prevent radical elements from entering the country, although ports would remain open and cargo operations would continue.

Drivers throughout District 2 were being warned to expect pop-up roadblocks on major arteries. Checkpoints had been reported on the Long Island Expressway and Route 27, the road to the Hamptons. There were also scattered reports of gas shortages, although I was pretty certain that was simply a way of cutting down travel between districts. Whatever, the roadblocks, checkpoints, and gas shortages were going to make my drive to the border a lot more complicated.

It was early evening before I finally got a response. The burner vibrated the correct code. A text message directed me to an online site, GobbledeeandGook.org, and provided a code. Gobbledeeandgook was a Wonderland site; it had been created for a single use and was linked to no other sites. You couldn't get there from anywhere else. I opened it and typed in the code. The procedure seemed way over the top; I half expected it to go up in smoke to the accompaniment of dramatic music after I'd read it. An area code 646 number appeared.

It rang three times. A pleasant male voice answered, "Gobble, Dee, and Gook. How can we help you?"

I hesitated.

The voice filled the silence. "How can we help you, Rollie?"

"I, um . . ." I had wandered into a new world and had to get my bearings.

The voice prodded me. "We're here to help, Rollie."

"Who is this?" I asked finally.

"I guess you could call me your travel agent."

I swallowed, then exhaled; it was going to take me some time to get used to all this. Even with all the excesses and insanity of Trump/Pence, I had never expected it would go this far. None of this seemed real. In fact it didn't even seem possible. "How . . . how do you know what I need?"

"You reached out to us for help, remember that? We know you're on the list, so there aren't a lot of options." There were hundreds of people in the same situation, the voice explained, trying to get out of the country before they were detained. The majority of them from the East

Coast were heading north. To assist them, a rudimentary "underground railroad" had been created and was cranking into operation. "We can get you to Canada," the voice said with confidence, "but it's going to take a little time."

A priority list had been established, he told me, and unfortunately journalists were considered category 2. Seats were limited, and politicians and celebrities, opinion-makers whose names people recognized and might respond to, people who could help build the resistance, went first. "I'm really sorry, Rollie, but even with what you've already done, it'll be a week or more before we can get you a reservation. There's not much we can do to help you before then."

There was no way I could wait that long. I played my best hand. "Listen, I've got some really important information. It's a story I've been working on." He was intrigued. I wasn't going to offer any specifics, but I did add, "It's the kind of story that has a chance of blowing Wrightman right out of the White House."

After a long few seconds of silence, the voice had responded with some uncertainty, "Hold on."

I was passed along to two more people and made my case to both of them. At that moment the rest of the world was offering at best tepid support for the administration's regressive policies. European leaders were trying to balance ethics and economics, waiting anxiously to see how events turned out before making any commitments—and fully aware that opposition forces within their own countries also were watching and waiting. I was asked for more information. "Here's the deal" was as far as I would go. "If the evidence I have is confirmed and made public by a respected entity, like the Canadian government, there's no way Wrightman can win an election." I spoke with the confidence of a used-car salesman pushing a vintage Yugo. But I needed that ride. When I didn't get an immediate answer, I added, "And it'll make it really difficult for any democratic government to continue supporting Wrightman." If that wasn't sufficiently intriguing, I added, the United Nations, which thus far had been silent, would be forced to take a position. Worldwide condemnation, and with it a total loss of credibility, would have dire consequences: The word of the American government would have significantly less value in international relationships. "In other words," I said, "they would be Trumped."

While no single country was powerful enough to force change, the worldwide community acting in unison could put enormous economic pressure on the administration to restore fundamental rights.

In about a dozen different ways they asked me for details about my evidence. I couldn't blame them, but I also wouldn't tell them. If it leaked, and anything was possible, my trip would suddenly become a lot more difficult. I must have made the sale, because they finally handed me a priority ticket. "You leave tomorrow morning. You'll be all right tonight?"

I'd figure it out, I said. Because of my unusual circumstances we agreed I'd have to drive Van. My first "conductor," I was told, would be waiting for me outside the Zawadi African Art Gallery on U Street NW the following morning. I'd recognize that person because they would be wearing a faded red *Make America Great Again* hat—backward.

I spent the night at the McDonald's hookup. I finally got a text from Jenny: "I'm okay. Very busy. (smiley face) We're trying to get to M. Love you much. Stay loose." Stay loose? That made me smile. Run, she was telling me, run.

"On my way, eh!" I responded. "Save the last dance for me." Followed by three heart emojies.

It was a long and restless night. On a scale of 1 to 10, the comfort level of Van was slightly less than "Are you kidding me?" It would have been cramped even without Mighty Chair. Fortunately, Chair was foldable. Just before sunrise I'd gone outside and watched the day dawning over the gas station across the street. Light crept into dark crevices, as if the world were opening its eyes. Shadows came alive and began crawling, their morning stretching. I started thinking, which given my present circumstances probably wasn't the smartest thing to do. It occurred to me that my whole adult life had been a series of goodbyes to people and places. I started counting the number of places I'd lived for more than a month and quit when I got to twenty-two, although I knew there were more. They ranged from an heiress's mansion in the Hamptons the summer between college and grad school to an air-conditioned tent outside Khwaja Rawash Airport in Kabul. I'd seen the sun come up in every one of those places. Some people kept photo albums—I had my sunrises. I was, I realized, a collector of beginnings; I'd watched the day arrive in just about every imaginable environment. I'd seen those shadows crawl down skyscrapers in a cold New York dawn and seen a burning yellow ball ignite the desert. This one had arrived boldly; it wasn't one of those wimpy ones that couldn't decide between shades of gloom. This one was a bright yellow Crayola. *Here's the day. Take it. Make something out of it.*

Its warmth lulled me to sleep; I was awakened by a man yelling into the squawk box that he wanted two Bacon, Egg, and Cheese McGriddles—without cheese. He was adamant that he did not want the cheese. I went back inside Van, hoping the unlikely sight of a guy in a large wheelchair asleep in the rear parking lot of a McDonald's had not attracted unwanted attention. That was stupid. A rookie-fugitive mistake.

Forty minutes later I was gliding past the African Art Gallery. No one was waiting there. That didn't surprise me, not with overly zealous law enforcement agents reveling in their new power. I drove past the store and made three right turns. When I came around for the third time a woman was standing there, her MAGA hat on backward. She was wearing baggy jeans and a light jacket, comfortable traveling clothes. Her hair was pulled back into a bun, but I recognized her instantly: Laura from the meetings. I stopped at the corner and sat there; she took a casual look around, and when she was satisfied it was safe, she walked over to Van and got in. "Fasten your seat belt," she said as she flashed a cheerful smile. "It's going to be a bumpy ride."

18

In his own bumbling way, George W. Bush's secretary of defense Donald Rumsfeld got it exactly right when he said, "There are known knowns; there are things we know we know. We also know there are known unknowns; that is to say we know there are some things we do not know. But there are also unknown unknowns—the ones we don't know we don't know."

If knowledge is power and ignorance is bliss, I was one dumb happy fella.

You have been riding right along with me every step of the way. I've kept you completely informed; what I knew and when I knew it. But to badly paraphrase Rumsfeld, I had no way of knowing what I didn't know. The White House had done a good job scaring people into silence. However, as I was about to find out, there was one vital piece of information that I was not aware the White House knew that would change my plans.

The government had found out about the evidence I had in my possession. Months later I pieced together what had happened. But I think it is only fair to reveal it to you now. It will help you understand what happened next.

It turned out I had been right about Hack Wilson. As I suspected, he was a contract employee for government intelligence agencies. A high-level hacker. To confirm Brain McLane's theory, Hack had reached out to

several people he worked with regularly and trusted, asking if my interpretation made sense as well as requesting additional samples of code to
use in his own analysis. Two of the coders he approached worked at the
NSA. This possibility had never occurred to me. What are the odds, right?

To test McLane's concept that individual coders left footprints that
could be identified and used to trace back to the source, NSA senior
engineer Paul Steingruby converted several segments of code he had
written several years earlier into this "language." He graphed the code.
His initial reaction, when that sample turned out to be a close match
for Hack's submission, was that he had disproved the concept. The fact
that old code he'd pulled out of his desk drawer was a close match to
Hack's sample indicated that the results produced by this method were
not sufficiently unique to have any real probative value.

It was later that night, when he was home watching an old episode of
NCIS that turned on an amazing coincidence, that he started getting very
nervous. It seemed like too much of a coincidence that Hack would give
him two pieces of code he had written without being aware of it.

While I was greeting the sunrise in McDonald's parking lot, Steingruby was at his desk, running additional comparisons. His panic grew
with each failure. This method made sense, it worked. Within hours his
fear had become reality: Someone had matched a nonsense code he'd
written as a favor for a high school hackers' competition to the code
he'd written for his old commanding officer, Artie Hunter. I can imagine the panic that ensued: Somebody had just connected him to the
most recent Crime of the Century.

He called Hack. I know all this because Hack told me. He and Steingruby had known each other for years; they had worked together on
a number of classified projects, had even dated sisters for a brief time.
Without thinking about it, Hack told him that this guy he worked out
with at the gym, guy named Rollie Stone, the Detroit whistleblower,
had asked him to check it out. Nah, he didn't know where the two segments had come from or what they represented. "I told him you were a
good guy who had asked me to do him a favor."

"It's an interesting concept," Steingruby told him in what Hack described to me as an offhanded manner. "But it isn't an especially good

way of making a valid comparison. There are just too many variables. It might work in very limited situations, but I don't think any competent person would have much confidence in the results. Computer coding just doesn't work that way. A talented hack is virtually untraceable."

Hack thought that report was really interesting. That didn't square with the work he had done. To test Brain's theory, he'd run two segments of code he had previously written using the kid's method and found repetitive characteristics in them that he hadn't known existed. Peaks, valleys, and intervals. He had identified his own footprint and it was there in every segment of his own code that he tested.

Which is why alarm bells went off when Steingruby reported a different conclusion. He was much too casually dismissive of a technique that Hack had seen produce positive comparisons in his own lab. "Thanks a lot, Paul," he said, then just to be cautious added, "That's pretty much what I decided too." To reinforce his little lie, he'd told Steingruby not to bother returning the samples: "Just go ahead and toss them."

Which is why the next morning Hack told me he believed the method was valid; the two codes I gave him had been written by the same person or group.

But now you know what I didn't: the government was aware of the danger.

What happened next is conjecture. There are a few pieces I know to be accurate; the chain might be a little bit different, but the end of it is the same. In some version, here's what must have taken place. Steingruby couldn't be certain his dismissal had ended Wilson's investigation. He called his contact in Hunter's office; who knows, maybe he called the vice president directly.

The vice president would have shared this information with people on his need-to-know list. NSA director Bobby Satin would have been on the list. Rip McCord probably would have been on it. Rocky Penceal at Homeland Security certainly was informed. The president? Who knows, plausible deniability plays an important role in American politics.

I'm guessing some of those people found the whole story farfetched; and perhaps a beard to cover the horrendous possibility that there was a traitor on the inside.

I have been told, and I'm sorry but I can't share this source, that Homeland Secretary Penceal did some checking and found that two of his agents already were tracking me. Agents Corbin and Russell reported that while on their way to pick me up they both had sustained minor injuries when their car was hit from behind at a traffic signal. They were informed that locating and apprehending me was no longer their primary assignment, it was their *only* assignment. Penceal told them, and this too comes from a trusted source, "I don't want to hear you stopped to take a piss until this guy is in your custody."

Somehow, I don't think Dickie was really looking forward to taking that piss anyway.

Although I was not aware of it at that time, within several hours I had become the most wanted man in America. After allowing sufficient time to pass, agents Corbin and Russell had informed headquarters that I was on the run. (I'm positive the usual jokes were made at Homeland Security headquarters: Actually, he's on the wheels! Ho-ho. He can't run, but he can't hide either! Ha-ha.) As a result, a BOLO, a be on the lookout for, was forwarded to all law enforcement agencies, which now officially included enrolled militia.

I knew how all this worked. I'd been on the inside of a coordinated search several times for stories. This notice would include my credit card numbers, known phone numbers, type of vehicle and license plate number, maybe even the manufacturer of the stripped-down Mighty Chair. My driver's license photograph and all pertinent information would be sent as a BEAT to the 700,000 police officers on the LET NET, the restricted access Law Enforcement Twitter Network. The U.S. Marshals Service definitely would be brought into the search. The popular TV show *The New America's Most Wanted* quickly prepared and began broadcasting a two-minute segment. I know for certain that Dickie and Frannie visited Howie in detention and offered inducements peppered with subtle threats in an unsuccessful effort to convince him to help them find me. Knowing Howie, he'd tucked his thumb under his palm, surrounded it with his fingers, and suggested, "Talk to the hand."

While all this was shifting into full gear, Laura and I were two hours into a thus-far-uneventful drive. "Don't we even have a secret hand-shake?" I'd asked as she settled into the passenger seat, a line I considered a nifty icebreaker considering our circumstances. But then I added quickly, "I'm Rollie. Thank you for doing this."

"I remember," she said pleasantly. "I'm just going to take you the first leg. Somebody else'll take you from there." She glanced over her shoulder at the makeshift bedroom. "Nice." She flashed a smile. "Love the cat!"

"There's a refrigerator if you'd like something to drink. Energy drinks and water."

"Maybe later." She removed a tablet from her backpack and propped it up on the dashboard. It opened to an illustration of Julie Andrews singing happily as she led the von Trapp family to safety through a field of sunflowers. *Quite a whimsical choice,* I thought. She clicked to Google Maps and typed in an address. "We'll get whatever notifications we need from here." She put out her hand. As I started to respond, she said, "Give me your credit cards and your phone, please."

I started to object, but then saw the wisdom in her demand. There was no way I could use my own credit cards. I handed her my wallet. "I've already gotten rid of any phones that could be connected to me."

She went about her business efficiently. After removing all my credit and debit cards, she put one in: "That's your debit card," she explained. "The code is all sevens." It had been issued to Randy Yellin, and there was $250 on it. "Use it when you need to, but whatever's left when you get to Canada, we need back." She pulled off my E-ZPass and replaced it with a new one from her backpack, dropping the old one into a foil pocket. Then she leaned back and told me, "Okay, let's get this show on the road."

Google guided us out of Washington. As we headed north, I glanced one last time in my rearview mirror. Storm clouds the color of a dense ocean fog were rolling in, dull and lifeless, swallowing the remainder of the blue sky. The Washington Monument stood against it like a sharpened pencil poised to write on a slate ceiling. I took one deep breath, filled my cheeks, and exhaled slowly, then studied the road in front of me. But for just an instant my memory flashed a glimpse of Reagan's "shining city on a hill," when America was still a beacon.

I didn't see the address she'd keyed in, but wherever we were going, it would take us three hours and twelve minutes to get there. That's if we were lucky. I assumed Google hadn't factored in military roadblocks, which would make the trip longer. Like, possibly, the rest of my life.

I had a vague idea of the route we were going to take. Years earlier I'd shipped out from the Air Reserve Station at Niagara Falls for a mission that officially never happened. I'd driven up there from Bragg. I'd taken the little bit longer route, making it a pleasant drive through a lot of bucolic countryside. It got me away from the noise of the cities, serving as a sort of refresher course in real America.

We stopped briefly in the secluded parking lot behind a Kohl's in Middle River, Maryland, where she swapped my D.C. plates for a New York set and pasted small stick-on decals reading *Dr. Watson's Medical Devices* on both sides of Van. That was pretty impressive; someone had been doing some preparation. "I'll be right back," she said and disappeared around a corner. I guessed she was using the restroom. She returned in a few minutes. "Let's go," she said, slamming the door. "C'mon."

I was curious. "What'd you do?"

She held up a $10 bill. "I sold your E-ZPass to a trucker. C'mon, let's go."

Now that was pretty impressive. "You really think all this is necessary?"

"Who knows?" She shrugged. "We're just making it up as we go along." She looked at me and smiled for the first time. "Welcome to New America."

As we skirted Baltimore I finally began to relax. "Can I ask you a question?"

"That is a question," she pointed out. She had a really confident attitude, but I noticed that her nails were either cut or bitten short.

"How many runs like this have you made?"

"Counting this one?" She pursed her lips. "Two." The "railroad," she explained, had been organized by former New York governor Andrew Cuomo, who had turned down the opportunity to flee to Canada and supposedly was moving around the country in disguise, setting up safe houses and way stations. "He's become an almost mythical figure," she said. "You know, like Sasquatch." I noticed she had a very pleasant voice, feminine with a backbone. "There are all these stories of him popping up all over the country. People claim they've seen him driving an Uber, pretending to be a power company lineman, even walking around wearing dark sunglasses being led by a guide dog."

The farther we got away from Washington, the more relaxed she became. She was an actress, she said, which allowed her to move easily and often without attracting government attention. That's why she had been recruited.

Suddenly it all clicked. That's why she had looked so familiar. "You're the cell phone girl!" I said with the delight of recognition. I repeated her line from the ubiquitous commercials, imitating the pseudo-sultry voice she used in those spots. "Everybody else is just talk. We're the whole deal." We laughed together, and for a brief moment the tension was lifted.

Laura, it turned out, was her real name. "Actually not my real real name," she clarified, "but my real *stage* name. Somebody else was registered with SAG under my name, even though that wasn't really their name." She considered that, dismissing it with a chuckle. "That doesn't make a lot of sense, does it?"

"Ah, show business."

She had spent the prior eight months working at the National Theatre. She had done a variety of roles, her favorite of which had been a witch in *The Crucible*. She hadn't been picked specifically to be my escort, she had just had the day off from work, but it was fortuitous that we'd already met. She explained the procedure to me, cautioning that everybody was new to this, so we might have to make some adjustments on the run.

"Literally," I said.

She would go with me to the first station, which was just on the fringes of Pittsburgh. If we were stopped, we would claim we were in a new relationship and sneaking away for a brief vacation. "That's when I blush and steal a glance at you," she said, stealing a glance at me.

Assuming Pittsburgh hadn't been compromised, she would hand me off there. She didn't know who would take me from there, but they would have their own cover story. "When you reach the border, you'll be instructed when and where to cross safely. Canada's being great about all this, they haven't announced it publicly, but they will offer political asylum to anyone who puts one foot down . . ." She looked at Mighty Chair and paused, probably wondering if she had said something offensive. "Well, you know what I mean."

I didn't interrupt her, occasionally tossing in a "Really?" or "Wow." Apparently the resistance was a mildly warm bed of rumors. The latest rumor was that Homeland Security was compiling scores on everyone. "Like the Resistance Olympics," she said. According to this story, watchers were reading and rating social media posts, 1 point meaning it had no interest to the government, 10 meaning it was highly critical of the government. An average over 7.5 got people moved to a more active watch list. "Finally," she said with some pride, "I'm a ten!"

I smiled as noncommittally as possible.

We stopped for gas south of Pittsburgh. Laura paid in cash. When we were back on the road, she sent a coded text message to the stationmaster confirming the delivery was going to be on time. She was mildly perturbed when she didn't receive a confirmation. "It happens," she said, staring at her phone. She shrugged. "We're all so new to this stuff."

I nodded. No big deal. Growing pains. Working out the kinks in the system. Screwups were part of the process. But just in case, I began checking my mirrors more often.

On the highway, it was difficult to feel any change. The countryside was still beautiful, the farmlands still green, the red and silver silos framed against the Mediterranean blue sky. The only noticeable change were the military and militia vehicles that passed us regularly, most of them flying two or more American flags. Twenty miles closer she tried Pittsburgh again. Then she sat staring at her phone for a response that didn't come. There was a hesitancy in her voice as she admitted, "I'm not sure what to do." She told me the protocol: If she did not receive an acknowledgment, she was to assume the station had been compromised. "Mistakes happen," she said hopefully. "That's probably all this is. There's a dozen reasons they didn't get back to me."

Paranoia, I adore ya! I wasn't interested in the benefit of the doubt. "Do you know any of these people?"

"No." I caught her biting her thumbnail, her shoulders hunched protectively over her phone, willing it to ring. "Let's drive by there and see if anything's going on."

I pushed myself up, but I couldn't get comfortable. WWBD? I was already working out a new agenda as we reached the city. Armed soldiers were standing guard in front of banks, churches, and public spaces, but not nearly as many as I'd seen in Washington. From what I could see, people seemed to be ignoring them. "Make this next right," Laura said, pointing. "It looks like it's a few blocks up. I'll tell you when but don't slow down."

We approached an intersection. An MP was directing traffic with ex-aggerated verve. I was enjoying his performance until I saw that the traffic signal directly over his head seemed to be working fine. There was no reason for him to be there. My Special Ops spidey sense was sending me an alert. There wasn't much I could do about it without drawing attention to Van. It was too late to turn off. As we drove past him, I made a point of casually looking away, as if I was checking traffic coming from the side street. The light was red, but the soldier whistled insistently and waved me through. Laura leaned forward. "Next block," she said. As we drove past a pizza shop, she glanced casually inside. Then she pushed back into her seat and looked straight ahead. "Keep going!" she snapped, that pleasant voice gone. "Keep going."

In an instant I was back in the Stan, driving a Humvee down a rubble-strewn street. Hyperalert. No panic. I tightened my grip on the wheel; I maintained my speed. *Pay no attention to me, just out for a drive.* I watched the doorways and the windows. Glanced at the rooftops. Checked the cars in front and behind Van, vehicles coming toward us. At any instant I was ready to slam down on the accelerator and hasta la vista, amigo. "What happened?"

She was already putting new data into the iPad. "Make the next turn. Right or left, just get off the street."

I made the next right, then the next left onto a parallel street. No one was trailing us. "What'd you see?"

She twisted to face me, leaning back against the door. Her voice now riddled with uncertainty, she said, "There was supposed to be a sign in the window, three slices for two, if it was good to go. It wasn't there."

I ran my tongue across my suddenly dry lips. "Now what?"

She wiped her palm across her brow and bit down on the nail of her pinkie, probably trying to clear away the confusion. "I don't know." She tried to calm herself with a deep breath; then she slammed the heel of her hand against the dash. "This fucking iPad won't take this address. God, I hate these fucking things." She slammed it a second time, then pushed back in her seat and folded her arms in frustration, looking like a petulant child.

I looked at her and smiled.

"What?"

I held up my hand defensively. "Nothing. Honest. In the movies this is where I say, 'Now I'm stuck with you for a few more hours,' and you stick out your tongue at me."

"This isn't a joke, Rollie. This is . . ."

"No kidding. Wow. And here I thought we were having such a good time together." A blue-and-white police car, sirens screeching and emergency lights in full "watch out, here I come" mode raced by going in the opposite direction, followed by an old-fashioned army jeep failing to keep up. "Why don't you grab us both some water, please."

She ducked her head and climbed into the back, returning seconds later with two bottles of sparkling water and her composure. "Sorry."

I nodded my acceptance. "It happens." Then, after a beat, "Look, all of this, nobody believed it was possible. Soldiers patrolling the streets, people getting arrested for criticizing the government? That's not supposed to happen here, not in America. That's . . ." There were too many examples to choose one. "But it is happening here and so now we've got to deal with it. Being pissed off is what we should have been five years ago, when fucking Trump was selling out our values. It's too late to waste time on what we should have done. Right now we've got to focus on what we can do." I turned my head and looked right at her. "And that means getting me to Canada."

That probably didn't come out exactly the way I intended. "Really? What exactly do you think I'm doing here?"

"No, wait, you're right. That's not what I meant, least not that way." I stared straight ahead, the road unfolding into the distance, the clouds moving north with us. "I'm sorry, Laura. Look, it isn't easy for me to ask for help. It never has been. Even before I was Rolling Stone." I took a thoughtful breath. She deserved to know the truth. "This isn't about me. There are other things going on, things that I can't tell you about. But I have some information, some papers that have to get to Canada. That's really what you're doing here. Believe me, it's not because I'm some kind of big shot."

She looked at me skeptically. "Is that from some movie?"

"No. It's true."

"And if you told me what it is . . ."

We finished together, "I'd have to kill you." I pointed at her iPad. "Go ahead, try it again."

We drove north on I-79. Laura sent a message to "Mom," informing her that she had decided not to stop at her aunt's house in Pittsburgh. Minutes later "Mom" acknowledged it without an explanation beyond a warning to be cautious. "Weird," was all Laura said, shaking her head.

We had been on the road for almost four hours. The drive from Washington to Buffalo could easily be made in seven hours, considerably less if you were pushing it, but I was careful to stay at the speed limit. I picked a random car and locked in a comfortable four car lengths behind it, reminding myself to go easy on the accelerator. We stayed off main roads when possible, driving through the farms and fields and small towns of the American countryside. I'd driven across the country several times through college, on road trips and new assignments; I'd traveled through the mountains in the East, across the endless prairies of the Midwest, and through the desert and stunning beauty of the West, and always with excitement and anticipation. As corny as it sounds, I'd always felt connected to it in some deep and inexplicable way, enjoying a profound sense of pride that this was my country. All of it. From the traffic jams of Manhattan to the bait shops of Louisiana, a special bond held us all together. No matter where in the country I traveled, whoever I'd met along the way, it was all home. And I was the product of it all.

"What are you thinking?" Laura asked.

I sighed. "Nothing really. You know."

"You gonna miss it?"

A gust of sadness hit me. "I've been missing it for a long time."

I glanced at the clock. It was after five o'clock. We were in decent shape, I figured. I still had no reason to believe that anyone other than two seriously angry Homeland Security agents was searching for me, and nothing I had seen from those two indicated they would be able to find me. The last time I'd seen them they were doing the pain dance on the bathroom floor, so I was fairly confident they would be taking the next few days off. Even if Homeland Security was interested, they didn't have the slightest idea where I was heading.

Canada was the logical destination, but if they had profiled me, they would not expect me to act logically. And even if they knew for certain I was heading for the northern border, there were literally hundreds of roads that would get me there. Laura had done a smart thing dumping my GPS on a trucker; if they were tracking that, they by now were heading in a completely different direction. The Marshals Service might well be monitoring my credit cards, computer and ATM usage, and phones, but I had stayed completely off the grid.

What else? There always was something else that could be done. I was running through my checklist for the umpteenth time when Laura asked, "What do you think this is all about?"

Here we go, I thought, *road trip talk.* We'd skipped right over favorite movies, places we'd lived, worst vacations, dates from hell, bad jokes (Me: What do major-league ballplayers and dieters have in common? You: I don't know. Me: Plate discipline. You: Huh?), even questions about my disability; heck, we hadn't even harmonized on a single Beach Boys song. We'd just gone from zero to infinity, smack-dab from "Does that come with fries?" to the meaning of life. "What particular this?" I asked warily.

She turned in her seat to face me, but this time did not push back. In body language that meant her defenses were down. "Wrightman. I just don't get it. Why's he doing all this?" She shrugged her left shoulder. "I mean, he's destroying everything this country stands for. Why?"

She couldn't have asked something easy, like what would it be like to visit a black hole? "I wish I knew," I told her. I flipped a hand into the air, stumbling for an answer that made sense. "Maybe he really believes this is necessary to reunite the country, save it from being ripped apart between right and left. Maybe he really thinks this is what he has to do to protect the country from terrorists." I looked at her. "Or, I guess, he simply could be a megalomaniac . . ."

"Or a narcissist?"

"Or a narcissist," I agreed. "Or he has an inferiority complex. Or it's better than working on an assembly line in Dayton. Or some department secretary has pictures of him *in flagrante delicto* with a moose and is bribing him. Maybe he's insane, who knows. It could be any of those things, or all of them."

"But do you think he understands the damage he's doing?"

This was shaping up to be just another one of those lighthearted discussions about good and evil, original sin and the essence of man. Another question hit me: Could Dr. Freud have driven while explaining the psyche? "I don't know," I admitted. "Questions like that are why psychiatrists can afford swimming pools.

"Whatever his reasons, I'm pretty certain he doesn't see it as damage. I'll tell you what surprises me. Wrightman is a pretty bright guy. He was a decent senator. Middle of the road, go along to get along. Nothing like Trump, for example." I glanced at her—no reaction. I continued. "Trump was easy to figure out. His megalomania left him unburdened by self-doubt, his insecurity made him a bully, his lack of common knowledge made it easy for him to destroy tradition without the slightest guilt, and his ignorance made him the champion of poorly educated and easily manipulated people. For him, being president was as easy as dating was for Neanderthals. But Wrightman . . ." I shook my head.

"So what do you think he's gaining from this? I mean, he's already the most powerful person in the world."

I knitted my lips into a straight line and shook my head. "Honestly, I don't have the slightest idea. It doesn't make a lot of sense to me either. With some of these guys it's obvious, like Kim Jong Un or Saddam— they had to hold on to absolute power for their own survival. But that's not what's going on here, is it? There's endless possibilities—lifestyle, riches, vengeance, self-defense, you know, if we don't conquer them they'll destroy us. Sometimes it's a necessity. Before World War II the Japanese needed access to cheap oil to expand. Then there are your religious zealots spreading their message of peace through murder.

"Money? He's already a very wealthy guy. What's that quote . . ." I dug into my Bible file, which in fact was pretty thin, and pulled up a go-to quote: 'For what shall it profit a man, if he should gain the whole world, and lose his own soul?'"

She buried a laugh in the back of her throat. "I'll bet you say that to all the girls."

We shared another flash-smile. Then continued speculating without reaching any conclusion for several more miles, finally acknowledging that the why of it made no difference.

We were breezing along into the late afternoon, not quite feeling groovy, but I still had slim hopes for a Beach Boys medley. And then that old spoilsport Cher had to interrupt. Laura and Cher had been getting along quite well; Laura had even asked Cher for help in avoiding traffic on our new route. About an hour earlier I had told Cher to scan police reports to see if my name came up. "Rollie," she said suddenly, "I have found your name in a report."

Shitfuck. "Cher, what?"

Several years earlier Y had hacked Cher into several law enforcement communications systems, including the LET NET, just as in earlier days reporters would monitor police scanners. Maybe it wasn't entirely legal, but it was a good tool when I was working on a story. Cher reported, "A high-priority BEAT has been issued on the Law Enforcement Network. This includes all pertinent information. It also mentions a white van with handicapped license plate number WP4106. Two photographs are attached. Suspect is believed to be north of Pittsburgh. If spotted, officers are to contact Homeland Security immediately."

"Cher, thank you." I assumed she was done.

She was not. "Rollie, I have not concluded my report," she corrected. "Officers are informed the suspect has in his possession sensitive documents. Suspect is to be searched and all documents are to be confiscated but not read."

"Cher, thank you." I very quickly analyzed that information, considered all the possibilities, and came to a valid conclusion: I'm fucked! I ran through my options; throwing myself on the floor and kicking my feet in the air while I whined was definitely out. That left pretty much everything else.

"Rollie?" For the first time there was fear in Laura's voice.

"Not good," I said. "Very not good." I made my first decision. "Listen, they don't know you're with me. Soon as we get to the next town, I'm letting you off. You'll have to figure out how to get back . . ."

"Oh, don't be silly." She dismissed that thought as if I were suggesting buying the twenty-roll package of toilet paper at Costco rather than trying to prevent her from going to prison for aiding and abetting a federal fugitive. Things clicked into place in her mind pretty quickly. "You're right, they don't know I'm with you. So they're not going to be looking for a couple. We've got good IDs. They don't have the right plate number. We got the Dr. Watson's signs on the van." In those few seconds she had convinced herself. There was real confidence in her voice as she said firmly, "We can still do this, Rollie. We just have to be smart and careful."

Apparently my best Bogie wasn't sufficiently convincing. Laura was not getting on that plane with Victor Laszlo. "Ho-kay," I agreed, breaking it into two syllables to hide both my relief and gratitude.

With Cher's alert, the plans we'd made were abandoned. We had to assume that the main highways and border crossing points were being heavily patrolled. Law enforcement had my information. In a strange way, though, the advantage had shifted a bit. Until a few minutes earlier, I hadn't been aware that a massive search for me was in progress and we had been driving right into the spider's parlor. But we were aware of that now and could take precautions. All they had was the full cooperation and participation of every law enforcement officer, soldier, and militia member covering the entire East Coast, while we had almost a full tank of gas.

This presented a whole new set of problems I hadn't anticipated, starting with getting through customs. I could no longer be Rollie Stone. Even Chair might need a new identity. My famous Rodney Dangerfield imitation probably wasn't going to work, so somehow I'd have to get ahold of new identification. Laura was reading my mind; her brow furrowed and her left cheek crunched up, pulling her mouth to the side. A full McKayla. "We're gonna have to get some new identification," she said. She looked at me. "Don't worry, they'll figure out something."

"Here's what we're going to do," I said evenly. "They don't know that we read their BEAT. So instead of going north, which is what they've got to be expecting me to do, let's work our way west."

It was amazing how quickly my mind made the necessary adjustments from being uncertain exactly where I was going to not having the slightest idea where I was going. We got off at the next exit. We were just outside Lake City, Pennsylvania, a suburb of Erie. "We should stop and figure this out," I said. "Let's find a diner."

We followed Laura's iPad to Leo's Own Diner, a shining silver imitation railway car directly across a rutted road and a seedy strip mall from Lake Erie. Exactly the kind of place you might run into Jack Reacher. The parking lot was about a third full, which seemed about right for early evening dinner. The handicapped spot at the far end of the parking lot was vacant. Perfect. For me, Leo's main attraction was its long ramp that rose to a side door.

As we entered, the waitress, a solidly built woman who seemed a bit old for her yellow pinstripe uniform and Converse high-tops, was moving from table to table with a dishrag and a coffeepot. When she saw us, she pulled a chair away from a table and beckoned us over. "I'll be right with you," she promised, laying down two menus and continuing her coffee rounds.

While Laura hit the ladies' room, I glanced around Leo's Own. The cash register was sitting on the bakery display case, next to the main entrance. A counter ran almost the entire length of the diner, fronted by evenly spaced round swivel seats with glittering red plastic tops. The one directly in front of me had been repaired with gray duct tape. Several booths covered with the same tired red vinyl were built in by the windows facing the road and the mall. At a right angle to the booths were three small square tables. Two flat-screen TVs over the counter were set to a Cleveland Indians game; the sound was off, and the captions were too small for me to read.

We were seated at one of the three tables. I tried but failed to remember the last time I'd slid into a booth. A kid about ten years old, sitting in a booth with his family, was leaning into the aisle to get a better look at Mighty Chair. He had a straw in his mouth, and every few seconds he'd straighten up and say something to a man I assumed was his father. The man responded by looking at me, then playfully slapping the boy's hand.

The menu offered typical diner fare, any dish made anywhere in the world, from grits to fajitas to moo shu pork, all of it guaranteed delicious and prepared in fifteen minutes. Laura returned; she'd put on pinkish lipstick, taken her hair out of the bun, and added just enough eye shadow to make her appear simultaneously younger and more mature, a woman's trick I'd never quite figured out. "You know what you want?"

"Everything looks good," she decided, perusing the menu. She lifted her eyes over the top and caught me staring at her. "So?"

"You can't," I said, locking eyes. "Everything is too much."

She opened her mouth to respond, but it was our waitress who said, "Sorry." She took a pencil from behind her ear and held it ready by her pad. "What can I do you for?" The greeting *Leo Says Hi!* with an illustration of a smiling man in a yellow pinstripe shirt waving at us was printed on the name tag pinned to her shoulder. A handwritten slip of paper inserted in it identified her as Midge. Woven leather straps hung from her glasses, as if her face were inside parentheses. Laura asked, "What have you got that's gluten free?"

I buried my face behind my menu so she wouldn't see me laughing. Here we were, right in the middle of our escape, and she was concerned about gluten. Midge paused before responding, staring at Laura as if she recognized her but couldn't quite place her. Then as Midge pointed out the yellow starbursts that identified gluten-free choices, Jenny popped into my mind. *Nice going, mind,* I thought. *You trying to tell me something?* Maybe it was some kind of defense mechanism kicking in, maybe it was a test of my loyalty, but as attractive as Laura was at that moment, I desperately missed Jenny. I wanted to talk to her, tell her where I was and where I was going, but mostly I just wanted to hear her voice and know she was okay. That we were okay. The second I got across the border I was . . .

"Sir?" Midge was impatient, tapping her pencil. "What can I get you?"

I ordered. As we waited, we began planning the next few hours. She had not been assigned to take me to the border, that was supposed to be Pittsburgh's job. "I don't know anything about it," she said. Then she put her hand on top of mine and said confidently, "We'll just have to figure it out when we get there. There are a lot of navigators up there, and Mom'll put us in touch with them."

We talked about going west but decided the longer we stayed in the country the greater the chance we would be spotted. As there was no "best option" we agreed to go north and figure it out when we got closer. Considering the precautions we would be forced to take, there was no way of even guessing when we would reach the border. As my mother used to tell me, we'll be there when we're there. Whenever that was, we would wait until either morning or evening rush hour, or maybe a day or three or six, then slip across in the traffic. Just in case, though, she asked, "You have anything in there that might be a problem? Any pot? A gun?"

I coughed into my fist. A gun? Well, *there's* a problem. But until we reached the border, there was no reason to dump it. "We'll be fine," I told her, waving off the question. Adjust and adapt; and when necessary, give 'em the old one-two.

Midge filled our water glasses. "Food's coming," she said pleasantly. "Kitchen's just a little backed up."

When she was gone, Laura leaned into the table and asked, "What about that whatever it is that I don't know about? Is that something we need to worry about?"

"No, nothing." I pointed to my forehead. "It's here." I could have pointed to my ass too, as I was sitting on it.

Ten minutes later we were still waiting for our meal when people started shifting in their seats to look at the TV sets. "Turn up the sound, Dusty," a woman with a helmet of blond hair in one of the booths shouted to the counterman. Dusty gave her a serious look, an "I know what I'm doing" look, then reached up and did so. A somber President Wrightman was speaking from the Oval Office, a look of deep concern on his face. The chyron at the bottom of the screen, in bold letters large enough for me to read, stated ominously: LIVE FROM THE WHITE HOUSE: PRESIDENT TO ANNOUNCE EXECUTIONS.

19

We missed his first few words. "Quiet!" that blond woman yelled sternly, and all conversation stopped. The kitchen crew came out and stood behind the counter, looking up. The cook was distractedly wiping his hands on his stained apron. Dusty raised the sound just in time for us to hear the president announce "arrests in the attempted assassination of President Wrightman and the murder of Treasury Secretary Farber."

"Yes!" the boy's father blurted and was immediately hushed.

The president said he refused to "give these people the political platform they want. The attention they were willing to kill for." He paused to let that sink in. "Therefore, I am not going to announce their names or provide any details about them. But I can tell you their participation was part of a larger effort against the American people, and their apprehension makes all of us safer tonight."

The president put down the papers from which he had been reading as the camera dollied in for a close-up as he obviously began reading his heartfelt remarks from a teleprompter. "The evidence against these people, there are two of them, is overwhelming. And when confronted with it they confessed. The question that I had to answer is: What are we going to do about that?"

He paused and looked at his hands, which were clasped prayerfully on the desk. "Rather than put the country through that turmoil, God knows we've got enough on our plate right now, we convened a military tribunal. Our finest military leaders gave these people every opportunity to defend themselves, but they were unable to do that. So after a hearing these two people were convicted, unanimously convicted . . ." I couldn't help but admire his TV presence. After a pause and a deep breath, he finally looked directly into the camera and continued: ". . . and sentenced to death. And just like President Abraham Lincoln did at another time of great turmoil, I have decided to accept the recommendation of this military tribunal and order that these people be hung."

I was stunned, absolutely stunned. Just like that he was throwing out the Fifth Amendment. He was ignoring more than two centuries of precedent, destroying what was left of the American legal system. Due process? Habeas corpus? Trial by a jury of your peers? Miranda warnings? Gone. Welcome home, Star Chamber.

Laura reached across the table and took my hand. I let her. Maybe even needed it.

"Believe me," the president continued, shaking his head in dismay, "what I am about to say brings me no pleasure. But after consulting the Justice Department, I have made the determination that for the first time in the history of this great country these executions will be televised." He paused again, and Leo's erupted into a smattering of excited responses.

The kid had wiggled out of the family booth and was standing by the counter, looking up at the president with adoration.

"We aren't quite certain yet when this will happen. This is America, and under our laws these two people are entitled to all their possible legal remedies before being executed, so it will be at least another day or two."

When he'd finished, Leo's sprung back into life. It was as if he had announced Black Friday was being extended. A roar of excited chatter rose and filled the place as clattering plates and relieved laughter created harmony. Midge delivered our now slightly cold meals and apologized. Naturally we understood, that's just the type of good Americans we were. More than anything else, though, the truly frightening thing about it was the sense of normalcy. The president of the United States had just announced the end of American jurisprudence, and people in a typical American diner in a typical American town responded by asking for another slice of that delicious lemon meringue pie.

Laura and I kept our voices low, leaning across the table in conversation as we ate. We laid out a panoply of options, none of them especially great. The counterman had turned down the sound again as talking heads began earnestly discussing the speech. "Put the game back on," someone shouted, and Dusty clicked through the channels until he found it.

It was almost nine o'clock when we were ready to leave. We'd decided to drive through the night to get to Buffalo. We would try to make contact with the resistance there. Laura paid our bill in cash. As we approached Van, I told Cher to open the side panel. The ramp extended and lowered to street level. "Want me to drive?" Laura asked.

"That's all right, it's easier for me." I rolled into the driver's tracks and locked Mighty Chair into place. Laura climbed into the passenger seat, adjusted her seat belt, and placed her tablet on the dashboard. I turned on the engine and put Van in reverse. Warning bells indicating something was behind me chimed rapidly. I glanced at the screen.

Two police officers were standing in the night haze of the rear camera. They were standing legs apart, holding their extended weapon with both hands, pointing at Van. "What the . . ." I said, then started pounding the wheel. "Fuck!"

The night exploded into red and yellow swirling lights. Four police cars squealed to a halt, trapping us in Leo's Own parking lot. Searchlights lit up the area brighter than an August afternoon. I could see police officers scrambling in every one of my mirrors. A bullhorned voice ordered, "You are under arrest. Do not move. Everybody in the van come out with your hands raised." I buried my face in my palm, took a long, hard deep breath, and smiled wanly at Laura. "I'm sorry."

"Oh god," she said. She laid a hand on her chest. "Oh my god."

I took several measured breaths, trying to gain control. I put a hand on Laura's wrist. "It'll be okay." Then I shifted into park.

Seconds later Van's side-panel door slid open and the ramp extended. In those yellow searchlights it probably looked like a scene out of *Close*

Encounters. I drove Chair down onto the parking lot gravel. Laura followed me out. The spotlights blinded us both, but we kept our hands raised. Somebody shouted, "Get on the ground!" I shaded my eyes and looked into the blinding lights and shrugged helplessly. Softly I said, "Cher, turn off." The less they knew about Chair's capabilities, the better it was for us. Laura laid down on the gravel, her arms extended. I kept my hands high in the air. They came out from behind the protection of their vehicles.

It became obvious very quickly that none of these officers had ever arrested a suspect in a wheelchair and weren't certain how to proceed. While a female officer frisked Laura, another cop ran an electronic wand over Mighty Chair. The wand crackled like a terrestrial radio in a mountain pass. Every inch of the metal chair triggered a warning. The cop finally gave up and patted me down. I thought he looked embarrassed as he did so. Other officers hand-searched Mighty Chair and swarmed through Van. As far as these officers were concerned, we were terrorists, and clearly they feared we might have some type of booby traps. A big cop with a blubbery face gingerly unhooked my backpack, laid it on the ground, and opened it cautiously. Right on top was a black plastic kidney-shaped container with a tube running into it. Admittedly it was an odd shape and that tube could have been carrying wires. He took a step back and pointed at it with his weapon, demanding, "What the fuck is that thing?"

"That's my urinal tank," I told him. "Go ahead if you want, open it."

He grimaced, as if he was too close to a decaying body part. Using the barrel of his gun he moved it to the side and searched the rest of my backpack. The other officers stepped back, several of them covering their mouths. "Well, look at this," he said with some delight, drawing attention as he pulled out my cowbell. It clearly had captured his fancy. He happily clanged it several times until he was ordered to "put that damn toy away."

A sergeant read us our revised rights. He held a card at arm's length and squinted, then reluctantly put on a pair of tortoiseshell-framed reading glasses. "We have been authorized by the Department of Homeland Security to detain you until further notice . . ." No mention of the right to remain silent or the right to an attorney. Gone. The protection from self-incrimination. Gone. Instead, ". . . as duly authorized law enforcement agents we have the right to take any and all actions we believe necessary to carry out our orders." The sergeant lowered the card and said in a sad attempt at a Southern twang, "'Nother words, your ass is grass and we are the lawn mower."

This "warning" was only slightly different from the notice I'd been given by the feds. I guess we were being "detained" by local authorities until we could be "taken into protective custody" by the feds. There is something chilling about the fact that authoritarian leaders believe they need to create a facsimile legal system to do whatever it is they want to do.

There were nine officers, eight men and a woman. The patrons and some of the staff from the diner had come out to watch the proceedings. That little kid was standing in front, his father's hands on both his shoulders, smiling and pointing at me. From the bits I could overhear, these officers had no idea how to proceed. They were trying to determine if Mighty Chair would fit into the trunk of a squad car. Apparently, they were waiting for Homeland Security agents to arrive and take us into custody. I wondered if it would be Corbin and Russell. I admit it, part of me was hoping it would be.

Laura was standing next to me. Tears were dripping onto her blouse. I whispered to her, "You're just a hitchhiker I picked up . . ."

"I don't care about me. It's you . . ."

"Hey!" A young officer waved his flashlight through the night. His nameplate identified him as Officer Gunn. "No talking, you two."

I should have been scared, but I would be lying to you (for dramatic purposes) if I said I was. I can't explain it, maybe it was my inner Reacher. More likely it was because I had been in several equally serious situations and somehow managed to get out of them, but rather than wasting time feeling sorry for myself or worrying about the consequences, I was already churning out possible solutions.

After a lot of back-and-forth on their radios, Laura was put into the back of a squad car. And me? Their problem was how to transport me and Mighty Chair. Have I mentioned there are certain advantages to being disabled and that I am not above exploiting them? Rather than lifting me into a squad car the sergeant decided to put me in Van's rear compartment. "Can you drive this thing?" the sergeant asked patrolman Gunn.

"'Course I can," he responded confidently. "Anything's got wheels, I can drive it." They tied my wrists to Mighty Chair's arm using plastic cables. I didn't bother introducing them to Cher. I don't think she would have approved.

They spent several minutes trying to figure out how to get me into Van. Finally they loosened my right hand and I rolled up the ramp. But even at this moment, with everything going on, the thought of what was about to happen amused me.

While I was locking myself down in the back, Gunn opened the driver's side door and climbed in. It was only after he was in the driver's well that he realized there was no driver's seat. He looked around, as if one might suddenly materialize. He frowned, trying to figure out what to do. He knew there had to be a solution, but as hard as he concentrated, the answer eluded him. He didn't want to embarrass himself by asking one of the senior officers, who had put him in this predicament. He finally reached what probably seemed to him to be the only logical conclusion: he would have to drive standing up.

If my hands weren't tied down, if I hadn't been under arrest in the back of Van, if Laura hadn't thrown my phone away, I would have started taping this. This definitely would have been a highlight on *America's Funniest Home Videos.*

Gunn steadied his feet and grabbed ahold of the steering wheel with both hands. He inhaled deeply for courage, both shoulders rising in determination. He carefully avoided touching any of the gizmos mounted on the wheel, having no idea what they might be for, then squatted down into a sitting position and turned on the engine.

He took another apprehensive breath, then released the emergency brake. He put Van in reverse and then . . . and then he was completely stymied. If he sat on his haunches, his foot couldn't reach the accelerator. He thought about that, then glanced over his shoulder at me. I smiled and waved one tied-down hand from my wrist. I think my disdain made him even more determined to figure it out. There was only one option: He balanced himself on his left foot while stretching his right foot forward until he reached the accelerator, looking very much like he was performing a slow-motion Kazatsky, the famed Cossack sitting dance.

For an instant he was actually able to retain his balance, but then he tipped over. Van, now in reverse with the emergency brake off, rolled backward into a squad car. The crowd cheered.

"Gunn!" the sergeant screamed. "Put the fucking brake on! Put on the brake."

Gunn got out muttering. Several of the other cops turned their heads so they wouldn't be caught laughing. Eventually a lieutenant showed up and took charge. His name tag read *L. Carty.* He was a perfect bronze color and came fully equipped with a sense of humor. He asked me to drive Van, which would make everyone's life easier, then cautioned me about trying to escape. "But if you do, I'm warning you," he threatened, tilting his head toward Gunn, "you better take him with you."

I rolled Chair into the rails behind the wheel and locked down. We drove in a convoy, three squad cars in front of me, three behind, all of them with their light bars flashing. It was as bright and colorful as a party in my friend "The Mush'es" basement in high school. Gunn rode shotgun with me, watching me drive with the hand controls. "That is definitely cool," he finally said. "Man, I never would have figured that out."

"Oh, sure you would have," I said, as if he were a friend. I went through each of the controls for him, demonstrating how they worked. And when I was done with that I asked, in the same friendly conversational tone, "How'd you guys find us anyway? That's good police work."

"Thank you, we are pretty good, you know, for a small town." He paused, then filled the silence. "Okay, I'll tell you. We didn't. The marshals called us and said you were over at Leo's and we had to get right over there and arrest you." That was interesting but not helpful. I'd screwed up somewhere, and without knowing exactly where that was, it was possible I'd do it again.

"They don't tell you how they do that stuff, I guess."

Gunn was pretty talkative once you got him going. "It's some kind of secret voodoo shit. They got all this spy stuff. All I know is they told us they seen you going into Leo's."

Thank you very much, Officer Gunn. Cameras. That's interesting. Drones maybe, but I doubted that. There'd be no reason to fly drones in that area. Satellite images? Possible, satellites could read license plates fifty miles away, but Laura had changed the plates and there were a lot of white vans on the road. They saw me going into Leo's? Not Van, me. It had to be surveillance cameras. Had to be. We'd used them all the time over there to gather intel. I wasn't really up-to-date on new techniques and capabilities, but I was pretty sure they were keyed for characteristics. Hair color. Height. Gender. Wheelchair. That was a problem. Once we got out of this, I'd have to figure out how to present a different profile.

Laura was in the cruiser directly in front of me. At intervals she would twist around to make sure I was still right behind. To my surprise, rather than being taken to the station house, we pulled into the parking lot of the Good Night Motel. In its defense, the Good Night did not pretend to be anything more than what it was, a rectangular-shaped lump of cement built to be an inexpensive alternative to more popular places near the lake. It offered beds and air-conditioned rooms. It reminded me mostly of the practical motels outside every military base in the world, paper-thin mattresses available by the night or the hour afford-able on an enlisted man's salary. No frills, no thrills, we called them.

Laura and I were escorted into a small room. Gunn was ordered to stay with us. The room had pale yellow walls and a single thick-curtained front window that looked out onto the parking lot; it contained two single beds, a bureau, and a desk. There was a large wood-framed mir-ror above the flimsy desk, a night table between the beds with a lamp and alarm clock on it, a closet, and a bathroom. Over each bed was a cheap print of flowers in a vase that somehow was sadder than empty space would have been. An old Sony Trinitron TV sat on the bureau. An ancient but still functioning air conditioner clunked every few seconds. *Truth in advertising,* I thought. Years of disinfectant seemingly had soaked into the walls and seasoned the air. The doorframe was just wide enough for Mighty Chair to squeeze through.

While Lieutenant Carty made sure we were safely settled, I asked him what we were doing there. "Don't we have our rights as American citi-zens to be taken to jail?"

Carty didn't even try to hide his displeasure at this whole situation. Everything about him read professional, from the polished shine of his shoes to his politeness. "We're just doing what they told us to do. I don't know why, they said they didn't want you on the books. There's two Homeland Security guys coming to pick you up, and they told us to keep you safe and secure until they got here."

Laura looked puzzled. "What does that mean, 'not on the books'?" She turned to me. "Can they do that, Rollie?"

Carty appeared to be embarrassed by his own answer. "Yeah, well, turns out we can. But I promise you, it doesn't mean anything except you get worse towels and better food than you'd get with us." He tapped his chest as if confirming a pledge. "I promise you, nothing's going to happen to you long as you're in our charge. Officer Gunn here is going to stay with you for the first shift. One of our people is gonna be outside too. You have any problems, you need something, tell Gunn and he'll find me." He seemed reluctant to leave, finally saying apologetically, "Believe me, I don't like this any more than you do. But this is just the way things are now and we have to get used to it." He couldn't even meet my eyes as he said sadly, "We're just doing our job."

"So I guess this means we don't get to make a phone call?"

Carty got my little joke. "Where do you think you are, Mr. Stone? Canada? They told us to bury you so deep the Chinese would have to dig you out."

"How 'bout me?" Laura suddenly spoke up. "My mother is expecting to hear from me. That I'm okay. If she doesn't get a message, she'll . . ." She smiled at the irony. "She'll call the cops."

Brilliant! Apparently the last thing the cops wanted other cops to know was that we were in police custody. The lieutenant thought about it for a minute, then made an executive decision. "Okay, go ahead and send Mom a text that you're okay. But just that, okay? Please?"

"Say hello from me," I added.

After making sure the message Laura sent to "Mom" was sufficiently innocuous, Lieutenant Carty turned to leave. Gunn stopped him and asked in a loud whisper, pointing to me, "What am I s'posed to do with him?"

Carty leaned closer to him and replied in an equally loud whisper, "Your job."

When Laura was done sending her warning message, she plopped down on the bed. The bedsprings squeaked. She asked me, with enough bravado to be reassuring, "You always take girls to seedy motels on a first date?"

"Of course not," I admitted. "That's usually the third date. You should be flattered."

"Hush now," Officer Gunn ordered.

"Oh, come on," I said. If possible, I'd been taught, establish dialogue with your captors. Maybe it was time to wheel out my collection of bad jokes? In a tone dripping with friendliness I suggested, "You know, as long as we're going to be here for a while, we might as well get along. What's your name?"

"It's not important."

I couldn't resist. "Okay, now we know what it's not. The real question is what is it?"

Laura helped me move onto the bed closest to the door. Then she rolled Chair into a corner. Gunn was sitting Western-movie style facing the back of the wooden desk chair at the base of my bed. His crossed arms were resting on the top of the chair back. "I'll tell you what it is," he snapped. "It's none of your business."

Too easy. "Can I call you 'nonie' for short?"

Gunn's mouth opened and closed like a fish gasping as he searched for a clever response. Giving up, he settled for "You know what? You're not funny."

Talk about a meatball. I was getting ready to crush it when Laura admonished, "Rollie. Don't." She turned her attention to Gunn, asking pleasantly, "How long have you been a police officer?"

He considered the consequences before answering, finally deciding it was not a trick question. "Just about four years." Laura got him talking about himself. He had a girlfriend and they'd talked about getting married, but she wanted to wait until she finished at the community college. She was planning on becoming a nurse or a dental hygienist because she liked to help people. So they'd compromised: their *Second Life* avatars had gotten married. He actually blushed as he acknowledged, "But, you know ..."—raising his eyebrows salaciously—"getting together that way isn't all that much."

Watching Laura ease him into a pleasant conversation was fascinating. The two of them were close to the same age, but she had quickly taken control. She completely won him over. It took me a minute to figure out her trick. It was obvious, there was no trick. She was genuinely curious about his life. In his fumbling way, it suddenly became clear to me, Gunn was explaining how all of this had happened in America. The young police officer had small dreams. He had grown up on a farm (hence his delight at discovering my cowbell), and all he wanted was the middle-class American life he had been promised: a woman who loved him, a comfortable house, some kids running around, mowing the lawn on Saturday morning, complaining about visiting the in-laws on Sunday. And he had seen those things slipping away, beyond his reach.

He had become a police officer, he explained, because it was good, honest work. It offered stability and provided him an opportunity to help people. "It was okay the first couple of years," he said, "but it's much better now, since President Wrightman. People just look at us differently now. They really respect us, you know what I mean. They know we're their first line of defense against the terrorists. People like . . ." He pointed at me.

Laura ignored that. "So you really like the president?"

"Love him," Gunn said firmly, sitting straight up in that chair. "The man said what he was going to do and he's doing what he said he would do." Not only did he respect the president, his whole family did. "He's doing a damn good job protecting this country. Maybe we're not in favor of everything he's doing," he continued, "but you know what, nobody's perfect."

Laura asked, "What about all the rights the government has taken away? Doesn't any of that bother you?"

He shut his eyes and shook his head. "Truthfully, we don't even notice that. Most of that comes from people who like to complain about everything. They're just angry 'cause they can't complain. Me and my family, we're just regular people minding our own business, so that stuff doesn't affect us."

As their conversation continued, I drifted a few hours into the future. There were certain assumptions I could make: Homeland Security agents, presumably Dickie and Francis, were on their way. They would take us into custody and move us back to Washington. We would be detained there indefinitely and questioned. I wasn't overly concerned about that because I was pretty confident it would never get to that point. What did concern me was Laura. How was she going to respond when the time came? I looked over at her; she was waving her hands descriptively, making some point. Young Officer Gunn was nodding in agreement, completely won over by her. She was giving him what he needed most: attention and respect. Attention and respect, it didn't seem that hard; but apparently it was.

Anyway, there was nothing that I could do until the agents got there; and when it was time, I needed to be alert, so I willed myself into a light sleep. When I opened my eyes, the sun was shining and Gunn was gone. Another officer, Sergeant G. Hicker, tall and blond with thinning hair, was sitting in Mighty Chair. "This is pretty comfortable," he said pleasantly. "I ordered you guys some coffee. I sure need some."

A few minutes later the coffee, doughnuts, and a bagel for the officer were delivered to the room. Laura was wide awake; I couldn't be sure she'd slept at all. "You okay?" I asked. "I mean, considering."

"I'm fine, I'm good."

Hicker continually checked his watch. I assumed he was anticipating the arrival of the agents. I was wrong. At nine A.M. he turned on the TV. "This is gonna be something to see," he said. He opened the door and waved the second cop inside. "Come on in, it's starting."

I shot a quizzical glance at Laura, who shrugged. "What's going on, guys?" she asked.

Officer G. Hicker pointed toward the TV with his coffee cup. "The execution's on."

As if on cue Aaron Copland's stirring *Fanfare for the Common Man* blasted through the room. Officer Hicker flicked through several channels to see if there might be a different view, but they were sharing the same feed. The establishing shot was directly in front and above the stage—in the balcony, I guessed. The scene was somewhat reminiscent of *Hunger Games,* although rather than taking place outdoors, this was in a theater.

I recognized it right away, having spent a lot of hours there. "That's the Kennedy Center," I said, "the concert hall."

The second Lake City officer looked like he was younger than Gunn. He was tall and so thin that his uniform hung on him as if it were still on the hanger. His name was Stillman. He sat down in the desk chair, which now was facing the TV, and leaned forward with his elbows resting on his knees. He was so completely absorbed in the broadcast we could have walked out.

By now most of you have probably seen this live or online. The ratings rivaled the Super Bowl. Obviously many people wanted to watch it several times, as the video broke every YouTube record. This was my view from room 117 of the Good Night Motel. The stage was dimly lit. Three people dressed head to toe in black stood together on the left side of the stage, with their backs to the camera. A sleekly designed minimalist burnished metal gallows had been set up centerstage. A series of mirrors were arranged diagonally behind it, making it appear as if the gallows faded into infinity. A small sign was affixed to the front of the gallows, but at this distance, on that TV, it was impossible to read it. Everything on the stage was monochromatic, which made the large American flag at either end stand out boldly. Whoever was choreographing this had done a great job; it looked like a rock concert for ghouls.

"This is unbelievable," Laura said.

"Isn't it?" Stillman replied with excitement, looking over his shoulder at her and grinning broadly. His face was pockmarked, and several protruding teeth were chipped—a look that suggested he excelled as a human beer bottle opener. "Like, amazing, right?"

The anonymous announcer asked the audience to rise and join him in reciting the New American Pledge. Stillman stood; Hicker looked at him, then looked down at his own shoes. Following that, the announcer introduced the president, drawing out his name as if this were pro wrestling. "Eeeeee-yan Wrightman!"

I propped myself up against the headboard. As much as this disgusted me, I have to admit to some fascination. I was watching a televised hanging. This could have been taking place in Iran or North Korea or so many other places lacking a working legal system, but it wasn't: This was here, in what had once been America. I couldn't take my eyes off the screen.

The president received an enthusiastic welcome. As he came onstage he pointed at someone in the audience, as if he had recognized them, and smiled, then waved to the audience. After basking in their applause, he held up his hands for quiet. "Thank you. Thank you, my friends." He paused long enough to take a deep and meaningful breath, then looked up to the rafters and admitted, "I never thought I would say these words, but it is not a pleasure for myself or the first lady ..." He pointed to her sitting in the front row and smiled reassuringly; as the audience cheered for her the camera caught her kissing her palm and blowing it to him. "... for us to be here with you. Unfortunately, it is absolutely necessary. It was a wise man who said, 'Where the rule of law breaks down, there is chaos.'"

"He's damn right about that," Officer Stillman agreed loudly.

Wrightman reminded Americans that we could not relax our vigil because "there are evil people right in front of you, whose sole purpose is to bring harm to good and decent folks." "You're damn right!" Stillman said, indicating the TV.

As the camera dollied-in, he spoke directly "to those good people who might wonder why we are broadcasting this historic event. I understand your reticence. Let me assure you this is nothing new. This country has a long and proud history of public executions. Only recently have we begun hiding executions behind closed doors, as if we should be ashamed of defending the right of all Americans to live safely ..."

As Wrightman continued, the director cut to different locales around the country, showing people of all ages gathered together in small groups, watching in awed reverence. From the headquarters of New Orleans's Pete's Pistols militia headquarters to a bus station in Aurora, North Carolina; from a high school gymnasium in Hopping, Arizona, where students filled the bleachers, to a bowling alley in Yukón, Oregon, the image was eerily similar: no one was talking, every eye transfixed on the broadcast.

"Let the word go out," the president concluded, "that from this day forward, to friends and foes alike, wherever they may be, that the torch has been passed to a new and tougher generation of Americans. Ready to defend this country and its leaders, whatever it may take, whatever we have to give, no matter the cost."

When the president left the stage, the entire audience rose in respect, cheering wildly. In our motel room Stillman once again popped up out of his chair, shaking his fist in support. I glanced at Hicker, still sitting comfortably in Mighty Chair, holding his Styrofoam cup in his hands. Our eyes met and he shook his head just slightly enough to make his point: *I can't believe this shit any more than you can.*

When the ovation ended, followed by a few overly enthusiastic hoots, the announcer said gravely, "To officially pronounce sentence, ladies and gentlemen, the Vice President of the United States, Arthur Hunter."

In contrast to the president, the Hun was somber, reflecting the gravity of the situation. He took a folded sheet of paper from his jacket pocket and said to the absolutely silent theater, "Mr. Attorney General, will you reveal the prisoners please."

The total lack of any musical accompaniment was far more dramatic than any theme might have produced. If there was ever going to be a hanging chic, this was raising the bar, or dropping the noose, to be more accurate. A curtain rose at the top of the gallows revealing two prisoners wearing long-sleeved work shirts and jeans, their heads covered with black sacking. It was impossible to determine anything about them: age, race, gender, even the color of their skin. They could have been anybody. Four men, in some type of shimmering black fabric, stood behind them, one at each elbow. Their hands were clasped behind them, chins jutted upward.

"I can't watch this," Laura said. "This is . . . I can't."

I reached across the divide between the beds and took her hand.

"You know what," Stillman said with some annoyance, twisting in his chair, "maybe you should. Then just maybe people like you would appreciate how good you got it here. I don't know what you did, lady, but you wouldn't be here if you'd done what was right."

Before she could reply I squeezed her hand. She looked at me and I shook my head.

The screen went black, with the exception of the two prisoners, who were illuminated in pin spotlights. Nooses dangled loosely around their necks. Their hands were tied together behind them. "Prisoners," Hunter read, "after a fair hearing you have been convicted by a legally constituted panel of committing acts of terrorism against the people of the United States. You have been sentenced to be hung by your necks until dead."

One of the prisoners folded at the knees, but the people standing behind each caught an elbow to prevent the condemned person from falling.

"Look at that coward," Stillman said derisively, shaking his head in disgust.

That old cliché "the silence was deafening" has never been more appropriate. Occasionally someone in the audience coughed. Hunter said in a surprisingly calm voice, "Bring prisoner number one forward."

As the prisoner who nearly collapsed was dragged forward on his knees, remote shots from the different locales appeared on the screen, as if they were showing all the nominees at the Academy Awards. A young student in the Hopping, Arizona, gym was leaning forward, his chin resting in his hand, his foot tapping restlessly. In the Aurora bus station, an attractive black woman was watching a monitor with equal intensity. In the bowling alley a group of men were gathered in the lounge, beers for breakfast, their heads craning upward toward the TVs above the bar. In the militia headquarters about a dozen Pistols, wearing ceremonial coonskin caps, were standing at attention saluting the TV.

As the noose was being placed around the prisoner's neck, the camera slowly panned the entire stage, then pulled out of the shot all the way back to the top of the theater so the entire stage and front rows of the audience were visible. "Mr. Executioner."

Talk about random thoughts. I remember wondering where they had found an executioner on such short notice. I was a bit surprised the executioner wasn't shown. I wondered if that was in his or her contract. Then I wondered who had negotiated that contract. Do executioners have agents?

The pin light tightened until the prisoner was the only thing visible, as if he or she were standing in their private sun. The noose looked like a thick rope necklace. The executioner waited. The tension grew. The prisoner was sobbing and muttering something unintelligible. Still, they waited.

Without warning, soundlessly, the prisoner dropped out of the spotlight, which remained locked on the suddenly ominous void. My whole body jerked involuntarily. I expected to hear a thump from the trapdoor, but it must have been padded, which made it even more brutal. The audience gasped, then cheered.

Cheered.

"Jesus," Laura whispered.

"Yes!" Stillman shouted almost simultaneously.

The reaction of the people in the insets was mixed. The Hopping teenager's mouth hung open. The black woman crossed herself. The men in the bowling alley lounge cheered. The militia members shook hands.

G. Hicker wordlessly crumbled the Styrofoam cup in his hand. It made an odd squeak. He threw it toward the wastebasket but missed. It bounced off the wall and settled on the frayed carpet.

The dangling body was not shown to those watching at home.

As the pin light faded to dark, a second pin light simultaneously came up on the second prisoner. That person took a bold step forward, then stood rigid, defiant, head held high, facing straight ahead as if staring at the audience through the cloth hood. Standing motionless in the spotlight, the prisoner looked like a statue of nobility.

The trapdoor opened. This time the sharp snap of the prisoner's neck cut through the silence, followed by the straining cries of new rope.

The stage went black—impenetrable black. Seconds later, accent lighting beneath the gallows brightened, backlighting the bodies rotating slowly, as if dancing in the slowest motion. They were reflected in the rear mirrors, creating an infinitely long chorus line of black-clad bodies, hanging, turning in unison. At that moment I had no doubt the director was going to be nominated for an Emmy.

The hall was silent for several seconds. Then one person began applauding, which grew quickly into a great wave of approval. It grew louder and louder in approval. The chant began, *Wrightman! Wrightman! Wrightman!* It ended when a beaming Vice President Hunter appeared at the podium and waved them quiet. "That concludes our purpose here this morning," he said, his voice flat and void of any emotion. "I hope this serves as a warning to all who would do harm to this great nation that this is the inevitable fate that awaits you. God bless America."

Officer Stillman stood up, turned, and looked right at me. "Now that's what I'm talking about."

For the first time, Hicker spoke. "Stillman," he said, "shut the fuck up."

"Sir?"

Hicker closed his eyes, maybe debating the consequences of revealing his feelings to a true believer. "I said that's enough. You've made your point."

Stillman glared at him, then backed down. "I'll go watch outside."

Hicker turned to Laura and me. "It's not gonna be much longer. Want me to leave the TV on?"

"Sure," I said. Hicker was quickly absorbed in the post-hanging special report on Fox. Audience members were being interviewed as they left the Kennedy Center. I heard someone describe it as "a great day for America, so tastefully done." I rolled over on my side and faced Laura. "You're doing great," I told her.

"What are we going to do?" she asked. "What's going to happen?"

I smiled, maybe just slightly more confidently than I felt. "Trust me."

20

I looked at Laura and thought of Jenny. They were very different women. They would respect each other, but probably wouldn't be friends. I was carrying Jenny with me. Several times every day, too often at the most inopportune times, she popped into my head, and I wondered what she was doing at exactly that moment. It was never good. Worrying about her was an emotion that served no useful purpose, so finally I used an old visualization I'd been taught during interrogation training: I envisioned an old-fashioned steel safe, the type with a big spinning lock, then balled up my fears, put them into that safe, and closed its door. That generally worked well, but this time I could see droplets of anxiety leaking from beneath the door.

One cup of coffee wasn't nearly enough; I dozed, the image of two dangling bodies twisting slowly in a million mirrors pasted on the inside of my eyelids. I woke up when Lieutenant Carty returned about noon. "Those agents'll be here soon," he said.

He helped move me back into Mighty Chair. I let him give me more assistance than I actually needed—another way of making people feel good. I had just gotten comfortable when Corbin and Russell walked in. Rather than gray suits, they were in casual clothes, but both of them wore jackets that covered the weapons they would be carrying. Dick looked at me and grinned ugly. I couldn't help myself. "Laura, look who's here! Hey, buddy, good to see you standing upright."

Corbin ignored me, handing his credentials to Carty. "And this is Agent Russell. I'm assuming your people did a good search?"

Carty glanced at the ID, then gave it back. "We brushed over them. They're clean." He got ready to leave. "You people going to need anything else from us?"

"Nope. That'd be it."

"Okay." He stopped at the door and looked at me. "Good luck," he said.

Russell locked the door behind him, then looked at me. "Now go ahead and smile again, asshole."

"You're drooling," I said, making sure I got all their attention. In their anger and anticipation, they completely ignored Laura.

Dickie put a restraining hand on Francis's shoulder. "Me first." He took two steps toward Mighty Chair, then stopped beyond the extendable arm's reach. He stepped to the right before coming any closer. Then tentatively ran his hand over Chair's right arm to see if it contained any other surprises. Chair sat impassively. Dickie moved closer and ran his hand down the seatback with more apprehension than I'd seen on the faces of bomb disposal techs in the desert. He was treating Mighty Chair as if it were a dangerous sleeping animal, capable of striking when aroused. "Show me your hands," he ordered.

I held them out; he tied them together with a plastic twist. When he was certain I wasn't capable of triggering any defenses, he began a thorough search. As Gunn had done, he opened my backpack and lifted out the black plastic tank. "That's my urinal tank," I told him. "Help yourself."

He held it gingerly in both hands, away from his body, and shook it. When he felt the liquid swishing around, he put it down and continued digging through my backpack. He pulled out a shirt, which he patted down; a battery-operated toothbrush, which he shook in case it was hollow; and my passport. He put the passport in his jacket pocket— "no need for this anymore"—and replaced everything else. Then he methodically went through each of Mighty Chair's pockets, receptacles, and bags.

He reached into a deep side pocket and Cher suddenly started giggling. "Stop. It tickles."

Corbin leaped back, ripping his hand out of the pocket as if he'd dipped it in lava.

Thank you, Y, I thought. But what I said was "Hey, don't blame me. I'm just sitting here."

"Fuck you, Stone." After completing his search of visible storage, Corbin hesitated and thought about it. "Gimme a hand," he told Russell. They struggled to move me onto the bed. I didn't resist, but I didn't help, either. "You stay right there," he said sarcastically, chuckling at his own humor. Then he continued his search. After going through the visible storage places, he warily lifted Chair's foam seat cushion. And discovered the manila envelope. "Well, now what might this be?"

I took a guess: "Inca treasure?" Apparently no one but me thought that was funny. Corbin lifted the clasp and pulled out two graphs. He stared at them, having no idea what he was looking at; he turned them sideways, but they still made no sense to him. He folded them in half, then again into quarters, slipping them in his pocket with my passport.

Dickie tossed the cushion on the floor. "Now isn't this something," he said. The plastic seat beneath the cushion had been divided into five shallow storage boxes. He slipped his index finger into a flush mount ring and lifted the lid. He moved the contents around, found nothing of interest, and replaced the lid. He grasped the second ring and pulled open the second box—and took a step backward. "Whoa." He looked at me with an I-didn't-know-you-were-that-kind-of-guy surprise. He took out my revolver, raising it triumphantly into the air. "Well, lookee here," he said with appreciation for his own professionalism. "Look what I found."

I frowned. "Darn. Now what am I going to get you for Christmas?"

"Go ahead, funny man," he said, pointing the gun at the muted TV. CNN was showing highlights of the executions. "Let's see how funny you are when you're starring on that show." He checked the gun. It wasn't loaded. Another steel-lined box contained eight rounds. An emergency repair kit and a collection of bolts and screws filled the final box. Corbin then got down on his knees and began searching Chair's underside.

"Careful," Russell warned him.

I told him, "Don't unscrew that white cap."

Corbin hesitated. "Why? What's in it?"

"Silicone. That's what keeps the chair lubricated." The reservoir actually did contain silicone, but its real purpose was to create a slippery trail if I was being pursued. It was Y's homage to Bond, James Bond. Dickie hesitated, wondering if I was playing reverse psychology, or perhaps this was a double reverse. Did I want him to open it or not? Was it a trap or was there an escape tool in there? I almost hummed a dramatic theme. He left it alone and continued his search. I smiled with what I hoped looked like relief, not because I was relieved but because I wanted to screw with him.

He finished his search and stood up. For the first time he spoke to Laura. "You got something to say?"

"I'd like to know what's going on. Why am I being held here?"

Corbin looked at Russell. "You want to tell her?"

Francis crinkled his nose. "Let it be a surprise."

"Okay," Corbin said. "We got to get going. C'mon, Stone, mount up."

"I'll help," Laura volunteered, coming around to the other side of my bed. She leaned down and I swung my arm around her shoulders. She leveraged me to my feet. Mighty Chair was only a few feet away and Cher could have brought him over, but instead I struggled to get there, playing up my disability for the agents. As we got close, Russell put his foot on Chair's seat and pushed it back against the wall. Laura glared at him with what I guessed was as much hatred as she could muster, then dragged me a few additional feet until I collapsed into the seat.

"Francis," Corbin said to Russell without taking his eyes off me. "Take the young lady out to the car. I've got a few questions I need to ask Mr. Stone."

First question, I was pretty sure: How'd that one feel, you bastard?

"I'll go with Rollie," she said firmly.

"No, no, you won't. In fact, you'll do exactly what I tell you to do when I tell you to do it."

She stood her ground. Damn, she was terrific. But I didn't want to see her get hurt. "Do it," I said. "Go with him." She considered her options. "Please," I said.

The fight drained out of her.

I nodded. "Go. I'll be okay."

Corbin waited until we were alone, then let his hatred boil over. "Now you're mine, asshole." He took a step toward me. I smiled mischievously and let my bound hands hover over Chair's controls. Corbin stopped, then circled around behind Chair. There wasn't much I could do. I relaxed and closed my eyes. I was ready for it.

He slugged me on the side of my head. I went sprawling onto the cheap carpet. I went with it rather than trying to resist, letting the force of the blow power me forward. "You fucking traitor," he cursed in a guttural roar, then kicked me hard in the kidney. That one hurt. "You're gonna fuck with me, huh? That's what you're gonna do? Fuck with me?" I pulled myself into a fetal position, protecting my face and stomach, my hands and arms cupped over my head.

Corbin wound up like a punter and kicked me in my leg. I didn't feel a thing, but I screamed in pain. For effect. The old give-'em-whatever-they-want-to-hear. He kicked me again, this time in my lower back. Okay, that was a good hit. He kicked me again. Then he began punching down at me. The kicks and punches came in a frenzy, over and over and over, but he quickly tired himself out.

Here's something important to know: Your head and face, your hands, and your balls are the most vulnerable. The rest of your body is easily repairable. I kept my head tucked safely under my arms, my body folded protectively over my groin and let him punch himself into exhaustion. Those long mornings in the gym paid off; I felt every blow and reacted convincingly enough to satisfy Dickie's need for revenge, but few of them caused any significant pain or damage. The thing about fighting that they don't tell you in the movies is that when you hit someone, you also hurt yourself. The human body is surprisingly solid: hit certain parts of it hard enough and you bruise your own hands and feet. If you're not in great shape, you might pull a muscle; punch or kick someone wrong and you can break the small bones in your hands and your feet. So after taking the first few hard shots, you start holding back to protect yourself. And having taken a serious blow to his ego and his honkers, the Big Dick hadn't entered the fray in primo condition. His anger petered out pretty quickly.

As he was whaling away, I noticed that Vice President Hunter seemed to be watching from the silent TV. In that instant I flashed on the meeting in his office. *I warned you,* I heard him thinking. A kick caught the back of my hand, ripping off some skin and bringing me back to reality. Blood was flowing from several cuts. But an interesting thing happened: As I was being pummeled, part of me long buried was savoring the thrill of being involved in a brutal physical confrontation—although admittedly not so much being on the receiving end. Corbin had kicked through the barriers of decency I'd erected, kicked down my walls of civility. The adrenaline bursting through my body masked most of the pain; instead I was feeling a kind of primal joy that I hadn't experienced in years. For a second I started to push myself onto my feet to get back in the fight.

Then I remembered. That wasn't going to happen. I hated the fact that I couldn't stand up and smash the shit out of this prick, hated it, but this beating had awakened something primordial that I'd left behind in that collapsed building in Fallujah.

Corbin stepped back. He was breathing heavily. My shirt and pants were ripped and bloodstained. I was moaning, rolling on the floor, hoping I wasn't overacting. "Try me again, asshole," Corbin threatened between breaths, leaning on the bureau for support, "and you won't walk out of . . ." He coughed some mucus out of his throat. "I'm telling you. We're taking you back, and I promise you, you're gonna rot there."

"Go fuck yourself," I said through gritted teeth, doubled over, convincingly in pain.

Corbin straightened his clothes. Smiling, satisfied, he bent down and ripped the plastic ties off my wrists, then stepped over me and opened the door. "Now get yourself back in that chair." He started to close the door, looking back at me curled up on the floor. "And don't try climbing out the bathroom window." There was a meanness in his eyes as he added, "Whoops. I forgot." He was laughing at his cleverness as he closed the door behind him. I heard him say loudly, "He'll be right out. Soon as he straightens up."

I rolled onto my back and lay there, gathering my strength. I could feel some liquids on my face and chest; I hoped it was sweat. "Cher," I finally said in a rasp, "come here." Mighty Chair rolled to the sound of my voice. I rubbed both wrists then picked the cushion off the floor and tossed it onto the seat. Then I grasped Chair's arm, as if it were a bar in the gym, and used it to get to my feet, then swiveled into the seat.

I sat there for several seconds. For Bourne or Reacher, this beating would have been a minor inconvenience, forgotten by the end of the chapter; but for me it hurt like a son of a bitch. I wasn't about to forget it. My left shoulder was screaming for attention, but I didn't have time for it. I had to move quickly before they came back to check on me. I grabbed my backpack and put it on my lap. I reached inside and took out the plastic urinal tank. I kept it on top because it usually discouraged people from searching any deeper. I opened the tank, which in fact was not connected to Chair and was filled with water. I lifted out the plastic bag protecting a compact Glock 42 and a six-round magazine. I loaded it, put the empty bag inside the tank, put the tank back on top, and hung the backpack where it belonged.

I slipped the gun under my seat cushion, took one last deep breath, and said, "Cher, let's go, please."

On the still-muted TV a slow-motion replay of the hangings was being shown while talking heads silently provided expert analysis.

I came out of the room in slow motion, slumping, a man defeated. Laura gasped when she saw me. Quite dramatically, she tore herself loose from Russell and ran over to me, hugging me with more conviction than she'd ever shown. "What did they do to you? Oh, Rollie . . ." As she hooked her left arm around my neck, she slipped Hicker's bagel-buttering white plastic cafeteria knife into my hand. "Are you okay?"

Corbin pulled her away from me. "We all get it," he said dismissively. I noticed for the first time that he was moving slowly; he appeared to be waddling more than walking. The adrenaline that had allowed him to beat on me was slowly dissipating, and his body was remembering his pain.

Russell was leaning against the government car they'd driven up from Washington, a white Chevy Caprice, combing the remaining strands of his hair, adjusting his jacket. Doing the victor's dance. "Nice of you to join us, Stone," he said, with a knowing smirk on his face.

It was only as the agents got ready to leave that they realized their problem: Just like the Lake City PD, they had not anticipated the difficulty in transporting a detainee in a wheelchair. They spent several minutes fruitlessly debating if Mighty Chair would fit into the Chevy's trunk before giving up that idea. They debated renting an SUV or van, but finally decided it would be safe and considerably easier to let me drive Van. Just like the Lake City PD, Corbin volunteered, "I'll ride shotgun with superschmuck." Laura would go in the car with Francis.

As Laura climbed into the Caprice's caged back seat, Dickie asked, "You okay to drive?"

Was I okay? You kidding me? That was an essential part of my plan. You're damn right I was okay to drive. "I think so," I managed.

As we watched Van's ramp rattling flat on the pavement, Corbin poked a warning finger at me. "Let me tell you something, pal. I wasn't kidding about riding shotgun. I don't know exactly what you've done, but you pissed off some pretty important people. They had the whole world out looking for you. When they told us to come up and get you, they made it clear they didn't give a flying fuck about how we brought you back."

He took a pack of Juicy Fruit from his pocket, slid one out for himself, and offered one to me.

"No thanks."

Corbin unwrapped it and put it in his mouth, savoring that initial rush of flavor. "Damn, that's good. Like I was saying, they told me that where you're concerned there're no rules. Do whatever I had to do. Do it twice if I felt like it. Nothing was ever going to bounce back. So here's my point, you screw with me . . ."—he tapped his index finger on his chest to emphasize that *me* meant him—"you're gonna die." He raised his eyebrows as high on his head as he could to reinforce that warning. "You try anything with that chair or this van, it's pretty likely that girl is gonna die too.

"Now listen up, I don't want to shoot you. Far as I'm concerned, right now you and me, we're even. But I have to tell you the truth—if I do have to shoot you, I will enjoy it." He forced up both sides of his mouth in his phony smile. "Capiche?"

I capiched. As Corbin played Dirty Harry, I hunched my shoulders and didn't look up, showing him I was as beaten up on the inside as was visible on the outside. But I had been genuinely affected by Laura's willingness to risk her own safety to slip me a weapon, if you believe a plastic knife is a weapon. It was a wonderful gesture; she had no way of knowing it wasn't necessary. I had laid out my plan a while ago. The only part that had been missing from it was the feral anger that once had made it possible for me to do brutal things without hesitation, to look some jerk with a bloated sense of self-importance in the eyes and pull the trigger. But I had it now. It was back.

Rollie Stone, journalist, was a different man. That was by necessity, but also by choice. Life was easier once you backed away from the edge. On some of those sleepless nights I'd had brief reminders; for an instant I was the trigger, walking down a rubble-strewn street, ready to snap. Jenny had caught me there once, asked about it, and I'd joked my way out of it. Rollie from my first life, I'd explained, paying a brief visit.

But he'd come back to stay on the floor of that motel room. Each kick, each punch had opened the door a little wider, and he'd rushed back in. Welcome home, baby.

The girl is gonna die too? Really? Fuck you very much. I was going to enjoy this a lot more than I had anticipated. I could feel the bulge of the Glock under me as I cowered. I wanted to make sure Big Dick was confident, even cocky.

"Now let's get the fuck out of here," Corbin finished.

While Mighty Chair slid into its rails and I locked down, Corbin belted himself into the passenger seat. To be extra safe he made a big show of taking his weapon out of his shoulder holster and putting it in the passenger door well, making it impossible for me to reach it while still keeping it easily accessible. He called Francis on his mobile to confirm he was "ready to roll with Rollie," and advised him we would be stopping for gas within an hour. "We'll stay in the right lane. Just keep up with us."

We took the highway. No diversions, a reasonably straight shot to Washington. I didn't even bother asking if he wanted to detour slightly to visit the Liberty Bell. It was a bright sunny day—it probably would be remembered as a good day for a hanging—and Corbin was enjoying the ride. He'd accomplished his mission and undoubtedly there would be goodies waiting for him. Regional assistant? Probably not out of the question. He played with the radio, settling on an easy listening station. Barry Manilow was singing a mournful arrangement of "On the Sunny Side of the Street." Good, the boredom had gotten to him even sooner than I'd expected.

Corbin turned to me. "So what exactly was it you were trying to do? How come you're so important?"

I glared at him. That punch to the side of my head had rattled my noggin and my brain was still banging around in there. Or something was causing the throbbing pain. I didn't say a word, just glared at him.

Corbin couldn't stand the silence. "I mean, come on, with that chair and everything, what could you be doing?"

Ah, the beauty of low expectations. I picked my words carefully when I responded, "We're taking back our country."

"Oh?" Once again he raised his eyebrows; apparently that was his go-to expression. "You think so, huh? Let me tell you something, pal," he continued, his voice rising. "That ain't happening. This country is just fine, thank you. There are some people like you trying to cause trouble, but thank God we have people like me to stop you."

Okay, so maybe the rumors are true. People are starting to fight back. I checked my rearview mirror. The Caprice was holding steady four car lengths behind. I turned and looked directly at Dick, then yawned. I yawned long and loud, my mouth opened as wide as I could manage, and sighed.

It took a few seconds to register, but then Corbin yawned. To get to Lake City that early, he and Russell must have left Washington in the middle of the night. The early afternoon sun glaring through the windshield added to that sense of fatigue. But Dick kept babbling, maybe to help himself stay awake. "I haven't seen Americans this united since . . . since whenever. Oh, man." He yawned again. "I mean, nobody's saying that Wrightman is the brightest bulb in the chandelier . . ." He lazily pointed his finger at me. "You didn't hear that from me. But c'mon, look what all those smart guys did; Kennedy and Bush and Clinton and Trump . . ."

I looked at him skeptically.

"Okay, maybe I'm just kidding about Trump. Just wanted to make sure I had your attention." He rattled on for several more minutes, continuing his long monologue on the state of the nation: People were satisfied, the economy was coming back, there was a feeling that someone smart was in charge, and "You got to admit it. There are more great shows on TV than ever."

Just to make sure he knew I was still in his game I interjected an occasional *uh-huh* or *Really?*

Corbin was describing his favorite Netflix series, something about earthlings trading places with their duplicates on our mirror planet (which ironically was how I sometimes felt in Wrightman's America), as we came around a gently sweeping bend. I checked again; the Chevy was steady in position. The road grade was rising and we were heading directly into the sun. Dickie leaned forward and snapped down his visor, and when he settled back in his seat, he turned and looked at me and saw the Glock in my left hand, pointing at his head.

He started to reach . . .

"Don't." I was completely calm. Calmness equals control; a lack of emotion in your voice is far more threatening to someone than screaming at them. Long as it's backed with a gun, of course. "Don't. Fucking. Move." The first hour of the first day of Special Ops training, we had been taught the importance of establishing and maintaining total control. Drill Sergeant Millard Dearing had reminded us every day, "The choices you make at the beginning will determine the actions you'll have to take at the end."

Corbin's right hand began edging toward the door pocket.

"Do it, and I swear to God I will put a bullet in your head."

He lifted his hand. "You shoot me and Russell'll shoot your girlfriend."

"Maybe. But how is that gonna help you?" He dropped his hand in his lap. "Good. Now here are the new rules. You do exactly what I tell you to do and you'll be fine. You'll end up back in D.C. and they'll give you another assignment and eventually they'll forget all about this one. You'll get to be a wise old agent, telling stories around the book burnings. But try to be a hero today . . ." I frowned. "I will kill you."

Corbin had lost his bravado, so he retreated to threats. "You know what they'll do to you if you shoot a federal agent, right?"

"Yes I do, Dick. I most certainly do. Exactly the same thing that they're going to do to me if I *don't* shoot a federal agent. Either way, I'm fucked if I get caught. But you, you've got a choice to make. You can be a live agent or a dead hero."

Corbin entwined his fingers in front of him and snapped them back, running scenarios in his mind. I was way ahead of him. There wasn't one of them in which he emerged in a better situation. Even if he got his gun, what was he going to do with it? Shoot the guy driving the van?

"You ever check out my background?" I asked him. Watching him while driving was difficult. I needed to change that equation, take him out of the game at least temporarily.

"No. Why? What was I going to find out, you're some kind of bumper chairs champion?"

"Yeah, well, you know." I sneaked a quick glance at him. "You scared, Dickie?"

"Of you?" He half laughed, half sneered. "You kidding me?"

"Good. Here's what I want you to do," I said, still evenly and firmly. "Hold out your right hand with your palm facing down and spread your fingers." He hesitated. For the first time I raised my voice. "Don't fuck with me. Do it now."

Corbin turned slightly in his seat and did exactly as directed. He fought to stop his hand from shaking. In one move I took hold of the steering wheel knob with my gun hand, then with my right hand I grabbed Corbin's trigger finger. I pressed down hard on his knuckle with my thumb while yanking the finger upward. An oldie but goodie. It sounded like a piece of kindling crackling in a fire, followed instantly by Dick's agonized scream. "What the fuck! Oh, Jesus Christ, that fucking hurts! You broke my fucking finger."

I waited until his shrieking dissolved into whimpers, then told him, "Now reach down into the well with your right hand and give me that gun." With a completely unnecessary but totally enjoyable sneer, I added, "Capiche?"

We used to refer to snapped fingers as tweets to the soul. It definitely got your attention, and if not necessarily your respect, your obedience. Corbin was sweating from the pain, but he did exactly as ordered, picking up the gun with his thumb and middle finger and handing it across his body to me. He covered his right hand protectively with his left hand as tears ran down his face. "Hurts like a bastard, right? But you're lucky. It'll heal up. Maybe you won't be tapping your chest for a few months . . ."—I demonstrated, tapping my chest with the Glock as he had done minutes earlier—"but give it a little time and you'll be ready to shoot anybody you want."

I slipped his gun under my seat cushion. I checked again. Russell was staying steady. We passed a large sign promising food and fuel, exit right in two miles. About a mile later I put on Van's right-turn signal. A few seconds later Russell's signal light clicked on. *Good boy,* I thought. "Okay, here's where it gets interesting," I told Corbin. "You fuck up, I promise you, bad things are going to happen." I told him exactly what I wanted to do, throwing in all the requisite threats.

The exit was a long two-lane ramp ending at a traffic light at the crest of a rise. There was an off-brand gas station with a small market about two hundred yards down the road on the right. While we were stopped at the light, I told Corbin, "Call him now." This was the most delicate part of the plan so I doubled down. As he picked up his phone with his left hand, I reminded him, "Believe me," I said evenly, keeping any hint of exaggeration out of my tone, "I got nothing to lose. Whatever happens to me, I will kill you."

Corbin hit the keyboard with his right pinkie. I watched in my rearview as Russell answered. Corbin came acceptably close to sounding normal. He told Francis that before filling his gas tank he should escort the female to the restroom.

"You sure?" Francis asked. "That's not what the regs say we're supposed to do."

Corbin took a deep breath, fighting the pain. "It's on me." He closed his eyes. "Just do what I tell you, Frankie, okay?"

"Well, what if she doesn't need to go?"

Corbin pressed the phone against his chest and looked at me. "Tell him to tell her this is the only time we're stopping. Her boyfriend says take advantage of it."

He repeated it exactly. The fight was gone out of him. He was in survival mode.

As we pulled into the gas station, I remember noticing that the price of gas was unusually low, back to pandemic prices, and thinking that was another trade-off to keep people docile. Funny I should remember that. I drove around to the side of the market, as far away from the pumps as possible. There was a row of empty parking spots on my left and I parked in the one farthest away. The Caprice pulled in on my left, meaning Agent Russell had to approach the van on the driver's side. I looked down, as if fumbling for something in my lap, but with my peripheral vision I watched Russell get out of the car and lock it with a remote. Laura was sitting calmly in the back seat. Russell waddled around the back of his car, putting his jacket on to cover his weapon. His badge was hanging from a lanyard around his neck. He came over to the van, his head down.

As I rolled down the window, I backed up Mighty Chair several inches in its tracks, giving me a wider field of vision. For the next few minutes I was going to have to be Bourne again. Keeping both agents in view was tricky, but I didn't need the details, I just had to be aware of motion. Russell rested his right arm on the doorframe and leaned in. "What's going . . ."

The Glock was in my right hand, resting on Chair's arm, pointing directly at Corbin. There was about eighteen inches between us, can't-miss distance. If I fired, I'd hit something. As Russell leaned into Van, I raised my left hand and jammed Corbin's gun right under Russell's chin and pushed up hard. "Don't. Fucking. Move."

"Do what he tells ya," Corbin shouted. "He's nuts. He broke my fucking finger."

"Whatever you say," Russell stammered, starting to raise his hands.

"Put your hands down," I told him. "We're gonna do this by the numbers. One, take the remote out of your pocket and open the car."

"What's two?" he gasped as I moved the gun into a slightly better position. Its barrel fit almost perfectly over Russell's Adam's apple.

"There is no two. Either you do exactly what I tell you or you die in a gas station parking lot."

We were in a good spot. Anyone looking in our direction would see someone leaning into a van having what appeared to be a friendly conversation. Then they would have seen an attractive young woman getting out of the rear seat of a white Chevy and joining us.

"You okay?" I asked her.

"I'm good."

"Pat him down. He's got a gun on him somewhere."

Russell tried to look at her without turning his head. His eyes were pulled so far to his right, they threatened to disappear into his ears. "Don't touch me there," he said. "It's in an ankle holster."

She was shielded from view by the Caprice as she bent down and found his weapon.

"That's it?" I asked.

"My other one's in the glove box." He cleared his throat and asked in a voice so thin it could have been coming through a straw. "Think maybe you could ease up a little."

As I'd learned in dark rooms, that's what fear sounded like.

Corbin shifted in his seat enough to attract my attention. I turned and he recoiled, raising his hands in supplication. I noticed his index finger had swelled up like a balloon. He saw me looking at it and pulled it back. He obviously had accepted the fact he was dealing with a crazy guy. "I'm not doing nothing," he swore.

"I got him," Laura said. We exchanged a quick glance. She smiled confidently. She was enjoying this, whether it was simply retribution or maybe a feeling of finally being able to fight back, a new part of her had been exposed, and clearly she was enjoying it.

I wasn't certain how to proceed. Getting to this point had been my primary objective. I had a sort of vague plan, but I lacked sufficient knowledge to fill in the gaps. I didn't like that. Contrary to the cliché, the best-laid plans usually were the ones that worked. I had no choice, though—we'd just have to solve each problem as it popped up. What was certain was that Dickie and Francis would be traveling with us, at least partway. "Get his phone," I told her.

"I'll do it," Russell volunteered and started reaching into his pants pocket.

"Stop," Laura snapped. I could see she shoved the gun into him a little harder. He kind of rose up on his toes, and I realized she was pushing it between his butt cheeks. My, my, what an interesting woman.

"Okay. Okay."

She reached into his pocket and got his phone.

I told her, "Lock him in the cage."

"Give me your handcuffs," she said.

"One hand," I warned him.

Using one hand, he took the cuffs off his belt and handed them to her. She cuffed his hands behind him and pushed him into the Chevy's cage. When they turned, I confirmed my suspicion—she had the gun rammed up his ass.

When he was secured, I gave my full attention to Corbin. "Your turn. Here's what you're going to do. Type out a message to your boss. Tell him you're on your way back to Washington with your prisoners. You'll be back later tonight. Don't send it. And please, don't be a smart guy. I honestly don't want you to get hurt."

He showed me the typed message. "Okay, send it."

I told Laura to toss both agents' phones in a rusting green dumpster. If anybody at headquarters got hinky, they wouldn't be able to ping these phones to locate us.

Twenty minutes later we were back on the highway, the Chevy trailing Van, but once again heading north. After retrieving the graphs and my passport from Corbin's jacket pocket, Laura had duct-taped him to the passenger seat, his arms at his side. It wasn't a total mummification, just three times around, sufficient to keep him restrained. As she was wrapping him, he pleaded, "Watch my finger. Careful of my finger."

We drove into the early evening, not pushing it. I-70 flowed into I-90, straight to Buffalo. The twilight sky was the bluish-black of the bruises on my arm, where I'd been kicked. In the distance, lightning was backlighting a cloud bank, but if there was thunder it was muffled by Van's air-conditioning. Corbin was quiet, probably wondering about his next career after this debacle. No matter what I'd told him, this wasn't going to be a career builder for him. Finally he asked, "C'mon, Stone, where'd you learn this stuff?"

I thought about it before responding, wondering what the benefit-loss ratio might be to telling the truth. We probably had more to gain if Corbin appreciated the danger he was in. "Special Ops," I said. "Multiple deployments, numerous missions. Mostly in the sandbox." I glanced at Corbin. "Multiple KIAs." I didn't mention attending the University of Ludlum and Child.

"Yeah. I figured something like that. Me too. I mean, you know, I was just a grunt. I was there for the Surge. We were in some deep shit." He paused, waiting for me to respond. I got it, two GIs shooting the shit, brothers-in-arms. But I didn't say a word. Corbin was my prisoner, not my pal. D. I. Dearing again: "Never kiss someone you might have to kill."

Once Corbin started talking, he wouldn't shut up. Maybe it made him forget the pain of his broken finger. Eventually he came back to the starting line. "So c'mon, what'd you do to rate priority handling? Which one of those assholes did you piss off?"

I brushed him off. He didn't need an answer. "I told you," I said, "I fought for America."

"Yeah, I got that. That's what you said."

I looked straight ahead, into the past. "That was then. This is now."

"I don't get it."

"I know," I said, finally glancing at him, "that's the problem."

21

They know," Laura said. There wasn't a quiver in her voice. It was as much a report as a question: What do we do now?

The only thing that surprised me was how long it had taken them to figure it out. We'd been on the road more than two hours. Anybody looking at us would simply have seen four people in two vehicles driving northwest on side roads at a casual pace. But the reality was a whole lot stranger than that. The first vehicle was a specially equipped van being driven by a man in a wheelchair carrying evidence that would reveal a massive government plot to seize unlimited power while a veteran Homeland Security agent sat duct-taped to the passenger seat. We were followed by a modified Chevy Caprice in which the entire law enforcement module had been installed, including a supercharged engine, a reinforced chassis, and a steel partition separating the front and rear seats. The car was being driven by a gun-toting attractive young woman, an actress who had appeared in several commercials and supporting roles at the National Theatre, while a fuming second Homeland Security agent was handcuffed in the secure back seat.

Laura had been monitoring the radio in the agent's car. She had ignored the repeated radio calls to the car. But when she heard the all-hands alert, she had used her phone to call Cher. "They called it a code red plus. Then they gave your description and said you were armed and dangerous."

Corbin was smirking. He turned his head, which was essentially the only part of his body he could move. "You're fucked," he said confidently.

I thought about that for several seconds. I had to admit he had a point. Then I responded, "You know, this reminds me of a story I once heard a comedian tell. He said he'd bought his son a chemistry set that came with all kinds of weird chemicals. After that, every time he tried to punish his son, the kid would hold a test tube filled with some liquid over his head and shout, 'We'll all go together!' So if I were you, Dickie, I'd start rooting real hard for the home team."

What I learned several days later was that Canadian immigration authorities also had heard the alert. They immediately shared it with leaders of the American Resistance Movement (Canada), Barack's Battalions. Among those people who received printed copies was Colonel Martin Shaw, formerly Detroit PD, with whom I had worked in exposing the Detroit Massacre. Marty Shaw had driven across the border with his family soon after the introduction of the New American Pledge and helped organize the opposition.

The code red plus designation had puzzled him. Somebody was pushing the panic button. The *plus* meant the rules were suspended—get this guy whatever it took. Border patrol agents, area military, regional militia, and local law enforcement were ordered to join the search, to secure the border, guaranteed overtime. Personnel on the four bridges crossing into Canada were doubled and officers were told to inspect every vehicle approaching the control points. Look in every car. Ask questions. Officers were dispatched to the bus and train stations, as well as the airport. They were told Roland Stone was "wanted for participating in acts of terrorism against the American people." I had to be stopped and nobody much cared how, "Subject is believed to be armed and should be considered highly dangerous. All necessary steps, including the use of force, should be taken to apprehend Stone and his accomplice or, if the situation does not permit that, to terminate this threat to national security by any means possible."

Shaw knew that was total bullshit. He knew me. We'd sort of worked together; I'd established my bona fides with him. What he didn't know was why? Why was the government so desperate to stop me that it had basically said, *Go ahead and shoot him*? Ten thousand resisters, more than that, had already swarmed across the border without attracting anywhere near this level of attention. Why me? What made me so different? So important? There was only one logical answer—it wasn't me. It was what I had with me; I had some information or materials in my possession that the Wrightman government did not want made public. It had to be physical evidence, Shaw guessed, otherwise I could have called it in.

Whatever the reason, Shaw decided, bless his soul, that I was going to need assistance. Under his command ARM already had helped numerous people safely cross the border, but this one was going to be a lot more complex. They did not have a shred of information about when or where I was going to try to cross. That wasn't so surprising, neither did I.

I didn't have a clue how we were going to do this. Nor did I have any idea Shaw and his people were getting ready to help me. He had set up his headquarters in the banquet room of Arthur Lem's Oriental Palace, a Chinese restaurant on the Canadian side of Niagara Falls. He had sat down with his best people over General Tso's and spring rolls and laid out the situation. My disability made it even more challenging. Given my limitations, I wasn't going to attempt an off-road crossing. I wasn't going to be strolling through the woods or over fields in my wheelchair. "What are we going to do to help this guy?" he'd asked. "Anybody got any suggestions?"

"Yeah, I got one," one of his top aides, Saul Wolfe, responded. Shaw loved telling this story. Everybody looked hopefully at this guy, who suggested between bites, "Next meeting we should get some pork fried rice too."

Had I been at that table I probably would have suggested extra sweet sauce. But I had more pressing problems, like the entire U.S. government mobilizing to stop me. Laura was monitoring the radio and the reports were growing increasingly ominous. The situation seemed surreal; the pursuit of the truth had made me a criminal in America. If I was careless or unlucky in the next few hours, I was going to end up locked away. Worse than Howie—it was going to be keep the key, throw Rollie away.

I cut off those thoughts. They weren't doing me any good. Toss 'em in that safe. Focus, focus, focus. Be in the moment. I began making my mental list. One at a time, I reminded myself. Don't try to do everything at once. Solve one problem at a time: Don't kill the army, kill the soldier. First, we had to get rid of the Homeland Security vehicle. And quickly. Next we'd have to get rid of Van. I hated that thought, but they had its description, so there was no possible way we could drive it across the border. Then we had to get rid of the agents.

Where it was possible, we mixed into local traffic. Hiding in plain sight. As we approached Buffalo, it suddenly started pouring. The rain came out of a clear night sky and lasted only a few seconds, as if we had driven under a misplaced waterfall. I started to say something about it to Corbin but caught myself. Big rule: Don't humanize your prisoners. I glanced at him. He was staring at his hand, testing how far he could flex his finger, then grimacing in pain. We passed a digital billboard, which announced in vibrant colors that Brad Paisley was in town, performing at the KeyBank Center. Two shows. I checked my watch, it was almost eight P.M. The first show was about half over. Brad Paisley was an unexpected bonus, Canadians would be driving back across the border after the concert, probably after eleven o'clock.

In the Intel classrooms at Benning we would game scenarios—the what-ifs. Dungeons & Dragons with tanks and missiles. This would have made a pretty interesting challenge: a clearly defined objective, identifiable good guys and bad guys, limited time and resources, extreme consequences. It would have been fascinating to see what we could have come up with, I mean if my life and freedom weren't at stake here.

What would Bourne do? Or Reacher? Or even Bruce Willis's John McClane? That's a big problem with life; there's never a good screenwriter around when you need one.

Although clearly Laura and I were outpersonned, we did have some factors in our favor. The feds had to cover four bridges, train and bus stations, and an international airport, so they would be stretched. They had no idea when we were going to try to cross, or even if we were still heading for Canada. The smart play would be to lay low for a few days, so they would have to keep juggling their resources to ensure they had fresh people on watch. The smart play? I chuckled. When did I start recycling noir talk? I tried to remember the attention curve we'd been taught, after how many hours did people start getting distracted? Seven or eight, I thought, but I wasn't certain. Then the feds couldn't be sure how many people I was traveling with; I certainly could have picked up some additional people, even some kids, to scramble their equation, so they had to search every vehicle. And maybe my biggest advantage, they would be looking for the average guy riding a normal chair; they had no concept of what me, Cher, and Mighty Chair were capable of doing.

For Christmas several decades ago, I'd bought my parents a clunky computer and set them up online. I wanted to be able to stay in contact with them wherever I was in the world. It worked out perfectly. I was able to maintain contact throughout all my tours and my mother became a champion Lexulous player. I have been paying for it ever since, literally, and it remains among the best investments I've ever made. After my father died in 2014, I refused to cancel his account. That seemed just too final for me. Instead I kept him alive in cyberspace. When I realized the marshals would be tracking my account, to avoid detection I had Cher log on to the net using my father's account. I had no trouble remembering his password, because it was what he had always called me. Ironically, it was Sonny.

Cher took advantage of Sonny, providing all the necessary background information I needed. I got the details about the crossing points, what to expect at customs, anticipated traffic and wait times, currency restrictions, and local trivia. For example, seven people have gone over Horseshoe Falls (one of the three falls and the only one belonging to Canada!) in a barrel. Four of them lived, three died.

There were four bridges between the United States and Canada. The Lewiston-Queenston Bridge was three miles north of Niagara Falls. The Whirlpool Rapids Bridge probably was the quickest to get across, but using it required a NEXUS card; so it was mostly for residents commuting back and forth. My Homeland Security badge (Thank you, Dickie) might work, but I wasn't sure it was a chance worth taking.

The Rainbow Bridge was limited to noncommercial traffic and permitted pedestrians to walk across, while the main highway, I-190, led directly to the Peace Bridge.

Corbin had been quiet for quite a while. His head was pushed back against the headrest, his eyes were closed, and he had an amused smile on his face. "What's so funny?"

He opened his eyes and looked at me. "I'm listening to what she's saying and I'm wondering how you think you're going to get across the border. By now it's crawling with cops."

I agreed, "I was just thinking that myself." I smiled at him. "That's when I started wondering if you can float."

His smile disappeared.

I checked my mirror. Laura was right there, right in position where she was supposed to be. I wondered what was going on in her mind. At this point any woman not shaking in her 'Boutins would have to be a little crazy. She was doing an amazing job. When we met, she was a well-meaning supporting stage witch, and in only a few hours she'd become an accomplice in the kidnapping of two federal agents and stuck a loaded gun up a federal agent's behind. She was currently driving a stolen government vehicle assisting a wanted fugitive attempting to escape to a foreign country with evidence that might overthrow a president.

And all of it with a minimum of makeup!

Well, whatever we were going to do, it was time to start doing it. We had to get the agents' car off the road. I put on my signal light. One exit was the same as every other. Time to go. I'd recently heard a pop philosopher sum up contemporary American culture: "All roads lead to Mickey D's!" In my experience that was pretty accurate; get on any main road and eventually you'll end up at a McDonald's. As promised, in less than ten minutes I was looking at those Golden Arches. Those signs once boasted how many millions, then billions of hamburgers had been served. They no longer included that information; I wondered if they'd run out of numbers.

This Mickey D's was on the corner of a strip mall. The lineup of stores was typical for a middle-class residential neighborhood. In addition to the McDonald's it included a stationery store; a Chase bank with two ATMs in front, which was right next to a Citibank, which also had two ATMs in front; a pizza shop; a children's shoe store; one vacant storefront; and most important, a twenty-four-hour CVS. There were a few cars in the lot. Inside the Mickey D's, a man was swabbing the floor. Two people were working the ATMs.

I parked at an angle in front of the empty storefront. I'd learned my lesson; if it did have active surveillance cameras, which I doubted, I didn't want them reading our plates. I took two regular spaces rather than one handicapped spot—and felt great about it. Laura pulled in right next to me at a similar angle.

I watched Laura turn around and say something to Russell before getting out. I rolled down my window as she approached Van. "Nice parking job," she said.

"Cher, play rap, please." The rap bopping through Van's speakers made it nearly impossible for Corbin to overhear our conversation. I didn't especially like rap, but I figured it would irritate him, and that was good enough for me. "What were you saying to him?" I asked.

"I was just being honest with him. I told him I didn't know how stable you were, so if he decided to make a fuss, he probably was putting his partner's life in danger." She leaned on the window frame and spoke-whispered. "You wouldn't really shoot him, would you?"

I was pleased she'd made it a hypothetical question. That made it much easier to answer. "I'm not sure." I lowered my voice too and told her exactly what I wanted her to do. Cher had provided the information I needed. She was nodding as I gave her the list. As she turned to go, I put a restraining hand on top of hers. She paused, with a question in her eyes. "ATMs all have cameras," I reminded her, "so keep your head down. You don't want to show up on the intel network." I had no idea if those cameras were tied into a facial recognition system, but we had to assume they were.

Laura repeated my instructions, then started walking away but stopped and came right back. "What?"

She leaned inside my open window and kissed me. "We are gonna do this, aren't we?"

I watched her walk away. "Cher," I said, getting comfortable, "what's the traffic doing?"

It was kind of a cool plan. All it had to do was work. While Laura was shopping, Cher skipped around to various news and talk stations. Most of the stories were still focusing on the executions. The networks supposedly proposed moving the next hangings to prime time. There also were rumors that cable stations were preparing to make a substantial offer for pay-per-view rights. There wasn't a word mentioned about fugitives on the road.

She returned about fifteen minutes later with two large plastic bags filled with goodies, among them two prepaid phones. "That was all they had left," she said. She had activated both of them and made the necessary phone call. "It's done," she told me. "About forty minutes, they said."

We had a lot to do in that time. I drove Van around to the rear of the mall. It reminded me of the late-night patrols we used to make into Indian country. It was dark and lonely, and the shadows faded into deeper shadows. A bare bulb over the rear door of the McDonald's illuminated a black and green plastic mountain of garbage. The covers of several dumpsters were open; a cat leaped out of one of them and disappeared into the night. I parked under a spreading willow, leaving myself enough room to lower the ramp with space to squeeze in one car between Van and a high white stucco rear wall. Laura squeezed the Chevy into that space. I could see her in the front seat, turning and pointing Russell's gun right at him. Damn, I was proud of her. It was pretty obvious she wasn't especially comfortable with the gun, but hey, it was a gun. You didn't have to be comfortable to fire it and probably hit something. He hunched his shoulders and involuntarily raised both of his legs protectively as high as he could. I heard her warn him, "We're getting out of this car. I'm going to open your door and you're gonna get out and you're gonna get right into that van. You understand that?"

"Yeah. Yeah. Then what?"

As cool as if she had spent her whole life waiting to say this one line, she told him, "Then I don't have to shoot you."

With a big smile on my face I said, "Cher, open the side panel, please."

Chair was still locked in the wheel well, but I was pointing my Glock at the Chevy's back door. "Move," I said. "Now."

Laura opened the Chevy's rear door and stepped back several feet, holding her gun in both hands. Van was shielding all this from anyone passing in front. She kept her weapon pointing at Russell's chest as he wiggled out of the car and managed to get into Van's cabin. He sat on the carpeted floor. "Now what?"

I told him, "Lay down on your stomach. Not a sound."

Laura climbed in after him. I said, "Cher, close the door, please."

Corbin asked as if he were a curious bystander, "What's going on?"

Laura bound Francis's legs together with the duct tape. He actually lifted his legs to help her, resigned to the situation. "Check his pockets," I told her, tossing her a blue canvas duffel bag with a Nats logo I'd gotten at the 2019 World Series. "Put everything in this."

She looked at Russell and said reassuringly, "I'll be careful, I promise." She took out his keys, wallet and badge case, some loose change, a plastic toothpick, several individually wrapped white Life Savers mints, and slips of paper on which he had written some notes. She dumped everything in the bag.

With both feds secured, Laura reached into her plastic bag and pulled out a family-sized bottle of CVS Health Maximum Strength Nighttime Sleep Aid and a bottle of water. "How many should I give them?"

"What does it say on the bottle?"

She read the instructions. "Take one before going to sleep." She looked at me.

Corbin said firmly, "I'm not taking any of that shit."

I ignored him. "I don't know. Three? Four? Four should be okay."

Laura opened the safety cap, cut through the foil cover, and fished out the ball of cotton. She tapped out three gel caps. "Let's do three." Russell was lying on his back in the cabin, hands cuffed, legs taped, but to his credit he was still holding on to the last remnants of defiance. He locked his mouth closed and began moving his head. She knelt down next to him. "Open."

He continued rattling his head. "*Nnnnnnnnnnnnnnnnn . . .*" he responded through gritted teeth.

She shrugged. "Your choice," and reached down to grab hold of his balls.

"It's open. It's open!" he shouted, opening his mouth wider than Sea-World dolphins at dinnertime.

Honestly, how could you not be impressed by a woman like that? "Thank you." She dropped the three gels into his mouth and gave him enough water to wash them down. "Show me," she said, as if talking to a child. He opened his mouth again. "Thank you. Good night." Then she looked at me; her eyes were dancing with joy. She was finding places inside herself that she had never touched.

She duck-walked to the front and shook out three more gels. "How about you?" she asked Corbin.

He kept his mouth shut.

I poked him with the Glock.

Through his closed mouth, he mumbled something I could make out as "You gonna shoot me for not opening my mouth?"

I reached down and took hold of the index finger on his left hand.

He opened his mouth.

Laura repeated the process. Dickie washed them down. "Nighty-night," she said. She turned to me. "How long?"

I shrugged. "Twenty minutes? Half hour?"

"Perfect."

Things were humming in our own little world. People were racing around the region like pieces in speed chess. It probably was a good thing we didn't know what was going on, as we might have changed our plans. They had positioned officers at highway entrances and exits. Then they began knocking on doors of every hotel, motel, and Airbnb between Lake Erie and the border. Additional officers were assigned to patrol the Peace Bridge, the closest crossing into Canada. As I later learned from an admittedly gleeful source, Rip McCord was so confident his people would find us that he told Vice President The Hun, "If he so much as farts, we'll hear him."

On the Canadian side of the border Barack's Battalions also had been mobilized. Saul Wolfe actually had come up with a very crazy plan, but everyone agreed it was more effective than General Tso's. Shaw had little confidence Operation Egg Roll, as they were calling it, would make any difference, but lacking anything more promising he went with it. Thanks primarily to Arthur Lem, who had agreed to provide free wonton soup, egg rolls, and barbecued ribs to all participants, they had recruited several dozen people.

In Van's cabin, Corbin and Russell were fighting to stay awake. Corbin was screeching Maroon 5 songs in a dreadfully off-key screech, but as the pills kicked in, he was slowing down. He was at the Drunk Maroon 5 stage. Laura had duct-taped his legs together, moved the passenger seat as far back as it would slide and lowered the backrest so he was no longer visible through the side window. Russell was fading even faster, having been reduced to "Puff the Magic Dragon."

As the agents faded into sleep, Laura dug into her CVS bag once again. She took out a spray can of Jerome Russell B Wild!!! Temporary Hair Color. She covered my shoulders with a cloth and sprayed my hair the same light brown as Corbin's. As she worked, I asked her where she had learned to handle a gun like that.

"Did you hear me?" she asked, her enthusiasm bubbling over. She lowered her voice and practically growled as she repeated her tough-girl line: "Then I don't have to shoot you." She laughed with delight. "That was just so great." She lowered her voice another octave into Darth Vader territory and said again, "Then I don't have to shoot you." The laughter slowed and she caught her breath. "I don't know anything about guns. I hate guns. That's the way Angie Dickinson does it in the reruns of *Police Woman*."

Finally she finished and took a step back to admire her work, almost banging her head on Van's roof. "Nice," she decided. Moving back another few inches, she reassessed the result. "It's okay." Then, to convince herself, "Yeah." Nodding. "Yeah, it's a . . . okay." In the daylight, if someone were looking carefully, it was an easily detectable paint job. But at night, under artificial lighting, if I wore a baseball cap, it probably was good enough. "Almost time," she warned, checking her watch.

The parking lot was bordered on one side by a line of trees. I moved the van to the front of the lot, directly beneath the tree canopy, close to the main road. I figured a van left overnight in the rear of the lot would attract more interest than one parked right up front for everyone to see. Hide in plain sight. Laura drove the Caprice out of the lot down a long, quiet residential street and parked. She checked the street signs to make sure it would be legal for at least a day, then hurried back to the mall, being careful to stay out of the streetlights.

It was time to go. Russell was snoring loudly. Corbin's head was resting on his shoulder; he'd definitely have a stiff neck in the morning. I took a long look around. There were a lot of memories stored in that van. I rolled down the ramp one final time. Then I sat there for a moment. "Thanks, Van," I said, patting its side as Cher buttoned him up. "You've been great." Then I turned Mighty Chair around.

Laura was waiting in front of the CVS. "They're out cold," I told her, then added with as much confidence as I could muster, "By the time they wake up, we'll be eating maple syrup and saluting Mounties."

We stood in the dim light of the twenty-four-hour just about everything store, waiting as calmly as possible. Two cars, one a local police cruiser, the other a white sedan with no markings, went racing past heading in opposite directions, their lights flashing, sirens whining.

Our ride was late. "It'll be here soon," I said, hoping I was right. Laura rested her left hand on my left shoulder and tapped nervously. I reached across with my right hand and took hold of it. A minute later she checked her watch again. She was dripping anxiety on me. But there wasn't much we could do except wait.

Finally a black Ford F-150 pickup truck turned into the parking lot. "That's it," she said excitedly, pointing. "There it is."

The pickup came to a stop almost directly in front of us. I looked inside. There was no one driving it. It had the aura of an alien spaceship; we just stood there, staring at it, not quite sure what to do. "You ever drive one of these?" I asked.

"Do they even call it driving?" she wondered.

Okay, I admit it, it spooked me. "How hard could it be, right? I mean, they definitely wouldn't rent them if it was too complicated."

"Right," she agreed, bolstering her own confidence. "We're two intelligent adults. We can figure this out."

Let's be honest, how many of you have not driven your own car? I had never been inside an autonomous vehicle. But the availability of self-driving SUVs and pickups had been big news within the disabled community. Arranging transportation has always been a major hassle for people with handicaps, and this was a vitally important step toward further independence. Among the many advantages offered by autonomous SUVs and small trucks is that they provide sufficient storage space for the necessary supportive equipment—in my case, Mighty Chair. We were lucky: Buffalo's first It-Drives-U franchise had opened three months earlier and had an F-150 available. We'd used Corbin's credit card, hoping Homeland Security hadn't thought to put an alert on it. The pickup had been dispatched to the CVS to pick us up.

I was going to drive. Or whatever you call it. Law enforcement had to be looking for someone in a chair or riding as a passenger. Seeing me sitting behind the wheel of the pickup, my hands on the wheel, should provide cover for us. Laura opened the driver's door for me and I muscled into the seat. I took a minute to look over the dashboard. I don't know exactly what I expected to see, but this definitely wasn't it. It looked pretty much like every other vehicle I'd ever driven. The dashboard was covered with quality faux leather and highly polished black plastic. The steering wheel was tightly wrapped with black leather, and all the necessary gauges and monitors were in front of me. The infotainment center, which controlled everything from performance to radio station, was in the middle. A gearshift was on the center console.

The media display made controlling the truck relatively easy. I worked my way through the options to Truck Bed Operations, then lowered the tailgate and extended the built-in ramp. The directions were so easy even an adult could understand them. While most wheelchairs are stored by pushing up the middle of the seat, bringing the two sides together, because of its technology Mighty Chair had been designed to close up from the top down. "Cher," I told her, "fold up." Within seconds the backrest lowered over the seat and pistons lowered it. As this was taking place, Cher was doing a passable Margaret Hamilton, crying, "I'm melting. I'm melting." And as it lowered to the ground, I could see the resemblance to the Wicked Witch's melting. Thanks, Y.

Fully compressed, Mighty Chair resembled a rectangular ottoman about two and a half feet high. Laura grasped the handle and wheeled it up the ramp into the truck bed, secured it with crisscrossing bungee cords, and covered it with the canvas sheet she had requested. The entire process took about ten minutes. A couple of people coming in and out of the CVS had glanced in our direction but didn't seem to be paying any undue attention. There was nothing we could do about it anyway. This was hardly a perfect plan.

As I raised the rear gate, Laura got into the cab's passenger seat. It seemed like just a decade or so earlier she was climbing into Van's passenger seat and introducing herself. She looked at me, sitting behind the wheel as if I was actually driving this thing, and forced a wan smile. "Can o' corn," I said.

She scrunched her face into a question mark. "What?"

"It's okay, it's a saying."

"Oh. Okay." She reached into the CVS bag one more time, this time pulling out some cover makeup. "Lean over here." I followed instructions and she began covering the visible bruises as best she could. When she was done, she handed me a pair of oval reading glasses in a black plastic frame and a baseball cap bearing a cartoon image of Abbott and Costello above the words: "Slowly, I turned . . . Niagara Falls, New York."

The glasses and cap completed my nerd look. "Here we go," I said, running my hands over the console like a pilot figuring out how to get this 757 off the ground. I pressed and pushed and turned until the GPS appeared. I didn't have any specific location in Canada to plug in, so I went to my usual fallback position. Assuming every city has a Main Street, I said distinctly, "One Main Street, Niagara Falls, Ontario." Then I added, "Take the Peace Bridge." A female voice accurately repeated the address.

After considerable thought I finally had picked the Peace Bridge essentially because why not? It was the closest and busiest crossing. With 160,000 vehicles crossing every day, agents had little time to make thorough inspections. It also was the obvious choice, so I hoped Homeland Security would assume I was too smart to use it and instead was heading for one of the less traveled bridges. Reverse reverse reverse psychology!

The GPS gave me a choice between the fastest and shortest route or toll roads. I went for the quick. The system told me it would take thirty-eight minutes. I hit "approve guidance" and the truck slowly accelerated. I took my hands off the wheel and held them in midair, hovering enough to quickly grab the wheel if necessary, getting accustomed to the reality that I was not in control. "This is really weird," I said, my tone somewhere between amazement and amusement. Sitting behind the wheel, watching it turn, created an odd sensation. As the truck picked up speed, I found myself instinctively reaching for Van's hand controls, and only after realizing they weren't there did I accept the reality that I wasn't driving.

It still felt very uncomfortable, though.

The GPS guided the truck through several middle-class residential neighborhoods. Trees and front lawns, well-kept houses, a father and small daughter walking their dog. Squirrels dashing across the street. Everything appeared calm and normal, a warm summer night in suburban America. Then we turned onto a street being searched by the local militia. Who knows? Maybe they were looking for me. It was a block of one-family brick and wood homes built, I'd guess, in the 1950s. An old-fashioned suburban block lined with mature trees whose roots were pushing up the sidewalk. The houses had aged well; they were narrow and deep, with a four-step brick stoop climbing to a landing, windows on either side of the front door, a driveway on the left leading to a garage at the rear of the house. Many of these houses had covered entries; several of them had added wider windows and second-story dormers. Most of them had lined their front with bushes, and two or three also had window boxes, one of them filled brightly with red and yellow flowers. The driveways were gravel, asphalt, or cement. I could see basketball hoops on most of the garages.

I rested my hands on the steering wheel. A young man peered into the cab. He looked pleasant enough, except for the semiautomatic weapon on his shoulder. After deciding that we were normal Americans, not some traitor in a wheelchair, he smiled and gave us a one-finger salute as if tipping a nonexistent hat as we drove past. Laura smiled back and gave him a little wave in return.

Members of the militia, all of them dressed in black pants and black shirts and wearing red armbands, were standing in groups on the sidewalk or on landings. They carried flashlights, and several of them had rifles slung over the shoulder or hanging across the chest. At a glance they looked to be a wide span of ages. There were several women, some of them patrolling with children. One young boy was carrying a Little League–sized baseball bat.

Some front doors were open, but most were not. As we drove past a dark house, two men were attacking a closed door with a sledgehammer. A little farther down the block, the Blackshirts were beating a bloodied man, who was on his knees, shielding his head with his arms. An older woman walking a big dog was waiting patiently to get past, watching with obvious curiosity as she was held back.

With our windows up and the air-conditioning on, most of the sounds were drowned out, giving the scene a slightly apocalyptic feeling. An occasional muffled scream and the shattering of glass provided a terrifying reality. Laura and I avoided looking at anything with more than a cursory glance, no matter how compelling it was, being careful to avoid attracting attention. Just a guy and a gal in their pickup.

And then we were on the next block and the next block. We kept our voices very low when we discussed our plan, even though we were alone in the cab. Laura gathered the paperwork we'd need when we got to customs. The GPS indicated we were eleven minutes from the bridge. "I always wanted to see Niagara Falls," she said.

Marty Shaw later filled me in. Just as we were getting ready to make our run, he received a text message reading: "Hi, Marty, the plan is in action. The turnout is stronger than we expected. Will keep you informed." He replied with a question: How many? The answer was more than three hundred men, women, and some children, an incredible and unexpectedly large number given such brief notice in the middle of the night. Organizations had rallied their members who were racing, okay, progressing steadily, toward the border. They had not been given specifics, they were told they were needed, then told where to assemble.

"I couldn't believe it really was happening," Shaw told me. "It was pretty incredible."

The F-150 carried us around a long bend, and as we reached the summit, the beautifully lit Peace Bridge appeared in front of us. It sat like a jewel against the black sky, its LED lights programmed to create a green and lavender necklace across the Niagara River. The river itself was relatively still, the reflection of the bridge rippled only slightly by a small boat easing gently upstream.

Laura took a deep calming breath, filling her cheeks, then slowly blowing out a long stream of air. The next few minutes were going to determine the next few years of our lives. At least. She took my hand and held it.

"We're okay," I said, staring straight ahead at our future. She could not hear me thinking, *I hope.*

22

It was late, almost midnight, but traffic was backed up leading onto the Peace Bridge. That didn't surprise or concern me. Long-haul truckers prefer driving at night and there had to be a sprinkling of Canadians returning from the Paisley concert. But the real problem was created by the orange cones set up to funnel every vehicle into the maze of checkpoints. Law enforcement was putting on a full-bridge press. Border patrol agents supplemented, I guessed, with Homeland Security and local cops were stopping and talking to every driver. Other officers, some of them holding bomb-sniffing and drug-detecting dogs on long leashes, were circulating among cars and trucks.

It was a loud mess. A few exasperated drivers had begun banging on their horns; they were quickly joined by many more, creating a cacophony of noise that must have irritated the already harried officers. A BMW and a Mercedes racing to fill a vacated space had banged bumpers and the drivers had gotten out and were literally bumping chests. Officers were trying to pull them apart. Two other cars had overheated and were cooling on the side.

All good. The more hectic it was the better for us. I had figured out how to drive, or more accurately not drive, the pickup. The driver could assume control of the system at any time simply by turning the steering wheel or pressing on the accelerator or brake, just as cruise control could be overridden in traditional vehicles. As long as we were mired in the traffic jam, we were okay. The truck stayed a safe distance behind the vehicle in front of us, moving whenever it moved. The only problem I could foresee was what to do if that car in front of us moved out of range while we were being interviewed. Without being able to put my foot on the brake there was no way I could prevent the truck from moving forward. That would be awkward. But we had no choice; I had to be behind the wheel, maybe the last place law enforcement would expect me to be.

They were doing a pretty thorough search. Officers were leaning into every vehicle. Each of them had a photograph and were trying to match it to anyone in the vehicle.

I turned on the radio, just two normal folks out for a midnight drive. "You think there's a station playing soothing cop music?"

"Just remember who we are," Laura reminded me. She held her hands locked together in her lap, although several of her fingers appeared to be struggling to get free.

The truck was moving perfectly, maintaining the gap between us and the sports car in front of us. Thoughts were running through my mind like those endless banners at the bottom of a news report. What did I miss? What if the cops ask us to get out of the car? Should we have taken a different bridge? Maybe I should have gone west and crossed in a different state? I was responsible for Laura, so when should I surrender to save her? My paranoia shifted in high gear: What if Cher thought it was funny to yell out she was being kidnapped? None of it was productive, but every effort I made to lock them away failed.

We eased into the traffic. As we slowly moved forward in the long line leading to the first checkpoint, I noticed a blue van to our right had a handicapped sticker affixed to its rear bumper. "That poor guy," I said, pointing it out to Laura, "he has no idea what he's gotten into."

The red car moved forward, and we closed the gap. I had gone for country on the radio and was trying to whistle along with Brad, but my throat was too dry and I kept blowing air. We stopped next to a new Kia Sorento; it was a hatchback, and I noticed a wheelchair sitting in the cargo space. *That's a coincidence,* I thought. *Two in a row.*

About five minutes later we reached the first checkpoint. I kept both hands on the wheel. As I turned down the radio, a New York State trooper leaned into the cab. He was an older, pleasantly round-faced man. He was holding a clipboard; the photograph on top showed me sitting in Mighty Chair at my desk at the *Pro*. I was smiling whimsically. A tower of Dunkin' cups rose from one edge. It actually was kind of flattering. "Evening, folks," the trooper said politely. "Sir, may I see your identification, please."

I made a big show of reaching into my back pocket for my wallet. I opened it wide enough for the trooper to see the badge, then removed Corbin's Homeland Security ID card and handed it to him. The trooper looked at it, looked at me for comparison, then looked at the ID again as if he wasn't convinced. "What's all this about?" Laura asked with big-eyed innocence, leaning across the console.

The trooper ducked down to get a better look at her but did not ask for her ID. Obviously this was just a preliminary check. "We got a heads-up out on a suspect," he said pleasantly. "A handicapped guy in a wheelchair."

I kept watching the red car in front of me. As long as it stayed within the gap-distance we were okay.

"No luck?" Laura asked.

The trooper took off his tan Stetson and frowned. "Not so far. Funny thing, though." He waved his hat at the traffic jam. "It's like all of a sudden every Canadian in a wheelchair decides to go home tonight." He handed me Corbin's ID and stepped back. "It's like a wheelchair convention." He put his hat back on and squared it. "Thank you, Agent Corbin." Then he turned and waved the car behind us forward.

Laura's dye job had passed its first test. Corbin was taller and thinner than I am, but when you're seated behind the wheel in a dark vehicle, it's pretty much impossible to determine height and weight. Most important, I was driving what appeared to be a standard pickup, while this guy they were looking for would be driving a specially equipped van or, more likely, be a passenger.

A wheelchair convention? Either we were in the middle of the greatest coincidence in history or there were forces at work I knew nothing about. "Now isn't that interesting," I mused as we finally moved forward.

"What was he talking about?"

"I'm not sure."

But more and more, as we were absorbed foot by foot into this traffic jam, I felt like I had been transported to some kind of disabled wonderland. Once I began looking around, it seemed like every other vehicle was transporting a chair. We were in a veritable sea of SUVs and vans and modified station wagons; there were other trucks, pickups, and rented box trucks with their rear door rolled up. Another pickup slid past us in an adjoining lane; a young man was sitting in a wheelchair in its bed, engrossed in a book. "Look at that," I said with growing excitement. I didn't know who or how, but the community had been mobilized. "No way that can be legal."

Laura was equally perplexed. There was a look of absolute wonder on her face, like she had just opened her closet door and discovered E.T. "You think that's illegal," she said, looking in her side mirror. "Wait'll you see what's coming."

Seconds later a motorcycle with a sidecar squeezed past on our right; the sidecar had been modified to hold a wheelchair in place. A teenage girl wearing a crown was sitting in the chair, as if it was her throne, and as the bike passed the pickup, she waved to us with the beneficence of a queen.

It was extraordinary. I had never experienced anything like this; no one had. While many people trapped in this mess were furious, at least some others realized they were caught in the middle of something very special and were enjoying it. Several people began honking in a rhythm, the traffic jam version of synchronized clapping. I banged on our horn. I couldn't help it.

The noise level rose as others joined in, either for the fun of it or because they were majorly pissed. Laura shouted to me, "You ever hear anything like this?"

"What?" We laughed in unison. "This is crazy," I shouted.

We passed a convertible with its top down and two chairs balanced on the rear seat; a boy and a girl somewhere in their mid-teens were holding hands, big smiles on their faces. We stopped at a second checkpoint. A female trooper looked at me as I handed her Corbin's documents. She glanced at it as she looked around me at Laura. She stared at Laura, then bit her bottom lip as if perplexed. Then she began nodding in recognition; pointing Corbin's documents at Laura, she said, "I know you. You're that whole-deal girl. Wow."

Laura smiled back. "Everybody else is just talk," she agreed.

Without looking at me the officer handed me back the documents. "Nice meeting you," she said, still smiling.

As Marty Shaw told me, his people had decided to flood all four crossing points with wheelchairs. It was the only plan they could come up with that might have an impact. Their objective was to overwhelm the system; to confuse, delay, and frustrate. Rather than allowing law enforcement to search for the needle in the haystack, they were building a haystack out of needles.

They had requested assistance from every organization for the disabled in Ontario. To help a political fugitive attempting to escape from the United States, they explained, they wanted as many wheelchair-bound people as possible to cross one of the bridges into America, then return through a different checkpoint. It wasn't much of a plan, he admitted, but given the complete lack of information as to where and when I would try to cross the border, it was their only shot. There was nothing the authorities could do to prevent it.

And there we were, smack-dab in the beautiful middle of it. We continued moving steadily toward the next checkpoint. Every vehicle was being stopped, many of them were being searched, papers were being examined. I put on the baseball cap and glasses. Laura turned up the radio. We were two cars away. Then one. An immigration officer with a somewhat grim look on her face leaned into the car and took a quick look around. "Hi," she said, somewhat distractedly, "May I have your passports, please?" It appeared she had already dismissed us in her mind.

I was watching the car in front of us. Just stay there, I thought, please, stay there.

Laura handed me her passport. After Wrightman had given law

enforcement the power to stop anyone at any time to examine their identification, people had begun carrying their passports, residence documents, or national ID cards with them at all times. I put Laura's blue passport on top of Corbin's ID wallet and handed them both to the officer. Then I made a point of leaning over and turning down the radio. Look at me! No disability here!

"What's the purpose of your visit?" the officer asked in a perfunctory manner.

Laura smiled, her cheeks blushing. "Pleasure," she said, giving it a sensual connotation.

I coughed nerdishly. "We're staying with some friends," I corrected, then turned and looked at Laura. "You know, for the night." Just as the trooper had done, the officer tried to match my face to the ID, but clearly was struggling with it. Up ahead, cars were moving forward. I wondered if I could get away with lifting my leg up with my hand and dropping my foot on the brake. "What's going on?" I asked, then took a shot: "I don't remember seeing it backed up like this."

The officer glanced back at the wall of headlights pointed at her. She had to scream to be heard above the honking. "Some kind of training exercise," she lied. "You know, the new regulations and all." She tapped Corbin's ID. "Agent Corbin, do you happen to have your passport with you?"

I shook my head. "No." I pointed at the document wallet. "They give us that in lieu of a passport. I think you guys have a similar thing, right? What do they call it?" I frowned, struggling to remember. Ah, I got it! "A courtesy document."

She had a confused look on her face. She looked at the ID again, tapping it on her extended finger as she considered how to respond. She began looking around for assistance. The traffic up ahead was moving. The gap was widening. "Jack!" she called to another customs officer. "Could you come here for a sec?"

Jack came over. Jack was round all round, a small round head on a round body, as if someone had placed a basketball on top of a beachball, then put a hat on it. "What's up?"

She handed him Corbin's ID. "Ever see one of these?" He glanced at it, then looked at me and held it. I looked right back at him, not wavering at all. Nothing to see here. Jack frowned, considering it. The red car began moving, the car behind me honked. It was joined instantly by several others, and the wave started growing once more. It was too much for Jack. I was starting to roll forward. The car was starting to move. Jack handed the wallet back to the female officer. "It's fine." He shrugged it off, his whole demeanor expressing, *What are the odds?* He looked at me, "Have a good night, sir." He pointed at the honking driver behind me and started walking purposefully toward him.

The officer handed me our documents. I gave them to Laura just as we started rolling forward, into Canada.

I let loose a deep breath and turned to Laura. Tears were snaking around her cheeks and rolling down her face. I squeezed her hand. "Pleasure?"

We crossed the border. When we reached Canadian customs, we were stopped again. An immigration officer with a bushy mustache approached the truck. Officer Dudley Do-Right! I turned off the engine and just sat there. "Welcome to Canada," he said. "May I see your identification, please?"

I have no idea where my response came from. He gave me a quizzical look as I told him, "Take me to your leader."

At that moment the population of Canada became 39,215,878, plus two. I leaned over and kissed Laura. Not a romantic kiss, not even close—a thank-you kiss. The sense of relief I felt was enormous. I was filled with relief, with joy, until I looked over my shoulder and saw my country across the river.

I stopped the car in the breakdown lane. We just sat there for several minutes. I was completely disoriented. It was as if I was being wheeled out of Walter Reed again, but this time there was no Howie standing there with a big smile and open arms ready to help me remake myself.

Until that instant I had been mission-focused. I hadn't permitted my emotions to color my judgment. But suddenly the sadness I felt was as close to overwhelming as anything I had ever experienced. It hit me with the intensity of a collapsing building. It was completely disorienting. I covered my mouth with my palm, biting the inside of my cheeks. I wasn't leaving a place. Instead I was accepting the painful reality that the day of America exceptionalism was done. Everything good that happened in my life, everything, I owed to my country. I am who I am because I was born in America. I was shaped by its greatest values. Maybe the reality of America was never anyone's idea of a utopia. Hunger and homelessness were always with us; there were too many places where poverty was a way of life and education was a dream; distrust, racism, and hate divided us; no one would claim we had ever reached that place envisioned by our founders. We were more like Oz or Shangri-la; our best days were always over the next horizon, beyond the cotton clouds. But until Trump took office, we had never stopped striving to get there, never stopped pursuing those goals of true human decency and equality.

During Trump's final year in office protesters had hidden inside the Statue of Liberty when its museum had closed in the evening, then somehow made their way up to the torch, where they sabotaged the wiring. They had made a symbol of the symbol—turning off the torch of liberty. The Parks Department claimed it was an internal wiring problem and the story never received wide circulation. But that's what happened. The Democrats had promised to relight the torch. It was to be the symbol of the country once again becoming a beacon for people in need. Never happened. Instead it has remained dark and empty. That was the way I felt inside.

"We got to go, Rollie," Laura said.

"Yeah."

The Canadians had developed a protocol for dealing with Americans claiming political asylum. We were escorted to the small office of the regional director of immigration, Ontario, still close enough to the border to see the innocently twinkling lights across the Niagara River in Buffalo. With assistance Laura had rolled Mighty Chair off the truck. As easily as opening a convertible couch, Cher had snapped Chair back into position. When it was done, Cher sighed loudly, then told me, "That feels better."

The Canadians laid down a sheet of plywood to serve as a makeshift ramp, allowing me to get over a raised sill and into a small soulless cinder-block building. There were five small offices on either side of a narrow corridor. We were escorted into the second office on the right side. It was standard bureaucrat: a gray metal desk with a narrow table behind it; a bookcase with government manuals on its shelves; two chairs in front of the desk. A hot plate with a coffeepot was on the table. A rattling air conditioner was leaking water into a plastic container on the floor. "How can we help you?" the official asked with a locked-in-place smile.

Here was a sentence I never expected to say: "My name is Roland Stone and I am requesting political asylum."

Joel Dictrow, he said, offering his hand and trying a little too hard to be more welcoming than officious. He picked up a pen and blank sheet of paper. Dictrow was a tall thin man with tired eyes and a spotted complexion, but when I said my name, he stopped writing and stared at me. "Please wait," he said, as if I had turned on a switch, and scurried around his desk and out of his office.

We sat there for quite a while. Every few minutes a different person would stick their head in the door or walk past the window and pretend to be ignoring us. "You have any idea what they're doing?" Laura asked.

"Calling the Welcome Wagon?" I shrugged. "No idea."

Finally a group of people arrived noisily and pushed into the office. A trim man stepped forward with a big smile on his face. "Mr. Stone, my name is Marty Shaw. Welcome to Canada."

He held up a bag he was holding. "We brought you some moo shu if you're hungry." Shaw sat down behind the desk. "I think we have a lot to talk about." He looked at my bruised face. "You okay?"

It still hurt when I smiled. "I am now."

I introduced him to Laura, referring to her as "my tour guide."

He took us through the events of the night. It was a pretty incredible story, and if I hadn't been sitting there, I doubt I would have believed it.

Laura and I ran out of steam pretty quickly. We'd been running on adrenaline for so long that the relief deflated us about as quickly as a tire hitting a pothole. Exhilaration became exhaustion. We shared an awkward moment when Marty Shaw checked us into the Foxhead Hotel and asked if we wanted one or two rooms. Laura and I looked at each other and responded almost simultaneously, "Two." We laughed.

"You need some help?" she asked. "You know," indicating Mighty Chair, "with everything." That was odd, it was the first time she had referred to my disability. I admit it, I wondered if that was really what she meant or was she asking a different question entirely.

I considered the possibilities. "I'm good."

The next afternoon we began the legal process. I was officially requesting political asylum, I said, claiming that if I was deported to the United States I would be arrested and prosecuted as an enemy of the state. I turned to Laura. Her head was lowered and she didn't say a word.

"Miss?" the Canadian official prompted her.

She shook her head.

"What?" I asked.

In a soft voice, looking at the floor, she said, "I have to go back."

I was incredulous. "What are you talking about?" I said. "You can't go back. They know who you are now."

There was a complete absence of drama in her voice as she responded, leaving no doubt that she had thought this through and made her decision. "We have to fight them, Rollie. I'm not going back to Washington, that would be crazy, but there are a lot of other places I can help. This is just the beginning. We're just getting organized. You, you can fight them from here; you can write and make a difference. I can't, and I have to do what I can."

I ran a complete inventory of all applicable movie lines, searching for something ironic or amusing that would take the edge off the moment. Sadly, "Wow" was the best I could do, which was woefully insufficient. I even said it a second time: "Wow."

I asked her to stay a few more days to work with me in releasing the information we had brought with us. It was going to create significant problems for Wrightman, I hoped, and I wanted her to get the credit she'd earned. But my real purpose was to try to convince her to change her mind. There was nothing good waiting for her in the United States.

We worked through the days, slowly climbing through the levels of the Canadian government intelligence apparatus. I found myself humming Brain's codes so often that my lips began hurting. Gradually I began to get some traction. We went all the way from incredulous to interested.

I hesitated to call Jenny. That decision had nothing to do with Laura. There was no good ending to this conversation, so I put it off as long as possible. I waited until the next evening, hoping she would be home. Home, at her apartment. As I dialed her landline, I felt the same insecurity I had in junior high, when I was calling my crush to ask her to go to a movie. My butterflies were wildly flapping. Part of me hoped she wouldn't answer so I could just leave a message. Even as the phone was ringing, I had no idea what I would say. I figured the words would just come out. She answered, "Rollie?"

"Hello, Jen, it's me."

She screamed, literally screamed, then started crying. In one great burst she unloaded her fears that had been growing the last few days. Are you all right? Where are you? What happened? They've been here three times to ask if I've heard from you. I spoke to Howie and he's holding up . . . She caught herself, snapping back into her surprised and excited mode. She missed me so much, she said.

"I miss you too," I said, "so much," surprising even myself by how much I meant it. Well, that was an interesting revelation that I didn't know I was feeling. I played with that thought: Did I miss the comfort of what we had or did I miss her? You know what, it made no difference. I missed it all.

"With everything they're doing . . ." She dropped the rest of that sentence. The government crackdown had caused everyone to think carefully about their words before they said them aloud. Both of us were aware there was a strong possibility that agents were listening to our conversation or that it was being recorded. There were questions that couldn't be asked and wouldn't be answered. As Jenny calmed down, we began maneuvering around them.

The reality of life as a wanted man was new to me, but I could make certain assumptions. For one thing, the people I cared most about were in jeopardy because I cared most about them. For the first time this thought censored my words: The government of the United States of America was my enemy.

"I'm safe, Jen. I'm in Canada." I didn't tell her anything at all about my escape. Which meant I didn't have to tell her anything about Laura. Not that there was anything to tell, of course, but women being women . . .

Jenny was talking again and I picked up her thread mid-sentence. Apparently rumors about me had been spreading on the Hill, although no one seemed to know where they were coming from. Supposedly I had been caught fleeing the country with stolen classified documents, or I had been seriously injured in a highway accident, or most absurd, I had turned government informer. She finished with an upward inflection that suggested I should fill in the blanks, to which I responded, "You know I can't talk about any of it."

This was an incredibly frustrating conversation. We both had to talk around what we wanted to say. But as we spoke, I picked up hints from the things she said, as well as the way she said them, that made me believe she finally had picked a side.

She had applied for permission to visit Martha and had been told it was possible. When she expressed concern about Martha's well-being, a pleasant woman at Homeland Security had reassured her that this was all temporary, and suggested that Jenny should pretend "the congresswoman is just on a little vacation and will be home soon."

She started talking about "the show," the hangings, asking me if I had seen it. "I did," I told her, being careful not to say, "*We* did." For the first time I heard her suppressed anger. Her grandfather had seen similar executions while serving in Europe at the end of World War II, she said, and it caused him to despise the governments that had permitted it. I got her point; her grandfather had lost a leg at Guadalcanal and been discharged. He was not in Europe in 1945. She was referring to a different war. This war.

We spoke for almost an hour. After the first twenty minutes or so it actually began feeling almost normal. Eventually we reached the part of the conversation about us. Her request for a new security clearance was being vetted. If she received it, she might be able to visit me. But as a

condition for approval, she admitted, she had agreed to notify Homeland Security when she heard from me. *Notify,* she emphasized, which
was little more than an acknowledgment we had spoken. Somehow I
didn't think the government was waiting breathlessly for that notification. She was still working on the Hill, assisting Martha's appointed
successor, although as she pointed out, since the establishment of the
military districts her workload had been considerably lighter.

It was a long and difficult conversation. The only thing I had established for certain was that my feelings about Jenny were real and deep. I
didn't see any easy answers, but I wasn't giving up either. I told her I would
call again soon and hung up. That empty feeling I had feared hit me. I was
completely disoriented; I was sitting in my hotel room looking around
for something, anything, that was mine. "Well, Cher," I said. "That wasn't
so hot, was it?"

"The temperature is seventy-two degrees, Rollie. Would you like me
to turn up the air-conditioning?"

I chuckled. At home she was able to remotely adjust the temperature.
Even Cher was discombobulated.

I started reviewing my conversation with Jenny, trying to see if I had
missed anything she had tried to tell me. I also felt a little dishonest at
not mentioning Laura. Escaping from America was one thing; doing it
with an attractive woman put a whole different slant on it. I suspect my
real fear was that eventually she would find out about it and begin wondering why I hadn't mentioned this other woman. Fortunately, Jenny
wasn't a jealous woman, so I did not expect to hear her asking, "Why
didn't you want to escape with me?"

Next time we speak I'll tell her, I decided, definitely next time.

Laura had finally agreed to stay in Canada for several more days,
helping me get organized. My legal status remained unsettled. The
Canadian consulate had informed the American State Department that
it had received a request for political asylum from an American citizen
named Roland Stone, providing the dates for my immigration hearing
if the government wanted to contest it.

In response, the American government had filed an array of criminal
charges against me. Corbin and Russell had been found safe and sleeping

in Van. As a result, I was being charged with assaulting and kidnapping federal agents, drugging federal agents, the theft of a government vehicle, impersonating a federal agent, theft of official government documents, and treason. The government added that it expected to file additional criminal charges in the future. Therefore an official request for extradition had been sent to the Canadian government.

I would not be going home for the holidays. Or, as I ruefully told Marty Shaw, "No noose is good noose."

I didn't wait to deliver the message I was carrying. I wanted to get it as widely distributed as quickly as possible. It took the Canadian government three days to clear it for dissemination. Apparently there had been several government officials who did not want it made public, knowing the political repercussions it might cause.

On our sixth day in Canada, I was sitting in a conference room at the Canadian Broadcasting Centre in Toronto, four empty Tim Hortons cups piled in front of me. I was joined at the long highly polished oak conference table by Shaw and two lieutenants, representing the self-proclaimed Government of the United States in Exile and journalists from the major Canadian newspapers and TV stations. This meeting was being taped for broadcast. Knowing that it would be seen in the United States, we decided Laura should not be in the room.

I began telling my story, although I gave a fictitious version of how I had obtained the code. One cold March night more than 250 years ago a mysterious man in a red coat had appeared on the streets of Boston and had urged the patriots to stand firm, leading directly to the Boston Massacre, arguably lighting the first flame of the American Revolution. In my story the mysterious man in a red sports jacket had reappeared on the streets of Washington. Claiming to be a coding genius living in a western state, he had handed me evidence that Flight 342 had been cyjacked by the Wrightman administration to terrify the American people into demanding Congress grant war powers to the president. "That's something you know all about, Marty, don't you?" I said, passing out copies of the graph.

The journalists in the room looked puzzled. Marty told the real story of the Detroit Massacre video.

"That's it," I finally concluded, "that's how we got here. Questions?"

The room was silent as the reporters considered the possible impact of my claims. This was a pretty significant accusation, and the evidence seemed pretty flimsy. Several of them probably wondered about my sanity. They looked at each other, waiting for someone else to speak. Finally an associate producer of the evening news, Robert Hugall, asked the obvious question, "That's quite a story, Mr. Stone. But is that all your evidence?"

In response I withdrew from one of Chair's pockets a cone-shaped device resembling a small, sleek megaphone and slid it over the right arm. "Cher, display the Word document music, please." Within seconds Chair projected a slightly out-of-focus image of the graphs on the far wall. Part of the image overlapped a wall map of Canada, so I moved Chair slightly to the right. "Cher, focus, please."

The focus sharpened. I explained the general concept, using the example of finding similarities in fingerprints. Then, using a laser pointer, I traced the top line. "This is a portion of the code the cyjackers used to take control of Flight 342. It was released by the government. And this ... Cher, next slide, please." The next slide clicked into place. I traced it with my pointer. "This is the code supplied by the NSA to a national hacking championship for high schoolers." The similarities were obvious; it was like looking at two images of the same mountain range. "There just isn't any doubt these two codes were created by the same person or people. We do know this code, the competition code, was created at the NSA. Now, listen up ... Cher, play the tones, please."

As Cher played both segments, I conducted the music in the air. While not perfect harmony, there certainly were recognizably similar elements, including rests. "Cher, play them together, please."

As she did, Hugall said with disgust, on tape, "The bastards. Fucking bastards. They were willing to kill all those people ..."

"I don't think so," I corrected. "I don't think they intended to kill anyone. My guess is they'd worked out the solution before they got started. They just fed it to the pilots."

One of the reporters confirmed, "This is all on the record, right?"

I nodded. "Go ahead and sing along." I looked around the table. "Other questions? Anyone?"

Another reporter raised his pen. "Yeah I got one. Where'd you get that cool wheelchair?"

It took two additional days for the CBC to sufficiently verify the details of the Flight 342 story to go with it. The story became headline news pretty much throughout the world, with the exception of the United States, where it was deemed "fake news" being spread by anti-American interests. In the States, the increasingly popular pop-up pirate sites translated and reprinted stories from the foreign media, many of them referring to me as "journalist in exile Roland Stone." Several British and Canadian musicians sampled the samples; building songs around them, ranging from the rapper Payday's "Fuck That Wrongman" to folk-rocker Dondi O.'s "Ballad of 342."

The world speeded up. So much was happening so quickly it was hard to absorb it all. Other nations had to act on this information to squeeze the most possible benefit from it. Since Trump, the power scales had been disrupted and had not yet settled, and this served to once again put a fat finger on the weight pan. The United Nations Security Council proposed censuring the Wrightman government for "human rights abuses against its own citizens," but that was vetoed by the American representative. Far more destructive were trade sanctions imposed by the EU and Russia, which threatened to significantly impact the fragile economy. China took a more measured approach, announcing it was monitoring the situation but warning the Wrightman government against any further attacks on the American people. In France, a *petit peu taquin*, an internet petition asking for the return of the Statue of Liberty, garnered more than a million signatures.

I turned down almost all interview requests. As much as possible I wanted the facts of the story to be the focus, not the personalities. I especially didn't want to bring undue attention to my friends and family still living in the States. I wanted to reach out to Hack, but it was just too dangerous. So, Hack, if you're reading this, thank you. I'm sorry I couldn't tell you what it was all about.

My biggest fear was that government investigators might track down and identify Brain McLane. I didn't dare reach out to him, knowing full well any attempt to do that might instead lead law enforcement directly to him. He'd understand, I was sure about that. That's why he was Brain.

With the cooperation of the Cuomos we were able to move him and his family out of the country and get them settled in Canada. He's already been awarded a full scholarship to McGill. Without that, I never would have mentioned his name in this book or given him the credit he has earned.

There was no way of knowing exactly what was going on inside the Wrightman administration. Stuff, that was for sure. And turmoil and confusion. A lot of *oy vey iz mir* and agita. The administration had made a massive effort to beat the story by posting all kinds of denials, claims, and comments. They rolled out the head of NSA, two cabinet secretaries, the pilots and passengers, but it was one of those stories that just stuck. Vice President Hunter, describing himself as angrier than a dog setting on an army ant mound, told the official media that he personally guaranteed "we will get to the bottom of this story, no matter who is responsible, and that person or those people will pay for it. There is nothing more important to this administration than the safety of the American people, and we will continue to do whatever is necessary to protect them."

Yeah, right, I thought. Just more lies. I was reminded of what *Daily Bugle* reporter Frank Weimann had once written about Donald Trump: "He lied so easily and so often that we were no more surprised about another lie than we were when the sun disappeared in the evening." For a brief period at the beginning of his administration, Wrightman seemed to make an effort to tell the truth, but apparently that had proved too difficult. He figured out pretty quickly that a significant number of Americans would happily accept lies that squared with their closely held beliefs. So that's why I was surprised . . . no, *surprised* isn't even close; I was stunned, completely shocked a week later when Mighty Chair's trumpets blared and Cher alerted me that an important story was breaking. I was sitting in my new office at the CBC, Horton cups at a solid seven and climbing, when the story broke.

I flipped on the monitor and began reading:

(AP) At a hastily convened press conference in the White
House, Vice President Arthur T. Hunter announced his
investigation into the cyber-hijacking of North American
Airlines Flight 342 had led directly to President Ian
Wrightman. When confronted with irrefutable evidence
that he had been involved in a conspiracy to terrorize the
American public into submission, President Ian Wrightman
had offered his resignation to House Majority Leader Alan
Susskind, which was immediately accepted. At 5:34 PM
(EST) Vice President Hunter was sworn into office as the
48th President of the United States by Chief Justice John
Roberts.

The disgraced president and former first lady, Charisma
Wrightman, their three children, and two grandchildren had
been escorted by the military to their hilltop cabin, where
they will remain under guard for their own safety.

The newsroom erupted. Oh, at that moment I missed Howie so
much. That sound, journalists at work, was his music. I looked around
for someone to share this news with; there was no one. There was
no Howie. No Jenny. No Frankie B. Laura had left that morning for
"someplace warm," refusing to tell me her destination but promising
to maintain whatever it was we had. I felt alone in the noise: just me,
Chair, and Cher.

Press secretary Eunie Kaufman's office continued to issue updates. A
statement issued by President Hunter reassured Americans:

At a time when our national institutions are being challenged,
it is necessary to take this difficult step to protect all
Americans from enemies both domestic and foreign. Former
President Wrightman put American lives at risk in an effort to
extend his power. Until we have confirmed that this was an
isolated effort and have arrested all involved, I have asked
Congress to suspend temporarily those provisions of the
Constitution that might be used to further spread disharmony
or incite rebellion.

> The former president has asked me to convey his deepest
> regrets and shame to all Americans for his misguided
> actions. He is cooperating fully with law enforcement. Until
> further notice he will remain with his family under cabin
> arrest. There will be no further statements.

I read and reread the release, trying to grasp the ramifications. My phone started ringing, my social media accounts quickly overflowed. I had no illusions: This was a coup. And I was the spark that had set it off. As I sat there, literally twiddling my thumbs trying to absorb this news, the realization hit me with the shock of The Rock dropping suddenly through my ceiling tiles and smacking me with a folding chair. This had been Hunter's plan all along.

It wasn't Wrightman, it never was Wrightman. It was Artie Hunter. From the beginning it had been Hunter. Wrightman had remained what he had always been, a political matryoshka—a brightly painted Russian nesting doll, hollow on the inside, which opens to reveal several increasingly smaller brightly painted dolls, each a different guide enabling him to be whatever the voters needed. Polished on the outside, empty inside—a perfect vessel to be filled by Hunter.

I thought about that odd meeting I'd had with Hunter in his office at the beginning of the administration. It had made no sense to me then. I couldn't figure out what he'd wanted with me. Now I was beginning to get it; he was laying the groundwork. It had been a recruiting session, and I'd failed to make the cut.

There was no way he could have planned or anticipated the events of the past few weeks, but when I popped up with my little charts, he recognized the opportunity and seized it. I had created the perfect scenario for him, I'd given him the opportunity to be a hero. President Arthur Hunter was America's savior, courageously rescuing the country from a president gone power mad. My favorite line from Joseph Heller's *Catch-22* seemed appropriate: "Yossarian was moved very deeply by the absolute simplicity of this clause of Catch-22 and let out a respectful whistle."

Okay, time to get to work. I had stories to write, tales to tell. As

I shifted into work gear Cher began playing "The Battle Hymn of the Republic," meaning Laura was Skyping. I hooked in; she was in an unidentified American airport. I looked at the signs behind her, trying to figure out where she was. My guess was St. Paul, but I wouldn't bet my rented apartment on it. Her hair was cut student short and she was wearing a designer backpack. "You saw it?" she asked, with restrained excitement.

"I did."

"So what do you think?"

I hesitated. That was an easy question requiring a complex answer. What did I think? Got a week? "Well," I said finally, "I don't think I'm going to be competing on *Dancing with the Stars* anytime soon."

23

It took me several months to get my *eh*-game down. But gradually I became used to saying *zed* rather than *Z*; I took pride in the fact that William Shatner and Jim Carrey were Canadian and that Mr. Big was a chocolate bar rather than a TV character. I embraced Tim Hortons. While I continued to make fun of the Canadians' relentless good nature, I discovered that they did too; it was an essential aspect of their relentless good nature. I also learned that they also had suffered through strange leaders. Prime Minister Mackenzie King, who headed the government for twenty-two years, conversed regularly with his mothers' ghosts, often attended séances, and made national decisions based on reading tea leaves, shaving cream, and the responses of the three angels disguised as his dogs who offered advice by the way they wagged their tails.

All America has had to deal with were Trump/Pence, incompetent Democrats, Wrightman, and now Hunter. We should have been as lucky.

The positive news is that the resistance is securely established and has continued to expand. It is now operating in all fifty states, Puerto Rico, and the Virgin Islands. We have been working from here to offer as much assistance as possible. There is much about it that I can't disclose without risk to other people. But networks have been established and the opposition to the Hunter government continues to grow.

I do know that within the military there continues to be debate, and grumbling, about continuing to support an administration that has

abrogated the Constitution. Although thus far there has been no agreement about steps to take. I can report that there has been considerable
tension between the administration and the military and Hunter is
aware he does not have its absolute loyalty. But he is a clever man,
clever and devious. He has replaced the entire Joint Chiefs with his
allies, although he has been warned that their oath is to the Constitution, not the executive branch.

The United Nations has taken tentative steps to at least discourage the
Hunter government from further restricting civil liberties. (Although
that's like trying to close the barn door after the farm has been sold,
knocked down, and replaced by a soccer stadium.) In protest to the
recent limitations Canada has recalled its ambassador, replacing that position with a chargé d'affaires to handle legal matters. Ironically, Mexico sent additional troops to its northern border to assist Americans
attempting to escape into Mexico.

The good news *and* the bad news are that America's immigration
problem has been curtailed if not exactly solved.

I also can report that Laura, who no longer is Laura, has become a
key organizer and is moving regularly. I hear from her at odd times, and
she is careful to never even hint at her location. I can tell you she looks
good as a blonde, a brunette, a redhead, and with light-brown long or
short hair, depending on her appearance at the time. When I think
about her, when I wonder where she is and what she's doing, for some
reason I remember the beautiful final scene of Steinbeck's *Grapes of
Wrath,* in which Tom Joad, now a fugitive in America, sets his path:
"I'll be all aroun' in the dark. I'll be ever'where—wherever you look.
Wherever they's a fight so hungry people can eat, I'll be there. Wherever they's a cop beatin' up a guy, I'll be there . . . I'll be in the way guys
yell when they're mad an'—I'll be in the way kids laugh when they're
hungry an' they know supper's ready. An' when our folks eat the stuff
they raise an' live in the houses they build—why, I'll be there."

I've always loved the determination, the promise, and the threat of
that promise, and hold on to it still.

And Jenny. If this were a movie script the character instruction
would be: (*Rollie sighs deeply, caught in a flurry of confused emotions*). That

would be accurate. We speak regularly. I notice when I'm talking to her I find myself scratching my left palm, an old nervous habit I thought I'd left behind long ago. Our conversations are always like a mountain range in twilight; the peaks are impossible to miss, but the valleys are hidden. Maybe that's intentional. For two people whose careers are dependent on the ability to communicate directly, we have both been utter failures.

Neither of us can ignore the possibility (she says, I say fact) that Homeland Security is physically listening to or taping these conversations. I know I don't speak without first considering the impact of my words on her life. It's like America has become a universal party line. (For those who don't know, a party line was a single telephone line shared by many people that provided no privacy.) Like those nations we once fought, in schools and churches, in the entertainment world and on television, the government is listening for subversive conversation. No one really knows what is being recorded or who might listen to it or, worse, what the penalty might be. Those rumors about a subversive point system that I'd hear apparently proved accurate. It appears the National Computer Center search engines have been programmed to pick out key words or phrases, which are forwarded to the "Computer Bank of America," a division of the NSA, where someone listens to those conversations and decides if and what actions should be taken. In most cases, each time a person is cited a point or two is added to his or her score. Ten points gets you a pleasant visit from a district officer.

The Resistance supposedly circulates a list of the latest "key" words and phrases in a weekly blast, although if that's true I've never seen it. But Jenny and I avoid talking about the past as much as possible, as well as avoid talking about the future. Occasionally she'll give me a "crème brûlée," a sugarcoated version of some event, leaving it to me to try to figure it out. The best I can make of it is she hasn't dated anyone else; I know I haven't, either. It is strangely comforting to find yourself focusing on your social life in the midst of the American Apocalypse.

Through all this, I know how lucky I have been. I easily could be languishing in some form of imprisonment. I could think of many forms of torture by citing examples of American culture, but this isn't the place for humor. I simply set out to do the right thing; I had no intention or desire to overthrow the president of the United States.

I have been welcomed here and within weeks received several job offers. For the time being, at least, I have not accepted any of them. I am freelancing, appearing semi-regularly on Canadian television to comment on events in the United States, writing a regular column, and working on this book. The CBC has been kind enough to make an office available to me. In all of those efforts I have been trying to understand exactly how this could have happened in America. It may be too late to make any difference, it may not be possible to restore our democracy, but I refuse to accept that. And remember, I'm the cynic. What I am trying to do is prevent this incalculable tragedy from being repeated elsewhere.

I recently wrote an article for *Maclean's,* trying to sum up events, an article I believe is worth including here:

HOW IT HAPPENED

by Roland Stone, American in exile

In 2019, American scientists employed an array of telescopes to take the first photographs of a mysterious black hole. It was an extraordinary feat, comparable to photographing the date on a quarter in Los Angeles using a camera in Washington, D.C. So it remains astonishing that a nation capable of that feat could fail to see what was happening in plain sight: the theft of its most precious possession, American constitutional democracy.

Like all of you, I watched it happen. As a result of my efforts to prevent it, I am now living in exile in Canada. Since my escape from America I have spent considerable time trying to understand how it happened. And perhaps, to offer some suggestions about what happens next.

The United States had always been a noble idea, an experiment, determining if people from all the varied cultures of the world could live together in harmony and freedom. That big word, *united,* was often overlooked or taken for granted. It referred to an agreement between the states, and between we the people, that we would be governed by a set of laws enumerated in the Constitution.

That system of government given to us by the founders was ingenious: three co-equal branches with defined powers artfully designed to force cooperation and prevent any one of them from becoming dominant. In 1787, Benjamin Franklin described that government as "a republic," but only, he warned, "if you can keep it."

It worked. For more than two centuries it worked very well. The United States of America gave the world George Washington, Thomas Jefferson, Franklin, John Adams, Lincoln, and Teddy and Franklin Roosevelt. It was a nation that fought tyranny in the war to end wars, that defeated the Nazis and Communism, that invented suburbia and mass production and created the middle class. There were significant bumps along the way, and at times it was brutally unfair and unjust, but it had managed to bumble along with dents and scratches and deep chips. Until now.

Until now. Until us.

The experiment is done. Put away the incubator, it's failed. The "arsenal of democracy" is closed. The beacon of hope is extinguished. The question that needs to be answered is how. How did we let that happen?

The answer is more complex than navigating an unlit maze, with unexpected twists and turns that intentionally lead nowhere. It's easy, satisfying, and woefully inaccurate to blame the end of American democracy solely on Donald Trump and Michael Pence, or on Ian Wrightman and now Arthur Hunter. But that was just the last act. The demise had begun long before they arrived onstage and took advantage of the situation.

Beginning during the administration of George Washington, Congress has been steadily ceding its constitutional powers to the executive branch, most often citing an emergency situation. Those grants of power have always been temporary, just for a brief century or two. Eventually more than 700 of these so-called special powers had been granted—and until recently only one, the right given to Franklin Roosevelt after the attack on Pearl Harbor to confine Japanese American citizens to internment camps, was repealed. In essence, under certain conditions those laws gave the executive nearly dictatorial power.

Later presidents used those special powers to shape the nation's economy, to take us to war, even to suspend other constitutional rights. And almost always with the same rationale: These actions are necessary to protect the country from those who would do us harm.

It turned out that the people who would do us harm turned out to be us. Cartoonist Walt Kelly pointed that out in his strip *Pogo* almost fifty years ago, when Pogo himself observes, "We have met the enemy and he is us." Americans blithely ignored history, focusing our attention and our budget on protecting the country from external enemies, while in fact the most successful attacks on government have always been internal. The Nazis were German. The Stalinists were Russian. The Maoists were Chinese. The Khmer Rouge were Cambodians. We overlooked the reality that America had been given the greatest of all geographic gifts, a vast landmass bordered on its north and south by two benign nations and on the east and west by vast oceans that made the nation almost impregnable. No enemy force was going to storm the beaches of Santa Monica or invade Baltimore's fashionable Inner Harbor. We spent trillions of dollars preparing to defend the nation against an enemy that wasn't coming. Our military budget was greater than the nine countries that followed us—combined. Our enemies certainly could inflict death and damage from a long distance, but they could never gain control of the country.

So how did it happen? FDR once calmed a frightened nation when he said, with great confidence, "The only thing we have to fear is fear itself." Little did anyone realize how prescient he was, as fear became the weapon the enemies of democracy would use to destroy it. It was fear itself that we most should have feared.

Okay, fear and indifference.

In the 1980s two political operatives, Lee Atwater and Roger Ailes, changed the political equation. Until then Americans were passionate about politics but didn't take winning and losing elections nearly so personally. Atwater and Ailes brilliantly made elections an emotional experience, pressing the same emotional buttons as rooting for a sports team, and voilà! a political loss had the impact of a personal rejection.

That coincided perfectly with the creation of the tools they needed to spark their revolution, the home computer and the internet. There always had been a significant number of disaffected, alienated, margin-alized, and seemingly forgotten people in the country, Nixon's "silent majority." They were angry, bitter, and fearful that the world as they knew it was being taken over by some vague "them." These people were scattered, and until the creation of the internet, they had no way of finding one another. The internet allowed them to form into highly motivated tribes. It was not an especially large movement, not at first, but its members were zealots. Somebody finally was paying attention to them, and it felt oh so good. They recruited candidates or bent other candidates to their will, threatening them with their numbers. While they were not a majority, not nearly a majority, they turned out and they voted, while those people who so easily could have defeated them stayed home to watch TV or just didn't feel like schlepping to the polls.

That coalition of the disaffected gained power. To do so, they adhered to the phrase credited to French philosopher Jean-Paul Sartre and made popular by Malcolm X, "by any means necessary." The values upon which the republic had been built—among them truth, honesty, integrity and common decency—were cast aside, and what eventually was described as the "alternative truth" became acceptable. Where necessary, the electoral system was rigged through gerrymandering or worse, voter suppression. In some states with Republican governors, it would have been easier for me to beat LeBron one-on-one, without Mighty Chair, than it was finding sufficient voting machines in minority neighborhoods. The result of all that was Donald Trump.

A quirk in the nation's electoral system allowed the candidate who received a minority of votes cast to become president. Donald Trump was not the choice of voters, but their respect for the system allowed him to take office. That's the way the nation crumbled. Trump was not particularly well-informed or educated. He knew little about history or science, had difficulty with simple tasks like spelling, and had not been blessed with great intelligence or creativity. He was, however, a skillful liar. His greatest assets were that he was unfettered by the truth and lacked any moral clarity. (And the assistance of Vladimir Putin and a legion of Russian hackers. Whatever debt he owed to the Russians was paid off in policy decisions that weakened not only this country but the entire Western alliance.) The "truth" became whatever served his needs at that moment and by extension the needs of the Republican Party. The few ideas he did have were not supported by the majority, so for him to succeed, it became necessary to destroy the media. To roughly paraphrase George Orwell, he who controls the media controls the present. Who controls the present controls the past. Who controls the past controls the future.

An essential aspect of Ailes's strategy was to create an enemy that needed to be attacked relentlessly, causing members of the tribe to rally together against it. In Trump's case it was both and necessary to make that enemy the media. "The duty of the journalist," wrote the *London Times* in 1852, "is the same as that of the historian—to seek out the truth, above all things, and to present his readers not such things as statecraft would wish them to know, but the truth as near as he can attain it."

CNN's Jim Acosta once summed up the turpitude of the Trump administration by explaining, "Lying to the press is just another day at the office." There was no requirement within that administration to tell the truth if the truth did not support the goals of the administration. There were no penalties for lying or cheating or even stealing.

Trump repeated his big lies about the media over and over, and in this effort he had an unshakable ally: Fox News. Roger Ailes had cynically created Fox News with only one mission: to reinforce the often-unfounded beliefs of the radical right wing, to reassure those viewers that they were right and good and even godly in their fervor and those who disagreed with that were the enemy and must be smote.

It worked too. Fox News became the go-to place for aging white America. Opinion often disguised as fact was delivered in neat packages by indistinguishably attractive blond women and big-haired men no better informed than the viewers. The truth was whatever Fox told its viewers was the truth. Russia good; the Western alliance bad. Ailes raised pandering to new heights: Right-wing media told its followers what to believe; those people repeated it and were then congratulated by the right-wing media for their insight.

Trump and Pence successfully undermined the basic structures supporting American democracy, making the whole system wobbly. They staggered to the finish line. The well-meaning administration that followed tried too hard to be too much to too many, accomplishing little other than adding to the confusion and leading directly to the election of an Independent, Ian Wrightman, whose popularity arose mostly from the fact that he wasn't one of "them."

Trump had set the bar lower than the finals of the world limbo championship. The American public decided that any candidate provably breathing was an acceptable improvement. What Americans craved most was normalcy. Not great promises, not stirring rhetoric—normalcy. And that was Ian Wrightman, whose greatest attribute was that he was nothing special. His choice of Artie Hunter for vice president satisfied any concerns that Wrightman might not be tough enough.

By discrediting the news media, Trump had done the heavy lifting for Wrightman. The rest was easy. The Wrightman administration parlayed that into control of social media, limiting negative commentary, then utilizing influencers and faux polls to shape public opinion. He enlisted the support of the business and advertising community by eliminating burdensome and costly regulations, thereby ensuring that supporting the administration would be the most profitable position.

The still-unanswered question is, How much of what happened was part of a greater plan? Answering that would require knowing Wrightman's—and Hunter's—motivations. Was this simply a power grab or did they honestly believe these steps were necessary to save the country? I am reminded of the astute explanation given by an American officer in Vietnam after the bombing of the village of Bến Tre during the Tet Offensive: "In order to save the village it became necessary to destroy it."

I've never told this story, but after my participation in the release of the Detroit Massacre video, I received a phone call from a source high up in the administration. It was meant to be a warning to ease up my criticism of the administration. "You may not think so, but we're saving this country," this source told me. "Look at the polls, people love the president." When I questioned that, this person continued, "People want order and we're giving it to them. Let me ask you, you think the former Yugos wouldn't give anything to have Tito back? Ask the Iraqis what they'd give to have things the way they were when Saddam was in charge. Those people would kill . . ." That source caught him- or herself, but insisted, "We're doing what has to be done to keep this country together."

Maybe it doesn't matter if this was part of some greater plan or simply a response to opportunity. Maybe it isn't necessary to answer that question. We're here now. Whatever their motivations, Wrightman and Hunter could not have accomplished any of it without a willing collaborator, the American people. The American people allowed this to happen. No one can dispute that.

For the American people, the problem with saving democracy was that it simply was not particularly entertaining; it wasn't nearly as exciting as *Call of Duty VIII,* as intriguing as *The Voice,* or as suspenseful as *24.* Maybe if some entrepreneur had packed it into a video game, say *The Last Flagman: Showdown for Freedom* or a multipart saga that Netflix could produce, it might have attracted sufficient attention. But that didn't happen.

Americans had more important concerns than worrying about politics. Too many people were struggling to pay the rent or to buy a third TV and a thinner cell phone to pay attention to all that bickering. A 2017 Freedom Forum Institute poll found that almost 40 percent of Americans couldn't name a single right protected by the First Amendment; so protecting, among other things, the freedom to criticize the government ranked well below "visiting Disneyland and meeting Mickey" on many Americans' bucket list.

While millions of Americans did try to make a stand against looming tyranny, the majority believed that they were gaining vital protection in exchange for rights they barely used. It was a trade they were willing to make. As Wrightman explained in his second State of the Union address, "My greatest obligation as your president, as is guaranteed to every American by the Declaration of Independence, is to protect your unalienable right to life, liberty and the pursuit of happiness. If it should become necessary to temporarily suspend lesser rights to protect more precious rights, I give you my solemn word, for the benefit of future generations of Americans, we will do exactly that."

Or as late-night host Jimmy Jackson interpreted it, "Give up the right to complain in exchange for security? Can I make that same deal with my wife?"

Most Americans agreed it was a great deal. The late senator Daniel Patrick Moynihan coined the phrase *benign neglect* to describe a philosophy which postulates that leaving something alone will be more beneficial than focusing attention to it. This was far more sinister; it might better be termed *active neglect*. Americans made a choice, deciding that "You the government . . ." was preferable to "We the people," telling the government, essentially, you got my back.

In return, the American people asked one compelling question: Can we get fries with that?

That's a joke, the American people did not want fries with that. They wanted a Happy calorie-free meal, enjoyed in peace. And so they made a choice. If there is an indictment to be made, here it is: The American people didn't simply let this happen, they wanted it to happen. Congress might also have risen up to defend and save democracy, to stand strong against this coup, but then it wouldn't have been Congress. Instead it followed the will of the people who had elected them. The people wanted Congress to do nothing, which coincidently was its area of expertise. Fortunately, this was a situation in which Congress had substantial experience; it had been surrendering its powers to the executive branch long before any citizen thought of it. History had seen this before, as Edward Gibbon wrote in his *History of the Decline and Fall of the Roman Empire*: "The image of a free constitution was preserved with decent reverence: The Roman senate appeared to possess the sovereign authority and devolved on the emperors all the executive powers of government."

The result of this docile acquiescence was that Wrightman and Hunter successfully consolidated their power. Their takeover was complete. Only once before in American history had Benjamin Franklin's warning, "We must all hang together or, most assuredly, we will all hang separately," been more appropriate. When he said it, he meant it literally; history had made it figurative, a plea for unity; and now it was both literal and figurative. Americans actually are at the end of the rope.

As a practical matter, daily life in America has not been fundamentally changed, as long as you support the government. The vast majority of people still get up in the morning, go to work, and come home to their family at night. The economy is struggling, as the rest of the world has been very cautious to negotiate trade agreements; although that probably will change soon, as China has already praised the "new continuity and stability President Hunter has brought to the American government." There are people there for whom life actually has gotten considerably better; the nation has been hammered back together in a way that has not been possible for decades. The years of raucous dissent are done. The screaming at one another is done. Mostly now, America resembles the legendary Frankenstein, an assortment of ill-fitting pieces stitched together but somehow breathing and walking.

The word *democracy* is derived from the Greek *dēmokratiā,* meaning *dēmos* (people) and *kratos* (rule). The people rule. If you know that, it is accurate to say that democracy in America is in a coma, if not brain dead. It has been suffering from many years of abuse and neglect. Says the cynic, there is little hope for recovery.

The United States of America was a promise made to all the peoples of the world that there was a place where the greatest ideals of man could be realized; it was always slightly over the horizon, just beyond reach, a dream more than a reality, but a place worth striving to find.

Sorry. Better luck next time.

That's it. Here I am, still sitting in front of my laptop. I got it all down so no one will forget how it happened there. The rest, of course, is up to you.★

★ Cher asked me to leave you with this practical advice: "Make sure your bolts are fastened tightly, your surface is brightly shined, and all your parts are oiled, eh." And buckle up, it's going to be a bumpy ride.

Acknowledgments

I would like to express my appreciation and my admiration for Thomas Dunne, formerly the greatly esteemed proprietor of Thomas Dunne Books. This book was born in his mind and he was kind enough to involve me and has been incredibly supportive throughout the entire process. He handed the actual editing off to Steve Powers, to whom I remain indebted for his enthusiasm, his support, his skill, and his good nature. I also am greatly appreciative of the work done by Steve's assistant, Lisa Bonvissuto, who was always there with a smile in her voice and properly encouraging words. I also greatly appreciate the work of my editor Sarah Grill, who came into the action late in the game, picked up the pieces skillfully and gracefully, and brought it to the finish line.

Matthew Glenn and Jerry Stern (with whom I have been friends since he moved into my neighborhood in fourth grade) read various versions of this story and offered advice and storage space!

Everything I do is possible because of the love and support of my beautiful wife, Laura. (Anybody looking for the best personal trainer and yoga instructor in the country, she's it!) But more importantly, to me, she has been my greatest cheerleader and most astute coach throughout all the books we've done together. How lucky I have been to find her and for her to marry me. Rollie should have been so lucky!

I also appreciate the work of our sons, Taylor Jesse and Beau Charles Stevens, as well as our polite Chihuahua, Willow Bay, for creating a home in which I could happily type-away!

Finally, it was Brian McClane, to whom this book is dedicated, who educated me about the daily struggles of the physically handicapped. I am reminded of some of the courageous people I have known in my travels, who have a different and harder path through life. Among them was Kyle Pablo, a fellow Yankee fan, who remains in my heart. In this new world we hopefully are creating it is my hope that we not only are including the accommodations they require, but that we are welcoming them to complete participation. Disabilities separate us; admittedly at times I wasn't sure how to form a friendship with a man or woman with a disability. And then I learned it begins with "hello."